SPACE HACK

BONNER LITCHFIELD

CHAPTER 1

KEVIN STOOD at the edge of the hangar bay, all alone. The fact that he was down here by himself should have been reassuring. That meant nobody on the ship knew his whereabouts at the moment. But the still silence screamed at him to run. And every part of him agreed. A prickly apprehension ran up his spine. His knees trembled as he willed himself to breathe.

The massive hangar was shaped like a honeycomb, larger than a gymnasium or even an outdoor playing field. High overhead, a solid white glow illuminated everything.

Each wall was comprised of cog-shaped steel plates that interlocked like puzzle pieces. Huge silver floor tiles, cold and solid under Kevin's boots, spread out before him in a symmetric pattern of gleaming rectangles. Kevin figured each tile to be fifty times his mass. If he hadn't felt puny and insignificant before, he did now.

The hawkers—single-person fighters—were lined up in the center of the hangar. Two hundred of them, arranged in ten uniform rows. Waiting for a command to get things started. Basking in the glow from the ceiling, each one was a swift predator with a single black eye and a sleek white body with red trim.

They all seemed to be staring at Kevin, mocking him, threatening, anticipating his next move. In fact, the hangar felt like a giant booby trap ready to grind his bones to a powder if he dared to take a single step forward.

These thoughts were just imaginary bullshit in his head, sure, but they were also byproducts of his fear. Thoughts could be dispelled; cowardice, not so much.

Even the lightweight body armor he was wearing was no help. This was a suit that turned average dudes into studs. Black and imposing, it bulged out in all the right places and made the wearer look like a superhero. Or an imposter. Even though it had been custom fitted to his slight frame, putting it on always made Kevin feel like a worm in a snake's skin.

And that made all the difference. Other recruits got reckless when they wore the armor. Kevin stayed scared. He'd never worked up the nerve to launch himself at a target with full abandon, always fearful of the impact. The possibility of a bruise or a sprain made him want to puke.

As did wearing his helmet right now. With the dark face shield almost touching his nose, the smell of neoprene—that and knowing he was breathing filtered air—gave Kevin a sense of drowning. The slightest malfunction, the tiniest crack or compromise, a pinhole-sized opening anywhere, and he was a goner. Never mind that the hangar was sealed tight as a drum, that he could walk in here naked as the day he was born and breathe just fine.

Even his weapon felt heavy and useless, hanging on his right hip like an extra appendage. A painful reminder of his ineptitude in the practice simulator, and validation that he didn't belong. Small wonder that he always got singled out during drills. And small wonder that he couldn't hope to do what he'd come down here for.

Directly behind him next to the door he'd just come through, the palm reader's red circle dared him to set his plan in motion. One touch. That's all it would take. The thick metal doors on the other side of the room would slide apart. The hawker of his choice would be Kevin's to command.

Except—his lack of manhood had rendered him immobile. Hell, his boots, for all intents and purposes, were welded to the metal floor. Unable to press on. Unable to turn tail and run. He stared at his feet, searching for an answer in the polished chrome.

A soft hand on his shoulder made him cower and yelp. Worse still was the echo of his own voice inside his helmet. Hearing himself squeal like a little girl was beyond demeaning.

"Relax, Kevin."

His blood raced when he recognized the girl's voice. Tonya Verdi. She was wearing the same black combat gear as Kevin with one huge difference: her body enhanced the armor, not the other way around. With her face shield raised, her bronzed skin glowed in the white light. Her easy smile caused gooseflesh on Kevin's skin, followed by a surge of hopeful lust that he immediately dismissed as impossible fantasy.

Tonya gave his shoulder a reassuring squeeze.

"Wh-what are you doing here?" Kevin stammered.

Her brown eyes had a flirtatious gleam, as if sneaking into a restricted area was just a lark. "I could ask you the same thing," she said.

"Nothing." Kevin looked down and wished the massive floor tiles would swallow him up. "Nothing at all."

CHAPTER 2

Join the Armada!

Seemed like a good idea at the time.

In Kevin's homeland, some folks mined carbon. Others worked on assembly lines building nanotubes for circuit boards. All of them low-paid grunts. His mother took great pride in never having missed a shift in twenty years.

Consequently, nobody there cared a whit for logic or abstract thought. No call for people who could embed instructions into those nanotubes they manufactured. No. Cushy work of that kind was reserved for those with rank and privilege on other worlds. So for Kevin, it was suck it up and spend long hours doing menial labor, sit home and starve, or . . .

It began with aptitude assessments to determine how a candidate might be of maximum service. On the physical tests, Kevin failed miserably, to the point that he thought they'd reject him on the spot. Even though the Armada was rumored to have a rejection rate of zero.

However, his proctor's face went slack with disbelief when he finished the math and logic modules in a fraction of the allotted time. They'd even given him a signing bonus (ten thousand in bit-gold) along with a letter of recommendation for a research and development post in the prestigious outer realm. He'd have to go through standard training, of course. A mere formality. Then he'd trade in his body armor for a mug of strong coffee. In fact, his biggest venture would be the walk from his workstation to the break room.

That's what they kept telling Kevin right up until the moment they assigned him to this warship. *We need bodies for combat*, they said. That was the revised version of their story.

He'd spilled all of this personal history to Tonya during their first week onboard. Tonya! Even an attempt to make eye contact should have turned his brain to mush. Yet somehow, someway, for reasons Kevin couldn't fathom, she had the opposite effect on him. Her mere presence was like a truth serum, loosening his tongue and causing him to dump his thoughts out for inspection. Well, most of them.

And here she was in the hangar—actually touching him!—this drop-dead gorgeous girl with easy charisma and sex appeal. She unlocked Kevin's face shield and raised it so that they were face-to-face. "I know what you're up to," she said. "And I get it." Her flirtatious gleam had vanished. She looked earnest and serious. A bronzed goddess of empathy.

Kevin felt his face redden. Tonya had come down here to rescue him, apparently. Because she was a friend, and she was protective of him.

Not that he could ask for a better bodyguard. In hand-to-hand combat drills, she was top in their unit. None of the men relished the prospect of locking up with her—not on the mat in the gym, anyhow.

Kevin felt desire and awe whenever he watched her in action. Particularly the calmness in her face. She could have a two-hundred-pound man trying to take her head off and her expression remained as placid as it was at this moment. And while he had no way or proving it one way or another, Kevin often sensed that she was toying with her opponent, that she could render anybody on this warship unconscious in a skinny minute, including their drill instructors.

And now his silly escape attempt was done. Over. Finito. Tonya was about to take him by the hand and escort him back to his quarters like a little lost boy. At least that's what Kevin anticipated as he dropped his eyes from her steady gaze.

She lifted his chin, forcing his eyes to meet hers. "You're doing the right thing," she said. "You don't belong here. And they should know that. Idiots! You have a gift. It takes a special kind of person to sit by himself and not only problem solve but create. To them, you're just another warm body."

Kevin stood straighter. Tonya had that effect on him. Likely, he was just feeling the heat she gave off and attributing it to himself. But beggars couldn't be choosers. Kevin would take what he could get.

"If that's their value system, they don't deserve a man of your talents," Tonya said.

Kevin nodded, even though he'd never considered himself *too good* for the Armada. His exit plan had nothing to do with retribution or elevating his own station. He was simply fleeing a situation that he couldn't deal with even with Tonya babysitting him every step of the way.

Then he looked across the hangar at the closed hatch. It might as well be a million miles away. He forced himself to look at Tonya, hating himself for exposing even more of his weakness to her. "I can't do it," he said.

Tonya's generous mouth tumbled open as she smiled that easy smile of hers. She touched his face. The black glove on her hand left a sweet aftertaste on Kevin's lips. "We'll do it together," she said.

"But I can't let you go AWOL," Kevin protested. Not that he could stop her from doing anything.

"Not me," Tonya said. "You. We'll get you out of here, and they'll have no clue where to find you."

"But—"

"What you really need is someone to close the hatch doors when you leave," Tonya said.

She had a point. If the ship's scanners picked up an unexpected blip…way better if the hangar doors were closed. Something Kevin wouldn't be able to do from a launched vessel due to security protocol.

Her fingers encircled his right wrist. "C'mon, Kevin. You've got the power, dude."

His pulse hammering into the deafening silence, Kevin stood breathless as Tonya pressed his hand against the palm reader. He imagined a real shock to his fingertips. Silly. Because the glove emitted no electrical current. Nanotubes embedded in the glove read the wearer's DNA and generated an encrypted code for the palm reader to evaluate. A double authentication protocol that was both glove and wearer specific. Kevin hoped he'd mimicked it successfully.

The red circle on the reader turned green, indicating a big thumbs-up.

"Your chariot awaits, sir," Tonya said. She offered up a playful faux curtsy.

Well, yeah. He'd programmed the glove for elite-level clearance. That enabled unfettered access to anything in the hangar, including permission to pilot any of its vessels.

Even though he'd never actually flown before. This was not shaping up to be a good plan.

Tonya reassured him. "Hey. You've got this," she said. "You're going to Innes. Right?"

Kevin nodded. The Innes sector was a short jaunt from here—important because he had no food or provisions. It was also neutral territory beyond the jurisdiction of the Armada and every other faction. An equal opportunity offender, there was no extradition from Innes. Consequently, the entire sector had gotten a reputation as a haven for outlaws. However, Kevin just needed to buy some time to put together a new identity and figure things out.

"You don't have to know how to fly a hawker," Tonya said. "Just download your course map and let autopilot do all the work."

"What about when I get there?" Kevin said. This was a hell of a time to be asking questions like these.

"The hawker will just disengage in the general vicinity and float in orbit. No problem. A barge or a space station will see that baby and drool. They'll tow you in no questions asked. They'll probably take your ship as payment for their services, but you don't know how to fly it anyhow. So what the hey!"

Tonya leaned in and kissed him full on the lips, making the hair on the back of his neck stand up.

"You've got this, Kevin." She gave his hand a reassuring squeeze.

"You've got this."

CHAPTER 3

THE SOUND of the hangar doors whooshing open made Kevin's crotch draw up into his abdomen. This was like the start of a wild carnival ride, when you knew you'd made a mistake buying a ticket. Too late to turn back now. You could only hope to make it out in one piece. And not puking all over yourself would be an added bonus.

There were no safety restraints in the cockpit. Kevin's body armor adhered itself to the bucket seat. The dark windshield had closed over him, allowing him a view from every conceivable angle. However, the holographic touchscreen would be far more reliable for monitoring his surroundings.

Monitoring being the operative word in this case. The onboard computer was doing the actual flying. Kevin was a mere passenger. His weapon was stowed behind the seat within reach. Hence the expression, *riding shotgun*.

He didn't realize he was space-bound at first. He was waiting for a g-force kind of pressure. Something slamming him into his seat. But it was as if the hawker was stationary and the scenery shifted around it. The hangar disappeared, suddenly replaced by stars and darkness.

Kevin licked his lips, the taste of Tonya's kiss still lingering. She was right. He had this. Hell, he'd just outsmarted the Armada. How cool was that? Maybe they'd think twice about treating personnel like livestock in the future. Probably not. But one horse had sure as hell broken out of the corral.

With much of his angst at bay now, he reflected on how he'd pulled this off and laughed out loud in the empty cockpit.

New recruits were allowed a small amount of personal tech, all subject to screening, of course. Things like family holograms, books, music, and a few games like chess and poker.

And all executable programs were formatted with a specific data structure to allow the computer to find, parse, read, and run them. It was all about storing and retrieving data using pattern matching.

Kevin's Throwdown game, book reader, and slideshow all had innocuous header data. Armada AI had scanned them for malware and found nothing. But Throwdown, a space dogfight game, tied it all together. The game itself was dull, void of cool scenery and storylines. Just two ships fighting it out on a black background with a few distant stars thrown in for looks. Tonya always blew him up with ridiculous ease when they played it together.

Once the game launched, however, the seemingly random stars in the background formed a pattern of coordinates that served as a template. Using this template, Throwdown touched (but did not execute or launch) photo, books, and poker executables, pulling in partial instructions from each of them. The result was a worm built from bits and pieces of each. As the players duked it out on a cheesy star field, it compiled and launched itself into the network.

The worm didn't do any damage. A smart virus didn't kill its host, after all. Didn't eat data. Didn't touch a damn thing. All it did was pry and look. And giving Kevin kernel-level access was like throwing chickens into a fox's den.

Still savoring his victory, he checked the rear camera and watched the warship disappear from visual range. He wasn't totally in the clear yet—but the being out of sight produced a heady sense of liberation. Already, he'd dared to venture far beyond his courage level. All because Tonya had shown up at the last minute and talked him into it.

———

The hawker picked up speed, a fast acceleration that pressed Kevin hard against his seat. His stomach lurched. After all, he was putting his life in the hands of the onboard computer. All he could do was sit and wait.

Closing his eyes, Kevin concentrated on slow, steady breathing. The pressure of the seat against his back began to feel more inviting, and he began to find a sense of security in the inertia that held him in place. This was cruising speed. A far cry from full throttle, better known as *balls to the wall.*

He opened his eyes and gazed at the distant stars in the black beyond. Somewhere out there, the first jump was waiting. And it was up to his ship's navigation system to find and traverse it.

Still, he needed to at least stay somewhat engaged, even as a focused bystander. It was way too early to check his progress. But he pulled up the holographic map just the same. *Never too soon to start preparing.* That was something the drill instructors loved to yell as they jarred recruits out of deep slumber.

Kevin studied the 3D representation of his projected course and identified his current location by the blinking orb that didn't seem to be moving. It was going to be a long journey. Monitoring his progress was going to be a lot like watching metal rust.

The map would morph into new shapes and patterns based on his location. There were no compass points in deep space. No concept of longitude or latitude, north or south. Not even up or down. This was computer-based interpretation of *were, are,* and *would be.* And a single-person hawker's computer could only handle one iteration at a time.

He licked his lips again and thought of Tonya. Not a smart thing to do while careening through open space. On the other hand, no further action was required of him. At least not for a good long while. Still, shit happened sometimes. What shit, Kevin couldn't say. But he at least needed to quit dreaming and stay completely awake. With all of that in mind, Kevin resolved to remain alert—but at the same time, allow his emotional mainspring to unwind a little.

Approaching Jump Sector 1XQ-to-3AP.

Kevin almost wet his pants when he heard that system prompt and saw it flashing on the map. That meant he was coming up on the first of two wormholes. All according to plan. Except: he thought he'd reached this first wormhole way too soon.

Or maybe not. After all, he was nervous and uptight, his thoughts bouncing in a hundred different directions. And nobody could keep time in his own head. That's why time-keeping devices had been invented in the first place. Well, duh! All he had to do was look at the time elapsed. Almost half an hour. Or for his needs: fifteen hundred and eleven seconds and counting—it had to be that granular.

Kevin ran some of the math through his head. (He'd always been able to solve complex equations without a calculator, to the disdain of his classmates, which had led to more than a little bullying.) Based on his calculations, maybe he'd gotten here too soon. Maybe not. *Real conclusive,* he thought in disgust.

Actually, he *could* conclude that his arrival time was in the realm of reasonable expectation. Course maps were, after all, based on spatial relationships between faraway objects: warships, planets, wormholes, entire galaxies. And nothing stood still. Which required the mapping algorithm to make incessant adjustments. *Deviation shift* was the technical term. And course mapping handled that without issue.

Okay. So nothing to panic over. Yet the nagging voice in the back of Kevin's brain persisted. Call it instinct, call it paranoid. His gut—in fact, the very marrow of his being—insisted that something was amiss.

That sector identifier also gave him pause. *1XQ-to-3AP.* Probably no big deal. Software developers were often gearheads that overengineered everything to the nth degree. They couldn't even count to eleven without dropping their pants. Why simply count two wormholes using integer values 1 and 2 when you could come up with a hash code to make yourself look smart?

Then again…

Well, it couldn't hurt to check. In other words, don't trust what the map is telling you. Go one step further than just reading the heading labeled *Innes* that floated reassuringly above the holograph. That meant paging forward through the map itself, all the way to the final destination. Which would bog things down a bit. Quantum brain farms on a warship or space station could churn through the map data without breaking a sweat. But a hawker's computer was going to struggle. One reason why pilots had restricted access—why they weren't allowed to monkey with things like this.

A fire burned in Kevin's chest. He was under no such restriction!

But when he placed his glove on the palm reader to invoke his elite access, a telltale beep sounded. Access denied.

No. It had to work. He'd given himself root-level privileges. Generals couldn't get at the shit he could. But no. It was shutting him out. He pressed down again in vain, still getting the same *Invalid User* response.

Tonya!

She'd squeezed his hand while she kissed him. Just a quick firm grip. And, of course, he'd been working with limited supplies, so this glove he'd made to circumvent system security didn't have the reinforced microfiber of a true battle-ready glove. Tonya had busted his nanotube seam, goddammit! She'd set him up. He wasn't a passenger. Or even cargo. He was a prisoner— stuck on this course to who-knew-where, and there wasn't a thing he could do about it.

There was one hope. The computer had allowed him to pull up the hologram of his current route. That implied that anybody sitting in that pilot's seat had at least minimal access. Hell, he could probably read books or play games on his way to wher- ever he was really going if nothing else.

Kevin queried his personal account. Nothing doing. Tonya had locked him out.

But this vanilla pilot account. Maybe it had access to his personal tech. After all, it wasn't locked down. He knew the program ID of Throwdown. If he could force terminal-level access…

Kevin pulled up a virtual keypad and typed furiously. Yes. He was in. Well, not really. He could launch his worm-building apps. But doing that was all too little too late. It took hours for the worm to make inroads once the build occurred.

There had to be another way—there always was.

If only he had time…

CHAPTER 4

APPROACHING JUMP SECTOR 1XQ-TO-3AP. Calibrating entry pattern.

Now things had gotten real. In a few minutes, the wormhole would be in sight. The map would collapse into a spinning obelisk. Final adjustments would be made.

Then the spins.

It would be like flying into a swirling funnel with a spout that never lined up straight. Hit the sides, and the ship would disappear. It wouldn't blow up or disintegrate; it would just cease to exist.

Not as bad as it sounded. Annelida's Law stated that regardless of size, shape, or mass, any object that matched a wormhole's rotational pattern would be literally sucked through to the other side. It was a concept akin to a boulder passing through the eye of a needle. A phenomenon unprovable by any known science. Yet there it was. Just measure the wormhole's rate of rotation—easy to do with its gravitational ebb and flow—and spin your vessel at that exact same speed. Really not hard at all. Autopilot had it covered.

The map began to collapse in on itself. That meant the

required readings had been gathered; the system was working on synching up with the wormhole now. *Might as well ride it out,* Kevin thought. By now, the Armada had to know that one of their hawkers was missing. So it would be a really good idea for him to disappear.

The Innes sector would have been nice, but that wasn't going to happen. Kevin placed his glove on the reader, willing his elite-level menu options to reappear. A futile waste of time. All he could do was sit back and enjoy the ride at this point.

Something wasn't right.

The map should have been compacting itself. Instead, it was spreading outward till the hologram almost wound up in Kevin's lap. That couldn't be good.

Then Kevin realized it was splitting into two distinct entities melded together. Holy crap. Two interconnected obelisks were forming. That explained the *1XQ-to-3AP* naming scheme. He was about to enter a cosmic juncture: an intersection of two (sometimes more) wormholes.

A cold sweat formed on Kevin's prickly skin. He was going to throw up right here and now. Holding his breath, he closed his eyes and unclenched his fists. Then he exhaled slowly and tried to relax, even though it seemed that he was being lifted out of his seat by pure panic.

The second wormhole meant added complexity. Running two sets of calibrations wasn't so bad in itself. The real bugaboo was entering the second wormhole immediately after being shot out of the first one. That second spin pattern had to kick in at that exact moment or else…well, there was no else if something got botched.

No big deal. There was at least a ninety-percent chance of making it—and that assumed worst-case scenarios across the board. So probably all good.

Probably…

"Screw that," Kevin said to the empty cockpit.

He still had those executables that he could jury rig. Throw-down, book reader, slideshow, and poker. Kid's games with adult consequences once their true power was unleashed. He could easily take over the hawker's computer system, even though he'd been locked out. But there wasn't enough time for that.

And speaking of time…he'd caught a break by having to traverse a juncture instead of a garden-variety wormhole.

Yeah, a real break.

No, really. There was added complexity now, which slowed down the calibration process and brought him a little extra time.

One thing about that: if he stayed on this side of the juncture, the warship would find him. That was an empirical fact. But he didn't have the nerve to go through that maze of matter in front of him, regardless of the odds being in his favor. Just like that time in training—he'd been unable to jump off the platform into the net fifty feet below. They rode him hard over that one too.

Okay. Setting aside the cowardice of his decision, Kevin instructed his programs to continuously launch one another. Furthermore, he created a continuous launching loop in the same execution space as each of the calibrating modules. It didn't take long. Both obelisks froze almost simultaneously. In fact, the entire map became more of a wispy cloud than a holograph. He'd just put the brakes on an uppity kidnapper. *Try and lock me out*, he gloated. *Just try!*

The thought of it gave Kevin a thrill. Despite the stress of time constraints, his fear of getting caught by the Armada and the inevitable consequences, an electric thrum vibrated up his spine and made a pleasant tingle in his groin. He wasn't aroused; just excited and empowered. The sensation put an almost pleasant taste in the air he was breathing and made him feel way less puny and feeble.

And he was psyching himself up for nothing. So far, all he'd really been able to do was grind a single program to a halt. A far cry from gaining access to any meaningful functionality. He could eventually carve his way through the onboard security, sure, but that could take hours. Time that he didn't have.

Scolding himself for almost getting carried away, Kevin bit his lip and choked back a sob of desperation. He was beyond pathetic. A loser on every level. Couldn't compete with any of his fellow recruits, couldn't handle life in the Armada at all. Forget that they basically lied when they recruited him. So loser plus-plus. He'd gotten played. By them. Worst of all, by Tonya.

Look at him now! He'd officially screwed up this whole liberation effort—but good.

Stop it, he said to himself. *Think, dammit!*

One thing was certain: regardless of adverse circumstances—risk, limitations, any of that shit—scared was the absolute worst state of mind for tackling problems. You examined your options, came to a decision, then executed it to the best of your ability. Fairly simple for Kevin in the techie world of computers and code—in the real world, not so much. Then again, this *was* the real world.

So what to do? Well, for one thing, he needed to gain access, to manipulate executables, to pull up restricted data. But with no time—

Especially if you never get started on it, Kevin chided himself.

Okay. He had an objective: to regain admin control of this ship's computer system. More specifically, to replace the autopilot course that was chauffeuring him into some unknown cosmic juncture with his original course to the Innes sector. He could attack that problem one of two ways: somehow recreate the encrypted hash generated by the (now ruined) nanotube in his glove, or fool the system into loading his Innes course map some other way.

Only he didn't have any idea where to start. Not a clue.

So what the hell did a combat pilot do in a situation like this? Hey, wait a second. That was a legitimate question. Say he was forced to land somewhere—on a planet, asteroid, space station, didn't matter—and get out of his ship. And something happened. Probably nothing embarrassing like a hot girl like Tonya making a fool out of him. But still...the Armada was all about covering possibilities. And shit did happen. So what was a logical Plan B in the event of a lost or damaged glove?

Kevin tasted blood and realized he was chewing the inside of his cheek. He was waning away from conscious thought because he hadn't taken a decent breath in at least half a minute. That was his problem. He was trying to think his way out of an impossible situation and grinding his mental gears to a pulp.

And thus abandoning the very thing that might save his bacon: his lone talent—a gift specific to the world of computers. In this realm, others analyzed and sought; Kevin *saw*. Moreover, he didn't think when he was in the zone. He just played.

But play at what? The panic of the situation still clamored for attention. *You don't have shit for data points...*

"And that'd be true if I happened to be analyzing and seek-ing," Kevin said aloud.

Again—it didn't have to be that way. The fact that he was a fugitive in a ship he didn't know how to fly was irrelevant. Code was code, systems were systems. That was his domain. A place where he opened his mind and let the realizations come to him.

Envisioning a leaf floating downstream, Kevin let his mind slip into a zone. *The* zone. His fingers sped across the touch-screen as he rigged a new executable from his Throwdown-chess-solitaire combo tool. He was done in a matter of seconds. His new creation would dump the map data of his current course. A delicate operation. One false move and the map core would be irrevocably corrupted; the hawker's navigation system would be cooked, with possible collateral damage to other func-tions as well.

No problem. Kevin dumped the map and immersed himself in the winding web of quantum computation. Patterns emerged.

He quickly identified the oblong bulge that represented his current route back to the Armada warship. Then he found a qubit cluster in the shape of an inverted egg. Embedded inside of it was the user token for the hawker's default system account.

Based on his previous unauthorized access of the warship's computer files, Kevin knew what to do. It was a simple matter of querying the map reader with a course identifier and a valid credential object. The course identifier was no big deal. Just a simple hash, not much different than contacting someone socially with their name or handle. But embedding his now-defunct superuser credentials in that qubit cluster... Kevin stared at his useless glove and gritted his teeth. It would be nice to simply place his hand on the touchscreen and drop those creds right in there.

Waaaa-aaaaaH!

A low-pitched siren erupted. Kevin wanted to jump out of his seat and run.

Waaaa-aaaaaH! Waaaa-aaaaaH!

The noise was coming from the console. He was being hailed. He could block the signal, probably, if he could just manage to hear himself think. Except—his eardrums felt like cheese in a grater.

"Hey out there."

The obnoxious noise had vanished, replaced by an authoritative male voice.

"Can you hear me talking?"

Kevin stared at his feet and said nothing.

"Okay. Let's try it this way. This is William Whitehead, Technologist Grade Five, of the Armada warship *Touchstone*, contacting the pilot of hawker craft D005G. Do you copy?"

A couple of moments passed.

"We need verbal acknowledgment, Kevin. Don't make me do this the hard way."

"Yeah, I hear you," Kevin said.

"Good boy. We're sending instructions to your ship. It'll transport you back here all by itself. Like magic. What that means is: you ain't touching shit. So you'll want to put your hands in your lap and keep them there. Understand?"

Kevin stared at his boots and said nothing.

"That was a yes-or-no question, Kevin. Do you understand?"

"Yes."

"Very good. Now you just sit tight and we'll have you home in a jiffy."

CHAPTER 5

KEVIN DIDN'T KNOW what they'd do to him back on the warship. It was guaranteed to suck, whatever it was. Not that it had to be that way. He still had options. He could ignore Technologist William Whitehead's instructions and tamper. Call off the programs he'd launch and let the current map finish what it had started. He'd be through the juncture before the Armada warship could touch him.

Or he could get back in his zone—*the* zone—and let his mind flow into the system. It didn't take a genius to figure out that the *instructions* they were sending over was a map with a course back to them. Like as not, he'd be able to extract Technologist William's credentials out of their little care package. From there, he might be able to retrieve his Innes route, assuming Willie had sufficient access.

"Hi, Kevin."

Kevin's breath caught—Tonya's voice in his ear! Calm and assured. Also sexy as all hell. He stared at the console for a couple of seconds before he realized she was addressing him through the comm system in his helmet. Slick. Very little chance they'd pick up on that. It also meant she was in close proximity.

He didn't know the specifics, just that ship comms spanned great distances, helmet comms mere kilometers. Anyhow…Tonya close by! That was a wild and dangerous thought.

"Just listen to me, Kevin," she said. "Don't talk. Or they'll hear you on your ship's comm port."

Kevin nodded, ridiculously, knowing full well that she couldn't see him.

"I don't know what you did after takeoff—doesn't matter now—but we've got to get you the hell out of here."

Why should I trust you? Kevin almost said it out loud but managed to just think it instead. She was right about him needing to get the hell out of there. Only there weren't any options that didn't suck at the moment.

A new pane opened on the terminal screen, and Technologist William's course map swirled into focus. To snag those creds, Kevin needed to declutter his brain. Drop the ballasts of the physical world and submerge himself in the tech once again.

But he'd been instructed to sit still and not move…

Screw it. Screw Techno-turd Willie. Tonya too. (He could wish, anyhow.) He was already wet. Might as well take a deep dive at this point.

Allowing the map to load, Kevin began his analysis. The qubit hash on William's transmission was the exact same pattern as the map object he'd just finished dissecting. Same oblong bulge as the route back to the warship. Same inverted egg pattern that housed those keys to the virtual kingdom, so to speak. All he had to do was snag those creds and drop them into a map query, then he'd have his Innes route back online.

There was (at least) one possible glitch in that plan: William would be logged in as himself, of course. Ideally, before transmitting his map to Kevin's ship, he'd replace his creds with a default account that had minimal rights. But somehow—call it gut instinct—Kevin didn't think he was smart enough to think of that.

"Hey!" Whitehead snapped. "What the hell do you think you're doing?"

Kevin didn't answer. But that sudden distraction had thrown him off his game. He'd have to shut down all communications; no way he could stay on point with someone constantly yapping at him. Instead of being immersed, he was just skimming the surface now.

"What's going on, Kevin?" Oh, hell. Tonya again. Hard to believe he'd forgotten all about her.

"Last warning," William said. "You take your paws off that console or it's going to go really bad for you. I won't tell you again."

So they knew he wasn't sitting still like they'd told him to. Probably because the computer was transmitting back to the warship. Maybe as high-level as number of active users. Maybe more detailed. Or maybe they had eyes in here. He'd never researched a hawker's architecture in detail; only the course and autopilot programs necessary to fly him where he wanted to go. What if they had failsafes in place for stolen ships? Maybe Whitehead could shock him from a zapper in his seat. Or maybe flood the cockpit with deafening noise.

Kevin's heart raced. He could feel the sweat trapped inside the useless gloves he was wearing. *Go fast, don't hurry.* He told it to himself. *No panic. Don't get stupid.* The way out of this was to take a dive—a deep dive—into his zone and snag those creds.

"Okay, sport," Whitehead said. "We're doing it the hard way."

Then Tonya in the helmet comm: "Kevin! Talk to me. Please. I'm trying to help."

Kevin ignored them both. Tonya had gotten him into this pile of shit. Worse still—he didn't know what Willie Rectum meant by *doing it the hard way.* But it couldn't be good.

First things first...

It turned out that his ship's communication system had a

simple disable option. All he had to do was flip an on-off switch. At least he could hear himself think now.

He chose a more primitive means of squelching Tonya. "Give me a few minutes, Tonya," he said. "I've gotta do something. I'll let you know when I can talk."

Then he let himself sink back into the world of computing logic where everything made sense. Firing up the stealth tools he'd developed, Kevin carefully extracted Technologist William's creds from the map object he'd sent over. It was like working with volatile materials in a chem lab, where the slightest spill would blow the place up—exactly like that, because cooking the computer would turn this ship into a floating tomb.

Things got worse. He saw new processes spawning. Tentacles of logic reaching out like a giant squid. But not towards him (him being his account and the programs he was running in the space where he was running them). The invaders were stretching themselves into the outer regions of the operating system. Signaling outward. Into the hardware itself.

Kevin felt it happen. It was like a giant hatch slamming shut, sealing him underground. Blind panic took hold. He couldn't breathe…

No, actually, he could breathe just fine. He wasn't getting any air. They'd disabled life support, at least the oxygen part of it. Apparently, they had the ability to make things real bad for a thief.

"Kevin?" Tonya's voice was faint and distant. Bitch! If she hadn't screwed him (figuratively speaking, of course), he'd be well on his way to Innes, far removed from the warship's sphere of influence.

"Kevin! Say something."

"Can't…breathe!"

"Listen to me, Kevin." Her words had a muffled echo, as if she was talking to him from the opposite end of a long tunnel.

His face felt tingly, his head empty and light. Even his eardrums had gone numb.

"Kevin…"

Black spots danced before his eyes. A massive boulder was pressing down on his chest. And he couldn't get out from under…

"—Helmet."

Helmet! Tonya said…something about *helmet*.

"Kevin, your helmet!"

He heard it this time. Barely, but he heard her. *His* helmet. A lever on the right side of the faceplate. He just had to pull it down.

Kevin pawed at the side of his faceplate and got the vague feeling of something jutting out that he could push on. No good. He couldn't find that lever.

The black spots were getting larger now. He was drifting into an orbit all its own. It would be so easy to just let himself slip away—a leaf floating downstream…

Giving up, drifting off, accepting his fate…

He heard Tonya's voice, still distant but a bit more audible. "Find the indention at your jawbone. Press in and pull down."

Kevin pressed and felt—and felt his heart rate spike as his fingers floundered for something to pull down on. Then his index finger sank into a divot of sorts. Nothing that felt movable. Seemed like a solid alloy to him. But what the hell! He pressed and pulled till his knuckles cracked. And the spots converged into a dark veil across his face.

Then another soft voice. *Helmet respiration engaged.*

He could breathe. Holy shit. He could breathe!

"Kevin! Talk to me" Tonya's voice in his helmet was louder than before.

"How much air do I have?" Kevin asked.

"You're alright for now," Tonya said. Not an answer.

And that prompted a question: how she knew about the

helmet's respiration system. There'd been nothing about that in training. Even more important: how the hell was she communicating with him way the hell out here?

"Look, you don't have much time," Tonya said.

No shit, Kevin thought to himself. He had to get life support back online. And fast. Taking over William Whitehead's creds might still be his best bet. Thing is, they'd work for piloting functions like map loading, but, like as not, access to the mission-critical stuff like life support required elite access. Something he would have had if Tonya hadn't ruined his glove.

"C'mon. Talk to me, Kevin," Tonya said. "I know you're pissed, but this is not the time for silent scorn."

Kevin lost it. "Well, I really don't have time for your bullshit right now!" he shouted. "It's your fault that I landed in this pile of shit in the first place."

"And there's only one way out," Tonya said. "But you've got to listen—"

Kevin yelled even louder. "Why don't you shut the hell up?" That one made him dizzy.

From nowhere, a booming whoosh shook his ship so hard that it rattled. Kevin let out a startled squeal and immediately felt his face catch fire from embarrassment. From a short distance away, the other hawker spun on a dime and flew straight at him, stopping just short of impact.

"We're leaving together," Tonya said. "You can be pissed at me all you want, but it has to be this way."

"You're not a recruit," Kevin said. His ire was giving way to a throbbing headache now.

"You've got to be gone before the Armada gets here. If they get you…"

"Tell you what—you disappear and give me some peace and quiet. I'll handle the disappearing on my own, thank you very much."

"You don't have time," Tonya said. "Besides, I have elite access."

Of course she did. Compliments of Kevin's upfront work in this venture.

"And you're right," she said. "I'm not a recruit. Anyhow, that access you gave yourself made you a god. That's what I used to swap out your course map when you left."

"Any chance you might send it back to me?" Kevin said.

"That's just it." For the first time ever, Tonya sounded uncertain. "It's not working anymore. I can see your ship's computer node, but everything I send just bounces back. Which makes no sense. I mean, I have permission to do whatever I want."

"It's a firewall." Kevin knew without checking. "That asshole William put up a firewall when he killed my oxygen."

"Okay," Tonya said. "We're going to try something else. That's all. You'll need to lean forward and check underneath your seat. There's a black box under the housing."

"Whoa! Where are you going with this?" Kevin said.

"I know this is not what you want to hear, but there's an ejector lever inside that box. You just have to—"

"Say what?"

"An ejector lever. Look, I'll walk you through it. It's totally safe. Once you're clear, I'll do the rest. We'll ride double in my ship."

Screw that! Kevin decided before she was half finished. An open space pickup was beyond insane.

But then he got a warning beep, followed by an ominous message. *Helmet oxygen supply is running low.*

Tonya heard it too. "There's no choice, Kevin. And no time for arguing. So move your ass!"

She was right. He had to do something. And fast. He could make Willie's firewall look like tissue paper, if he only had time. Which he didn't.

It seemed that his only option was to trust Tonya. And worse: obey her commands.

But what if… Yes! He could rig the build itself. A one-shot deal. All he had to do was bump the poker executable up in the build order. Same concept as a train engine suddenly swapping places with one of the boxcars while rounding a curve. A guaranteed pileup. In this case, the faulty build would result in a stack overflow—the computational counterpart of liberating hydrogen from water. Boom! System resources blown out.

What would happen in this ship with the computer out to lunch? Well, hopefully, a reboot. *Hopefully!* Since the beginning of the digital age, computer operating systems *usually* rebooted themselves in the aftermath of system failure. *Assuming* the system was set to reboot on failure, which it *usually* was…

Kevin launched the build. The worm started to compile and balked. The displays went blank. Kevin felt a river of sweat running down his back and willed himself not to panic. His helmet wouldn't sustain him much longer, and he'd just taken out life support for the moment.

Then the system rebooted and came back online. Kevin saw that the default setting had plotted out a course to its home warship. He only had to load the map and invoke autopilot for that to happen.

He called out to Tonya. "I nuked the firewall. Send me the map."

Now he had options. He could extract his elite creds from her send packet and bid her farewell. Or, if time ran out, he'd just invoke the route she sent and follow her into that damn junction.

Waaaa-aaaaaH!

DON'T MOVE. A booming robotic voice reverberated through Kevin's ship. *YOU ARE SURROUNDED.*

Despite feeling like a trapped rodent, the analytical part of Kevin's mind calmly reasoned that he'd just rebooted, which had reactivated communications.

Then he saw the warship itself. Huge and imposing. Enough to make the emptiness of deep space seem suddenly full and crowded.

DISENGAGE ALL NAVIGATION SYSTEMS. DO NOT TRY TO RUN.

That one sent a jolt of dread through his body.

Finally, Whitehead's smug voice over the comm: "Hoo, boy! You two are in so much trouble."

CHAPTER 6

KEVIN KILLED communications (to hear himself think) and let himself sink down into the computer system. Just a light immersion. At least enough to see if Willie the Weenie was sending more virtual tentacles his way. Not that it mattered all that much. His only option—his only escape at this point—was going through the juncture.

Except, he was still afraid to try it. Probably *too* scared, in fact. Yeah, fear had frozen him stiff. Afraid to enter that juncture. And maybe even more afraid to tell Tonya to go on without him.

Out of nowhere, a group of hawkers—he couldn't tell how many—zoomed past him, rocking his craft like a rowboat in a choppy sea.

He watched them fade into the distance, dancing flickers on the horizon. Where was Tonya? Maybe she'd seen them coming and left through the juncture. One of the flickers froze for a moment. A flat disc of yellow and orange took its place. It glowed for a moment, then sputtered into nothing.

A space explosion. No noise. Only the momentary combustion of fuel and energy in a vacuum. Two more glowing discs appeared. Still another took their place when they vanished.

Tonya hadn't gone anywhere. They were attacking her. And getting their asses handed to them, apparently.

"Kevin!" Her voice filled his helmet comm. "Behind you." How the hell had she gotten on the other side of him? "I'm sending your new course now. Don't try any of your fancy techie tricks this time. Just let it—shit! Be right back."

She was gone again. And a squadron of fighters buzzed past Kevin in hot pursuit. There was no way for her to stay in his proximity long enough to send him a new course map. No way in hell.

And if she kept trying...they'd blow her up. No way around it.

Another column of fighters whizzed past Kevin to join the fray. More fiery discs lit up the black sky, closer and brighter now.

Kevin fumbled through menu options and found the view-port—basically a telescope with a zoom option. Even a vanilla pilot account ought to have access. He was right. Zooming in on the bright glow of exploding fighter ships, he spotted Tonya with at least a dozen of them on her tail.

Two more discs lit up. But she was surrounded. No way out. The only way they could lose was by shooting each other. There were that many of them.

She dove straight down. By the time they reacted, she was climbing at a steep angle. The force of that sudden direction change was enough to make Kevin dizzy just watching it. Up and over, then downward. Making her pursuers look silly. But everywhere she went, every blank spot on the horizon, there were more of them waiting for her.

"Coming your way, Kevin." This time her voice came over his comm. She was no longer bothering to hide the fact that she was in communication with him. Her ship swooped towards him, leaving a trail of glowing discs in its wake.

She was going to send him that map or die trying. Probably the latter.

As she approached, more Armada hawkers converged on either side. A crossfire. A hail of blue-green laser fire. It wrapped her ship like a net. She reacted with an instant duck-and-dive and somehow emerging unscathed. Well, almost. There was a vapor trail coming off her rear foil where a smoldering ember glowed and mercifully winked out. Man, that was close.

Kevin yelled into the comm. "Get the hell out of here, Tonya!"

"Not going to happen," she said.

He watched her make another wide loop with her pursuers in tow. There were more of them coming down from above. And up from below. A shit sandwich. She was embarrassing them with a lot of the same ridiculous moves she pulled off when they played Kevin's Throwdown game. But this was real life. And she couldn't stay ahead of them forever.

This time it was a three-way crossfire, but she managed to blast her way through more of them and escape momentarily. Everything was close now. The explosions were not just glowing discs anymore. Ships blasted apart, scattering shrapnel and debris. And even though space was soundless, Kevin still felt the pilot's screams.

Behind it all, the warship loomed dark and huge—an ominous backdrop for the carnage.

Three ships exploded in plain view. The flames went out, and Tonya hovered in front of him. Still not giving up. Intent on taking him with her. A death sentence with impossible odds. And it was his fault. Not that he could do anything to help her. Hell, even if he wasn't scared shitless, he didn't know how to fly a damn hawker—forget engaging an enemy in combat.

The fleet converged from all sides. She was toast.

Kevin's body betrayed him. Acting without forethought—something that he'd never done before—he loaded his default course map—Destination, warship!—and invoked the autopilot. His ship engaged so fast that he almost threw up in his helmet.

Just like that. He was flying back to the warship right through the middle of a space battle. And amazingly, they didn't blast him into smithereens; they were holding their fire, even getting out of his way.

He said his last words to Tonya. "Now you have to leave."

Then he killed all communications and went to work. There was a chance—a very good chance, in fact—that they'd catch him doing this last upload. If that happened, he'd wind up in deeper shit than ever. But he had a window, a flicker of opportunity. And he meant to take it.

CHAPTER 7

Pain woke him up.

He'd been dreaming of home—the last place he'd ever call a haven, safe or otherwise. But his dream was from another time when he was another person. Long before he discovered tech. When his grandmother was still alive.

He could smell her vegetable bouillon simmering on the cookstove in their small house. As a child, Kevin loved watching her stir the pot. The broth had a hearty flavor, sharp enough to clear your nose, yet mild enough to settle your stomach. He had no clue what was in it, being just a child, after all. Later, he would be afraid to ask.

She was singing an old ditty, humming every other line because she only knew half the words. Couldn't carry a tune in a bucket—but her gentle voice wrapped him up, shielding him from the hostile world. Here was a safe cocoon. No yelling parents. No bullies shoving him down in the mud or smearing pet shit on him. Just him and Gram.

He floated into consciousness. Gram was gone. His bunk solidified underneath him, a solid block with no mattress pad. No pillow either. Everything hurt. His ribs burned when he breathed; his joints ached when he moved. Even his hair was bruised.

The sniggers of his teammates leaving the barracks tipped him off to what awaited him this morning. And the rancid smell of piss confirmed it. They'd done it again. Now, they were headed for the chow line. And he was choking back puke.

Another glorious day in the Armada. Such was the life of a recruit who'd gone AWOL.

Every morning, before leaving for drills, Kevin had to make the barracks spotless. That meant missing breakfast. Not that he had an appetite anyhow. Not after the beating he'd taken last night. And not after his fellow recruits pissed all over the floor to make his life all the harder.

Checking first for signs of sabotage—anything from a knotted sleeve to glue in the crotch—Kevin pulled on his training uniform, a gray polymer skin suit that was highly breathable and durable. Then he unrolled a long piece of tissue paper, folding and wadding it as thick as possible. It was no use. The paper was absorbent but impossibly thin. No way to keep the piss from soaking right though to his hands.

These tissues accomplished nothing. They were useless. Lots of saturated paper wads later, the nanites would come behind him and disinfect the area. That was where the real cleaning took place. This exercise in drudgery and humiliation was simply an object lesson.

Did his punishment *have* to be so damn pointless?

There were labor camps. Mining colonies that were basically indentured servitude. Also outer-space construction projects that sacrificed safety for speed. At least those made logical, if not ethical, sense. But having him do this half-assed cleanup job...

"Hey you. Slaton!" The drill instructor stood in the doorway. Warrior First-Class Ellis, a square-headed fireplug with the intellect of a poached egg.

Ellis's uniform was brown instead of gray and bulged from

his light body armor. The Armada's coat of arms, a bright orange sword across a shield, was plastered across his chest; Kevin thought it had the look and feel of an arrowhead. Not that the Armada used swords, shields, or arrows for anything. Then again, some colonies based their emblems on extinct birds of prey. Pretty damn pointless.

"Those barracks aren't going to clean themselves," Ellis said.

"Yes, sir."

"Well, what the hell are you waiting for—moron! Don't stand there staring at me like a loser. Get to work."

Kevin balled up some tissue along with his resolve and got started. If he gently ran across all of the wet surfaces, spreading the piss as much as soaking it up, it'd be close enough. And the nanites would take care of the rest.

"What the hell are you doing?"

"Sir?"

"Is that how you address a superior?"

Dropping the tissue wad on the floor, Kevin stood up straight and saluted.

Ellis shouted hard enough to make Kevin's ears ring. "What is your problem, boy—you just threw trash on the floor."

"Yes, sir," Kevin agreed. He hoped the waver in his voice wasn't noticeable.

"Well, don't just stand there ignoring it. Pick it up!"

Another hell day. It was a solid wall of animosity. Cold and unyielding. He was totally isolated. Nobody to pick him up when he stumbled, no slaps on the back or words of encouragement. He wasn't going to make it. Especially without Tonya. He'd never realized just how much she'd protected him until she was gone. She never outwardly threatened any of the other recruits—not directly. But bullies wound up leaving Kevin alone.

Not anymore.

Choking back tears, Kevin bent to pick up the nasty wad of tissue paper.

"Slaton! What the—you're at attention, dammit!"

Kevin stood ramrod straight. Stomach in, chest out. Ellis stomped out of the room, but he knew better than to twitch. He could hear him yelling at somebody outside but really didn't pay attention. Instructor Ellis…Warrior First Ass!

Ellis stormed back in with four of Kevin's fellow recruits—three girls and a guy—in tow. *Really should have been listening,* Kevin chided himself. Not that he could have done anything to avert whatever humiliation was about to happen.

Ellis lined them up. "Anybody want to tell me what the hell is going on in here?"

Nobody spoke.

Ellis got nose-to-nose with the male recruit. Lance Hickson. A cool customer who always looked like he knew what he was doing.

"Talk to me, Hickson."

"Everything is in order. Sir!"

"You call this in order! This place is a sewer."

"Yes, sir."

Ellis moved over to one of the girls. "Well, what the hell are you going to do about it?"

"We're counting on Slaton. Sir."

"Relying on Slaton. And what is Slaton doing right now?"

"Sir! He's supposed to be—"

"Did I ask what he's *supposed* to be doing?"

"No, sir."

Ellis pawed at his sweaty face. His cheeks reddened. He was working himself into a lather, more disgusting to Kevin than today's puddle of piss. That was the bullshit they taught here. How to psych yourself into a homicidal state.

"I'm counting to three. And I'd *better* get my question answered. Or else—"

Erin Lane spoke up. "Sir! Kevin Slaton is doing nothing. He's just standing here, not moving a muscle."

"Very good, Lane. Right answer without overthinking it."

Encouraged, Lane continued. "Looks like he's got a poker up his ass."

Ellis nodded. Something like a smile flitted across his face. "I agree. And it looks like you've got a problem. Your barracks stinks. And nobody's doing anything about it. Give Slaton your tech."

"Sir? I don't understand."

"It's not complicated. Walk over to Slaton, give him your device, and grant access."

Kevin could feel Lane's hostility; it radiated off of her like heat from a dark surface. Her eyes told the story. She wanted to double him over with a strike to the gut, then mop the floor with his face. Or something to that effect. Handing him the device, she issued the voice command. "Grant access to Kevin Slaton."

"Well, don't just stand there, Slaton," Ellis said. "Take a seat." He gestured to an empty bunk by the door. "You're going to sit there and fart around with Lane's tech while your teammates clean up your mess, because that's the kind of lame excuse for a human being you are. And if you even look at them, you'll be spitting out teeth. Do I make myself clear?"

"Yes sir," Kevin said, not looking up.

He could feel their collective glares. No question about what was coming. They were already making his life hell; now they'd turn it up a notch. And all he could do was wait in dread.

On the other hand, they'd just given him a device. And it was hooked into the warship's network.

CHAPTER 8

Erin Lane's personal tech was entertainment only. Mainly a reader and a couple of socializer apps. What else? Recruits had no need for encoded messaging or advanced data processing. They were told what to do and when to do it. And those instructions were conveyed via shouting. So nothing for them to analyze or decide.

Kevin perused the apps, looking for a book or game. Something to distract himself. Something that would maybe piss Lane off a little less. But all she did was messaging and image posting. So he was stuck browsing through things she'd rather keep private—with the whole room as an audience.

It was as if he'd been instructed to pull down Lane's pants in front of everybody. The idea was to break recruits down, but also to bring them together and give them a common enemy—and who better to hate than a fellow recruit who'd tried to go AWOL?

The tiny device in his hand projected a hologram about fifteen centimeters tall. He knew better than to invoke stealth mode and risk Ellis shoving the device somewhere painful.

His ribs burning in protest with every breath, Kevin

reminded himself that air didn't really get thicker or gain mass, that the tension in the room had nothing to do with his ability to breathe. It was all in his head. Just like the hollowed-out socket in his stomach that deepened every time a pair of hostile eyes bored into him.

"C'mon, Slaton," Ellis prodded. "Crack open some of that good stuff."

Kevin sighed inwardly. This sucked just as much as the piss mopping job. But the realization that he didn't have the nerve to even attempt burrowing into the Armada's system—that burned his spirit to a crisp. Sure, he could tell himself his hands were tied. After all, the whole room was watching.

But they had no clue what he'd uploaded to the warship from his stolen craft. It was a snake in the cyber-shadows, ready to strike on his command. If only he had the guts…

He starting browsing through photos and messages. Erin Lane had stored no images from her past of friends or family. Not uncommon. A typical recruit was someone looking to abandon his or her current life for something better. The only thing Kevin had in common with these people.

Messages were a different story. This girl had a whole network of friends, all fellow recruits. Kevin was surprised at how much they chatted online given that they shared the same quarters. He could have easily eavesdropped on their conversations during the days leading up to his botched AWOL attempt when he still had tech of his own. But he'd had other priorities, like figuring out how to steal a hawker. And face-to-face conversations with Tonya, if he was really being honest.

There were several doctored images of Tonya. One of her performing fellatio on a gub, a huge porcine creature of the marshes. Another with her being ravaged by a sex-bot. Kevin's face reddened. His blood boiled. He wanted to bust Erin Lane across the chops, but he knew he couldn't cause any serious damage before she laid him out.

"Now that's what I call entertainment," Ellis said.

The four recruits paused their cleaning activity to laugh. "Keep going, Slaton," Lane said. "Open up everything. I've got nothing to hide."

There were messages about him too. Observations like: *Can't believe Tonya has a thing for that loser. Makes her feel special. Thinks she's sooo hot.* And another doctored image: this one with Kevin's head on a worm's body, crawling up Tonya's leg.

He deleted everything. Before he could stop himself. A reflex action. In one fell swoop, Kevin blew all of Erin Lane's apps and data away. The hologram faded into a blank shadow, waiting for its first input.

"You're dead!" Lane said.

She started towards Kevin, but Ellis blocked her path. "Where do you think you're going?"

"Getting more tissue to finish cleaning. Sir!"

"I think you can finish up with what you've got. Don't you?"

"Yes, sir."

"And Slaton, since you've nuked Lane's device, I guess you'll have to entertain yourself by watching them clean up your mess."

"Yes, sir." Kevin stood at attention and watched the seething recruits perform their nasty job. It was going to go bad for him later on.

And keep right on going bad.

Unless…

CHAPTER 9

NOBODY HARASSED Kevin during the last meal before sack time. Normally, he could always count on being bumped or tripped by somebody. But he made it all the way to a table without having the heavy tray knocked from his hands. Whatever they were planning, it was going to be *really* bad this time.

The chow hall made Kevin feel like he was eating in a closet. There was barely room for the food counter and four utilitarian tables. Had to be some inane mind game they played with recruits—forcing them to dine in close quarters to build comradery, or to just have them suffer together for the hell of it. The walls were a dark shade of green that blended with their dull gray uniforms like foliage and trees, stripping them of all individualism and shaping them into mindless cogs.

Their training squad was comprised of four six-person teams. Each team was assigned a number, not a name. Kevin was on team number four. And his teammates despised him. To them, he was a liability, the weak link, a twig that snapped under the slightest pressure. Always guaranteed to score in the bottom and pull down their overall average. No surprise there. Combat training in the Armada was based on physical prowess. And trying to mold Kevin into a fighter was like trying to freeze a blazing sun.

Team four was also down to five members with Tonya gone. She hadn't been popular with Lane, Hickson, and the others. But in competition against other teams, she could singlehandedly turn the tide in their favor, more than compensating for Kevin's weakness.

Everybody blamed Kevin for her absence, of course. Sure, he'd forced Tonya to leave. And it was also his fault that Instructor Ellis was an asshole, that galaxies died after billions of years, and that they always served the same tasteless shit here (over-preserved fruits and vegetables from vacuum-sealed containers and gray protein-enriched gruel). Kevin Slaton: scapegoat for anything wrong with anything.

His teammates weren't friends or allies; they were circling predators, watching and waiting, biding their time. And that was *before* the recent incident in their barracks, which was also his fault, according to their pea-brained logic.

Lane's messages and images, on the other hand… Yeah. He did wipe them out. Deliberately. No getting around that.

Kevin sat at one of the tables, shoulder-to-shoulder with two recruits from another team. From the next table, he could feel Erin Lane's eyes shooting daggers in his direction.

He knew what he had to do, and cursed himself for being unable to work up the nerve to kick things off. Being a coward sucked sometimes. In the past, however, he'd been able to justify it as self-preservation. There was some ancient saying about a coward dying thousands of deaths. Nope! A coward didn't die; he stayed alive and well, only without dignity, which was just a nice-to-have kind of luxury item anyhow.

But this was new. For the first time in his life, Kevin found himself in a situation where saving himself required a brave, fear-facing act on his part. Only he couldn't do it. All he could do was sit on that hard bench and stare down at the unappealing tray of food in front of him.

Thing is, he had nothing to lose. Absolutely nothing! No way in hell would his plan (or any other) make things worse for him than they were already. Yet when fear was engrained in your being, encoded into your DNA, as much a part of you as hair or eye color, with fingers of dread and cowardice intertwined throughout your guts, snuffing out the tiniest spark of fight or resistance, you were pretty much screwed.

Keeping his head down, Kevin forced down a spoonful of the tasteless gruel. It was hopeless. The more he tried to steel himself for action, the more he wanted to run and hide. How had he managed to steal a space vessel? Well, that entire operation involved running and hiding. This new plan was all about direct confrontation.

Again, he was pretty much screwed. Nothing to do but wait to be a victim.

What happened next changed everything. It started as a muffled giggle, then a ripple of laughter that spread from one table to another. Amanda Smith, another one of Kevin's team-mates, had turned her device all the way up, which could burn out the resistor beam if you overdid it (not that she knew or cared).

She was showing off a four-foot holo. A mocked-up image. Tonya with a snout and tusks changing Kevin's diaper.

Kevin's head was swimming. A scream rose in his throat; hot rage erupted in his gut and pounded in his chest. A tear splattered in the glob of gruel he'd been trying to force down. His vision blurred as all the laughing faces dissolved into a swirling sea of grins.

The two recruits on either side of Kevin had been snickering at his expense. One of them stuck out of a foot to trip him when he stood up. Kevin stomped down with his heel, evoking a snarl of pain and landing himself on someone else's shit list.

Without pausing, he walked towards the disposal window with his tray of uneaten food, still fully intending to get the hell out of here. Damage control time at this point.

"What's the matter, Kev?" Erin Lane called to him. "Need your girlfriend to wipe your ass for you?"

"She's probably been breastfeeding him!" Amanda shrieked.

Something snapped. Everything went white for a moment. Then Kevin found himself walking over to their table. He was going to do it—he was *really* going to go through with this...

Ridiculously, he paused to consider why the Armanda made food trays out of metal. Granted, there was an unlimited supply of iron ore on asteroids just for the taking. But why bother when you could synthesize polymers?

Then he was there. Standing at their table. Up close and personal, Amanda was still spewing laughter, oblivious to his approach, not that she would have taken him seriously. That was when sweet reason melted into molten lava.

Kevin swung the tray at Amanda's face. Bullseye! Her nose spouted blood. The impact reverberated from his hands to his elbows.

Then Kevin flung his tray at Erin Lane. She blocked it easily but wound up with a collage of gruel on the front of her uniform and a greenish legume lodged in her hair.

Kevin had quit caring at that point. A feeling he'd never known. No thought. No analysis. Just action. As foreign as jumping off a cliff or diving into a black hole.

"Dojo. You and me," he said. "Alone."

CHAPTER 10

If Kevin Slaton wanted to hide, the dojo was the last place anybody would ever think to look for him. This was where they trained for combat with weapons and bare hands.

The Armada's coat of arms, emblazoned on the back wall, was the first thing you saw when you entered. To the left were racks containing weapons and gear. Long synthetic staffs that left bruises with even light contact; fingerless gloves that allowed you to grab and twist but also punch hard without breaking a knuckle. Zap sticks crackled with bad intent and burned like a hot stove without leaving a mark. They even had gimlets, T-shaped handguns that bored precise holes through organic matter. For training purposes, the dojo's gimlets had been dialed back; a direct hit felt like a nail hammering into your body, but the pain subsided within minutes that felt like hours. To the right was the waiting area, where you stood and watched until it was your turn in the ring.

The floor was cream-colored padding with excellent traction for moving and darting. Just standing on it made Kevin want to run for cover. But he'd gotten things started, and he was going to finish this thing one way or another.

Who was he kidding? The dojo had always been a painful and humiliating place for him. This time would be no different. Lane was going to do all the finishing.

Except…this time it would all be worth it. This time, he'd gain something in the end besides pain and humiliation.

Right on cue, her voice pierced his thoughts. "Okay, tough guy. Let's see what you've got."

Face more intense than pretty, body more powerful than sexy, Erin Lane already had her shoes off. Her light-brown hair was tied back in a tight braid. Next to Tonya, she was probably the toughest member on their team. Hickson could hold his own with her. Kevin didn't stand a chance.

"I've got something to say." Kevin blurted out the words, hoping his voice didn't quiver.

"Sorry, pansy. Didn't come here to talk." Lane took a backward step to position herself between Kevin and the door.

"I can fix your device," Kevin said.

"And I can break you into eight-and-a-half pieces," Lane retorted.

"I'll fight you," Kevin said. "But first—"

"Look! You either square off with me right now or get the biggest hurt of your pathetic existence."

"You want to do without apps or entertainment for the rest of training?" Kevin said. "I can get back what I deleted. Let me do that, and then we'll settle up in the ring."

Lane's eyes were unsettling—the eyes of a rabid doe. "Why wait?" She started towards him, a steady and purposeful walk-down. "I can make you fix my apps *after* I beat the crap out of you."

"Not if I'm unconscious," Kevin said.

"You've got a point there," Lane said. "Because you're not leaving here under your own power."

Small and puny, weak and helpless, Kevin was food. Not prey. Food. Served up on a silver platter, he was a free snack that she didn't even have to work for. Erin Lane was going to rip him apart. That was a given. Kevin's only chance of success was convincing her to postpone her onslaught for the sake of having her device restored to full functionality.

Right now, she didn't seem too keen on waiting another second.

Without further thought, Kevin said the one thing—the *only* thing that might work. "I'm asking this one concession for me," he said. "For my own honor."

"You have no honor. Worm boy."

He walked towards her and didn't pause when she crouched into a fighting stance. "I'll make your device fully functional and get all your messages and images back. Then we'll be on equal terms."

"And then?"

Kevin walked all the way up to her, eyeball to eyeball. "After I fix your tech, maybe I'll fix you."

Surprise, and maybe a touch of uncertainty, flitted across Lane's face. She handed over her device. "Here you go, hotshot. I was going to shove this up your ass since it's useless anyhow. But let's see if you can live up to your words."

Kevin fired up the device. The holo function was dead, as was personal authentication. But the firmware was still intact. An empty vessel awaiting instruction. A personification of the ideal Armada recruit, Kevin thought.

Burrowing his way into the system kernel, well aware that Lane's account had zero rights, he pinged the warship's computer with a simple access request that contained a unique identification token. Credential authentication would never take place. Instead, a stealth process would recognize his message's unique signature and intercept it.

Uploading this worm to the warship's computer was the last thing he'd done out in deep space after forcing Tonya to leave him behind. Whitehead had been so focused on regaining control of the computer on Kevin's stolen ship, he'd neglected to monitor the data return stream. Kevin had embedded a packet with a special payload.

Several seemingly unrelated qubit arrays had arranged themselves into a virtual gateway, and Kevin's token would trigger a chain reaction, causing them to compile themselves into an executable that would attach itself to the operating system kernel and then start replicating. The result would be a worm or virus, growing and propagating with ever-increasing resource consumption.

Much like a human being infected by illness becoming weak, tired, headachy, feverish, and nauseous, the warship's computer would slow to a crawl and become nonfunctional. In bed. Out of commission. Calling in sick. Don't even talk to me right now.

And only Kevin would be able to stop it. His price for restoring control of their ship to them: freedom. A discharge.

This was what he should have done in the beginning when they screwed him over with this combat assignment. Way simpler than stealing a ship. And easier. Thing is, this approach involved physical altercation. Not exactly his strong suit. But he had no better option, and there was no turning back now.

Hearing Lane's restless breathing reminded him to look up. Her nostrils were flaring; she was barely able to restrain herself from attacking.

"Your account's rebuilding itself," Kevin said. "Another minute and I'm all yours."

"You've got that right," Lane said. She stalked over to the doorway and started stretching out, throwing lazy kicks over her head and punching the air.

Her device paused for another half-minute that felt like forever. She wasn't going to wait much longer. Then came the acknowledgment prompt. Kevin's program had assembled and launched. The die was cast. The process was in motion. In approximately five hours, the Armada warship *Touchstone* would be a giant piece of helpless space junk.

Kevin's heart raced as he looked again at Erin Lane. His triumph would come at a heavy price. Or maybe not. With his deep system access, he might be able to use Lane's device to activate training room boundaries. Dark lines representing invisible force fields would shimmer on the floor. Brush against a boundary and your whole body would feel like it was on fire. Throw your opponent against one…well, that really sucked.

Taking a couple of deep breaths, he reminded himself of the bigger picture. His main goal. Suddenly firing off an unauthorized process could tip off the system techs—mindless boobs like Whitehead. Right now, they'd still be able to contain Kevin's virus if they discovered it. In three hours, they'd have to bring the system offline for full decontamination. In five hours, it would be too late.

Kevin disconnected from the system and powered down Lane's device. "Got it working," he said.

Lane padded over, stalking her prey with the expectant gleam of a hunter. "Let's see it," she said. "I might let you crawl out of here if everything looks right. And I mean everything."

Kevin handed her the dead device. "Sorry," he said. "Guess I was wrong." Then he hit her full in the face, instantly regretting the throb in his knuckles.

No point in running, no point in hiding. What came, came.

CHAPTER 11

Space was a misnomer. Space implied wide open area, empty and vacant. Which also implied availability—as in not claimed or owned. Nothing could be further from the truth.

Commander Ralph Hudson stood gazing though the windowed wall of his quarters out into…not space, but *territory*. He clenched his fists and reaffirmed his reason for being. Everything his naked eye could see, and far beyond, was Armada property. *Our territory.*

Where the darkness surrounding the warship was concerned, size and area were irrelevant numbers. The warship's domain could be a pond, maybe an ocean, or just a droplet on a laboratory slide, depending on the observer's perspective. Didn't matter. What mattered was the white dot of every distant star represented a luminous boundary stake.

Exhaling till his chest and abs tightened and the pressure spread to his face, Hudson resisted the urge to inhale till he felt his heart slow down to a laborious oxygen-conserving grind. Then he took a deep breath and turned away from his viewport. He was in attack mode now, ready to wipe out whatever task or obstacle presented itself. *Stay on point,* he reminded himself. That was how you ascended through the ranks.

And speaking of *on point*, there was one point in particular poking him in the ass right now. Kevin Slaton. The asset. That's what high command called him. *The asset!*

Nobody, not even the captain, knew his true reason for being assigned to this warship. Hudson wasn't supposed to know either. But he had his sources. This kid, it seemed, was gifted in computers and tech. Which made him a useless pleb in Hudson's book, but that didn't matter. What mattered was his importance to high command. The admiralty.

They were so concerned about their "asset" falling into the wrong hands that they'd stuck him on a vessel that trained warriors. All very hush-hush. And they'd planned on keeping the little pansy unscathed (at least somewhat) by planting a top-notch bodyguard in his training squad to protect him.

A loyal officer would have shared this intel with his captain. Hudson wasn't loyal, and he wasn't sharing. Because he knew how things worked. If Kevin Slaton got injured or killed, there would be blame and repercussions. It wouldn't matter that their plan was idiotic, right up there with dropping a goldfish into a shark tank. Nor would it matter that Captain Arnold had no knowledge of what they were doing. She'd get blamed. That bitch! Especially since there'd been concerns voiced about the safety of recruits on her ship. (Hudson did indeed have his sources.)

Hudson's plan was simple. High command had handpicked a youngish Armada warrior with awesome combat skills and a natural aptitude for espionage as Slaton's protector. And thanks to certain contacts Hudson didn't officially have, that wonder boy had managed to get himself killed right before Slaton was due to be transferred to *Touchstone*—a stupid fight over a drinking game in some nothing dive in the Innes sector.

Enter Tonya Verdi. Sometimes too much secrecy meant too

little communication. Therefore, as far as high command was concerned, she'd been Slaton's assigned protector all along. But Hudson had paid her to kill the little shit. Half up front. The remainder when she did the deed. She was to make it look like an accident, negligence that should never happen in a training environment.

That's how Hudson planned to get Captain Arnold removed and take her place. Especially after the undeserving bitch leapfrogged over him to take what was rightfully his.

But this Tonya Verdi had screwed him royally (not in a good way either). Stealing the asset and escaping the ship...he never saw that coming. It had worked out well for Verdi, even though she'd been forced to leave her prize behind, because Hudson had planned to kill her in the end.

Never leave witnesses. That didn't work out as planned. Still, fallout from that shitstorm with the stolen hawker couldn't lead back to him. Probably.

Message alert.

It came through Hudson's private network, but not from a personal device from inside the ship or even from an exterior subspace channel. Then a grainy hologram popped and flickered as it assembled. But Hudson easily recognized the shapely Tonya Verdi.

"Hello Hud-do." Her mocking voice had a lilt to it, as if she was about to laugh. "Bet you never expected to hear from me again. Anyhow, you owe me the rest of my money. I'll contact you with details on where to send it.

"Oh, by the way, this is a timed alert I planted on the ship's computer. I've set up a few more of them as insurance. One will go to Captain Arnold; it's chock-full of shit you *don't* want her to hear about. I'll send you instructions on how to disable it once I'm paid. Later, loser."

The holo vanished. Hudson leaped out of his chair, wanting

to run but having nowhere to go. "Somebody's gonna die!" he shouted to the empty room.

His quarters suddenly felt small and confining. "Open door," he said.

Nothing.

He repeated his command. "Allow exit. Open door."

No. No!

He couldn't be trapped. Impossible. If he was being imprisoned or charged with an infraction, they'd send people here to arrest him…

He stared at the closed door, enveloped in a cold sweat that turned his stomach. The walls were closing in on him—that vast territory outside of the warship, a distant memory.

CHAPTER 12

For a brief instant, Captain Kalie Arnold missed being able to report her concerns to her superiors and let them decide what to do. It was her decision now.

Yes. She'd wanted this. The responsibility, the challenge, the constant grind of one problem after another. She'd had some baleful results of late: a recruit going AWOL, and a space battle in which her warship suffered massive losses.

It wasn't over yet. Because her gut was warning her that things still weren't right on the warship *Touchstone*.

She was behind closed doors in a small briefing room with only a desk and two chairs. Her private office away from interruptions. Just her and Jarrett, her senior adjutant. Jarrett was no longer fit for active combat, but his wisdom and experience made him invaluable.

Jarrett stood straight and rigid, watching her with his good right eye. His face was a mass of scar tissue. A circular disc covered the socket where his left eye used to be—before the optic nerve got fried in battle. "Shall I hail the bridge again?" he asked.

Arnold shook her head. "I want to talk to you, Jarrett. Tell me what you think."

"I don't understand—"

"Bullshit. You know exactly what I'm saying. So talk to me. Tell me what in the hell is going on."

"Everything's gone haywire, Captain."

"Right. Everything."

It had started with the meal service. They had some lame excuse about not receiving her order, even though the notion of Jarrett forgetting to send it was laughable. Then there were the reports that never came. And her briefing with less than half of the requested attendees.

All minor glitches. Nothing overly alarming all by itself. But put them together, look at them as a related pattern…

"What do you think, Jarrett—is the crew taking stupid pills?"

"No, Captain."

"Did they decide to be insubordinate just for kicks?"

"Umm…"

Arnold answered for him. "Of course they didn't. They're dedicated and competent. This is not a human problem."

The captain shifted in her chair and considered for a moment. "Sit down, Jarrett," she said. "You've been standing there, all stiff and rigid, long enough."

Always impeccably obedient, Jarrett issued the voice command. Acknowledgment was instantaneous. But nothing happened for about ten seconds. Finally, the chair floated over to him, but with fits and starts in its trajectory. As if it was rolling on wheels and getting stuck in patches of sludge along the way.

Was this a break in the pattern? The initial problem seemed to be related to ship-wide communication, or miscommunication in this case. But here was an unrelated piece of equipment with issues.

Or maybe *not* unrelated.

Arnold wasn't a tech, but she did have a working knowledge of a warship's AI. Any of the legless chairs that floated from one place to another had a basic navigation system built into the firmware chip inside of them. So a chair's floater program ought to be autonomous. It ran on simple logic: go straight to your destination; if you encounter an impediment, stop, go around it, resume course.

So why…

The navigation! Chairs and other items that moved on command pinged the warship's central computer to obtain their current position as well as their destination. It was a global positioning system specific to the warship itself, replete with restricted areas and safeguards.

"Sorry, Jarrett," Arnold said. "You're going to have to stand." She ordered the chair back to its holding area in the rear closet. Again, immediate acknowledgment followed by a long delay.

Arnold stood at her full height of nearly six feet. "There's a computer glitch affecting the whole ship," she said. "Here. Watch this."

She issued the voice command to open her door. Nothing.

Jarrett's good eye glared at the unopened door. "I'll contact somebody to get us out," he said.

"If you can reach anybody." Arnold patted him on the shoulder. She was three inches taller and projected a much greater height difference.

"No need to worry," she said. "We're not trapped."

Arnold pulled on a black glove. It was the same kind of glove that Kevin Slaton had used to steal a hawker. Embedded nanotubes read the wearer's DNA and generated an encrypted code for the palm reader to evaluate. A double authentication protocol. When she touched the palm reader, the door to her quarters slid open.

"That's hard proof, Jarrett," she said. "Any voice command that requires authorization gets routed through the main computer. In addition to evaluating my voice pattern, the computer gets a fix on my location and scans my physical image. That way, even an exact reproduction of my voice isn't enough to open the door. The nanotube in the glove, on the other hand, is DNA-specific. And the palm reader evaluates body temperature as well. So it doesn't need to check the ship's computer for verification."

Jarrett was already retrieving two micro communicators that attached to a uniform. Used during ground combat, they operated on an encrypted channel. You could be over fifty miles apart and still carry on a conversation. They also served as location trackers for orbiting ships.

"Good thinking," Arnold said. She affixed one of the micro-comms to her dark black uniform top. "I'm headed down to talk to the tech people. In person. In the meantime, your job is to distribute micro-comms to the commanders. They're to distribute them down throughout their ranks. Relay that as an order from me."

"Yes, Captain."

"You want to ask me something," Arnold said.

"How serious is this?"

Arnold's jaw clenched. "Probably just an annoyance," she said. "Nothing insurmountable by any means. Thing is, we can't live with *probably*. We have to know."

CHAPTER 13

Someone was outside his door.

Commander Ralph Hudson got his boots on and considered the situation. He issued the voice command to view his outside entryway and got back nothing. Just a single empty blank nothing. They were blocking him from access to anything outside of his quarters. No contacting anybody for assistance. No surveilling the situation from here.

Decision time. If there were four or fewer on the security detail outside his door, he could fight his way out of immediate trouble. But he had to do it now, while he still had access to weaponry. If he let them take him into custody, he'd be unarmed. Helpless. But killing or disabling his captors would necessitate getting the hell off of this warship and disappearing.

What to do?

A wave of dizziness almost made him puke. All of those swirling thoughts, racing tornadoes in his head. This was a monumental decision that had to be made in mere seconds.

Cursing his indecisiveness, Hudson kicked one of the solid walls and felt the impact reverberate all the way up his right leg. What a ridiculous situation! Action without hesitation—that was his mantra. He was *never* in a dilemma. Yet, here he was…about to be defeated by sick, cowardly panic.

A red X flickered over his doorway. An unsuccessful access attempt from whoever was out there. Not bothering to question why a security detail would have the slightest problem opening any door on a warship, Hudson got moving.

When in doubt—no! Doubt was not an option. Especially now. When every second counted.

Hudson armed himself with a handheld zap stick concealed against his ribcage inside of his uniform shirt. Also a gimlet, a T-shaped handgun that was ideal for carving flesh into charred ash. He hid the gimlet in his right boot. Whoever was searching him would find that first. But it would leave that person's neck exposed and vulnerable. As a last-second addition, he strapped a retractable carbide blade under his right sleeve. It wouldn't be detectable by scanners, at least not easily.

The second the door to his quarters whooshed open, Hudson assumed a fighting stance, ready to face down anybody who dared to intrude into his domain.

"Captain's Adjutant Fike reporting. Request permission to enter your quarters. Sir!"

That was it. One of the captain's lapdogs. A young punk with a milky face and a prosthetic right leg. He'd still be fit for battle if he were half a man. Instead, he preferred to let the bitch captain breastfeed him.

"What the hell do you want?" Hudson snapped.

Fike explained the apparent problem with the warship's computer system that was preventing intra-ship communication, among other things.

Internally, Hudson collapsed with relief. To Fike, he presented a scowl of disdain. "Why is that my problem?" he demanded. "You should be talking to the techs. Not me."

"Effective immediately, all warship personnel will be issued micro-comms for communication."

"No. What you need to do is pull your head out of your ass," Hudson said. "You've got some nerve. The computer's fouled up, and your idea of a solution is passing out micro-comms. Get the hell out of here!"

"Captain's orders, sir."

Fike maintained a stoic expression, but Hudson detected a glint in his eye. A well-hidden smirk. "If the captain has specific instructions for me, my channel's always open," he said. "She can contact me directly."

"Commander Ralph Hudson. Through me, as Captain Arnold's authorized agent of conveyance, you have just received a direct order."

Hudson thought of the zap stick, imagined it pumping voltage into this underling's neck. "You really want to watch yourself here, son."

"To confirm compliance, you must affix a micro-comm to your uniform in my presence. Please allow me to witness this action."

Seething with fury, Hudson snatched the micro-comm from Fike's hand and slapped it on his shirt. "Now get the hell out of here before I stick it someplace else," he said.

This time, Fike didn't bother to hide his smirk. He unclipped a synthetic pouch from his belt and laid it on a nearby table. "This package contains five hundred micro-comms," he said. "Captain Arnold also orders you to distribute them throughout your ranks." Then, before Hudson could react, he turned on his heel and vacated the room, closing the door behind him.

Hudson glared at the door, unable to remember the last time he'd been this angry. That loser—that pleb!—had just laid an order on him and left after getting the last word. His heart pulsated in his temples; he wanted to break something delicate, injure somebody, throw something heavy.

Taking deep breaths and wiping the stinging sweat from his

eyes, he reminded himself to stay cool and sit tight. For now. After all, he'd damn near overreacted. *Over a computer glitch!* He might have killed Fike over nothing. Then what? Thanks to the gods of the universe, whoever they might be, there'd been no time to activate his fake identity. A good thing. A *very* good thing. That was his failsafe. The absolute last resort if all else failed.

He'd obey the captain's orders and distribute those stupid communicators. Or, rather, farm that task out to his subordinates. But first, the dojo. He needed to burn some of the rage out of his system.

Hudson considered for a moment and decided it would be better to keep his weapons on him at all times—all of them, including the carbide blade. The prospect of being unarmed was just too much.

He issued the voice command to open his door.

No response. The door didn't budge.

Okay, he reminded himself. *It's a computer glitch. That's all.*

Touching the micro-comm on his chest, he hailed Fike. "Inform the captain that I'm unable to carry out my orders if I'm locked in my quarters," he said.

"You're not locked in," Fike said. "You can leave anytime. Sir."

"Well, the door won't open for me, numb nuts," Hudson said.

"No, sir. It's not responding to voice commands. Byproduct of the ship's computer issues."

"Listen, Fike! You get your ass over here on the double and get me out of here or I'll—"

"Commander Hudson, sir. Please use the hand scanner with your glove to enter and exit your quarters."

Hudson felt a ripping in the back of his throat and realized he was screaming. "Why the hell didn't you tell me that in the first place?"

"Begging the commander's pardon. I assumed you had deduced that on your own. Sir."

Hudson ended the communication. Fike had just managed to be insubordinate in a crafty, underhanded way. Hudson had forgotten the obvious: with the computer malfunctioning, you reverted to manual operations. So if he reported Fike for his insubordination, he'd look like an idiot.

Fike. He'd remember that name. It was burned into his brain. Fike! He was going to kill that upstart piece of crap.

But for now, he was an officer of the Armada, obeying orders and ascending the ranks.

CHAPTER 14

THE BRAIN OF THE WARSHIP, the cyber room, was located dead center. An attacking fleet would have to destroy the entire ship to take out the computer bank. And Captain Kalie Arnold would have much preferred fighting off an external attack to confronting the unseen enemy she was dealing with now. The very fact that she had to walk down here for a status report, instead of just hailing the cyber room from any comm portal on the ship, had her guts in knots.

She'd come alone, leaving Jarrett to coordinate the ship-wide distribution of communicators. Without announcing herself, she pressed her glove against the reader and opened the door. Then she stood and watched in silent observation.

Here was the nerve center. Literally the ship's brain that controlled everything from navigation and weaponry down to life-sustaining functions like oxygen levels. As a combat officer with rudimentary technical savvy, she didn't know how to interpret any of the colored lines and dots that pulsated across the room's six-wall honeycomb pattern (only that they monitored the very heartbeat of the ship), but their pattern just seemed… wrong. Way too sluggish somehow. And another thing: no holograms, nor any bustle of activity. In fact, most of the beige-clothed techs were sitting and staring with uncertainty etched into their faces.

It took a couple of seconds for someone to notice the open door (yet another issue) and see her standing in the entryway. At that point, the dozen techs ceased their inactivity and snapped to attention. She remembered one of them, a thin man with pale skin. William Whitehead, Technologist Grade-Five. Contrary to his name, Whitehead had a headful of thick carrot-colored hair. He'd been a key player in the capture of Kevin Slaton, taking a lead role from a technical standpoint.

Arnold didn't trust him, even though he'd had the training, passed the tests, proven himself to be reliable. Or, at least, hadn't proven himself unreliable. In the end, there was something about his mannerism that she didn't like. A cockiness bred from overconfidence and the false sense of security that comes from thinking you have an insurmountable advantage.

Her knuckles itched to crack his smug face. But Whitehead wasn't the problem. After Slaton's capture, she'd overheard him bragging to anyone who would listen about how he'd bested his quarry via the computer on the very craft he'd stolen.

And she'd overlooked it.

Instead, her focus had been on investigating Slaton's escape. And how an enemy agent with the fake name of Tonya Verdi had been able to pose as a recruit and get assigned to the *same team* as Slaton. No easy task. And impossible without inside help. They had a leak in their chain of command. And Arnold was going to find it. She had to.

That still didn't change the fact that she'd overlooked the obvious: William Whitehead's delusion—yes, delusion!—that he'd bested Kevin Slaton. With Whitehead sparring with him on a computational plane, she should have ordered a full battery of system diagnostics after the fact. Really, Whitehead should have been the one to do that; instead, he'd strutted around and boasted, poking out his bird chest till it was ready to split right down the middle.

No excuses, though. Whitehead had arrogance beyond his proficiency, but she was captain. Responsibility for the ship's wellbeing fell on her.

For two full minutes, Arnold kept everybody in the room standing at attention. Their nervousness was mounting; she could feel it in the air. Good. This was a potential crisis, and they needed some urgency in their thoughts and actions.

Finally, she spoke. "I'm here because I can't communicate with you over the ship's network."

Dead silence. Nobody spoke. A bunch of statues standing erect, not daring to flinch.

"Status update, please."

William Whitehead cleared his throat and tugged at the collar of his uniform. "After running the usual battery of diagnostics and finding nothing, I recommend a total reboot."

"Total as in everything?"

"That's what *total* means. Captain."

Taking two long strides, Arnold invaded Whitehead's personal space and glared down at him. "I know what *total* means," she said. "For one thing, I am in *total* command of you. Which means you will give me *total* respect or get your ass handed to you."

Whitehead reddened. But there was still a haughtiness in his eyes that Arnold didn't care for. Unacceptable.

She threw him against the wall and jammed her forearm against his throat. A collective gasp filled the room. Techies weren't wired for physical altercation. Nonetheless, they all remained at attention while Whitehead gurgled like an asphyxiated newborn.

"Case in point," Arnold said. "I could shut down Whitehead by choking him unconscious or crushing his windpipe. Two approaches with different results."

Instinctively, Whitehead grabbed at her arm. Arnold stepped on his toe, and he let out a high-pitched squeal—such a cowardly response. She could actually taste the bile-like disgust in her mouth. No fight, no fortitude. A pathetic excuse for an Armada warrior. Which, of course, he wasn't.

And neither was Kevin Slaton.

Pushing that thought aside for the moment, Arnold released Whitehead, and he staggered sideways, clutching at this throat. "What we do and how long we do it for matters," she said. "Anybody need another demonstration?"

Nobody did. So she continued. "I need details. How long would we be down during the reboot? I'm talking to you, Whitehead!"

Whitehead made a huge production of clearing his throat. "Three hours."

"And what ship's functions would be offline during that time?"

Whitehead stared at the floor and said nothing. The other techs shifted nervously, avoiding eye contact. These were smart people. Smart *asses*, more often than not, because their intelligence made them arrogant. Arnold considered picking two of them at random and cracking their heads together. But she already had them plenty scared. And fear didn't seem to be lighting a fire under anybody's ass. In fact, it was having the opposite effect. These pathetic excuses for men and women were cracking like cheap porcelain.

Because they weren't warriors. Never had been. That's not why they were aboard this ship.

Arnold softened her voice and pretended she was talking to a nursery full of cowering, temperamental children. Not a huge stretch, actually. "You're here because you're brilliant," she said. "I can't begin to understand the shit you work on down here. No clue. But I have to make decisions. And I need to understand what we're up against."

She approached one of them, read his name from his insignia, put a hand on his trembling shoulder. "Talk to me, Vincent."

"Catastrophic system failure," Technologist Grade-Three Vincent said.

"Does that sound right, William?"

Whitehead nodded weakly.

"Any idea what's causing the problem?"

Nobody spoke.

"Okay," Arnold said. "We'll come back to that. Exactly what does this three-hour reboot entail?"

Vincent spoke up. "Shields will come up automatically at three-quarter power. Also all environmental controls like life support and gravitational functions will continue. Everything else is offline. There's no way to calibrate thrusters or scan our surroundings. Even if the weapons array was functional, it couldn't pinpoint a target's location."

Arnold nodded. "Anybody in this room who's participated in a reboot raise your hand."

Nobody had.

"So new territory for all of us," she said. "One thing I do know is the ship's computer constantly monitors and adjusts environmental variables like air and simulated atmospheric pressure every few seconds. So where's the autonomy? How can we be sure the environmental controls will function on their own?"

William Whitehead spoke up. "Autonomy is baked in. The ship's computer doesn't control environmental systems. Not directly. Instead, those systems deemed critical to survival respond to messages (think of them as suggestions or adjustments) sent by the main computer based on readings from all over the ship. However, if those messages cease for a specified period of time—the default setting is ten minutes—critical systems simply switch over to autonomy mode. What that means is the environment gets maintained on kind of a bell curve. Air quality won't be optimal, but close enough for a three-hour stint. Same with the shields. They'll just lock in at seventy-five percent power."

A mousy girl with pinkish-blonde hair piped up. "That doesn't happen automatically."

"Sure it does," Whitehead argued.

"Shut up, William," Arnold said. Then, addressing the girl, she said: "What does happen?"

"The computer sends an interrupt message to the queue; it prompts specific functions like environment controls to ignore future messages from the main computer and run autonomously under their default settings."

"And the reboot generates that interrupt message," William said. "So automatic."

"So you say," Arnold responded. "But you've never seen it done, have you?"

"Captain." Another tech spoke up. "A trial reboot is part of testing when a ship's computer is installed. All standard protocol."

Arnold sized him up. He was a large, older man with the bored demeanor of a long timer who'd seen it all. "Not doubting the effectiveness of standard protocol," she said. "But that reboot test is performed on a fully functional system. Is it not?"

Nobody made eye contact.

Whitehead flushed crimson. "We have to do something. Captain."

"Shut up, William." Another long stride and Arnold stood face-to-face with the mousy pink-blonde. Agnes Jade, Technologist Grade-One. "Tell me, Jade, what happens if that interrupt message never gets sent?"

"In other words, if messages to the environmental systems just stop..." Jade squeaked. "I'm sorry, Captain. I don't know."

"Because that's never happened," the older tech said. "Even during battle, when resources are compromised, the main computer always sends interrupt messages to disengage with anything that can run on its own."

They were all speaking out of turn, without requesting permission. But Arnold let it ride.

"Permission to speak, Captain." William was pretty smart after all. Nothing like a good choke-slam as an attitude adjustment.

Arnold nodded.

"All communication with environmental controls will stop if degradation in the ship's computer continues; presumably, the main system would send an interrupt message before disengaging, but..."

"Could we kick off a manual interrupt?" someone asked.

William shook his head. "No dice. System resources are way too compromised for that."

Arnold relaxed her face muscles. Exuding calm was critical here, even though she wanted to blast the whole room out of existence. They had to do something. A reboot was risky. They ought to have life support during the three-hour window, but... She didn't have a better idea. No, *she* didn't.

"We need ideas," she said. "Fire up a combine board; start brainstorming. Jade, you maintain the list. If the combine board goes down, use old-fashioned parchment and pen. Everybody. Start talking. That's an order."

CHAPTER 15

Nobody ever joined the Armada to become a doctor. Theirs was not a care-giving mission. On warships, the medical staff was mostly comprised of warriors who had lost their taste for blood.

It had taken twenty years and over a hundred battles for Doctor Claude Gable to be done with killing and maiming. But it had happened. He'd gone from warrior to pacifist and hadn't dared to look back.

His transition didn't happen in space, where combat entailed strategic maneuvering rather than brute force, disintegrations rather than explosions. Nor was he affected by close-quartered combat where warriors chewed each other up by any means available, from zap sticks to bare hands. But more times than he cared to remember, he'd raided the surface of a planet and come face-to-face with the innocent, defenseless victims who didn't deserve what happened to them. He still had vivid memories of their wretched faces and screams for mercy that only fueled their conqueror's brutality.

And then he became the one who went too far…

That was the shit that haunted his dreams.

Looking down at Kevin Slaton lying comatose on life

support, he wondered what in the hell the recruiters were thinking. Granted, no green recruit really knew how to fight (even though most of them thought they did). All of them had a bloodlust that made them eager to learn. This boy, however, never should have been allowed to even sign up.

Kevin Slaton. Helpless victim. When they hauled him in on an air stretcher, the walls had suddenly closed in on Doctor Claude Gable. For the first time in his nine years of being a caregiver, he'd had to bolt from the room and puke. Not that the sight of Slaton was anything new to him. He'd seen countless ruined bodies up close and personal. But those bodies belonged to warriors who'd eagerly gone to battle.

Fair fight? Slaton never had a chance. That extra stomp to the head when he was down did him in. He'd taken the full impact. Nothing underneath him except a solid floor. She'd caved in his skull. And she might as well have been hitting a training dummy for all the defense he'd been able to muster.

The thought produced a fresh bloom of nausea in Gable's stomach, and he looked away, sickened all over again. The infirmary on the warship *Touchstone* had been his haven for nearly a decade. Repairing bodies, healing injuries. Making people better off, less damaged, mitigating their pain, even allowing them to depart from their lives with dignity. No longer. You couldn't seal off the past; it had a way of seeping in through whatever dikes you tried to maintain.

Gable tried once again to pull up a care-path hologram to plot out Slaton's plan of treatment. Nothing. Damn computer was still out to lunch. Consequently, there wasn't a hell of a lot of treatment to plan at this juncture.

For now, the patient was stabilized. He was hooked up to a bunch of tubes carrying fluids in and out of his body and a respirator that was breathing for him. Gable had him on a field unit that was typically set up on the fly during battle. But that was a temporary measure at best; to restore Slaton—no, Kevin. He was going to refer to this gravely injured recruit by his first name from now on. To restore *Kevin* to consciousness, they'd need a fully functioning care station that was hooked into the ship's network. Without that, Kevin was trapped in a coma.

Worse still: the time window for treating this kind of brain trauma was limited.

The door slid open. Jan Kirkman entered with a scowl on her pretty face. "Better leave it open," she said. "Entryways are misbehaving too."

Gable nodded absently and stared at Kevin, as if a stern look could fix him.

"Can't float a chair over here either," Kirkman said. "I guess we're sitting on wall bunks for the time being." She looked down at Kevin and sniggered. "That's what happens when you try to comb your hair with a sledgehammer."

"You mind shutting the hell up?" Gable snapped.

"Sure, whatever."

Gable knew he'd overreacted. Because Jan didn't care. Why should she? Kirkman was a field medic, whose job was to patch up the wounded during battle—enough to transport them out alive. To her, they were just organic wreckage, malfunctioning machines in need of replacement cogs.

But even though she had no personal stake in a patient's welfare, getting broken warriors functioning again was her contribution to the Armanda. She was damn good at her job, and her performance record meant a lot to her. Gable could use that...

"This one's going to be a challenge," he said.

"Like it matters," Kirkman said. She'd already dismissed Kevin as a loser, a recruit that didn't make the grade. Spoiled meat to be discarded, not worth the effort.

Pulsations of pain thrummed inside of Gable's skull. His stomach heaved. But he fought back the nauseating dampness that sweated out of him. Jan was right. From an Armada point of view, Kevin wasn't worth fixing. And successfully restoring him to health wouldn't erase the murky past, nor would Gable derive the slightest bit of absolution from doing so. He knew that. Yet letting another defenseless victim perish would make things worse somehow.

"Are all pretty girls as stupid as you are?" he said.

Kirkman responded with a glare.

Good, he thought. *I made her mad.*

"You think another chance like this one is going to land in your lap?" Gable asked.

"Chance for what?"

"To hone our skills, dumbass. You know…the concept of putting in work now to get a result later."

"And that result would be reviving…him?"

Jan technically didn't answer to Gable. But he was in charge of the infirmary, which gave him the final say in a patient's treatment. He could make her assist him. And she'd follow his instructions to the letter. But he needed more than her obedience. He needed her fully engaged.

"Suppose you were out in the field and Kevin was your patient," he said.

"The enemy would be doing us a favor."

"C'mon, Kirkman. Think of this as a drill. This could happen to any warrior. What would you do?"

"What you've done. Stabilize him on a field stretcher and get him out of there."

"And things go sideways. No transport. Broken signal. Under attack. Got to hunker down and wait it out."

"Then he's toast," Kirkman said. She gave Kevin a cursory look. A clear polymer shield provided a viewport into his open skull. "You've cleaned out all the bone fragments. But that divot in the front of his brain is mush."

"Impressive," Gable said. "Real astute observation."

"Hey, you wanted to play make-believe. If we were out in the field right now, I'd write him off. Hell, I'd probably have to unhook him to conserve resources."

She was right. This was no battlefield. No chaos, limited supplies, poisonous atmosphere, lack of oxygen, infection from alien races that could ravage a body in no time flat. But, with the computer gone, this also wasn't a real infirmary.

"What's your problem, Gable?" Kirkman said. "We both know that we can't synthesize a nanoweb without the ship's computer."

"It's not a question of *can't*," Gable said. "We'd never try. After all, here, in the infirmary, we'd have the computer. In the field, you'd have too much other shit going on to even think about it. But right now, in this room, with the computer down and time being of the essence, if we could somehow pull this off..."

"We'd be developing a new, unheard-of battlefield treatment," Kirkman said. "Cool."

"Very cool," Gable agreed. "If you're up for a challenge."

"Nothing to lose," Kirkman said. She glanced at Kevin. "For any of us."

CHAPTER 16

HUDSON LOOKED up at the Armada coat of arms, huge and imposing from above the dojo—a wrathful god overseeing its realm. As always, the glow of the sword ignited a flame in Hudson's chest. But it was the spatters of blood on the cream-colored floor that made him quiver in anticipation of what was about to happen.

Normally blood and sweat on the mat got cleaned up. And normally, he'd chew out a hundred people for their negligence, system glitch or no. But he rather liked this remnant of previous combat. Perhaps cleanup was overrated. After all, leftover blood provided a firsthand look at what could happen if you weren't on top of your game, a valuable training tool and motivator. Not that Hudson ever needed motivation.

His three opponents stood at attention, faces etched in stoic acccptance of what came next. No visible fear. But of course not; they were trained warriors. Still, Hudson could smell fear on a person. It had a distinctive odor. A cross between piss and perfume. It oozed from a man's pores, mingled with his sweat; it floated on the air with every breath he exhaled; it even wafted off the clammy surface of his skin.

None of their angst had anything to do with Hudson being their superior officer. In fact, nothing would land them on the shit list faster than going easy on him. But they could see the fire in his eyes, feel the heat from the wrath burning bright inside of him, and know for a fact that he was ready to flat-out fuck somebody up.

They stood ready. Lovett and Fenton, two studs. And Hare, a woman with more balls than most men. No weapons involved. No gloves or footpads either. This was going to be a flesh-on-flesh, bone-on-bone affair.

"Now!" Hudson shouted.

Lovett advanced quickly, a dervish of feints and weaves. Fast and sneaky behind a probing jab and kicks at varying heights. He was giving Hudson a lot to look at.

Pap!

Quick, snapping speed. A stinging punch grazed Hudson's face. Another fast combo followed.

Pap! A right jab, a kick from a weird angle.

A three-punch sequence.

Again. Pap!

Hudson moved just enough to avoid real damage. He wasn't superfast, but he was strong and solid. And he had the killer instinct of a shark. He was also willing to absorb pain to get to the end game.

Lovett feinted, then flurried. Right on cue.

Hudson snagged Lovett's arm and drove an elbow into his sternum, producing a satisfying crunch. Then he moved in close and tight, smothering Lovett's attack and ripping a series of hard shots to his ribs. Lovett sank to one knee, then managed to roll out of danger. Clearly injured, he tried to circle and parry as Hudson walked him down.

There was no shortage of guts and smarts in Lovett. In fact, the right thing to do would be to order him to stand down and let one of the others take his place. But Ralph Hudson didn't believe in right. Not with the thrill of combat pulsating throughout his entire being.

Lovett tried a leg sweep. Hudson countered with a hatchet kick to the knee.

Crack!

Hudson couldn't wipe the grin off his face if he wanted to. There'd be no more walking for Lovett without some serious reconstruction.

Game over. But he wasn't finished.

Advancing to a dominant position on the mat, he trapped Lovett's right arm behind his head. Now he was free to do whatever the hell he wanted.

From the corner of his eye, the other two warriors stepped forward on instinct, then stopped themselves. Exactly what you wanted in a warrior: dog pack loyalty to your mates coupled with the discipline to honor the chain of command. What was about to happen was really a waste. But Hudson was too far gone to care about resources right now. His first two blows spattered blood across the mat in a bewitching pattern of dark splotches covered by a fine red mist. This was artistry. This was transformative. This was true beauty. It was an ever-increasing surge of pleasure, culminating in a massive head rush.

Yes! He was being transported…

Everything went white. Then Hudson found himself lying on his back with his brain struggling to click into gear. Fenton and Hare were standing over him with zap sticks. His tongue was laden with the faint taste of burning rubber. Those two were going to regret ever having been born.

Fenton broke the silence. "Sir! We have an update on the asset, Slaton."

"Wh-what?"

"We have an update. You ordered us to interrupt this sparring session if any new information surfaced."

Right. The subject at hand. Hudson sat up and realized he had a screaming headache. "I know what the hell I ordered," he snarled. They'd done their jobs exactly as he'd instructed. Use whatever means necessary to interrupt him for breaking news on Slaton.

Thing is, that update that he'd ordered—that he'd been waiting on—was going to piss him off royally. He just knew it.

Medics were working on Lovett. Hudson wanted to get up and finish what he started, but he had other priorities now.

That pissed him off even more.

CHAPTER 17

Captain Kalie Arnold stood outside the cyber room and resisted the urge to interfere. The geeks were dutifully gathered around the combine board, brainstorming on what to do about the catastrophic system failure that was skinning the warship's computer system alive. And she had nothing to contribute to that effort.

But her fists clenched in frustration over the train wreck she was witnessing. This wasn't teamwork, nor was it collaboration. With William Whitehead still subdued from their earlier encounter, two older gurus were taking the opportunity to talk over everybody else. Worse still: they were talking down to their teammates. Under these conditions, the little girl with the pink hair wasn't going to utter a peep.

It turned out that this system failure had revealed a previously unknown problem: the specialist division, the techs, the ones in charge of the warship's brain, had near zero conception of teamwork. How had she missed it? Easy. She, and all combat personnel under her, had been focused on the battle tactics, strategy. Sure, they were constantly hitting up the eggheads for fresh statistics on rations and resources, as well as odds and probabili-

ties in simulated scenarios, but they mostly allowed the specialists to operate with autonomy. And now Kalie Arnold, ship's
captain, was witnessing the outcome: an asshole who thought he
knew everything lording it over everybody else.

Perhaps too little, too late, Arnold finally understood why the
Armada had acquired the asset, Kevin Slaton. Ironically, she now
had a preview of just what he might do to an enemy vessel. She
needed an update from Hudson, and she needed it fast.

But first things first. The immediate need was to get the
system back online. Somehow, someway. In the meantime, she
contacted Jarrett via micro-comm. "Anything from Hudson yet?"
she asked.

"No, Captain."

"Well, never mind, for now. We're getting nowhere here in
the cyber room. Can you find out if any of our warships are
within hailing distance?"

"I can get that info as of twenty hours ago," Jarrett said. "I
routinely download approximate locations to my device."

Arnold couldn't help smiling. "And what prompted you to
do that?" she asked, knowing full well how often she asked him
the whereabouts of the other ships in the fleet.

"I like to be prepared," Jarrett said. Then, after a couple of
seconds, he said: "The warship *Juggernaut*. They're not in hailing
distance, but they're in this sector."

Arnold stifled a groan. With almost double the crew of this
vessel, *Juggernaut* was under the command of Admiral Anson.
The last person you'd want to ask for assistance. *Juggernaut* was
a true fighting ship. No recruits ever. Its directive was conquer.
Nothing else.

"No other options?"

"Not in this sector. No point in checking other sectors, I
suppose."

"None at all," Arnold said. "Thanks, Jarrett."

She didn't need those cyber-room geeks to tell her that they couldn't perform the calculations for cross-sector communication. Traversing a wormhole or cosmic juncture with an encrypted message was something of an art as well as a science. It also demanded massive system resources.

In fact, contacting *Juggernaut* would still require a beacon—a direct beacon, not a juncture-navigating beacon, but a beacon nonetheless. That entailed firing an encrypted data stream that traveled at near light speed. Said data stream carried both sender and receiver signatures in its packet. Its broadcast was readable at four billion miles. So if you could hit a small solar system, that was close enough to work. Sounded crazy, but across the vastness of deep space, this represented pinpoint accuracy.

Arnold almost hoped that *Juggernaut* had left this sector already, or that *Touchstone*'s already-limited system resources couldn't handle that much load.

She grabbed Vincent and Jade from the cyber room. Just those two. Nobody else. (The pair of assholes running the show, drawing diagrams, contradicting one another while accomplishing nothing with their long-winded debate of theories and conjectures, never even noticed. She'd deal with them later.)

"Right now, in our compromised state, if we needed to send a direct beacon to a warship in this sector, could we do it?" Arnold asked.

"Sure. Any spacecraft's computer could do that," Vincent said.

Just use a spacecraft computer! How obvious was that? Every hawker and harrier onboard had one. Arnold silently chided herself for not thinking of it.

"Whoever fires up a hawker and sends the message needs to make sure the launch sequence doesn't activate," Vincent added. "Otherwise the hawker and its parent warship (us) would attempt to synch up, and that would bog the main computer down even more."

"What do you say, Jade?" Arnold asked. "Does that sound right?"

The mousy little girl's nostrils flared; her eyes had a faraway look.

"Jade?"

"That's it!" she squeaked.

"So you're in agreement with Vincent—"

"No! I mean, yes. Just…"

Arnold put a hand on the girl's shoulder. *That girl's heart must be pounding in her skull,* she thought. "Take your time," she said. "Relax. Take a couple of deep breaths."

Jade tried to follow orders, but she just wound up hyperventilating.

"Permission to speak," Vincent said.

"We're way beyond that," Arnold said.

"Jade. You've got something," Vincent said.

A bashful nod.

"Don't worry about sounding good," Vincent said. "Just spit it out. We'll decipher as you go."

Jade spoke in a loud whisper. "I know how to find out what's wrong with the ship's computer," she said.

CHAPTER 18

HUDSON'S KINGDOM WAS CRUMBLING. The walls of the dojo were caving in on him. He'd just found out that Kevin Slaton, the asset, was in the infirmary with the front of his skull missing.

Had to do it, you just had to take that risk, he chided himself. But how was he supposed to know that Tonya Verdi would try to abduct the asset? Worse still, her phenomenal dogfighting tactics in open space meant that she was connected to powerful forces. You didn't gain that skillset hijacking cargo vessels. Which led to even grimmer possibilities. She could be a Scythe Bearer in the Wraith Brigade, or even part of an internal plot within the Armada itself.

Hudson fumed inwardly. Someone else was going to take the heat from this shitstorm.

"Warrior First-Class Ellis reporting!"

Not really reporting. They'd brought Ellis to the dojo for Hudson to interrogate. And not really interrogate either. This was going to be a frame-up job, pure and simple.

Only…a flash of recognition gave him pause. He recognized Ellis, a solid, unyielding hammerhead who had risen to the top of his recruiting class through brute fortitude. Yes…a memorable recruit from Hudson's drill instructor days. And now, Ellis, Warrior First Class, had become a drill instructor himself. The Armada needed men like him. A warrior, and now a gatekeeper for a standard of excellence that had been slipping over time.

The medics were still working on Lovett. That and the blood spoors left behind by Slaton's misadventure made the dojo's normally pristine floor look like it belonged in an ancient torture chamber. But if Ellis was affected by any of the sights, sounds, or smells in the dojo, he didn't show it.

"I want to hear it from you, Ellis," Hudson said. "What happened with Kevin Slaton?"

"It is my opinion that he's unfit to serve in the Armada," Ellis said.

"Did I ask for your opinion?"

"No, sir—"

"Did I ask for your evaluation of Kevin Slaton as a recruit?"

"No—"

Hudson got in the shorter man's face, almost forehead-to-forehead. "I asked: what in the hell happened to him?"

"Slaton?"

"Yeah, Slaton. Dumbass!"

"He's in the infirmary," Ellis said.

"No shit," Hudson said. "And you're evading my question. What happened?"

"He was a discipline problem," Ellis said. "Never pulled his weight. Couldn't integrate with his team."

Hudson inched closer. Nose to nose. Spraying Ellis's face when he spoke. "You either quit playing games and tell me what happened or there's another stretcher with your name on it."

Ellis didn't flinch. Instead, his jaw jutted out and his eyes flashed with hopeful bloodlust. This guy wanted to quit talking and throw down. An Armada warrior through-and-through. Yet he remained at attention, maintaining proper decorum despite being under duress, despite wanting to settle this matter with an all-out rumble.

This was the kind of man the Armada needed. Not those gutless plebs and plotters who'd be more useful as cannon fodder. Botanists, chemists, cooks, tech support and the like.

It was a damn shame that somebody had to have consequences for what had happened to Slaton—a loser if there ever was one. But it wasn't going to be Hudson. Shit did roll downhill, after all. But maybe it didn't have to be Ellis either. Maybe…

Hudson backed away and softened his voice. "One of your recruits fucked him up," he said.

"Sir, I accept full responsibility—"

"No!"

Ellis never blinked. He stared at Hudson, wide-eyed but still respectful.

"At ease, Ellis," Hudson said. "Now tell me what happened."

"We all got the alarm. Injury in the dojo. Emergency. Slaton was lying there all by himself when we got there."

"So a teammate just left him for dead."

Ellis reddened. "He never was a team member. He's a fucking pleb!"

Hudson bit down on a grin. Bit down hard. He hated what he was forcing Ellis to do. So it was imperative that he keep a straight face. "We've got video footage," he said. "We can't review it until the ship's computer comes back online. But it's there."

"No, you don't. Sir. The dojo cameras are only activated to review training sessions. And since no official training was taking place at the time of Slaton's mishap—"

"You have no clue what's getting recorded. Or when," Hudson said.

Ellis responded with a glare and said nothing.

Hudson had expected nothing less. Of course, they had no

footage. He'd tried a bullshit bluff, and Ellis wasn't buying it. So now he was going to have to force the issue.

"You were one of my recruits," Hudson said.

"Yes, sir. You taught me what it means to be a warrior."

"So you remember the sparring sessions."

A curt nod.

Hudson gestured towards the still prone body of Lovett. They were preparing to physically haul him to the infirmary, the air stretchers being out of commission due to that damned computer. "I've gotten meaner with age," he said.

"Very good, sir. So have I."

Hudson wanted to kiss him. "Not you. Them. Your recruits. I'll have them brought in here one by one. Every last one of them. And I'm going to assume that everything coming out of their mouths is bullshit. So I'll have to beat the truth out of them till they're shitting blood. Then I'll really start hurting them."

Ellis glared pure venom. Good. At least he was onboard.

"Get me the responsible recruit," Hudson said. "I don't care how. Beat it out of them, or just ask nicely. But you *will* get me that person. That is a direct order. Do you understand?"

"Yes, sir."

"Get out of my sight then," Hudson snapped.

It really was a shame to ruin a promising recruit in favor of a pleb. But he wasn't going to let Ellis take the fall. Both the captain and the Inquest Unit were going to need somebody to piss on. He'd make a big show out of rooting out the offending party. After all, safety concerns had been voiced…

So that was that. Shit did indeed roll downhill.

CHAPTER 19

JADE AND VINCENT gaped at the sheer size and *strength* of the hangar bay. Solid floor, imposing walls; a collage of gleaming silver. They looked intimidated. Downright scared.

Hangar bays had never intimidated Arnold. In fact, she still recalled entering a warship's hangar for the first time. That had been years ago, but she remembered the surge of adrenaline and her eagerness to prove her mettle. But she had warrior blood coursing through her veins.

These technologists (sometimes called techs for short) were weak, sensitive intellectuals. Plebs—that's what most warriors called them. The strict definition of pleb was *ordinary people from lower social classes*. Well, these two weren't ordinary. Far from it. They were brilliant children with minds that could think rings around hers. Yet they were children nonetheless, incapable of growing up—of fending for themselves. They'd always be dependent on stronger people for protection. Which meant lower social status right there.

But that wasn't her problem.

They were here to try out Jade's idea, and they needed all of them to do it. Jade for the knowhow; Vincent to provide supporting knowledge and to keep her somewhat calm; and Captain Arnold because techs didn't have access to ships or hangar bays.

Riding on conveyor discs was not an option; they relied on the ship's computer for navigation. So with intra-ship transport down, they'd just completed a forty-minute hike to the warship's rear hangar—a venture that also entailed climbing down ladders due to lifts being out of commission. Even though it was the furthest distance from the cyber room, Arnold had chosen the rear hangar because it housed the larger spacecraft. All three of them needed to be inside a ship together, which eliminated a single-person hawker as a viable option.

On arrival, the hangar bay door had opened when Arnold pressed her glove against the access panel. Vincent had explained it to her. Something about decentralization of functionality, where the computer that unlocked the door had its own programming. It was tied to the main computer but able to operate autonomously in the event of a system failure. Like this one.

Presumably, the exterior doors to open space would also be operational regardless of the main computer's condition. That was a question that Arnold hoped wouldn't come up.

She led the two techs—a pair of wide-eyed babies—to a harrier craft that held a crew of ten. It came equipped with rear and side guns that an onboard crew utilized in teams of three. Perfect for strafing a planet's surface or even blasting open a larger vessel. However, it didn't have enough maneuverability to bottle up a single-person hawker.

She couldn't help catching her breath as the hatch to the harrier opened. It worked! Her bio-signs and the encrypted access key synched up correctly. All she had to do was walk up to it. Well, sure. You could wind up on an asteroid or planet and have no communication with anyone. The ship still had to discern you from other life forms.

That was the crux of Jade's idea. Ridiculously simple, yet by far the best plan that Arnold had heard thus far. To diagnose what had gone wrong with the warship's computer, they needed processing power. Which they didn't have. So they needed independent processing power from someplace else. As in the computers on their multitude of smaller craft.

They climbed aboard, Jade in the pilot's seat with Arnold as copilot. Not like they were flying anywhere. Vincent crouched behind them, despite the fact that there was plenty of seating available.

From here, the process was dicey. There was the operation itself, and there was also the task of priming Jade to be at her best. To act with confidence and not trepidation. But the sight of this pink-haired mouse quivering with fear in the impossibly large pilot seat instilled only doubt. *Serious* doubt.

That's why Arnold had known better than to send anyone else down here with these specialists. All it would take was a disdainful stare, a sneer, or even a heavy sigh at the wrong moment to spook them into uselessness.

"Okay, Jade. You're flying this ship. Just don't take us out of this hangar."

The little girl looked puzzled. "The computer won't let me past the status menu," she said.

"Oh, great," Vincent said. "This craft has been paired with this hangar. We're going to have to start the launch sequence and let it access—no, we can't do that."

Jade addressed Captain Arnold. "Launch sequence engagement means a connection to the main computer, which will create more processing stress. We really need to invoke the harrier's computer without triggering the warship's hangar protocol."

Arnold thought they were overcomplicating just cranking up an engine. "Why does the main computer even have to be involved?" she asked.

"It wouldn't be if we were away from this warship right now," Vincent said. "But ship security is about preventing any unauthorized exit. That's why every small ship gets paired to a specific hangar location. And once that happens, launch sequence protocol automatically kicks in. You're not going anywhere without permission from the main computer."

Arnold let an unrelated thought drift in. *Slaton had been able to bypass all of that somehow.* In his case, *asset* was an understatement. And *pleb* was an ignorant label. How often had opposing forces battled for supremacy in an incessant struggle to outthink, outfight, and outmaneuver each other and wound up in a bloody stalemate? Tech was the future.

Anyhow, back to the problem at hand: getting out of this tech-based fiasco in one piece. "There's an override," Arnold said. "I've never had to use it. We always just launch whenever we want. But I could force the system to bypass standard launch protocol."

"That'll still mean accessing the main computer," Vincent said.

"But using way fewer resources," Jade said.

Arnold detected a note of confidence in her voice. That was good.

"You can't be sure of that," Vincent said.

"No. But probably."

Vincent tugged at his chin and considered. "Yeah, probably," he said.

Jade explained: "If a launch request carries a known certificate of authentication, like an override by a senior officer, the system should bypass standard protocol. In other words, stop right there, tell the harrier it's okay to launch."

"The key word being *should*," Vincent added. "A well-designed system would do just that. However, there's a possibility that the warship's computer could exercise all of its authentication and authorization algorithms before finally evaluating the request as a potential override as a last resort. We really have no way of knowing."

"What do these algorithms do?" Arnold asked. "Seems like it's just checking identity."

"It checks against the encrypted creds in the data vault," Vincent said. "That's a fair amount of processing right there. Then, if it can't find a match, breach mitigation kicks in. Things like broadcasting a ship-wide alert, sealing all the exits. Lots of stuff going on under the hood."

"So my override might work, or we could wind up completely killing the main computer," Arnold said.

"But doing nothing can't be the answer," Jade said.

She had a point. This warship's computer would continue to lose resources until it went tits up and died. The worst thing that could happen was…those environmental systems didn't get the message to continue on their own (or operate autonomously, as the geeks put it).

Arnold contacted Jarrett. "Have those cyber room geeks—techs, actually—keep a close eye on system usage. I mean watch it like a hawk. If there's a sudden spike, start emergency protocol. Oxygen, environmental suits, the works."

Then she grabbed Jade's arm and looked her in the eye. "You're right," she said. "Doing nothing can't be the answer."

CHAPTER 20

THE DRILL INSTRUCTOR'S living quarters were a huge upgrade from those occupied by recruits. Four people to an apartment, each occupant having a private room.

In the common area, the walls were plain gray, but they were blanketed with an explosion of graffiti: names of previous occupants, places of conquest, remembrances of warriors departed but never forgotten.

Ellis propped his knee on a chair that no longer floated on command and explained the situation to his three fellow instructors. Unfit loser, Kevin Slaton, was in the infirmary with a fractured skull. And a recruit from their training squad was going to have to pay the price for putting him there.

Ally sat on a cushion with her back against the wall. She was a tough old broad with spiky hair and looked like part of the graffiti. "Seems pretty cut and dry," she said. "We sweat the truth out of our babies and serve up the guilty party."

"Here's the thing," Ellis said. "I think I already know who did it."

"So tell us," Ally said. "You should have done that from the start."

"But I think we should give them someone else," Ellis said.

They responded with blank stares. All three of them. Ally from her perch against the wall, Jackson and Talbot from opposite ends of the couch.

It was Talbot who broke the silence. "So the guilty party is one of your recruits," he said.

"There are no yours or mine," Ellis said. "It's our squad."

"Yeah, yeah. I know all that," Talbot said. "I've had the same training as you." He was relatively new, training only his third recruiting class. And, of course, he already knew more than any of the rest of them.

"Then you know this is about producing top quality," Ellis said.

"Actually, it's about *you* losing another team member," Jackson said.

True enough. The four of them shared a training squad comprised of four six-person teams. Except that Ellis's team had already lost two of its members: Verdi to AWOL and Slaton to injury. So he was in danger of having his team cut in half.

Why did that matter? Producing the squad's best team meant huge bragging rights. And the higher-ups noticed. There were also the personal bets that the drill instructors made among themselves. Which had obviously led them all to the cynical assumption that Ellis was trotting out a fine song-and-dance to keep his team's hopes alive.

Screw it, Ellis thought to himself. If their leaders wanted to sacrifice a future warrior over a pleb's mishap, might as well offer up Erin Lane and be done with it. He sure as hell wasn't going to get any cooperation from these rivals who were supposed to want the same thing that he did. Jackson was a glory hound. Always had been. Talbot had something to prove. And if he couldn't sell either of them, he wasn't even going to attempt to sell Ally. She loved breaking in newbies, to the point that she'd turned down several opportunities for advancement over the years. Trying to sway her with a convincing argument would be like chiseling a boulder with a feather.

"By strict definition, blaming what happened on anyone other than the guilty party would be dishonorable," Jackson said.

"No shit," Talbot said.

Then Ellis got a surprise.

Ally glared at Talbot. "You don't know what the hell you're talking about," she said.

"Fine," Talbot said. "Enlighten me."

"We rank our babies; we stage competition between our respective teams. What for? To win a bullshit bet? To get brownie points from our superior officers?"

"Here we go…" Jackson said with a groan.

"Hey!" Ally said. "At the end of the day, we're here to turn out combat-ready warriors. Not that any recruit is ever ready for real life-or-death combat without actually experiencing the real thing, but we have to start somewhere."

"And we hone those skills through competition," Talbot said. "*Fair* competition. Ellis is trotting out a line of shit about honor and purpose just to keep from losing his best remaining hope."

"Fine," Ellis said. "Fuck it. My team finishes dead last. I lose. That includes me paying off the bet. How's that?"

"I'm out too," Ally said. "You two can fight over the crumbs if you like; one of you can revel in a hollow victory."

Nobody spoke for several seconds. Ellis spotted Hudson's name splashed across the top right corner of one of the walls. That and Ally's support fanned an ember in his gut. This was where greatness began. This was a step beyond simply adopting the Armada's will as his own and hammering that mindset into recruits. Right here, in this room, they had an opportunity to shape the future—in a small way, perhaps, but shape it nonetheless.

"Well, I have to ask," Talbot said. "What about the dishonor of blaming anyone besides the guilty party?"

"*Touchstone* is a midsized warship with a crew of 2,000 warriors—those involved in actual combat—and 1,000 parasitic plebs," Ally said. "That's way too much dead wood."

"And it's gotten worse over time," Ellis said.

"You've got a point there," Jackson admitted. "If we have to sacrifice a future warrior on behalf of a pleb, we should cut our losses."

"Not should," Ally said. "*Must.* We *must* identify our weakest recruit. The runt of the litter."

"Okay. Fair enough," Talbot snorted. "In that case, I nominate Amanda Zimmer from team four. Another one of Ellis's finest."

Ellis seethed inwardly. A meeting in the dojo lay in the future for him and Talbot. But for now… "What exactly is your basis for choosing that particular member of my team?"

"Well, she got her nose busted by a food tray, compliments of your pleb with the fractured skull." Talbot smirked. "Not exactly combat ready."

"Fine," Ellis said. "Amanda Zimmer it is." A need had to be met, and he preferred to lose Zimmer instead of Lane or Hickson. Besides, this wasn't about him losing a team member. This was about laying aside personal ambitions and ego considerations in favor of the greater good.

"Not so fast," Ally said. "Zimmer's outperformed some of the other babies in our squad. Each of us needs to come up with a nominee from our team, then we'll narrow it down to the weakest of the weak."

"Still seems like this is Ellis's problem to deal with," Talbot said. "He's got almost half his team washing out."

"Shut up, Talbot," Jackson said. "Ellis and Ally are right. We've been putting way too much stock in completion rates and which team wins and all that other happy horseshit. I'm all about competition and kicking your collective asses, but we're supposed to be turning out warriors. *Reliable* warriors that we can count on in life-or-death situations. Not half-ass recruits we let pass because they don't outright fail."

What followed was a brief discussion. All four instructors picked their weakest recruit without hesitation. It was pretty easy to narrow it down from there.

CHAPTER 21

AN AGONIZING TEN seconds crawled by after Arnold overrode the launch sequence authorization. Nobody said a word. Arnold and the two techs, Jade and Vincent, were dead silent, not daring to even take a breath for fear of upsetting some delicate balance between luck and fate.

Nothing happened. No system spike. That was good...

But no response either. Just an empty void. She might as well have broadcasted her override into the side of a mountain.

Suddenly, the palm reader on the pilot's touchscreen lit up red.

"It wants your creds again," Jade said. Her voice was breathy. An urgent whisper. A hopeful prayer.

"I think that's good," Arnold said. She placed her glove on the touchscreen, and the control panel came to life. Access granted. All systems online and ready to rock.

"That's how it happens when we're out in the wild," Arnold said.

"Your override must have decoupled us from the hangar," Vincent said. "Makes sense. The warship's computer recognized a highly authorized, well-known override cert and kicked verification responsibility back to this harrier."

"That had to be what took so long," Jade murmured. She was already hunched over the harrier's computer, engrossed.

"Yeah," Vincent agreed. "Something that should have been instant took forever."

Arnold contacted Jarrett, who reported that the cyber room techs were still bickering and debating among themselves about what to shut down. (They'd have to address their team dysfunction after this fiasco was over, but that was a future problem.) Meanwhile, resource degradation continued, but at least it remained steady. No noticeable spikes.

She wanted to ask Jade if she was making any progress but decided against disrupting the little girl's concentration. Besides, next-to-no time had passed since she started. On the other hand, next-to-no time was all they really had.

As the minutes marched on, Jade's fingers moved quickly, her lips mouthing unspoken words, as if she was trying to coax the computer into action. Vincent made the occasional glance over her shoulder and grunted what Arnold assumed to be approval. He wasn't questioning her methods, at any rate. That was something.

Arnold got up and moved to the rear of the harrier. She gestured for Vincent to join her. From their vantage point, she could see at least a portion of Jade's screen. Arnold had never seen a display like this one. No touch options, icons, or menus, and forget voice recognition. Jade was typing in cryptic commands that didn't make sense. They weren't even real words. Just a hodgepodge of letters and symbols.

"What is *that*?" Arnold whispered.

Vincent avoided eye contact, his anxiety palpable.

"C'mon. What?"

"She's hacking the main computer," Vincent said in so soft a whisper that Arnold barely heard him.

"That doesn't sound good," Arnold said. "What's hacking?"

Vincent swallowed hard. Arnold couldn't read the computer screen, but she could sure as hell read people. The wheels in his head were spinning. He really didn't want to answer her.

"Hey!" Arnold gave his shoulder a firm shake. "I don't plan on stopping her or meting out punishment after the fact. But I do need to know what the hell this hacking is all about."

"It's an archaic expression," Vincent said. "Hacking is the ancient art of breaking into a computer system without being detected."

"And why have I never heard of it?"

"Because it never happens in this day and age. As in never ever. Systems have way too many safeguards built into them. AI processes that actually think like criminals. You're guaranteed to get caught."

"The recruit who stole a hawker…did he use this *hacking*?"

Again, Vincent averted his eyes. He wasn't *supposed* to know about Kevin Slaton. But William Whitehead had been involved.

"No doubt about it," Vincent said. "And he went well beyond just spoofing credentials. He actually created a new account with unlimited privileges. Not only that, he managed to pull it off without ever being detected. I mean, that's insane."

Arnold noted that he couldn't quite keep the admiration out of his voice. "You knew, didn't you?"

"About what, Captain?"

"Don't play games," Arnold said. "You knew that Jade was going to try and hack—Did I say that right?—hack into the ship's computer from this vessel."

"I assumed that was her plan," Vincent admitted. His face was flushed, his breathing unsteady.

"It's fine, Vincent. You and Jade have my blessing. This is a desperate situation, in case you haven't noticed."

"Thing is, there's no other way," Vincent said. "The computer will attempt to respond to anything it detects, be it an access attempt, program execution, explicit command, or what-have-you."

"And responses eat up resources," Arnold said.

"Yes, Captain."

"This way, she'll sneak in without triggering anything."

"Next to nothing," Vincent said. "Once she's in, Jade will start traversing the system logs to try to figure out what happened. And she'll be using the computer in this vessel to perform the actual search. That'll buy the warship's computer a little more life."

"Thank you, Vincent," Arnold said. "See if Jade needs assistance."

"Yes, Captain."

Arnold sat alone with her thoughts while Jade continued to work her black magic.

First Kevin Slaton. Now this.

Hacking wasn't exactly a thing of the past.

CHAPTER 22

ON HABIT, Kirkman almost jacked into the ship's computer with her portable field unit. More data was always better—except that the main computer was like a drowning elephant, liable to take any and all attached devices down with it.

Then she began scanning Kevin's skull for internal damage and immediately felt like an idiot. Internal damage…well, no shit. A fractured skull did tend to have that effect on a person. But field protocol was still field protocol. And Gable had suggested treating this situation as an exercise. A challenge.

Interestingly, but also understandably, Kevin Slaton's brainstem appeared to be more or less intact. Perhaps a bit swollen, but the nerve endings looked to be firing off their expected electrochemical impulses. That was a start.

"Let's try easing him off life support," she said.

"Isn't that a bit risky?" Gable asked.

"Hell yeah, it's risky," Kirkman said. "But the *front* of his skull got stomped. So the brainstem didn't absorb the full impact."

"There's still a lot of trauma," Gable said.

"I get that. But the sooner we can get him breathing on his own, the better."

Gable offered no further argument. He monitored Kevin's vitals while she turned off each life support function, one by one. It ought to work. Maybe, but not necessarily. The brainstem looked alright, sure, but assuming it could properly control vital functions like breathing and heartbeat was a lot like saying that a person with legs was guaranteed to walk.

Over the next twenty minutes, Kirkman got life support completely turned off but left all the wires and tubes hooked to Kevin in case they had to reinstate it in a hurry.

"His breathing is weak; pulse steady," Gable said. "He's still in danger, but he seems stable at the moment."

Kirkman bit her lip and refrained from mocking Gable with a smartass comment. Forming *any* emotional attachment to a patient clouded your judgment when quick and hard decisions were just plain necessary. To have any shot at all of bringing this kid back to life as something better than a mindless piece of meat, she was going to have to risk killing him in the process. No getting around it. But hesitating and second-guessing wasn't going to help anybody. Besides, was there really a benefit to him surviving in a catatonic state? Hell no.

She focused her scanner on the front of Kevin's skull, causing the frontal cortex to glow light green. This was literally a self-contained world. Clusters of orange and red flashed across the horizon, millions of synapses firing, sending and receiving signals—except, as she'd expected, that divot in the middle of his forehead was a wasteland. Just a dull, yellowish nothing.

"No big deal," she said to Gable. "It's just the part of the brain that controls thought and movement."

"I get it," Gable said. "You're giving up. The problem is beyond your abilities."

"Well, technically, I already did my part," Kirkman said. "He's breathing on his own now and somewhat stable. At this point, we'd transport him back for a genius like you to take over."

Gable didn't respond. His face was ashen, and his eyes had a hollow look of dread. This kid—this loser—was having a bizarre effect on him.

"Okay. Say everything was up and running on your end. What would you do?" she asked.

"Well, we'd use the ship's computer to synthesize a neural patch."

"That sucks even under ideal conditions," Kirkman said. "That's why we call them—"

"Don't say it!" Gable snapped.

Kirkman fell quiet. She didn't say meathead out loud, but she sure as hell thought it.

Meathead was a derogatory term for an unfortunate neural patch recipient. First they synthesized squishy brain tissues that did nothing more than fill an empty gap. Then they inserted a fine iridium mesh—a spaghetti-like mess of signaling cables that supposedly hooked everything together. Computer modeling did an adequate job of mapping everything out. But it was still a far cry from the correct gene expressing the correct protein to emit the right signal in the right place at the right time to the right recipient.

Some meatheads functioned pretty well. A few had to be locked up and only released in combat situations; they no longer gave a shit about anything at all. Others needed diapers for the rest of their lives.

"You know, we don't care about restoring our wounded to full health," Kirkman said. "We just patch them up and shove them back out there."

"That's a real pearl of wisdom," Gable said, his voice laced with bitterness.

"You're getting way too mushy about all of this," Kirkman said. "But that's not the real problem."

"Please enlighten me."

"As long as we keep doing the bare minimum, our methods are never going to improve. You've gotta innovate for that to happen."

"Hence the challenge I presented you with that you're obviously not up for."

"Bullshit. You're caught up in a personal crusade for reasons known only to you. You can play every form of mind game with me, but I still can't pull a brand-spanking-new frontal cortex out of my ass."

"Well, you got him breathing on his own," Gable said. "Thank you for that. I probably would have left him on life support. I'll just have to hope the computer comes back online before too long."

"Then you can turn him into a meathead," Kirkman quipped. "That's hopeful."

"Dammit! I told you…" Fire flashed in Gable's eyes. She could feel the deep-seated wrath bubbling up in him. He wanted to knock her sideways. Kinda a turn-on, actually.

"You tell me," she said. "What are the odds of a neural patch working across a damaged area that size?"

Gable said nothing.

"I've got an idea," Kirkman said. "But we'd be taking a huge chance."

"Absolutely not," Gable said. "A neural patch under these conditions is way too risky as it is. I'm not turning him into a mindless vegetable for the sake of trying out some wild idea."

"Again, what does he have to lose?"

"The chance for any conscious existence at all. I won't do it."

"Suit yourself," Kirkman said. She bit her lip, wanting to say more but thinking better of it.

CHAPTER 23

THE HARRIER WAS A SILENT TOMB. The only sound was Jade's anxious breathing. The air itself was thin, without substance. Every breath made Captain Kalie Arnold wonder about the ship's environmental system. Was it compromised? Well, that was inevitable. Several times, she'd caught herself breathing less. A senseless reflex action that only made her lightheaded.

Numerous times over the past hour, she'd resisted the urge to check on Jade's progress. The little girl was hunched over the console. Vincent sat next to her, watching and nodding. He was a picture of concentration, but a mere bystander. The fate of the warship *Touchstone* rested on the narrow shoulders of this pink-haired mouse.

Jade turned around and made eye contact.

"What?" Arnold jumped out of her seat.

"I found it," Jade said.

"Can you fix it?"

Jade was silent for a beat. Then she said, "It's not even a thread or a process. It's a massive blob of yuck that just keeps getting bigger and bigger. Imagine finding yourself buried in mud. The ship's computer is literally being smothered."

Arnold suddenly wanted to run screaming out of the hangar. She was scared. No. More than scared. She was fucking petrified. There was no fighting this deadly, silent foe that you couldn't see, touch, or feel.

"Did the log file tell you anything helpful?" Arnold was pretty sure she wasn't going to like the answer, but she asked anyway.

"No log entry," Jade said. "This thing totally evades detection."

Vincent chimed in before Arnold could ask the obvious question. "Jade found the invader by…unconventional means," he said. "But the ship's computer has no idea what's going on. It's like being submerged and smothered but completely oblivious to what's happening to you."

"I downloaded a piece of the invader to a handheld device," Jade said. "And it's totally invisible. The device has been working great for ten minutes. Nothing out of the ordinary happening at all. Except I know what to look for; I did download it, after all."

"Okay…" Arnold really didn't know what to say about that.

"How much longer?" Vincent asked Jade.

"Anytime now." She pulled up a holo on her device. A standard personal info app. Everything looked fine right up until it didn't. The images began to flicker. Jade pressed a menu option. Nothing happened. She tried exiting and everything froze.

"It happens fast on a handheld because there's a way smaller area," Jade observed. Then she entered a series of command-level keystrokes, and the device went dead.

Arnold's heart was stuck somewhere between her throat and ribcage. Her legs trembled. Sweat trickled down the back of her neck.

"What's the plan?" she heard herself ask.

Hearing herself say that brought a stab of pain to her right temple. She was the leader of this warship, dammit! A ship's captain never *asked* what the plan was.

She rephrased. "How do we get out of this mess?"

Even worse.

But the techs didn't seem to notice her near meltdown.

"That viral blob grows by writing itself to memory, data stores, all of that," Jade said. "The only way to stop it is to wall it in."

"Computationally speaking," Vincent added.

"Only it can't be a brute force approach," Jade said. "If we launch our own process—call it an anti-virus—to prevent that thing from expanding in new directions, it's going to change its signature and evade our blockade."

Arnold clenched her fists and listened. This was getting worse by the second.

"But I've figured something out," Jade said. "Whenever the virus expands into new frontiers, the newly morphed strands of code send back a success message. That's the signal to regroup and press on. No adjustments necessary.

"I think I can create an anti-virus that will block further spread but also send back a fake success message. Then that yuck-blob will think it's still propagating and growing even though it really isn't."

"What happens then?" Arnold asked.

"I'll have to kill a couple more of these handheld devices to say for sure," Jade said. "But I'm certain that it just keeps on trying to grow and expand ad infinitum."

"Which in itself consumes massive computing resources," Vincent said.

"Okay," Arnold said out loud to herself. Then to her techs: "Say you contain the spread; what does that get us besides an untenable stalemate?"

Vincent answered: "Once it's in a holding pattern and not rolling over us, we can start attacking it. Basically, overwrite it.

Zero everything out with pristine qubits. From there, we can begin to spawn untainted processes and get things somewhat functional."

"What does somewhat functional mean?" Arnold asked.

"Restoration will be a whole other challenge. A lot like rebuilding a strafed planet. There's shit that's just not there anymore."

He looked down and away, obviously cringing that he'd put it like that. Arnold couldn't have cared less. "Jade! Cut the chatter. You're talking my ear off."

The cute little pink-haired mouse responded with a nervous smile and remained silent. She'd given her update and promptly retreated into some imaginary safety zone. As if any place in the universe was even remotely safe!

Arnold softened her voice. Better to coax than to intimidate. "There's something you need to tell me," she said. "Just lay it out and we'll deal with it together. Okay?"

"We're past the tipping point," Jade said. Her voice faltered.

Captain Arnold took hold of her hand with a calming compassion she really didn't have. Jade's hand was damp, trembling, and weak as a baby bird's wing. "So tell me about this tipping point," she said.

"The ship's computer doesn't have enough processing power to attack this thing," she said.

"We don't know that for sure," Vincent said.

"But probably," Jade said. "Almost half of the ship's computer has been consumed. And given the virus payload and growth rate along with our current compromised state…"

Jade's face had become a collage of red blotches, a sign of super-high stress. Even in their current crisis state, she was afraid to ask for what she needed.

Arnold gave her hand a gentle squeeze. "You've got a plan, Jade. I know you do."

"To mount an attack of our own, we need a ton more

computing power," Jade said. "We'll have to use every small craft on this warship to jack into the main computer like I'm doing now."

Arnold gave her a reassuring smile. "That's no problem. I'm the captain. I can make that happen. Whatever you need."

CHAPTER 24

ELLIS WALTZED into the infirmary like he owned the place.

"How's the patient?" he asked.

"Not ready for visitors," Gable said.

"I'm no visitor. I'm his drill instructor. This boy is one of mine."

"I'm sure you're here out of extreme concern for his welfare," Gable said.

Ellis ignored the sarcasm. "Is he awake? Can he talk?"

Kirkman spoke up. "He's off life support, but—"

"We aren't going to discuss his condition with you," Gable said.

The two men locked eyes in a momentary stare-down. Then Ellis said, "I'm just here to help. Anything at all I can do, just let me know. In fact, you look tired. You should take a break. Get some sleep. I'll sit up with him. I'm no doctor, but if those lines on his monitor change, I'll come and get you."

"Thanks, but we can't do that," Kirkman said. "We'll tell Kevin you were here when he wakes up. I'm sure he'll appreciate it."

Ellis stared at her the way a hungry wolf would eye a piece

of meat. "What the hell are you doing here? You belong in the field treating injured warriors. Not coddling dead-weight plebs."

"Where I belong is none of your business," Kirkman said.

Ellis held up his hands in a passive gesture. "Let's start over. It's my right as his drill instructor to spend time with an injured recruit. Alone. Just the two of us."

"Since when?" Gable said.

"Since now," Ellis said. "We can do this one of two ways, easy or hard."

"You're not listening," Kirkman said. "This kid's unable to have a conversation with you."

"No problem. I'll do all the talking. People in comas respond to words of encouragement."

"That makes sense," Gable said. "You'd love a one-way conversation now that your recruit's been reduced to your level of intellect."

"Yeah, well...speaking of intellect, what moron voluntarily goes from warrior to...this? Oh, wait. That's not stupidity. That's gutlessness."

A spark of rage flashed across Gable's face. There for a mere second. Then his placid exterior resurfaced.

"I'm not leaving," Ellis said.

"Sure you are." Gable was calm and firm, as if chatting idly.

Ellis grinned. "Make me leave, Nurse Gable. Please. Go for it."

Kirkman stepped forward. She had grabbed a scanner off the medical tray. "Hey! Asshole! I've reversed the voltage on this puppy. I touch you with this and you'll dance like a scalded monkey."

Ellis touched the gimlet on his hip. "Might want to keep your distance, beautiful."

They were five feet apart. Gable calmly stepped between them and touched the black micro-comm on his chest. "This is

Doctor Claude Gable for Captain Arnold. I have an update on Kevin Slaton," he said.

Jarrett's curt voice responded instantly. "Doctor Gable. Hold for the captain."

Kirkman leered at Ellis. "Bet you didn't see that coming, asshole."

Then Captain Arnold came online. "Doctor Gable."

"Kevin Slaton is off life support and stable. We're working on repairing the brain trauma."

"And?"

"We're having to turn away visitors," Gable said. "I understand the concern for a fallen comrade, but he's not up for it."

"You understand nothing," Ellis said. He turned on his heel and strode out.

"Come back when you can't stay," Kirkman called after him.

"Short and sweet, what's going on?" Arnold asked.

Gable quickly told her about Ellis showing up.

"I'll have Jarrett convey the order," Arnold said. "Absolutely nobody allowed in the infirmary except you and Jan Kirkman. I'm also posting guards outside your door. And if Ellis shows up again, I'll personally bust his ass."

She clicked off.

"Holy shit," Kirkman said. "I didn't know you had a direct line to the captain."

"I don't," Gable admitted. "It was a bluff. I figured the captain's adjutant would make me hold. Which he did. I just wanted Ellis to think that Captain Arnold was expecting an update from me. I was downright shocked when she responded personally.

"Anyhow, that seemed better than bluffing him with a harmless scanner."

"He didn't know," Kirkman said. "Warriors think everything's a weapon."

"There seems to be a lot of interest in this young man," Gable said. "More than I know or understand."

"Doesn't take a genius to figure out that jughead was here to make sure our boy never wakes up," Kirkman said. "Not that he has a lot to worry about." She glanced over at Kevin. "Chances are he'll never string two sentences together again."

"Unless your idea pans out," Gable said.

"You mean the one you refused to even listen to twenty minutes ago?"

"Let's hear it," Gable said.

CHAPTER 25

IN THE DRILL instructor's quarters, Ally reared back against the wall and blended in with the graffiti. Ellis paced back-and-forth like a caged animal.

"If that coward hadn't run behind the captain's skirt, he'd be in worse shape than Slaton right now!"

"Gable didn't run," Ally said. "And the captain would have your ass on a silver platter if she heard that."

"I say Gable's yellow," Ellis snarled. "Besides, you weren't there to see what went down."

"And you weren't there during the Grunfeld skirmish," Ally said. "Gable was a beast of destruction in that one."

"Key word being *was*. He's too scared to shadowbox now."

"He's scared," Ally said. "But not of you."

Ellis turned beet red. His bristled head looked ready to erupt through the ceiling. In a frustrated howl of rage, he flung his hand blade; it buried itself in the wall, three feet above Ally's head, with a soft thud.

Ally maintained the same stoic, matter-of-fact smile she always had. "Let me know when your tantrum's over so that we can plot our next move," she said.

Given the current computer crisis, recruit training had been on hold. To keep all of the bored recruits in line, the instructors were monitoring them in alternating pairs of two. Ally's idea. This happened to be Jackson and Talbot's shift.

But the split shifts served another purpose. Ally and Ellis could now strategize alone. Fewer parties involved meant fewer stories to get straight and less chance of a slipup.

"We can't let him wake up and start talking," Ellis said.

"That's not going to happen anytime soon," Ally said. "In fact, it's probably not going to happen at all."

"Are you willing to just sit back and take that chance?"

Ally paused to consider. "Maybe I am," she said. "Even if they get him conscious, he'll probably be a meathead."

"Meatheads can talk," Ellis said.

"True. But it's his word against ours. Do we really want to draw attention to ourselves trying to fix something that doesn't need fixing?"

"Well, he's important enough to have Commander Hudson and the captain involved. There's no telling how high up this shit goes."

Ally chewed on her lower lip. She was a leathery battle-axe, everything about her totally by the book, except—she also had a crazy edge that made her scary as hell sometimes. She loved a good fight, the tougher the better, but she was also a cool, unflappable strategist and not averse to *necessary* risk.

"You and I can't get anywhere near Slaton," she said.

"We could just fight our way in," Ellis said. "Officially, we'd be doing it to prove that some numb-nuts coward-turned-doctor can't keep us from doing whatever the hell we please. Slaton would just be collateral damage."

"That's idiotic," Ally said. "The captain would have our asses. And Hudson wouldn't even pretend to help us."

Ellis grabbed one end of the dining table, intending to fling it, or at least flip it over. In one fluid motion, Ally was on her feet with both hands planted firmly on the tabletop. "No sense in taking it out on our furniture," she said.

"Goddammit!" Ellis roared. "Why didn't I just give them Erin Lane?"

"Because you're an Armada warrior, whose sworn duty is to turn out recruits of the highest quality. And those recruits are our babies. They're ours. They're part of who we are. So there was no decision. What we did was the *only* thing to do."

"So we just sweat this thing out and hope Slaton never wakes up, or that he can't say anything meaningful."

"Or we get someone else to take the risk," Ally said.

"Gunderson."

"Our fall guy," Ally agreed.

"Gunderson!"

CHAPTER 26

It felt irresponsible and just plain wrong. But Gable was helping Kirkman put her insane idea into action. Every step of the way, he wavered between amazement and disbelief. They were either going to forge a new medical frontier or turn the poor boy on their operating table into a mindless sack of flesh and bone.

One thing was certain: Kirkman wasn't half-assing this thing at all. She believed they had a real opportunity here, and she was leaving nothing to chance. No mistakes. Every detail, every new stitch to embed the ultrafine, electrode-studded wires into Kevin Slaton's brain tissue was flawless and precise. Her face was hidden behind the magnification visor she was wearing, but Gable could imagine the intensity in her brown eyes and her single-minded focus as she meticulously constructed a web of neural lace that dodged the delicate blood vessels and spread across the brain's surface like ivy.

Gable risked a nervous glance at the door. Two guards had arrived after his communication with the captain. They'd come quickly. And they'd explained that his glove could still activate the door's touch panel despite the ship's computer woes.

Still, a closed door was worse than an open one in many ways. No way to see or know what was happening outside. *Focus on your patient,* he reminded himself.

Kirkman raised her visor. "The web's in place," she said. "Any second thoughts?"

"I've been having second thoughts since we started," Gable said. A real understatement. When he performed surgery, he relied on practice and training. Kirkman was pretty much winging it here.

"Okay," she said. "We're ready for the big show."

Kirkman's bold idea. Tiny computer chips would be attached to the wires embedded in Slaton's brain. Said chips could receive and process the electrical action potentials—spikes—that signaled activity in the brain's interconnected neurons.

At least that was Kirkman's theory.

The end game was to turn these spikes into readable code that a computer could understand. That's where it really got crazy. After all, there was no computer or tech resource available to even begin such an undertaking. They'd have to be content to just hook everything up and hope Slaton's body didn't reject it.

Nothing else they could do besides that.

Not a thing.

CHAPTER 27

Pilots had arrived; every available computer in the rear hangar bay had been activated. And in each vessel was a tech whose job was to spin up an instance of Jade's anti-virus program when the time came. They had an additional duty: to monitor the system for…any strange anomalies—whatever those might be.

In fact, in every small craft throughout the warship, from the single-person hawkers to the ten-person harriers, the same thing was taking place. Instances of the anti-virus would be fired into the main computer in coordinated and contiguous blocks across the path of the advancing virus that Jade had dubbed the yuck blob. It would be a lot like burning a stand of trees to contain a forest fire.

Captain Kalie Arnold—decorated warship officer, veteran of multiple space battles, a true warrior who'd risen through the ranks, besting her fellow recruits, out-competing, overpowering, defeating her opponents through a combination of physical prowess, grit, determination, bravery, valor, honor, intelligence, and absolutely no quit or compromise—felt weak in the knees.

Here she was…*not* directing an attack—No! Rather, she was *watching* a frail little mouse go up against a massive force with no tangible substance in the world of living, breathing humans. Sure, she was in charge. She'd ordered the personnel down here, instructed the pilots on exactly what to do. Right—told them to fire up their ships; real leadership. A goddamn figurehead was all she was at the moment!

It was the techs who were going into battle. And all she could do was wait. She wouldn't even see the actual battle unfold. She might as well be hiding in a closet like she did as a girl when her uncle got too wasted to restrain himself.

Her skin got clammy; her throat tightened up. A cold sweat enveloped her.

Time to get a grip!

She was still captain, figurehead or no. If all she could do was stand here like a statue, she'd damn well do it. It was her duty to convey the might of an Armada warrior in her stance and in her demeanor. That meant not keeling over and puking all over herself even though she could taste it in the back of her throat.

Biting her lower lip till it bled, Arnold forced her food back down. She was captain, dammit. And her crew, this new crew, these soft intellectuals, needed leadership the same as a platoon of hardened warriors. So she walked from one small craft to another and tried to look like she had a fucking clue.

Then she climbed aboard the harrier that she'd claimed for Jade and Vincent. She could have just checked in on the micro-comm. Hell, there was no reason for her to even be here, except that she had no other priority at the moment. This was it. They had to win here, or there'd never be another battle to fight.

Besides, she was captain.

The pilot snapped to attention when she stepped aboard. She acknowledged his salute and told him to sit down. She'd assigned a pilot to every vessel in case their expertise was needed. Not that knowledge of how to fly a ship was likely to help with the task before them.

"How close are we to being ready?" she asked.

Vincent cleared his throat and deferred to Jade, who averted her gaze and looked distressed.

"Let's hear it," Arnold said.

"We're still waiting on test results," Vincent said.

Arnold glanced down at the half-dozen handheld devices on the floor. "How many of those do you have to go through before you know?" she asked.

"That's a question with no single definitive answer—"

"Vincent! Jade!"

Shouting got their attention and scared the piss out of them. Any louder and she'd have wound up peeling them off the ceiling.

"We've established a blocking pattern," Vincent stammered. "A map. Of where to deploy Jade's virus to maximum efficacy. We think we'll be able to neutralize the yuck blob, or at least slow it down enough for us to start attacking it."

"Then what are we waiting for?"

"Jade's not good with the results yet."

"Only sixty percent," Jade squeaked.

"What does that mean?"

"Sixty percent certainty of success," Jade said. She wrung her hands, and her eyes filled up. But she met Captain Arnold's steel gaze.

"And if we fail—never mind. Take as long as you need." Arnold smiled thinly. "Just hurry the hell up."

"Th-that's the problem," Jade whispered.

"Speak up!" Arnold said.

"According to my benchmarks, the yuck blob will grow past the tipping point before we're able to isolate a blocking pattern that's assured to be eighty percent or better."

Arnold ignored the pilot. He didn't matter. He didn't understand anything he'd been listening to, and he'd follow orders no matter what. Looking outside the cockpit, she surveyed what would be the scene of a full-on firefight in a hangar full of stationary battle craft. Where the enemy was invisible and pilots didn't matter.

"Do it," Arnold said. "Launch the attack. Or blockade. Or whatever the hell you call it. Every computer in every small vessel on this ship. Do it now."

Hell yeah. She was still captain.

CHAPTER 28

Commander Ralph Hudson's disdain clenched his whole body into a tight fist. The captain had put him in charge of front hangar operations. Babysitting a bunch of worthless plebs, in other words. To be spending even a single second watching them in action…hell, there was no action; they were just hunched over devices, typing and conversing.

A stationary shitshow. And if that wasn't bad enough, just being down here breathing the same air as them was beneath him.

The meaty part of his palm started to itch. Yeah, it would be great fun to walk up to a pair of those defenseless little runts and crack their heads together. Not an option. Even though he outranked everybody here, there were still too many witnesses. Anybody could be dumb muscle and throw his weight around. It took cunning and discipline to know how to pick your battles. Or create them.

Arms folded across his chest, feet planted firmly on the metal floor, Hudson considered the situation. It was tempting to just leave. There was absolutely nothing for him to do here. But he stayed put. Partly because word of his absence could get back to the captain, but mostly because they were working on the computer from right here in this hangar. He didn't understand what they were doing, didn't care either, but they were attempting to restore the main computer to health. A good thing for him to keep abreast of under the circumstances.

He was also in a hangar full of single-person hawkers. Right on the cusp of a fast getaway should the need arise. Granted, the vessels were all occupied. Plebs in the cockpit at the computer and a pilot wedged in with them for whatever stupid reason.

Well, he could pry them out of there. No problem at all. But only if escape became absolutely necessary. And only when the time was right.

In the meantime, there was nothing to do but watch and wait. And grit his teeth. And crawl out of his skin from boredom.

Hold up! Wait a minute…

A man had entered the hangar through the open door. Instant recognition. He'd know that insolent face anywhere.

Fike!

That condescending asshole who'd all but called him an idiot in his own quarters. Hudson's eyelid twitched. He was going to make that little bastard beg for death.

A blue flame ignited in the back of his brain, making his neck red hot. Hudson clenched and relaxed. Then he reminded himself to resist the urge to act right here and now. He wanted to knock Fike out cold, shove him in a hawker, and fly him off to somewhere real private. If anybody tried to intervene… Oh, what fun it would be to draw his gimlet and just start firing, blasting one loser after another out of existence. And if he took out some warriors in the process…oh, well.

Summoning all of his willpower, Hudson ground his violent fantasy to a halt. *Plan it out,* he reminded himself. Under normal circumstances—with none of this computer crisis shit going on— he'd bide his time and conceive an airtight strategy for Fike's demise. There were always accomplices to be had, some more trustworthy than others, but it was better to do one's dirty work alone; involving others created loose ends.

But this scenario was a blitz game. A very compressed amount of time for making all of his moves. This was it. The time to act was imminent.

Still, he'd have to watch and wait for now. If escape became necessary, maybe he'd abduct Fike and blast his way out of here. Otherwise, he'd just have to let plan B come to him. It always did.

Either way, he had a mission now. Something he could sink his teeth into—maybe literally. Standing down here with his thumb up his ass didn't seem so bad after all.

Hudson's jaw unclenched; his body loosened and began to unwind. The surliness melted from his face, replaced by an unfamiliar sensation.

He was smiling.

CHAPTER 29

It was delicate work, installing the computer chips. Fortunately, they were on a printed 3D sheet that provided a small margin of error for each touchpoint. In other words, a chip didn't have to match up perfectly with an individual electrode in the network of neural lace that was already installed. That made things a little bit easier, but not much. Kirkman couldn't just roll them out and slap them on. She had to seal each connection with an organic cement used for repairing flesh and severed arteries.

Gable assisted, using tiny forceps under extreme magnification to hold the delicate texture in place while Kirkman applied the sealant. They had been working for well over an hour. A long time to keep a patient's brain tissue exposed even in a sterile environment.

That only made the whole thing all the more nerve-wracking. To Gable, the hum of the monitoring systems hooked up to Kevin Slaton seemed deafening; that damn hum had set up shop in his head and cranked up the volume. And he could actually feel Kirkman's intensity as she focused on the job at hand. Funny…the stakes seemed higher in the infirmary than they'd ever been in the battlefield—for an obvious reason:

preserving life was far more difficult and tenuous than taking it.

"This is absurd," Gable said. "We ought to have staff in here assisting."

"You're kidding!"

Point taken. Warship *Touchstone* had over fifty capable members on its medical team. When the infirmary was filled with injured warriors, they operated like a well-oiled machine. Fast, creative, and mistake free. But they pretty much checked out if a battle with significant carnage wasn't taking place. Most of them used that downtime to fry their brains.

Gable applied a clamp and blinked the sweat out of his eyes. He couldn't help wondering what would have happened if he hadn't been here when this kid got his skull fractured.

"Forget about the challenge," he said. "There's no point in you trying to prove anything at this point. I mean, this will never be a field procedure."

"Of course it is," Kirkman said.

———

They kept going for almost another hour. At that point, Gable's hands were trembling, his body a knotted mass of tension. The process of performing one pinpoint attachment after another had become a marathon of tedium and delicacy.

Finally, the computer chips were in. The protective shield was back in place across the front of the patient's skull. Kevin was stable. For now.

Both of them were exhausted. Gable was sweating all over, and Kirkman's brown hair was dripping wet.

"Explain what you said earlier," Gable said.

"I have no clue what you're talking about."

Yeah. They were totally spent. As if they'd fought a battle—which, in a way, they had: for someone else's life.

"You claimed this could be a field procedure."

"Hell yeah!" Kirkman said.

"You're dehydrated. And it's affecting your brain," Gable said. "We just spent two hours in a controlled environment—"

"Not the chip installation, dummy." Kirkman paused to wipe her face with a white towel. "You are right about one thing. I'm thirsty as hell."

"Back to your arrogant and unsubstantiated claim…" Gable said.

"It's so damn simple that it's easy to miss," Kirkman said. "And a case study like this one doesn't come along all that often."

"He's a patient, not a case study."

"Whatever. The meathead wrap—sorry, brain patch—that you've been installing has to be mapped to a valid set of simulated brainwave patterns. Which means it has to be done aboard a ship because nothing in the field has that kind of computing power. But we can prefab this neural lace in a variety of sizes, and I can install it anywhere. The computer chip hookups will happen *after* we get the fallen warrior back here."

"Still not getting the distinction," Gable said. "Maybe because I'm so tired. But what have you gained?"

"We quit making dumbass guesses on which synapses wire up with which and just plug in one side of the connection. Stabilize the patient. Save the hard stuff for later. The swelling can go down, the body can acclimate to the implant. All good."

Gable nodded at Kevin. "But his frontal cortex is still shot. He can't have a coherent thought."

"That's later, gator. When the system's back online and we have techs to put on the job… Think about it. We can convert his brain waves to computer code. Then we can run it, analyze it, push changes back to the microchips. With this new way, if Kevin here thinks it's cool to drop his pants whenever he sees a girl, we can troubleshoot the problem and fix it."

"All largely theoretical," Gable said.

"That's life. Now let's find some grub."

Gable thought that was the best idea he'd heard in a long time.

That's when one of the guards at the door walked in.

CHAPTER 30

THE LIGHTS in the rear hangar seemed to flicker momentarily. Maybe computer related; maybe not. Captain Arnold didn't know which systems were dependent on the computer. Not a hundred percent. An issue to address in the future if there was a future to be had.

Or maybe those popping light flashes came from the headache that was grinding at her temples. Hard to tell.

Her hair bristled, and her entire body itched to strike out at something. Anything! This was what being led to slaughter felt like. Threatened and cornered with nothing to attack. A defense-less animal. Biting back on a scream of futility, she willed herself to think, once again reminding herself that she was captain.

Another flash of light caught her eye. This was no pain-induced illusion. It came from inside the harrier closest to the space portal. A sudden flash followed at once by darkness.

Arnold ran over to Jade's vessel and climbed aboard. The pilot snapped to attention, but Jade remained focused on the computer console.

"Sit down," Arnold said. "Jade?"

"The containment's working. We can start attacking the yuck

blob. But it's jumped over to two small ship computers. One here. Another in the front hangar."

"Jumped over! What does that mean?"

"Somehow it managed to get past our firewall. It means that two hawkers have dead computers now."

"When you say 'dead,' you mean wiped out?"

"Killed as in totally nuked," Jade said. "Affected computers will have to be rebuilt if not swapped out completely. And that would take—"

"The question is whether they can still function with the computer gone..." Arnold mused. "Shit. There's no way to initiate the startup sequence."

"I'm sorry, Captain." Jade cowered as if she'd just been slapped.

"It's not your fault," Arnold said. "You were following orders."

Indeed. The blame for this problem was on her, not Jade. A crew of engineers and mechanics had been deployed to every hangar bay on the ship to assist where possible. So far, they'd been standing around with their thumbs up their asses. Because this was a computer-related issue—Right? Wrong! This was a survival issue that involved everyone.

Captain Arnold shouted across the hangar at the chief engineer. "Wong! Get over here. Is there any way for our small ships to operate without a computer?"

"No, Captain," Wong said. "There's no way to initiate the startup sequence."

Jade, the frail little pink-haired mouse, looked up from her computer screen. "You could bypass the computer altogether and reroute the flow of control," she said.

Wong's dark brow furrowed. "That's the most ignorant thing I've ever heard. You should remain silent in matters you know nothing about."

Arnold's hand shot out and twisted Wong's ear. "I'm the

ignorant person who summoned you," she said.

"Not you, Captain. This—owww!"

"I can rip it off," Arnold said. "Then you won't have to listen to any more ignorant ideas."

"Apologies, Captain. And to you…Jade."

Arnold released her grip on Wong's ear. "Explain to me why we can't operate our battle craft without computers," she said.

"A computer is mission critical," Wong said. "Not only does it prevent theft, but it also calculates the rotation patterns necessary to traverse cosmic junctions. And provides navigation across deep space. And also detects the approach of allies or foes from far away."

"But physical operation—maneuvering, firing weapons, split-second decisions under duress—are in the hands of the pilot," Jade said.

Arnold nodded. Jade was right. Indeed, the vastness of space as a playing field coupled with the immediate needs of the present made computers untrustworthy in battle situations.

"With all due respect, Captain, jury rigging a vessel to solve an unrelated problem with the warship's computer is a waste of resources and would simply create more problems for us."

"Not true," Jade said. "If you could disconnect the computer —leaving it operational, of course—a small ship could be flown out of here even if the computer got bricked. And if the computer was still operational, it could be reconnected once it was safely out of the yuck blob's communication range."

Wong continued his protests. "Captain, this idea is reckless. It carries a great deal of effort and risk for very little gain."

"Yeah. Well, we'll take every little gain we can get at this point," Arnold said. "Get your people on it. To be clear: find a way to physically disconnect and reconnect a small ship's computer from the controls. Go! That's an order.

"And Jade, quit worrying about containment or jump-overs

or any of that shit. Kick the shit out of that yuck blob. Throw everything you have at it."

With her orders dispatched, Captain Arnold felt a weariness creep into her bones. For the first time in her life, she was experiencing fear for which she had no answer. She trudged over to the hawker that Vincent was on for the hardest task of all, one she could not delegate. She was about to send a distress beacon to Admiral Anson of the warship *Juggernaut*.

CHAPTER 31

Dr. Claude Gable paced the floor, casting nervous glances at his comatose patient, Kevin Slaton. The guard posted at their door had given him a message—and with it came one hell of a decision to chew on.

He hadn't made eye contact with Kirkman yet.

"Well," she said. "Are you going to keep me in suspense?"

"Someone else is here to see Kevin."

"That's easy," Kirkman said. "Not just no—hell no!"

"You're probably right…" Gable said. But his voice lacked conviction. And he was still pacing in that slow circular pattern.

"I'll send him packing," Kirkman said. "You stay here and knock out a few more laps."

"Wait."

When Kirkman looked at him, her intent brown eyes softened into something like pity. "Get a grip," she said. "You can't be a good-natured doormat to everybody who wants something. There's no upside to this. None at all."

She meant well. But her voice carried an extra touch of compassion that didn't need to be there. That hard-nosed bitch sensed that something was broken inside of him. Well, something *had* broken, but it wasn't anything that Gable ever wanted back. He wanted to explain to her that causing no harm, attempting to make another person's life a little bit better, treating others with kindness and compassion…none of those things made him a doormat.

And how's that worked out for you so far? That thought hit him out of nowhere like a thunderbolt on a clear day. Gable buried it. He'd gotten good at that too.

"This visitor's a fellow recruit," he said.

"I don't care who it is," Kirkman said.

"Look, I really think that a visit from this kid would help both of them."

"There's no nanites with the computer down," Kirkman said. "So we'd have to manually disinfect the hell out of him. We, meaning *you*. I'm not doing it."

"I can handle medical protocol," Gable said. "I am a doctor, after all."

"And you're also aware that our patient is here because somebody stomped on his skull."

"I'll be right here the whole time," Gable said.

"So you've already made up your mind."

"I think so."

"You really believe those bullshit myths about talking and hand-holding?" Kirkman huffed. "Look at him, Gable. He's out cold. He'll never have a clue anybody was here."

"Gunderson will know," Gable said.

"You mean that kid waiting outside," Kirkman said. "The one that you're referring to by name."

"Yes. And *kid* is an apt description," Gable said. "And he's nobody's henchman. I took one look at him and knew he was in the bottom of the recruiting class with Slaton here. The last person anybody would recruit to do their dirty work."

"Remember that planet where they planted plutonium in

those cuddly-looking wooly bear colonies? Hell of a chain reaction there."

"This kid's no threat," Gable said. "The guards will search him before letting him in. And I'll shine a light up his ass and check for plutonium."

"That's real funny," Kirkman said. "I just hope this doesn't come back to bite us."

CHAPTER 32

To Hudson, there was only one thing worse than watching those plebs, a herd of soft-shelled slugs, plod their way through fixing the damn computer. That was watching Fike, one of the captain's lapdogs, strutting around giving orders. The official bullshit storyline (according to Fike) was that he was *relaying* instructions from Captain Arnold. Which relegated Hudson to the role of bystander.

Bystander worked better overall. Hudson could watch, wait, and act when the time was right. Still, he was itching to rip Fike's head off his shoulders. But he had to stay cool and exercise restraint, at least for now. Dealing with Fike was a luxury action that had nothing to do with his next right move.

And the next right move…

Well, the data on the ship's computer could be a problem if they were able to fix the computer. Still—full computer recovery seemed highly unlikely at this point. Even then, the datastores would be suspect at best. Especially after Hudson got his people in place. There might even be an opportunity to destroy said data and blame it on this incident.

On the other hand, if the computer rolled over and croaked,

what would that mean for the ship's environmental systems? Not a pleasant thought, and not a situation he planned to stick around for.

So with multiple possibilities, some better than others…you hedge your bets. Prep for as many outcomes as possible.

Rule number one: when in doubt, arm yourself.

Grabbing his handheld device, he reached out to one of his contacts (who had no official association with him). No hologram materialized. Instead, Hudson found himself face-to-face with a jiggly mass of orange slime with a curved slit across its middle that had to be a taunting grin. Then his device went dead.

Unacceptable!

He marched over to Fike, who was immersed in watching over the plebs, and stuck the device in his face. "What the hell's going on here?" he said.

"That's why we're using micro-comms ship-wide," Fike said.

Hudson glared down at the smaller man. "Answer my question."

"Your handheld device just got bricked by the yuck blob that's attacking the main computer," Fike said.

Hudson pounded the micro-comm on his chest. He'd only put it on in compliance with a direct order from the captain. "So what good is this stupid black patch?" he asked.

"Well, their range is twenty miles—not so great in the field, but awesome on a ship. You ID yourself the moment you clip it on; that enables you to have a conversation with a specific person. Most importantly, they're not hooked into the computer."

Hudson said nothing. This time he definitely picked up on the underlying condescension in Fike's voice. His entire body flexed and strained against its yoke of conformity. He couldn't kill Fike right this second. But soon. Soon…

Then the little shit turned away from him as if he wasn't even there!

"Fike!"

"Sir."

"Did I dismiss you?"

Fike snapped to attention, awaiting instructions. Impeccable compliance.

Hudson left him standing in place and stomped out of the hangar. Technically, Fike was supposed to remain at attention until Hudson came back and dismissed him. That wouldn't happen. Hudson would bet the house on that. On the other hand, Fike was already at the top of his shit list. There was no action he could take to make things any worse for himself.

CHAPTER 33

ROLF GUNDERSON LOOKED like somebody who would trip over his own feet. He had a bulbous nose, pale skin, and red frizzy hair. One ugly dude. But that wasn't what bothered Jan Kirkman. There was cruelty in his eyes…this guy looked to her like somebody who might torture a helpless animal just for fun.

Sometimes those idiots who screened recruits put way too much stock in having a mean streak. Granted, the ability to hurt and kill without forethought was a must. However, few of the Armada's enemies were helpless. So survival was mostly about how you handled yourself with the odds stacked against you.

And yes, if the computer had been up and running, Kirkman would have pulled his records. And she would have found out that Gunderson was a lanky, clumsy bully who'd hoped the Armada would give him a chance to kick people around. Turned out that he'd gotten in way over his head, getting a lot more abuse than he was able to dish out. Indeed, spineless bullies like Gunderson had a bad time of it in the ranks.

But with no computer records available, all Kirkman had was her bad vibe about him. He'd already been sanitized; they'd had him strip off his uniform and change into a sterile lab suit. Still, she patted him down once more just to double-confirm that he was unarmed. The creep seemed to enjoy that. His breath stunk to high heaven, and his body was clammy and cold to the touch.

"So you and Kevin are good friends?" she said.

Gunderson responded with a blank look.

"You don't give a shit about him at all," Kirkman said.

"Yeah! Sure I do." Gunderson's right eyelid twitched. A nervous tic, or maybe a tell.

"I have a hard time picturing the two of you hanging out together." Well, yeah. A clod and a geek never hit it off.

Gunderson grunted. "When can I see him?"

"When she gets done grilling you," Gable said.

It was no use. Kirkman's gut kept telling her that letting this guy in was a horrible idea. But Gable had made up his mind.

"One more time," she said. "Who are you here to see?"

"Uh, I told you already."

"You're full of shit," Kirkman said.

Then to Gable: "He doesn't even know his alleged friend's name."

"Bitch! I can't think with you coming at me…"

His eyelid was twitching in earnest now. That's when Kirkman decided to throw him out on his ass. It would piss Gable off. Maybe he'd kick her out too—never let her back in. She'd be shut out of the next phase in Kevin's recovery where they wired up communication between the ship's computer and her implanted neural web. Fuck it. She wasn't letting this guy near him.

"C'mon," Gable said. "It's alright. Just follow me."

Just like that! He led Rolf Gunderson into the infirmary where Kevin was lying helpless and unconscious. And Kirkman was left wondering what in the hell had just happened.

CHAPTER 34

A TOMBLIKE SILENCE blanketed the rear hangar, and a cold fist in every gut bore testament to the urgency of the battle that raged inside the deep recesses of the computer.

Twenty minutes had passed since Captain Arnold last conferred with the techs. Their report was disturbing: a precarious—yet not totally lost—position. They'd stalled the yuck blob's forward progress, but their attempts to destroy it had failed. The yuck blob gobbled up any new qubits they fired at it and surged at their defense barriers with ever-increasing ferocity. Overall, the sum total of their efforts was a firebreak of sorts. A containment measure designed to stop the flames from spreading but little else.

Twenty minutes…

Arnold dreaded another status update. A feeling of solemn angst assured her that the news wouldn't be good. For the first time in her life, she preferred ignoring a problem to facing it.

All of this as she strode over to the harrier for a fresh report… She could have just used the micro-comm on her chest, but these conversations needed to happen face-to-face, eyeball-to-eyeball. Besides, the crew needed to see a commanding presence. They might be losing the battle, but you never turned the tide with surrender.

Jade looked up from her terminal. Vincent remained head down, keying in a series of arcane characters and studying the resulting onscreen messages.

"How bad is it?" Arnold asked.

"It's going to take over," Jade said. Her voice was steady. She didn't flinch or look away. Her statement was an empirical fact.

"Any hope?"

"None. We can slow it down—a lot, in fact—but eventually it'll run us over. We're not going to be able to stop it."

Arnold paused to think for a moment. Wong and his crew of engineers had been able to jury rig several small ships. Manual controls would continue to work when the connection to the computer was broken. They were working on a circuit board that would enable them to reconnect to the computer at will. Simple as plugging and unplugging. A future innovation for small fighter ships (if they lived to share it with anyone). Funny how great achievement seemed to emerge from a crisis.

But what of the warship itself?

"I think it's time to revisit the discussion about just how autonomous those environmental systems really are," Arnold said.

This time, Jade said nothing.

"I'm recalling our conversation in the cyber room," Arnold said. She was referring to her briefing with the techs about system slowness. That seemed like years ago now.

"The entire tech team agreed that the environmental systems were autonomous, that they functioned independently of the main computer, and that they would come back after a reboot even if the main computer didn't. You also stated that this behavior was somewhat theoretical because such a process had never been tested out here in space."

Jade nodded. Her jaw quivered, but she didn't flinch. "A

reboot is too dangerous now," she said. "The yuck blob would block the shutdown process; same concept as a parasite keeping its host alive."

"What happens if we continue on our current course?"

"Another theoretical scenario," Jade said. "The environmental systems *ought* not to get attacked. But they do have some communication with the main computer, to report current status if nothing else. And this monster can slip through the tiniest crack…"

"Recommendation?"

"I don't know if it's physically doable…" Jade said.

"Let me worry about that," Arnold said.

"The surest way to protect our environmental systems is to shut them down," Jade said. "Shut down environmental systems. We'd have to have a way to survive without them."

"No shit," Arnold said. "What else?"

"We let the yuck blob run its course. Quit fighting it. Even help it along. It'll brick the ship's computer the same way it bricked those handheld devices. At that point, it'll be like a fire without oxygen. Nowhere else to spread or go. At that point, we can bring the environmental systems back online."

"And be stranded on a warship without weapons or navigational capabilities," Arnold said. "Congratulations, Jade. You've made major contributions to a plan that's probably going to kill us all."

Surprisingly, the timid little mouse giggled.

Arnold smiled back for a moment.

"Hold off the yuck blob for as long as you can," she said. "I want to get as many ships as possible unhitched from their computers. The more escape options, the better."

CHAPTER 35

THAT UGLY GUNDERSON kid stood hovering over Kevin Slaton. Kirkman didn't like it at all. It was like watching a dimwitted weasel who'd cornered a baby rabbit by dumb luck rather than cunning.

"Talk to him," Gable suggested.

Gunderson responded with a blank stare.

Kirkman edged in closer, placing herself between Gunderson and Kevin.

"She keeps crowding me," Gunderson said.

Kirkman took a half-step back, but she stood by Kevin, ready to pounce at the first sign of trouble.

"Let's all sit down," Gable said. Then to Kirkman: "Why don't you bring a chair over for our guest?"

"You do it," she said. "I'm good right where I am."

Shaking his head, Gable went to the other side of the room to fetch a third chair. "Can't summon it with the computer out to lunch." He tugged on the hovering chair; it clattered on the floor. "Looks like we're going to have to eject the legs. If I can find that never-used button."

The two chairs they'd been using were still floating next to

Kevin's air stretcher. "I wouldn't try either of those," Kirkman said. She really didn't care if they were trustworthy for sitting or not. She wasn't about to allow Gunderson to get that close to her patient.

"Uh, I don't mind standing," Gunderson said. "But can I at least see him up close?"

Kirkman sidled up to him. "Look, asshole. I can smell dirtbag all over you. So you move one inch closer to Kevin and I'll rip your balls off and feed them to you."

Gunderson quivered. A huge tear rolled down the right side of his face. "I just wanted—" His voice caught. "Kevin's my friend." He was sobbing in earnest now.

"What the hell!" Gable strode across the room and glared at Kirkman.

"Look, when I get a bad vibe, I get cautious."

"I'm sorry." Gunderson wiped his nose with the back of his hand. "I'll just leave."

"You'll do no such thing," Gable said. "Just take a quick break. Collect yourself. Then visit your friend."

He turned to Kirkman. "Maybe you should take a break too. Get some rest. I'll handle things here."

"If you don't mind, I'd prefer to stay," Kirkman said.

"Kevin needs positive reinforcement," Gable said. "I know you think it's bullshit. But attacking a grieving friend just for caring doesn't help anybody."

Kirkman's resolve weakened. She felt like a prize asshole. It seemed that the sobbing Gunderson was really hurting and that he had legitimate concern for Kevin Slaton, however unlikely a friendship between the two of them seemed on the surface. Maybe she'd been overreacting. But her gut didn't lie, even though it totally contradicted what she was seeing.

Thing is, she didn't know Rolf Gunderson's sociopathic depth. She didn't know that as a child, he'd used this same ploy to gain access to his little brother's beloved kitten. And that nobody had cried harder at his cousin's funeral than Rolf Gunderson, following her fatal accident caused by him.

"I'd really prefer to stay," she said. "I won't say another word. I'll stand off to the side. But I'd feel a lot better being here."

"Never mind. Just never mind." Gunderson headed towards the door. Gable quickly intercepted him. Ushering him back to the air stretcher, he spoke with quiet compassion. "Just talk to him. Tell him who you are. Let him know you're here."

"Uh, Kevin. Hey. It's me. Gunderson… Your buddy."

That set off Kirkman's alarm bells. If they *were* friends, there'd be no need to remind Kevin of that.

She stepped towards him.

Gable cut her off. "Enough, Kirkman." He was facing her with his back to Kevin and Gunderson.

"Gable!"

"No, really. Give it a rest."

Kirkman lunged towards the air stretcher. Gable restrained her with some strange pressure point that made her legs all tingly and immobile.

He didn't see Gunderson behind him with his hands around Kevin's throat.

CHAPTER 36

WAKE UP. You're dead!

Kevin found himself clawing at black nothingness. Not with his limbs, but with yearning thoughts. He wasn't floating or falling, nor sitting or standing.

He was just anywhere, everywhere. Nowhere.

In a void. A blank null of nothing.

All alone except for his panic invoked by the sheer emptiness that engulfed him.

Kevin tried to speak but couldn't.

No matter. There was no sound. No smell. Nothing to touch or feel. And without the blackness, there would be nothing to see.

He was going away. Dissolving. Becoming nothing.

Wake up. You're dead!

A shout. A cry for help. An impulse firing within himself again and again. And all he could do was claw at nothing and scream in silence.

CHAPTER 37

"GABLE! He's strangling Kevin, you dumbass!"

Kirkman fell to her knees, immobilized by whatever combat witchcraft Gable had performed on her. "Turn around!" she shouted.

But Gable didn't turn around. Instead, he dropped into a defensive crouch. Real fast.

Kirkman heard heavy footsteps. Ellis, that asshole drill instructor who'd shown up earlier, had burst into the room with a spiky-haired woman she didn't recognize. This gal had badass bitch written all over her.

It all happened in a couple of seconds. Gable reached back and clamped down on Gunderson's neck, all the while keeping himself in front of the gimlets that the intruders were pointing.

Her face icy calm, Badass Bitch zapped Gable in the chest. He dropped like a rock. Then she blasted a hole in the back of Gunderson's head. His body flopped to the floor. Totally limp. A clean kill. No blood. Just smoldering ash where Gunderson's skull used to be. The smell of singed hair permeated the air.

Kirkman's legs still tingled, but she had mostly recovered.

She struggled to her feet and stepped over Gunderson on her way to Kevin's bedside.

"His windpipe's collapsed," she said. "Damn you. He can't breathe."

There were also two bodies at her feet, but there was nothing to do about them. She was vaguely aware that these trespassers could waste her as well. But her focus, at the moment, was on Kevin.

"Might as well step away from him," Badass Bitch said. "He's done for."

Ignoring her, Kirkman quickly assessed the situation. There was organic cement, also forceps and magnifying lenses, as well as razor-sharp scalpels, on a medical cart next to the air stretcher. Her medical kit was leaning against a nearby wall. She rushed to grab it.

Rough fingers dug into her arm. Ellis. The drill instructor who'd tried to get in here already. "Listen up. The kid's done. Let it go."

Kirkman tried to drive her heel into his shin, but Ellis tightened his grip and smiled. White pain shot through her arm bicep and exploded in her skull. Tears blurred her vision. But she saw Gable moving. He was alive!

Gable tried to stand but lost his balance. He grabbed the medical cart to steady himself but only succeeded in pulling it down with him. The cart and all of its contents clattered to the floor as he fell down.

"So much for the big bad warrior," Ellis sneered.

"Shut up, Ellis," Badass Bitch said.

"Well, look at him. He's—ahh!"

Ellis let go of Kirkman's arm. His hands covered his face; a stream of blood flowed freely through his fingers.

Gable was standing now. "C'mon," he said to Kirkman. "We don't have much time."

Kirkman rushed to grab her medical kit. Permeating her

distress over Kevin's situation came a glow of satisfaction. Gable had grabbed a scalpel from the capsized cart and flung it with pinpoint accuracy. She couldn't help marveling at that.

"You're going down for this," Ellis said.

"Get over yourself," Badass Bitch said. "You're lucky he didn't put out an eye or cut your throat. Gable must be losing his edge."

Gable looked down at Kevin. "There's going to be serious reckoning for this, Ally."

So Badass Bitch's name was Ally.

"Doesn't have to be," Ally said. "You didn't know that Gunderson was unstable. Too bad we got here too late to stop him."

"You just better hope he lives," Gable said.

Ally shrugged. "In the meantime, you mind if I borrow some skin graft to patch this guy up?"

"Don't expect any help from us," Kirkman snapped.

"You should have killed him," Ellis snarled. "None of that quarter-power shit."

"Oh, shut up already," Ally said. She led Ellis out of the room, presumably to work on his lacerated face. Kirkman hoped he'd look like shit after.

In the meantime, there was Kevin. He hadn't had oxygen in well over a minute.

CHAPTER 38

Kevin sensed a world around him. Almost saw it. Knew it was there. But he had no way of occupying it. This nonexistence. Death? It was crushing him. Shrinking his space. Compacting him smaller and smaller. He felt himself—his actual self—yearning and reaching. But an invisible vise was squeezing out his very essence, crushing even the tiniest hint of life.

Something was constricting his very being, keeping him from existing, from occupying space. Kevin tried to breathe, but he couldn't feel anything; tried to hear, but everything was dead silent; strained to see, but it was no use. No darkness, no light. Just a blank nothing. He kicked and flailed, but he couldn't feel himself move.

And all the while, longing to survive…

To be!

Then full-on panic.

And…

Nothing.

———

Then—just like that!—something.

It might have been an hour. Could have been a minute. Or a split second that spanned an eternity.

His environment started to materialize. One detail at a time. It started out totally blank, nothing to see, feel, or touch. Then a hint of color. His vision— Yes! He could actually see. Everything was blurry at first, then colors and shapes slowly materialized. A dark blue sky at day's end, a pink hue on the horizon, the outline of a forest across a series of distant hills. He was standing at the edge of a clear stream, the rocky dirt solid under his feet. He could hear the water lapping against the shoreline, smell the fragrant evergreens that towered above him. Two tall trees. They'd just appeared out of nowhere. The sky got deeper and denser; details in the trees filled in—gray bark and green needles.

And Kevin was no longer getting squeezed into nothing; he was part of a new world. He occupied space in it. He *existed* in an actual place now.

It was as if he'd been planted on a blank canvas and the scenery was being painted in around him. Or maybe the artist's brush was creating him too. He could feel his heartbeat, taste his breath in the crisp air. His feet were shod in sturdy boots; his hands touched his flannel shirt. Different clothes. Not his Armada-issued uniform.

So I'm not on that damn warship anymore, he thought.

Then he remembered. The dojo. Erin Lane. He'd taken the fight to her. For a moment. Then she'd countered with jarring blows to his face and ribs. The air and floor had swapped places. He'd landed hard, the air driven from his lungs…

"She kept going," he said aloud. "A beatdown wasn't enough for her."

Wake up. You're dead!

Maybe…

This could be an afterlife. Every sect, culture, subculture, race, creed, and religion had something to say about what happened to a person after he died. But nobody really had a clue; Kevin was convinced of that. After all, how could you really know?

Then again, how did I wind up here…

Maybe he was in a coma. Maybe he was dreaming this shit.

Something stirred in the water. A school of glistening minnows. Then chirping birds in the trees above him. Actual birds. Kevin couldn't see them, so he assumed they were hidden in the high branches. Or in the thick foliage that had suddenly sprung up along the stream and around the trunks of the trees.

Kevin closed his eyes. Counted to three. Opened them again. He breathed deep of the clean air, holding it in his lungs, savoring its essence, and decided to quit worrying about the what and where of this place. Screw it. Being here beat the hell of out being on an Armada warship.

Then he noticed a clapboard cabin with a shiny tin roof that had solidified about thirty yards from the water's edge. It was nestled atop an embankment with a cobblestone path leading up to its entrance. What startled Kevin was its color: a deep, blue-toned gray.

Something was off.

He'd never been to this place before, nor any place like it. Hell, he'd only seen a stream with actual water in vids. There'd been trees where he'd come from, sure, but none this tall and certainly not this many in one place. No way was this a coma. Couldn't be. His mind would never concoct a scene like this one.

And yet…

A strange feeling of familiarity washed over him. A sense of sanctuary and security, a feeling of a home that he'd never had but always wished for. Somehow, instinctively, Kevin knew he didn't have to worry about food, shelter, water, clothing; none of that. And that the cabin, his base of operations—he knew that too—had everything he needed.

What surprised him most of all was the fact that there was no surprise, that this place was just as he expected it to be, even though he had never known it existed.

Maybe this *was* an afterlife, a *good place*. A port of refuge all his own, away from danger and adversity. Call it paradise, eternity, the hereafter. Even heaven!

I'll take it, he thought. *Whatever this place is, it's an improvement over anywhere I've ever been before.*

His new world continued filling in around him. Rocks and pebbles, grass and weeds. A cloud muted the orange sunlight. It seemed to rise from the depths below like a giant mushroom. There was anxious chirping in the trees above, followed by a mass of fluttering wings. Birds taking off, getting the hell out.

He took another deep breath. A tingling in his boots reverberated up his shinbones. The surface of the stream quivered with tension. Everything seemed to be vibrating in anticipation of... What?

Kevin chided himself for worrying. Still, he couldn't shake the feeling, the foreboding—the certainty—of something massive and destructive heading his way.

CHAPTER 39

Kirkman sweated as her heart pounded in her ears. Centering her focus, she blocked out her surroundings and focused solely on Kevin's collapsed windpipe. This was the same as operating during a battle, except that a warship's infirmary was supposed to be a safe haven, not a combat zone.

No time to repair the damage. That was later. For the moment, she made the requisite incision in the front of his neck and inserted a breathing tube. Her fingers were fast, her mind a steel trap of concentration. Had she been timing herself, she would have been pleased with her sub five-minute finish. But she wasn't smiling. Her face was a mask of angry concern.

Gable was propped up against the wall, watching her work. Getting stunned by a gimlet blast would do that to a person. He remained alert. Kirkman guessed it would go bad for Ally or Ellis if they came back. But she also knew that his nerve endings had that weird zap aftershock of raw numbness.

She checked Kevin's pulse. It was a pathetic threadbare beat with zero conviction. Not the heartbeat of someone willing himself to live or fighting to rise above death. Of course, the fact that he'd started out in a coma didn't help matters any.

Then her heart sank. "He's still not breathing," she said.

Gable's face betrayed his frustration that he couldn't help her.

"I'm gonna try shocking his system," Kirkman said.

Gable wiped his brow. "A shock would kill him in his condition," he said.

"He's practically dead already," Kirkman insisted. "I have to do something."

"Check him again," Gable said. "You just inserted the tube a minute ago."

"And he's not breathing!"

"Check him again."

Leaning in, Kirkman studied Kevin for a moment, then listened intently. It was there. Kevin's short, shallow breaths were barely detectable. But he was breathing.

"Okay. He's breathing again," she said. "But it's not enough. He needs life support to get stabilized."

"I'll be able to help you in a minute," Gable said.

"Bullshit. Your nerve endings are shot. You'd have two left hands with all thumbs right now."

Gable looked at his hands, a disgusted expression on his face. "You're right," he said. "I've got no touch at all. Funny. It doesn't take touch or finesse to split a man's face open."

"That dirtbag's not a man," Kirkman said.

Gable grunted and pulled himself to his feet. "Doesn't matter now," he said. "Our focus right now needs to be on taking care of Kevin." He looked at Gunderson's dead body. "And cleaning up this mess. I'll get him out of here. You get Kevin fixed up."

"Those creeps might come back," Kirkman said.

"They won't. Ally got what she came for."

"Which is?"

"A dead scapegoat," Gable replied.

"She could have killed you too," Kirkman said. "Why didn't she?"

"Because she's damn good," Gable said. "It was a textbook play. She'd planned to kill Gunderson all along. I was just an obstacle to neutralize. Or she might think she owes me one for old time's sake."

"You trained under her, didn't you?" Kirkman said. "I'll bet you were one of her prize recruits."

Gable flexed his hands. "I need to get Gunderson prepped for disintegration," he said. "He doesn't deserve to lie here on the floor like carrion."

Kirkman didn't pursue it. Obviously, Gable could fight his ass off. That much was clear. On the other hand, he'd only resorted to violence in defense of a helpless victim. It had been a spontaneous thing, totally unplanned, without forethought. A premeditated fight was no longer in his repertoire. So much for his career as a warrior. The reason he'd become a doctor in the first place.

Back to Kevin.

She checked his vitals and was pleasantly surprised that his pulse had gotten stronger. She'd definitely leave the tube in his throat for the next twelve hours or so. In the meantime, she'd need to sit here and monitor him, especially since the machines had no way of notifying her of a sudden change in his condition, not with the computer down. Hopefully, he could stay off life support. That was never a good thing to have to resume.

It was going to be a long night. Or was this daytime? It was so easy to lose track of time in deep space with no sunrise or sunset to usher in mornings and evenings. Well, it was going to be long as hell, whatever it was called!

And they still hadn't eaten yet. Nope. The shitstorm started right when they were about to go for some chow. Now Kirkman realized she was famished and weak. Her eyes were losing their focus. She almost dismissed the flashes of light she saw as optical illusions brought on by hunger and fatigue, coupled with a headache that gnawed at her temples.

Flashbulbs popping. Reflecting off of the clear polymer shield that protected Kevin's frontal lobe.

No.

Lights were flashing *inside* Kevin's shield. It was the electrodes she'd strung across his brain. They were pulsating. An army of tiny fireflies come to life.

CHAPTER 40

Captain Arnold stood alone in a corner of the rear hangar. She was communicating with Jarrett via micro-comm. He was in the cyber room where techs had been researching all things related to shutting down a warship's environmental systems.

"There's no precedent," Jarrett said. The lonely tuft of white hair on top of his head made him look like an ancient scribe. "In the history of the Armada, no warship has ever tried shutting down only the environmental systems."

"Because it's stupid and suicidal," Arnold said. (She knew that Jarrett hadn't dared say it, so she said it for him.) "But it's our only option. The alternative is to risk the yuck blob shutting them down for us. Permanently. So let's get on with it."

Jarrett conveyed the tech's findings. Based on command latency and message routing, a complete shutdown would take approximately forty minutes.

Insanity. Pure insanity. But it was all they had.

"Captain?" Jarrett said. "Are you still there?"

"Just give me a minute," Arnold said.

A minute… She would have preferred an hour, a week…hell, a whole damn year. But a decision had to be made. No more stalling. It was a choice between bad and worse. Well, the choice had been made. It was just a question of nailing down specifics at this point.

She contacted Jade via micro-comm, even though she could see her pink hair in the harrier's cockpit from where she stood. "I've got a number for you, Jade," Arnold said. "Forty minutes for a full environmental shutdown."

Thus far, Jade and her team had been firing everything they had at the yuck blob to stall its progress, even though their efforts were destined to fail. But they'd also been monitoring its rate of destructive spread.

"C'mon, Jade. Tell me something good. I know you can do it."

"Seventy-seven and a half percent," Jade squeaked.

That was the magic number. The ideal (or least horrible) time to begin environmental system shutdown was when the yuck blob had taken over seventy-seven and a half percent of computer resources. At that point, environmental systems would remain offline—safe from carnage—until the yuck blob totally bricked the warship's computer and died out with nothing else to eat.

"How long till we hit lucky seventy-seven and a half?" Arnold asked.

Jade paused a second. To consult with Vincent, Arnold surmised.

"About three hours," Jade said.

"Okay. Keep doing what you're doing. Update me every fifteen minutes."

She said it in a calm, authoritative voice, a *detached* voice, totally isolated from the surge of *Oh, shit!* panic rushing to her head. She engaged Jarrett again. "I've got a timeframe from Jade," she said. "Three hours."

"Captain, that's not—"

"I know it's not enough time, Jarrett."

Indeed. The warship had five decks, each of those divided into quadrants. Then there were the hangars and the bridge.

Suiting up for battle, reporting to your assigned station, be it a warship post or in a battle craft, required covering a lot of distance. Even connecting with one's squad could be a challenge at times. And with both the transport discs and lifts rendered inoperable, getting the entire crew into survival gear in under three hours was impossible. How pathetic their dependence on that damn computer for the most basic tasks!

I never saw this coming, Arnold thought.

They'd also have to have crew in place to assist the non-combat personnel (never to be referred to as plebs again, at least in her presence). Many of them didn't know the front end from the back end of survival gear—forget about wearing it for any length of time.

"Get a message to all ship personnel, Jarrett." Arnold dictated: *This is not a drill. Environmental systems will go down in three hours. Those in close proximity to their survival gear, suit up. Everyone else, await further instructions.*

"Captain?"

"Don't ask, Jarrett. I'll tell you when I know."

"There's one other thing, Captain," Jarrett said.

"What now?"

"Shutdown authorization has to be issued from the bridge."

"You mean…"

"That's right. You can't do it from the rear hangar. The commanding officer has to initiate shutdown protocol from the bridge. It's a failsafe."

"It's a pain in the ass," Arnold said. "But nothing's changed. Contact all personnel. Same orders."

She felt her heart pounding from yet another useless adrenaline dump. A key unsolved problem… An extra unexpected step in the process…

Every battle to this point had been convoluted.

CHAPTER 41

"GABLE! YOU'VE GOTTA SEE THIS." Kirkman felt giddy. She had no clue what the hell was going on, but was convinced that she was witnessing a phenomenon.

Gable was in the next room, preserving Gunderson's body for the inquest that was bound to follow the recent shitshow in the infirmary.

"Get your ass in here," Kirkman insisted.

Gable shuffled in, rubbing his eyes. Clearly exhausted. Getting stunned by a gimlet was bound to take a physical toll. "What's going on?" he said. "Oh, something went wrong with your neural lace. Those electrodes are blinking on their own."

"There's nothing wrong with the neural lace," Kirkman said.

"And you know that, how?"

"Because the electrodes are just dumb messengers. All they do is receive and transmit. And because I'm good; I know what the hell I'm doing."

"So this is a good thing," Gable said. "There's brain activity going on."

"More than that," Kirkman said. "They're flashing two different colors. Yellow and orange. Send and receive!"

"Then something's off," Gable said. "He's not sending or receiving anything outside of what's left of his skull."

"I think he's communicating with the ship's computer," Kirkman said.

"That's crazy, Kirkman. The computer is offline, in case you haven't heard."

"No, it's not. You can still connect to a computer that isn't working."

"And do what?" Gable said.

"I don't know."

"That's right. You don't know."

Kirkman wanted to scream. She had a trapped feeling of being walled in from all sides. It seemed like she could shout till she passed out and nobody would hear her. She closed her eyes, dug her fingernails into her sweaty palms, and really, *really* wanted to smack Gable across the face.

Why did she care what he thought? Or anybody else for that matter? Given that she had no way of proving herself correct… But she knew. She *knew*, dammit!

Gable's voice cut through her thoughts. "C'mon, Kirkman, nothing's changed. Either way, our job is to keep this kid alive and help him recover. Doesn't matter what kind of light show he's putting on."

Kirkman gritted her teeth. "When the computer's back online…then we'll see."

"Right. And in the meantime—"

"I know, I know…"

The same message reached both of them simultaneously. *Urgent message from Captain Arnold. This is not a drill. All personnel in close proximity to their emergency station will get into their survival gear immediately. All other Touchstone crew will stand by for further instructions. This is a direct order.*

Noise mitigation kept them from hearing each other's

message even though they were standing only a few feet apart. But they both knew they were receiving the same instructions.

Their eyes met. His gray eyes, her brown eyes. Then they looked at Kevin.

"There's no way we can get him into survival gear," Kirkman said.

"He didn't receive the order," Gable said. "But we did."

"Have you ever been ordered into survival gear on a warship not engaged in battle?" Kirkman asked.

"I have now," Gable said.

And that ended the conversation right there. The taste for violence might have left him, but following orders was still engrained into his very being.

CHAPTER 42

Kevin gazed into the distance, sensing the change before he actually saw it. Seeing the ginormous mass quivering across the horizon made him feel very cold inside. This was no earthquake, no force of nature. This was no avalanche that careened downhill with ever-increasingly velocity. Whatever it was, this thing was advancing at an even pace. No hurry. No pause. And eliminating whatever happened to be in front of it.

First it blotted out the sunset, then it devoured the furthest hills. More than that…the mass itself seemed to be growing. Consuming. That's what it was doing. Whatever it touched became a part of it.

And the vibration under his feet? The sheer size of this thing would cause that. But that idea felt…wrong somehow.

At any rate, he had to get the hell out of here. And fast. He needed to sprint in the opposite direction, but his legs were wooden and useless.

And leaving this place also felt…wrong.

He ought to be shitting bricks, but he felt strangely calm instead. Sure, he was scared as hell, terrified actually, yet his pulse was slow and steady, his breathing calm, and that all-too-familiar cowardly tingle in his spine was nowhere to be found.

I'm a total contradiction, he thought. *An optional programming object. Instantiate me as anything you want or nothing at all.*

The clapboard cabin beckoned. But he didn't have time for any detours. The sun no longer reflected off the tin roof because it was getting devoured one small piece at a time. That cabin would become his coffin if he was in there when this thing arrived.

All of these thoughts raced through his mind as he leisurely walked up the cobblestone path to the cabin's entrance. Might as well. Somehow, he sensed that running away from the oncoming disaster would be pointless.

So the cabin seemed as good an option as any. It had a familiarity to it that Kevin couldn't explain. His mouth watered, almost anticipating the aroma of Gram's vegetable stew in his nostrils, even though her rickety shack was nothing like this sturdy building with an unwelcoming metal door.

A metal door!

Great. He couldn't even get into the place. There was a touchpad, but Kevin didn't have a nano-chipped glove. Acting on impulse, he placed his bare hand on the touchpad, knowing it was useless.

The door whooshed open on silent tracking, and Kevin entered techie paradise. This was no woodlands cabin; the clapboard exterior was a mere facade. Blanketed by a soft blue glow, the room was equipped with a floating workstation surrounded by wall screens. A holographic computing cloud hovered just below the ceiling. Kevin's heart soared. Here was everything he'd ever need to create, build, experiment, discover. To just play!

He'd gone to heaven with hell fast approaching.

CHAPTER 43

The hum of approaching rovers…

That was a sound that Arnold had never dreamed of hearing *inside* a warship. But extreme problems called for creative solutions. Each of the warship's five decks had its own set of transport shuttles—small, speedy carts that were (of course!) computer controlled. And the lifts were disabled as well. With the crew unable to move quickly to the changing stations, their survival gear would have to be transported to them.

They had a plan. In addition to the ladders located at the front and rear of the ship, there was a wide stairwell dead center. Arnold had always considered stairs in a warship a waste of space. For as long as she could remember, the stairwell had served no practical purpose except for subjecting recruits to brutal weight-bearing runs.

Until now. The stairs connected all five decks. And rovers could climb stairs and turn the corners on every landing. (The larger vehicles, halftracks and mammoths, could be driven outside once the warship landed on a planet's surface. But they were way too big to maneuver inside the ship itself.)

It was still a complex operation. On each deck, the rovers

would travel to the changing stations, load up the survival gear, and deliver the right gear to the right unit on the right quadrant. There were makeshift teams of quartermasters, drivers, and record keepers assembled throughout.

Seventy minutes of Jade's three-hour estimated window had passed. They still had a fighting chance. They could maybe pull this off (if shutting down all environmental systems could be considered a win) while there was yet time to just let the yuck blob kill their computer and itself with it. Maybe, just maybe… they could make it in under the wire.

Commander Rison was in charge of bridge operations, not that anything was functioning up there; Commander Hudson was watching over the front hangar. Arnold didn't trust Hudson. No proof of any wrongdoing on his part. But she'd sooner swan dive into an active volcano than put her life in his hands. To that end, rover operations in each quadrant were being overseen by lieutenants, who sent their updates directly to her through Jarrett.

And now, Jarrett was hailing her. "Field Medic Jan Kirkman contacted me," he said. "It's about Kevin Slaton. I know we've got bigger problems, but—"

Slaton! She'd forgotten all about him. "Go ahead, Jarrett. What about Slaton?"

"Well, he's in the infirmary on an air stretcher. Still in a coma and breathing through a tube."

"And he can't dress for survival or batten himself down," Arnold sighed.

"There's more. His brain's lighting up."

"What?"

"That's what Kirkman said. They've hooked up some experimental mesh to his brain and now it's all lit up. Kirkman thinks he's pinging the ship's computer."

Arnold felt a huge fist in her gut. They were fighting against an invisible foe; that was bad enough. On top of that, a classified asset, very important to the admiralty, had gotten his skull kicked in. And now, a field medic had taken it upon herself to perform some harebrained experiment on him, which would probably end up killing him.

"Captain?"

"Sorry, Jarrett. Repeat." He'd been talking, and she hadn't heard a word.

"Kirkman wants you to reconsider shutting down environmental, at least in the infirmary's quadrant."

"And risk the yuck blob shutting it down for us," Arnold said.

"Not an option," Jarrett said. "Captain! I apologize for—"

"Nothing to apologize for, Jarrett. Give me a second."

Okay. Things had gone incomprehensibly bad. And losing this protege, this prized secret of the Armada that had been entrusted to the warship *Touchstone*, would make things that much worse. Assuming they were alive to experience any of the resulting blowback. Not only that—Slaton had caused this predicament. He couldn't be allowed to just slip away into the twilight.

"They have to get him to the rear hangar," Arnold said. "That's the only way. We can put him in a pressurized environment. One of the harriers."

"I'll contact Lieutenant Briggs," Jarrett said.

"You'll do no such thing. We can't spare a rover. And we can't afford to divert our focus either. Kirkman will have to walk him down to the rear hangar herself. I know it'll be cutting things close for them, but that's her problem."

CHAPTER 44

For a moment, the sight of Gable in his battle gear took Kirkman's breath away. Suits like this one were custom-made for up-close-and-personal ravaging.

The exterior was sleek body armor that molded to his muscular frame. It looked like a thin exoskeleton had been poured over him, but it could deflect heavy laser fire. Some weapons could cut through the material, but few societies had access to that level of technology. The hood and face shield could be activated by a mere touch, providing not only personal protection but also oxygen and pressurization for up to twenty hours without a recharge.

Kirkman's field medic suit looked somewhat plastic and robotic in comparison. But she could still move around in it, no problem.

"Impressive," she said.

"Haven't had this on in a long time," Gable replied.

"I figured you'd turned it in when you quit—became a doctor."

"It's mine to keep. Custom made for maiming and killing."

"And now just plain survival in a vacuum," Kirkman said.

Neither spoke for a moment. Gable's eyes shifted to Kevin, lying prone and unconscious on the air stretcher, the front of his brain still a Borealis of flashing lights.

"I contacted the captain," Kirkman said.

"What?"

"Through her adjutant, Jarrett. About Kevin."

Gable's eyes were daggers. "Questioning orders is never acceptable," he said.

"I was apprising the captain of a situation," Kirkman snapped.

"In an attempt to undermine what we've been ordered to do," Gable said. "Which is get ourselves prepped and wait."

"And let our patient die in the meantime."

"There's a bigger picture to consider," Gable said.

"I agree that the captain *should* consider the entire picture."

"That's not what I meant."

They glared at each other for several seconds. Kirkman imagined his gaze softened just a touch when their eyes locked, then dismissed that notion as wishful thinking on her part.

"Kevin can survive this shutdown if we put him in a small ship," she said.

"What?"

"Captain Arnold said it: he can be placed in a harrier in the rear hangar."

"The captain ordered us to do that?" Gable said. "Why the hell didn't you tell me that in the first place?"

"Okay, she didn't *order* us," Kirkman said. "But we *do* have permission. We're not disobeying orders if we do it."

"Do what, exactly?"

Kirkman paused before answering. "Transport him to the rear hangar and put him in a harrier."

Gable looked tired. Grunting, he sank into a nearby chair and rubbed his eyes. Probably still a little off from that gimlet blast he'd taken. "I assume transport means physically walking him down there," he said.

"That's right."

He looked at Kevin and sighed.

"I'm doing it," Kirkman said.

"Not a good idea."

"I'm still doing it. Try and stop me."

Gable looked up at her. Something like a smile flitted across his face. "The most direct route from here to the rear hangar is straight to the rear of the warship. Then down the ladders."

"He's dead weight," Kirkman said. "No communication with the main computer to plot out a levitation route. I'll have to roll him the whole way."

Gable stood up.

"Then I'm coming with you," he said. "Somebody's got to get him down those ladders."

CHAPTER 45

Hudson considered Captain Arnold's announcement that environmental systems would be going down.

Hmm… That means the computer's not coming back, Hudson figured. Good news if that was the case. His secrets would remain secret. Ironic, though…he no longer had anything to fear from the Inquest Unit, but he might also wind up losing luxuries like oxygen and gravity. One problem replaced with another.

Regardless of the problem at hand, being weaponed up was always good—and Hudson was in his body armor and armed to the teeth. He now strode around the hangar with not only his usual feeling of superiority but a certainty of invincibility. Nobody in here—not the plebs, nor the pilots stationed among them—could prevent him from doing anything he damn well pleased.

And that began with Fike. Hudson spotted him right away. That conceited rectum! Fike wasn't going to have any use for air or gravity or anything else…

Hudson cursed. He was being hailed by Commander Rison, who was stationed on the bridge. Rison was part of Hudson's network—a weak ally, but an ally nonetheless. So he had to answer.

"Hudson!" Rison's voice was stress-laden.

"Go ahead, Rison."

"I'm on the bridge."

"Well, no shit," Hudson said. Rison wasn't thinking straight.

"The captain's on her way up here."

"I've got my hands full down here in the front hangar," Hudson said, hoping to end communication right there.

"You know about the environmental systems shutdown."

Hudson found himself getting very annoyed. *Ship-wide announcement. How could he not know?* "What can I do for you, Rison?"

"Well, like I said, the captain's on her way up here to the bridge."

Hudson took a deep breath and resisted the urge to kill the communication in the middle of one of his own sentences.

"Captain Arnold's coming up here to shut down the environmental systems. That's oxygen, gravity simulation, cabin pressure. Everything."

"The entire computer's going tits up," Hudson said. "Or haven't you heard?"

"You don't understand," Rison said. "Environmental shutdown has to be invoked from the bridge by the ship's captain."

Hudson paused, heart thumping, suddenly interested, as if he'd just been jarred awake. "You're telling me that the environmental systems are going to be taken down deliberately, that the computer problems have nothing to do with it?"

Silence on the other end.

"Rison?"

"This is bad," Rison said. "I have grave concerns about pulling the plug on life support."

Like a shark smelling blood, Hudson sensed the fear in Rison's voice. Of course there was a legit reason for the captain's actions. Some way to attack whatever was killing the computer or at least slow it down. But Rison was scared shitless. Why else would he reach out to a peer in the face of a direct order? Normally he'd just obey without question. But this was a far-from-normal circumstance.

Hudson could use that. "You realize, of course, that the ship will be helpless. Just a floating blob of jelly with zero protection from anybody or anything."

"I know that!" Rison said. "Of course I know that. But what can I do?"

"Well, you *have* been given a direct order by Captain Arnold," Hudson said.

"Yes," Rison said miserably. "And I have no choice but to—"

"On the other hand," Hudson interjected. "No. Never mind."

"What?" Rison said.

"Well, orders are orders."

"C'mon, Hudson. Just say it."

"Sorry, pal," Hudson said. "I'm glad I'm not in your shoes."

"Just finish your thought," Rison pleaded. "Whatever you say stays between us. You've got my word."

Hudson bit down on a laugh. Rison was looking for a directive to follow. He was in unchartered territory and couldn't find his footing.

So he'd reached out to an alleged ally for reassurance. Bad move.

"I know one thing," Hudson said. "The shitstorm is just beginning. I mean, an Armada warship's been turned into a useless piece of crap. Think about it. We might as well be in a floating garbage can right now."

"Then I should go along with whatever that bitch captain wants?" Rison said.

"Not so fast. The shitstorm is barely getting started. Inquest Unit! Do I really need to walk you through what's going to happen?"

"Uh-h-h," Rison said.

"Ask yourself this: do you want to have to explain why you allowed all environmental systems to be disabled?"

"My answer will be that the captain gave me a direct order. It's on her."

"You'll be dealing with more than just the Inquest Unit," Hudson said. "Admiral Anson's going to ask why you'd render the entire crew helpless as newborn babies in the face of imminent danger. He'll wonder why you couldn't think for yourself in the face of an obvious breach of protocol. If you blindly trust the captain's fitness as a leader in this situation, what does that say about you and your future?"

Hudson held his breath while Rison stewed in silence. He'd either take the bait or retreat into the snug harbor of obedience and compliance.

"Suppose I refuse to let the captain onto the bridge," Rison said. "How would I justify that?"

Hudson released his breath slowly, savoring the taste of victory in a luxurious exhale. "We're talking about handicapping an entire crew when their ship's already a sitting duck," he said. "We might as well blast a *ripe for the taking* broadcast across the whole galaxy. By preventing that from happening, you'd be rescuing us all from total self-destruction. That's called taking initiative."

Rison paused before answering. "I appreciate your perspective," he said.

Yeah… Rison needed one more push.

"We are the Armada," Hudson said.

"The Armada is us," Rison responded.

Then together they chanted: "Always prepared to fight."

"Wherever the fight takes us," Hudson said.

"Wherever, whenever, whomever," Rison replied.

"Take it to them, brother," Hudson said.

"I shall!"

The transmission ended.

Rison! A sucker and an easy mark…

"Commander Hudson."

Two stern-faced pilots that Hudson didn't recognize had walked up on him. He'd been too busy smirking to notice their approach. Their weapons were drawn, and they'd spread themselves apart, one on either side of him, in a ninety-degree pattern.

And safely back in the wings, his face a mask of smugness, was Fike!

CHAPTER 46

Kevin explored the data matrix, the service cloud, the processor arrays. The elegant configuration that linked all of these things together was absolute perfection. If he could design a system from scratch, this would be it. This was way more than a computer. Here was a galaxy of swirling pointers that folded, modified, and manipulated with a mere thought.

It occurred to him that the cabin door and this workstation and whatever it was hooked into were all open and available to him. No need to finagle his way around security or firewalls. Total access. The how and the why of it was unimportant at the moment—a fleeting thought, easily cast aside. Instead, he was reveling in the warm caress of a world that made sense, that embraced him, made him whole, gave him a reason to exist among the living (whoever the hell the living were).

A kid turned loose in a toy store doesn't question how he got there or why the door was left open for him. He just plays.

Limited only by his intellect and imagination, Kevin considered where to start. He could build apps, compose algorithms. Innovate. Instead he began branching out, stretching quantum tentacles across his workstation's outer realm.

No system existed by itself; it was always part of a larger whole. Until it wasn't. Until that larger whole itself proved to be finite with its own inherent limits. Kevin would begin by determining boundaries, drawing borders around this new world where he'd been planted.

And from there? Pushing those boundaries, of course.

A twinge of angst stopped him for a moment, followed by a few seconds of concern about that other world. The one he'd just retreated from when he'd entered this cabin. It was under attack from some unseen, inexplicable force that looked to be unstoppable.

But that was a force of nature. Nothing he could do about that. Not a thing.

Couldn't outrun it. Couldn't attack it. Here was as good a port of refuge as any. And if this cabin got destroyed...well, he might as well enjoy himself in the meantime. It had been a long time since he'd been able to do that, and this might be the last chance he'd ever have.

Fatalistic logic. Something he'd never have been capable of before enlisting. So maybe the Armada had done something for him after all.

At any rate, Kevin immersed himself in the soft blue glow of the holographic data cloud and continued to reach and probe. He launched programs, ran scans, posted results to the surrounding wall screens, and then reran the decoded results through modified payloads. And all the while, he was becoming one with the system itself. In the zone. Touching and manipulating. Analyzing and expanding.

He reached far into the surrounding realm of clustered keys and indexed nodes. It was slippery out there. Volatile and unstable. Something was amiss.

He posted his results to the wall screens and reached further. The environment that surrounded him and his workstation had been damaged. Maybe through a system glitch that wrote out erroneous clusters that needed to be cleaned up. Or from a runaway program off the rails. Or even by a deliberate attack.

Instead of concern, Kevin couldn't suppress a surge of elation. The excitement brought about by the challenge that had presented itself to him. He'd been wondering where to start, what to do first. This was awesome. Finding and correcting the source of the problem was going to be a blast. Maybe he really *had* died and gone to heaven.

CHAPTER 47

CAPTAIN ARNOLD TOOK three warriors with her. They were halfway to the bridge. She reminded herself that it wasn't the end. They hadn't lost this strange battle—not yet, anyway. They were about to execute a ploy. Pure and simple. A tactic, a trap to cause their enemy to destroy itself.

From that perspective, shutting down environmental systems was not a mere act of desperation and could hardly be considered defeat. But it sure as hell couldn't be considered victory either. With every step, she imagined an invisible lifeline stretching ever tighter—the last vestige of certainty before she stepped onto the bridge, placed her gloved hand on the reader, authorized the shutdown…

These thoughts were running through her head when Jarrett hailed her.

"Captain, I'm patching in Fike. There's a situation in the front hangar."

"Keep walking," she told the warriors with her. Whatever the new crisis, she still had to make it to the bridge in time.

"Captain Arnold." Fike's voice interrupted her thoughts.

"I'm stationed in the front hangar. We've just placed Commander Ralph Hudson under arrest."

Arnold stopped walking. "Hudson is your commanding officer," she said. "Arresting him is… Do you know the consequences?"

"Captain. We're arresting Commander Hudson on suspicion of mutiny. I've captured a communication that proves he's deliberately undermined your command."

"Micro-comms run on private channels," Arnold said. "You're telling me you can eavesdrop on a communication?"

"There are ways," Fike said.

Arnold felt dizzy and wanted to sit for a minute to clear her head. "Never mind," she said. "What did Commander Hudson allegedly do?"

"I have it recorded, Captain."

Fike played back the final portion of Hudson's conversation with Rison.

Puking her guts out didn't exude leadership mettle, but that was exactly what Arnold felt like doing. *We can't even get a disaster to come off without a hitch,* she thought.

Then she snapped out of it. "Keep walking," she told her trio of warriors. Yeah, she'd have to deal with this one on the move.

"Walk me through it, Fike. How many warriors do you have on him right now?"

"Two. Their weapons are drawn; they're locked on him."

No! Arnold bit down on a shout. You'd need at least eight for him. No voice commands or warnings either. Just open fire and overpower him. Stun and be ready to kill if necessary. Like as not, he was in his body armor. He'd kill those two, no problem. And the others down there…he'd waste most of them too.

She walked faster.

Under normal circumstances, she'd accompany a team down there and give him the option of surrendering or getting taken out. In this case, her best option was to defuse the situation. Which meant no direct confrontation—yet again, dammit!

"Fike! Patch me through to Commander Hudson," she said. "And shut the doors to the hangar."

"Captain Arnold." Hudson's predatory baritone made her bones tighten. That's when she knew. There was going to be no reasoning with him whatsoever. Forget talking him into quietly laying down his weapons or any other nonviolent solution.

"I know you're armed, Hudson," Arnold said. "And we both know you can easily kill those two warriors facing you down right now."

"True. But I've got no call to kill fellow Armada warriors," Hudson said.

This was no good. She was fencing with a hyena. Arresting Hudson, meting out future punishment…none of that mattered. She had to get on the bridge. And she needed this situation in the front hangar resolved without loss of life.

Mostly, she had to get on the bridge.

She would have preferred to have him meet her in the dojo, one-on-one, despite the inevitable injuries to both of them. He wouldn't be able to back down from a direct challenge. But there was no time for that.

Again, she was fighting a different kind of battle. But cunning was a weapon she could hone to a sharp edge.

"Why do you think you're being arrested?"

"Games, Captain?"

"The hangar doors are shutting," Arnold said.

"I see that."

"You could probably kill everybody in there with you."

"Why this insinuation that I'd kill my own?"

Arnold ignored him. "It wouldn't help you because there's

nowhere for you to go. We'd have two full squads down there before you could cut your way out. And forget about opening the hatch doors to launch a hawker."

"Pray tell, Captain. Why *am* I being arrested?"

Arnold reminded her entourage to keep moving. They still had to get to the bridge. Then she returned her attention to Hudson. Fike's recording was enough for an arrest and investigation. But she wanted more. As in Hudson gone for good. It was time for mental warfare.

"The techs took a deep dive into the computer, looking for anything that might help us," she said. "Know what they found?"

"Enlighten me."

"Well, we know all about Tonya Verdi, the recruit that wasn't really a recruit." That was a true statement but also a mere generalization that might or might not mean a damn thing. A probing jab to see how he'd react.

Silence from Hudson.

"Anything to say?"

"How dare you, Captain! To suggest that I had any part..."

Arnold listened carefully. There was tension in his voice. Beneath his gusty bravado, a mere hint of underlying trepidation. At least that's how it seemed to her.

Let me be right! she thought. Lives were at stake.

"That's just the tip of the spear that's going to nail you to the wall," Arnold said. "They dug up some other shit that'll give the Inquest Unit wet dreams for the next decade. No time to go through it all right now with the ship about to be rendered helpless. They saved it off, though. To an external storage unit. Wasted some valuable processing cycles, but it was worth it."

Hudson started yelling, obviously for the entire hangar to hear. "I'm being detained under false pretenses!" he shouted. "I'm a loyal Armada officer and warrior, and I've been wrongly accused of crimes I didn't commit. I will not allow this to happen! Anyone in this hangar who participates in this treachery will pay and pay dearly!"

Arnold quickly contacted Fike on another channel. "Have your men stand down," she said. "Keep the doors shut, but do not engage Commander Hudson. Do it."

Then back to her conversation with Hudson. "Shut up, Hudson. They're standing down."

"I will not be anybody's scapegoat!" Hudson ranted, loud as ever.

He'd taken the bait. Maybe.

"What do you think's going to happen if you kill everybody in the front hangar?"

"That would be bad," Hudson jeered. "A thing like that happening on your watch."

"And you wouldn't make it off this vessel alive."

"Maybe I'll take my chances. In fact, go ahead and bid farewell to that little asshole Fike."

She almost yelled. Almost shouted…!

That would have signed Fike's death warrant. Instead, in a calm voice, she said: "There's a way out of this for both of us."

Dead silence.

"Keep walking," she reminded her entourage.

More silence. Ten agonizing seconds of it.

Finally, Hudson spoke. "Okay, little girl. Let's hear it."

CHAPTER 48

The outside beckoned.

Kevin ignored it. Everything was deteriorating out there—of course it was. Eventually, the mountains, the forest, the stream, even the sky *and this cabin* would be destroyed. But he couldn't do anything about that. He could, however, spend what might be the final hour of his existence engaged in the problems and puzzles of this cool new computer world he'd stumbled into. And he definitely had a challenge in front of him: track down the system instability and fix it.

Probing with his mind, focusing solely on the self-contained computing cloud in this cabin, a virtual bubble in and of itself, Kevin found that he really didn't have to focus at all. He was becoming a part of this thing, an inhabitant of this world. That familiar euphoria of visiting a realm where things made sense had returned.

Kevin had no sense of time. Didn't care. But he couldn't have tracked it if he did. It just happened. One second, he was examining the computing cloud that surrounded him and the processes that kept it afloat, then he knew that everything running in this workspace he inhabited was a base algorithm—

pure, untainted, pristine and unspoiled. His workspace was a self-contained system, an oasis of perfect symmetry.

He quickly wrote a series of test patterns. The instructions were simple: go out, pick an available memory address, read something, write something, delete. And send back result codes while you're doing that. Like probing tentacles, he launched them out into the surrounding desert, or whatever network of system nodes happened to be out there.

Several seconds and…nothing. Not possible. At least not in a functional environment. Each test pattern was too tiny and simplistic to not run instantly, even if the end result was an error code.

Going further, he compiled a batch of probes to simply ping the addresses of the test patterns he'd already launched. Find them and report back. Nothing more.

What should have been instantaneous took a minute, but results began trickling back to him. The nearby probes reported a status of *still running.* That was unthinkably slow. Then one of the test patterns finally finished on its own and returned a success code. That was about 10,000 times longer than it should have taken. And further out…nothing came back from any probe or test pattern, not even a crash-and-burn failure. It was as if they'd ceased to exist.

It didn't take a genius to figure out that everything worsened the further away he probed. So he carefully examined the outer edge of the cabin's computing cloud, the boundary of his oasis. As he worked his way out, Kevin uncovered flaws and cracks. Nothing major at first, just a misplaced qubit here and there, a damaged cluster of data. A piece of glass with a hairline crack in it.

Suddenly, he cursed out loud to nobody but himself. He'd forgotten a data pattern he'd been using as a baseline; it went right out of his head. He grabbed it from the cloud—again!—and saved it to a scratch pad on a nearby screen. No big deal. Except that he'd always been able to keep multiple pieces of info at the front of his mind. Now, his mind was skipping and popping, an idea just suddenly vanishing, a train of thought careening off unstable tracking.

Whatever. Even if he wasn't performing at his full potential, he was still having fun.

Except...

There was an inward bulge on the perimeter of the external qubit sphere. Slight and almost unnoticeable, but it was there. In fact, Kevin felt it before he saw it. Something out there was pressing in on his new computer world. His oasis.

Well, this was his domain. There wasn't anything he could do about what was happening outside of the cabin. But this thing, whatever it was, had picked the wrong oasis to screw around with.

CHAPTER 49

Hudson sat in the cockpit of his assigned ship. Assigned! Bile burned the back of his throat, leaving a bitter taste in his mouth. This was a pill too nasty to even consider swallowing.

Yet here he was.

A soft voice of reason in the back of his mind, his *Logical Voice*, was trying to reassure him that he'd made the best choice available, given his circumstances. He gritted his teeth and clenched the control stick till his knuckles turned white, wanting to drive *Logical Voice* into a corner and crush him.

This was no choice. This was coercion, plain and simple. Captain Arnold, that stupid cow! She'd put him here. Listening to a bunch of whimpering plebs. Thinking that downing life support—downing life support!—was a good idea. There was simply no scenario where she *deserved* to get her way, especially at the expense of her betters. *Damn that wrong-headed, hopeless, lucky, cowardly…* No. She was no coward. He had to concede that. But she was still a second-rate bimbo in the right place at the right time, who'd probably screwed her way up to outranking him in the first place.

Again, *Logical Voice* tried to point out that he was no longer under arrest or charged with any wrongdoing, that he was escaping certain scrutiny by the Inquest Unit.

"ARRH! SHUT UP!" Hudson roared at the top of his lungs, making himself a little lightheaded but knowing that nobody in the hangar could hear him once his compartment had been sealed. His heart pounded in his ears; sweat trickled down the back of his neck. Oh, how he wanted to hop out of there and wipe the grins off those smug faces. Especially Fike. They were all looking at him, knowing what had happened, waiting till he'd launched to laugh openly.

Well, the joke was going to be on them! He'd see to that.

———

That captain had laid it all out for him. Contact Commander Rison. Convince him to allow her onto the bridge. In exchange, Hudson would get a hawker of his very own and safe passage off the warship, freedom to go wherever he pleased.

"Or I could just kill everybody in this hangar," Hudson retorted. "There's a few here that can fight, but mostly plebs."

"The hangar door's closed," the bitch captain said. "Same with the outside hatch. And you don't have access to either."

She was right. He remembered Fike saying that palm readers were autonomous from the computer itself. And somebody had just closed the door to the ship, so that seemed to be true. He also knew that pressing the severed hand of a corpse (someone who had access when alive) on a reader was no good.

"Oh, and don't think about wounding anybody with access and using their hand," Bitch Captain said. "We can disable all entry and exit codes at the first sign of trouble."

Hudson's vision blurred as her condescending tone grated against him. Nobody talked down to him. Especially not a snotty bitch whose rank and position should have been his. Taking shallow breaths, nearly hyperventilating, he addressed the warriors with their weapons trained on him. "Back the fuck off!" he said. "I've just made a deal with your whore of a bitch captain."

Then he did it. He got on a three-way communication with Rison and the captain. "I did some digging on my own," he lied to Rison. From there, he talked the poor sap down off the ledge he'd put him on by endorsing shutting down life support as the best—hell, the only!—available course of action.

But before signing off, he dropped a clue. "Captain Arnold is in charge," he said. "We have to respect that."

Hoo, boy, he thought. *If Rison doesn't pick up on that, he really is a moron.*

———

The hatch whooshed opened. Hudson disengaged auto-launch in favor of manual control. One flick of the wrist would send him hurtling through open space before anybody could react.

He looked out into the dark vastness of the universe, letting the usual surge of empowerment course through his veins. The bitch captain had kept her word. That alone proved her too weak to command a warship—no further evaluation necessary. The right move would have been to cut him down in a hail of laser fire the second he convinced Rison to relent.

His hand twitched on the control stick. Payback time.

Savor the moment, he reminded himself.

CHAPTER 50

Rear hangar.

The entire tech team was attacking the yuck blob with everything they had. They were losing.

Eight of them were in a harrier; also a pilot who would maintain life support and a gunner with nothing to blast. Without having to suit up, the techs could focus on their main objective: buying time.

Jade was hunched over the computer in the cockpit. Vincent sat behind her, monitoring system status on his device. "It's getting worse," he said.

"I know," Jade squeaked. "We're losing. If we can just maintain long enough for Captain Arnold to do her thing on the bridge…"

"Jade, it's getting a whole lot worse."

"We're attacking with everything we have," Jade said.

"Jade—"

"We keep on fighting right down to the end till there's nothing left," Jade snapped. "That's it. Nothing else to do but battle it out. *Wherever the fight takes us.* That's the Armada way."

The other techs in the harrier had hooked their devices into the harrier's computer, forming a network of sorts. They were all engaged in firing fresh qubits at the yuck blob and maintaining their virtual firebreak, precarious as it was. And on other hawkers and harriers throughout the warship, other tech squads were doing the same thing.

And losing bad.

As in significantly worse than anticipated.

Needles of frustration prompted Vincent to stand instead of sit. He wanted to pace, but they were trapped inside this tubular box without a hell of a lot of room. Jade wasn't wrong. The only path forward was to keep attacking that yuck blob. All out. Reevaluating the situation was a luxury they didn't have.

No, Jade wasn't wrong. Except, she was buying into that asinine warrior credo of never backing down—to the point of glorifying your own death. They'd both had the training when they were recruited, albeit a much softer regimen than what prospective warriors had to endure. Apparently, that recruit who stole a ship and started this mess had been subjected to the full treatment. Vincent didn't get that at all. But that wasn't his problem, so why was he thinking about it at a time like this?

Thing is, Jade wasn't wrong, but she wasn't right either. Blindly pressing on was the best idea—sure, right up until now —but something had changed. Vincent couldn't say what, but the sudden drop in resources…there was a lot more to it than them losing faster than anticipated. Burying their heads and pushing harder just didn't feel right.

Because it wasn't.

"Jade!"

Vincent grabbed her shoulders and spun her around. "There's something else." He shoved his device at her. "A new variable's been introduced. Look at these numbers. This is more than just the yuck blob rolling over us."

Jade twitched her nose and studied Vincent's findings for half a minute. When she looked up, her eyes were expressionless, her voice dull. "Well, shit," she said. "This really sucks."

"Alright," Vincent said, making an effort to keep his voice down. "No need to panic."

But Jade had already turned around and resumed what she'd been doing. Vincent squeezed in behind her and looked over her shoulder at the console she was using. Her hair had a sweet aroma that cut through the stale air. "How did we blow the estimate?" he whispered.

"We didn't," Jade said.

That's when he realized she wasn't running new stats or rechecking their previous findings. Her sole focus had returned to fighting the yuck blob with all available resources, which were way lower than they were supposed to be at this point.

"Jade, dammit!" Vincent hissed between clenched teeth. "Captain Arnold's relying on our time estimates, and they're dead wrong."

Jade configured a new qubit cluster and spread it across a small section of the yuck blob's perimeter. "No," she said. "We're right."

"How can you say that? Obviously, resources are taking a way bigger hit than we ever imagined. You just said so yourself."

Jade never looked up. "I said, *this really sucks.* Nothing about our estimates being off."

What the hell! How could she be so obtuse? He wanted to shake her till her teeth rattled.

"Listen to me, Jade. Please. I'm begging you. We estimated the rate of spread and our capacity to stop it, but we never accounted for our own resources dwindling in the process."

"Sure we did," Jade said.

"Not enough," he said. "Nowhere near."

Jade turned around and looked him square in the eye, but she was a picture of resignation. "We calculated system degradation based on an over-aggressive yield curve that I padded by thirty percent," she said. "This new resource leak is something else."

She spun around and refocused on her work.

"Care to enlighten me?" Vincent said.

Jade ignored him.

"Look. This is not a game. This is life and death." Vincent was no longer whispering. In fact, his voice was loud enough to startle the people around him. He didn't care. "If there's another problem, we need to get on it. Like now! So quit being an asshole and tell me what's going on."

Jade shrugged.

"Fuck if I know," she said.

CHAPTER 51

HUDSON SLOWLY IDLED his ship towards the open hatch. He should never have been able to disable auto-launch. Those gawking idiots should have locked it down. Another mistake on the captain's watch. Apparently, she expected him to just sail out into the deep vastness of space with his tail between his legs—probably even assumed he was grateful that they'd allowed him to leave.

Stupid. Very stupid…

Keeping a light but firm grip on the control stick, he took a deep breath and focused on his objective. He'd have a split second to execute his maneuver. And he'd only get one chance.

This was where self-control was critical. It was hard not to soar off into a power binge and ride the high of what he was about to do. That wouldn't do at all; the task at hand demanded total concentration.

Because he was in the only vessel prepared to launch, the hatch would close as soon as he was clear of the ship. But not if he got his way—and he usually did.

Hudson gave himself a countdown. Three…two… He slammed the control stick full throttle and shot through the open hatch on a severe upward trajectory. Even as he did so, in a near-simultaneous movement, he flipped his ship into an inverted roll.

All in an instant.

Then he was firing into the hangar. A grin stretched across his face when he saw the control panel on the back wall explode. The hatch would have to be closed manually now. That wasn't going to happen. Because there'd be nobody alive to do it.

With the hatch open, an electrostatic barrier kept oxygen from leaking out. *Ha!* Hudson chortled. His laser fire would cut through the barrier like a hot knife through butter.

And the presence of oxygen provided an awesome bonus. Explosions! Not like a dogfight in deep space where a destroyed ship produced a mere flicker. He got to see flying shrapnel, gorgeous fire bursts, walls turning white-hot, dark smoke pouring from the wreckage. All up close and personal.

Best of all, those who weren't in ships were belly-crawling like the pathetic slugs they were, desperately seeking a safe haven that didn't exist. They'd had their fun mocking him! That's why he'd saved them for last.

If time had permitted, Hudson would have hovered outside of the hangar, reveling in their agony. But he didn't have that luxury. Even crippled, *Touchstone* was still a warship. So he wasn't taking any chances on a tractor beam snagging him or getting fried by a wide-area blast. Instead, he strafed the hangar with a final barrage, pausing only for a moment to admire his handiwork.

Fike was dead. Burned to a crisp like all the others. Here was a throwback to the superstitious cultures he'd encountered, those who lived in terror of an angry god. Well, maybe they were onto something. Maybe their beliefs weren't total bullshit after all.

Case in point: Commander Ralph Hudson had damn sure meted out some gnarly punishment to those unworthy souls who'd pissed him off. In fact, you might say the front hangar had become his sacrificial altar. His temples throbbed under a pleasant pulse that electrified his entire being.

This must be what omnipotence felt like. He was getting a mere taste. But there'd be more to come. Much more. He could feel it right down to the marrow of his bones.

CHAPTER 52

"HOLY SHIT!"

Vincent stared at his display in disbelief. They had just lost massive resources. Instantly, in fact. That was the bizarre thing. About thirty percent of their computing power suddenly ceased to exist.

His micro-comm was getting pinged right and left. So was Jade's. Every tech involved in fighting the yuck blob had the same question. *What the hell just happened?*

Cursing way too loud, he attempted a diagnostic scan, well aware that the scan itself would place excessive demands on their already-crippled computer. All systems still functioning. If you could overlook the fact that they were being systematically eaten away. So what the hell…

"Shut that off right now." Jade stood over him, chewing her lower lip as she glared—actually glared!—at his charts.

Vincent obeyed. He didn't agree with her decision, and he sure as hell didn't agree with being snapped at. But he obeyed the timid little mouse just the same.

"I get that we need the resources," he said. "But we've got to find out—"

"Already done," Jade said. "Something's destroyed the computers in the front hangar. All of them."

"Not something," Vincent said bitterly. "That damn yuck blob!"

"It's not the yuck blob," Jade said.

Vincent felt his blood heat up. For a moment, he actually wanted to yank a handful of that pink hair out of her head. "How the hell can you know a thing like that?"

"The yuck blob leaves a trail," Jade said. "Everywhere it spreads, it overwrites the computer's qubits with crap. If it had taken down all of the computers in the front hangar, we'd be able to at least go back and track its spread to that point. But that's not what happened."

"What else could it be?" Vincent said.

"It wasn't the yuck blob. That much I do know."

And with that, Jade walked back to her seat in the cockpit and immersed herself in her computer terminal.

There'd been something in her eyes… Distraction! Faced with instantly losing all that computing power—a game-changing moment that surely meant defeat—her mind was elsewhere.

Just then, the captain pinged his micro-comm. Captain Arnold herself!

"We've lost contact with the front hangar," she said. "But not before receiving a distress signal. Something is very wrong."

That was an understatement for the ages. But Vincent kept that thought to himself. In fact, he kept all his thoughts to himself because he didn't know what the hell to say. This was the direst situation imaginable, or damn close to it; his captain was reaching out to him. And he was tongue-tied.

"Vincent!" The captain's voice was calm but hard as nails. "You need to say something. Let me know you're still with me."

"Yes, Captain."

"Okay. Good. Now, we can't contact anybody in the front hangar. Jarrett's confirmed that their micro-comms are all dead.

As are the computers. At this point, we have to assume the worst." The captain let her words hang in the still air.

Vincent squirmed inside his own skin. He didn't want to know what came next—hell, he knew *exactly* what came next.

The captain continued. "What I need from you is an estimate. How much time do we have now?"

Shit, Vincent thought. *Shit. Shit!*

Taking a deep breath, he grabbed a pair of seatbacks to steady himself. "No use continuing to the bridge," he said. "By the time you get there, it'll be too late for a shutdown."

CHAPTER 53

THE BATTLE WAS OVER. They had lost.

Captain Arnold didn't need any explanation from Vincent on the ramifications of losing all computing power coming from the small ships in the front hangar; she knew what it meant. Shutting down the system wouldn't be necessary. They'd never get a chance. Not with over one-fourth of their resources gone. The yuck blob would see to that.

It also meant there'd be no coming back, that the entire ship's computer would be bricked. Dead. Unsalvageable.

Hence, a new phase of the yuck blob's siege. Now they'd have to deal with the ship's life support being knocked out on a permanent basis. So it was no longer a question of a plan of attack but a plan for survival.

And she was kicking things off with a stupid decision. Looking at the riveted steel of the warship innards—now tomb-like in its solidity—staring into the loyal faces of the warriors who accompanied her, she gave the order without a moment's hesitation.

"Front hangar. On the double!"

Four pairs of boots drummed across the solid floor as they

ran towards a lost cause. Arnold barked orders into her micro-comm, calling for a rover to pick them up at the stairwell. So they'd get there faster.

Dumb…dumb!

She contacted Wong. "How many ships have you jury rigged?"

"Eight so far," he replied. "Six in the rear hangar. Three in the port hangar, two in starboard."

That meant eight fighter craft would still operate if the yuck blob nuked their computers.

"What's the status on that circuit board?"

"We're close. But—"

"No, you're not," Arnold said and signed off. Viable options just kept on evaporating.

Regarding the front hangar: she couldn't reach Fike or anyone else stationed there; every small ship's computer in that bay had gone dead…and Hudson was involved. All of that meant the front hangar was a lost cause. So the right move, the logical decision, was to shut down every last resource—hawker computers, harrier computers, processes running on the main computer, all of it—then let the yuck blob kill their warship's computer and itself with it. All personnel should have donned survival gear by now. Of course, they couldn't stay zipped up in their suits indefinitely… She really ought to have Jarrett working on a rotation for food and sleep in the small ships.

But shutting down all systems meant certain death to everybody in the front hangar. Which was already a done deal. Probably. Once again, the right move, the *only* decision, was to shut everything down…

She ran faster, and the warriors with her followed.

Meanwhile, her mind wasn't going to shut down either.

Rational thinking during heavy exertion…so familiar. Bringing back memories of the Armada's intense training regimen. How she relished the challenge of drilling one daunting situation after another. And now—she faced the very real possibility that she was folding and failing in the midst of the real thing.

Check in with yourself. She'd preached that to her subordinates enough times! *What's really behind the decision you just made?*

The hum of an approaching rover prompted her to think faster. This was it. The last chance to change her mind and write off the front hangar. What was stopping her? *Check in with yourself.* Softness? Fear? Overvaluing human life to the point of clouding her judgment?

None of that.

It was a feeling. That was all. A feeling.

Screw the Inquest Unit! She could live with whatever repercussions awaited her following this incident (assuming she was still alive), but she couldn't live with going against her gut. And every fiber in her being insisted…well, it was impossible for her to decide any other way.

They were probably wasting time. Absolutely, she was putting the entire crew at risk with the undertaking. But they were going to the front hangar on the off chance that there were survivors who needed help. Period.

CHAPTER 54

Something didn't look right.

But that's all Kevin knew. He couldn't say exactly *what* didn't look right. The qubit sphere, the dome that surrounded the cyber world in the cabin he now occupied, was beginning to buckle. Whether that was right or wrong, he couldn't say. He *ought* to know, but there was a blank spot in his mind where that knowledge resided. Rather, the knowledge was there, but his brain was taking way too long to access it.

And how the hell did he know that, exactly?

Well, because this was what he did, anything process-related, automated, encrypted. If it had to do with computing, he could master it. Make it sing or dance a jig. He was a demi-god, and the cyber world was his domain. Therefore, that understanding…

Stop right there. A pattern had emerged.

He was struggling to put coherent thoughts together about the attack on his current environment and the problem it presented.

Yet he knew he was gifted in the realm of technology. Knew it instantly. No waiting. Not a shred of doubt. Didn't even have to think or remember. It was just there. Meta-knowledge—his knowledge about his own knowledge—was cached...somewhere.

So to sum up: he was an expert on managing qubit spheres of swirling holo-data, adept at spawning processes and weaving them together into a harmonious tapestry, a master of programmatic improvisation to the extreme, and he could worm his way through the narrowest and most hazardous firewalls. But he couldn't even begin to evaluate his current environment—a cyber geek's dream with all the functionality you could ask for—to even decide what was wrong, much less what to do.

That prompted the question of where his meta-knowledge (or knowledge about himself) was coming from, versus the inaccessible thoughts or ideas about his current environment. What was different? Both represented the same thing. Thoughts running through his own mind. Nothing else.

That was his first mistake. Thinking about the inner workings of his brain in terms of computing. True, the brain was an organic processor of data, a computer of sorts. But it was autonomous within a person's skull; it wasn't linked into a computer network; it couldn't be programmed or wiped out, or even rebooted like a computer system. And you sure as hell couldn't reconstruct thoughts and feelings to suit your needs—experience had taught him that.

Okay, he thought. *Let's go with that. What I know and remember, what I can and cannot do in terms of applied knowledge, has nothing to do with my physical mind. It's completely autonomous.*

Thus, something had to be different about the system hosted in this cabin. That was the anomaly. He could remember his recent actions as an Armada recruit—building programs, hacking the system, injecting the virus—all down to the most minute detail. But when he tried to apply this same technical knowhow here and now, the simplest, most fundamental concepts eluded him.

It wasn't that he'd forgotten them. Every memory or tidbit of info stored in the back of his brain was still there. Still there! That was the problem. Whatever thoughts he had (or tried to have) about *this particular cyber space that he currently occupied*—they were gummed up, impeded, buried in molasses. In fact, where *this particular space* was concerned, Kevin found himself unable to convert knowledge into thought.

And the problem wasn't his mind, which was autonomous and functional.

Or was it?

To make matters worse, he was getting a headache. Whatever was pushing down on the qubit dome was crushing his skull.

Which was impossible. Even if this cyber environment crashed and burned around him, his physical body would be unscathed.

Tell that to my aching head, he thought. And hadn't he felt the indention in the qubit sphere before he'd seen it? Not that you could trust your physical senses when it came to computing. Programs didn't have five senses. They didn't feel or care about anything at all. They just did whatever the hell you told them to do.

A stitch chewed at his side, even though he wasn't exerting himself at all. At that moment, a hairline crack appeared in the dome above him.

Kevin's heart sped up. Fear gnawed at him. Irrational fear, he hoped. He could feel his face getting hot as waves of anxious heat washed over him. But his skin was dry as a bone. He was sitting here, shitting bricks of dismay, without a single drop of sweat on him.

The rules of this strange new world where he found himself —particularly the rules of the cyber environment inside of this cabin—were different…how?

There had to be a pattern. Every aspect of computing had a pattern. No exceptions.

Until now.

The dome buckled again, sending another surge of pain through Kevin's head. This one should have blinded him. He shut his watering eyes, expecting his vision to blur. But everything in the cabin remained crystal clear.

Why is that? Kevin asked himself. *What does any of this have to do with me? And why does my brain check out every time I try to think about what's going on in this pl…*

The thought vanished. Just popped like a soap bubble. Once again, he'd tried to assemble all of the disparate pieces of info into some sort of conclusion, only to have his mind blank out completely.

Meanwhile, the crack in the dome continued to widen.

CHAPTER 55

Kirkman rarely walked down any of the ship's corridors without passing other crew members. But she and Gable were all alone, just them and Kevin. The hugeness of the ship had always meant a safe haven in the past. *Make it back to your warship and it's all good!* But now, with everything so silent and sinister, that massive all-encompassing security had turned into a vast wasteland. An advance aftermath of something bad that was about to happen.

The stretcher made things worse. Air stretchers could be moved by voice commands. A computer chip translated speech into physical direction. For example: up, down, left, right, forward, reverse, hover. Worked great in the heat of battle on a hostile planet. Not so much when the stretcher's AI was connected to a ship's computer that was being ravaged by a virus…

Kirkman had hunted down rarely used emergency wheels from the supply room and attached them. That meant pushing Kevin on a rolling bed. A primitive meat wagon rolling across the floor's unyielding surface. But there was no other way.

She pushed Kevin along and tried to quell her discomfort.

This was all wrong. The ship was supposed to be bustling with activity with the stretcher floating alongside them in total silence, not rolling on wheels that sounded like marbles in a jar.

At least Gable seemed to be walking without issue, looking hotter in his battle gear than she cared to admit. In fact, she almost forgot that he'd taken a gimlet zap a short while ago.

He was right. Their most direct route to the rear hangar was towards the rear of the ship. Mainly because there were no working lifts to get them from one level to another. Which meant going down the ladders. Two sets of them. And Kevin had to remain in a stable, horizontal position. That was critical. Throwing a patient who'd just had the front part of his brain repaired over your shoulder wouldn't work. Not to mention the breathing tube in his throat.

How the hell were they going to pull that off? That's what she dreaded more than anything, the proverbial end of the line where they'd have to admit defeat.

And do what? Leave Kevin and save themselves? Or was it her work, her neural lace, that she didn't want to lose? They were approaching the first set of ladders. She was about to find out.

They stood at the top of the ladder overlooking a platform fifteen feet below. What now? Neither of them had spoken the whole way over. So there was no plan.

She'd never forget what happened. Gable folded up the emergency wheels and held the stretcher with Kevin on it perfectly level at chest height. Then—amazingly!—walked down the fifteen-foot ladder using only his legs. Kirkman almost slipped on her way down out of pure awe. She'd seen warriors in action before, sure, but never a demonstration of strength and balance quite like this one.

Shit! She *had* forgotten. Gable's equilibrium was way too whacked for him to be going down ladders, especially with a delicately balanced load.

But he made it to the first platform. One ladder down, another to go.

"Do I need to go slower?" Gable said.

"Uh, no."

"Then stay with me on this next one," Gable said. "And be ready to flip the hover switch if I start to lose him."

His voice projected unflappable confidence. But there was a grayness seeping into his face, a tiredness in his eyes—telling indications that his powerful body could be on the verge of collapse.

"I don't think—never mind. I'm with you." Kirkman was pretty sure the stretcher's hover switch was useless, but there was no reason to tell Gable. He'd be more confident assuming a backup plan was in place, whether one actually existed or not.

The second descent started just as smoothly as the first. Kirkman stayed on the ready, one ladder run above the stretcher. She sensed Gable's slip before she saw it. The moment she hit the *hover* switch, Gable hit the platform below. A seven-foot fall.

"Gable!"

"I'm fine," he said.

Hover worked! Kirkman thought. *But for how long…?*

Gable got on his feet and climbed the ladder. His body armor had protected him from injury. Still, in his condition…

"Stay with me, Kirkman. Kevin may have to hover again."

But as he took hold of the stretcher, it dropped like a rock.

Gable lost his balance and jumped. He landed on his feet and somehow managed to keep Kevin from falling and even from rocking too much.

Kirkman slid down the ladder and engaged the wheels. "Holy shit, Gable! That was something else."

Gable collapsed on the platform, totally spent from the mind-bending effort he'd just put forth. But they'd made it. Well, practically. All they had to do now was roll Kevin to the rear hangar.

"Kevin's brain's lighting up...all over," Gable said between gasps. "Pulse is through the roof too."

Kirkman was incredulous. "How could you notice that while you were hauling him down?" she asked.

But Gable waved her off and lay flat on his back.

Kirkman checked Kevin's pulse. It was fast and weak, as was his breathing. A thin sheet of sweat enveloped his body. She checked the breathing tube. No issue there. He ought to be able to breathe with very little effort. And lying still and sedated meant near-zero effort beyond basic life functions. Maybe she should have used mind-impairing sedatives...

"All we can do is get him to the rear hangar," Kirkman said. "At least we'll be able to stabilize him. And there are techs." *Who could maybe break the link,* she hoped.

Gable grunted. "Go ahead without me," he said.

"No way. Not happening."

"I'll meet you there," he said. "I just need a few minutes. Kevin...can't wait."

"I'm not leaving you," Kirkman said.

"Go! I'll be right behind you."

Kirkman dropped to her knees and kissed him. Light and quick, but full on the mouth.

Gable allowed himself a flicker of a smile. "See you...soon," he said between heavy breaths.

Tears sprang to Kirkman's eyes. There'd been a ring of finality in his voice when he said that. Turning away quickly, she took hold of Kevin's stretcher and started pushing.

CHAPTER 56

It was distant.

But big.

Big… And…

…Distant.

A huge rocking…jol…ting…sensation.

From far…far…far…far…

And nothing…really…moving…here…

Kevin still couldn't think. That was his first problem, regardless of whatever else was going on inside or outside of this strange world he was in.

So he focused hard, looking inward at a recent memory.

Tonya!

A test thought.

partial-Result = await(concentrate-on=>the-thought)…

final-Result = append await(concentrate-on=>completing(the same-thought)) to partial-Result.

It took a full minute to recall the touch of her lips and her reassuring voice. *You've got this, Kevin.* Something that should have been instantaneous.

He tried another.

Erin Lane. Dojo!

final-Result = append await(concentrate-on=>first-thought) to await(concentrate-on=>next-thought).

Got it. She'd crushed his skull. And that recollection took eighty-six seconds and change.

He hadn't forgotten anything. His mind wasn't missing info. However, the mere act of a simple thought entailed the same effort as a five-hour exam.

Which meant...**await(concentrate-on=>and-on=>and-on=> and===>** *Brain screaming from exhaustion!* **stay-focused=>and-on=> and===>** *Failing!* **no stopping=>and-on=> and=?** *Slipping!* **hang-on=>and-on=>and-on=>and...**

Got it!

What if this place didn't physically exist like a city or a planet or even a rock?

Or **await(.......**

Kevin felt half-awake, both conscious and dreaming at the same time. A split feeling of occupying two spaces, each in a different way.

await(..............

His hands disappeared.

No. They just flickered out for a moment.

In fact, his body was fading out. It was still there, everything present and accounted for, all ten fingers and toes. But somehow dim. And threatening to become transparent.

Through his portal to the outside, he could see the distant mountaintop dissolving into nothing. This entire world, whatever the hell it happened to be...

await(.........

was being consumed.

await(.........

And him along with it.

await(.........

No use. He couldn't function. He was toast.

Or he could get back in his zone—*the* zone—and let his mind flow into the system.

await(.........

Relax.

await(.........

Let it happen.

await(.........

Not in a system, but *of it.*

await(.........

What purpose did an asynchronous process serve? It freed up the thread that had called it to perform other tasks while waiting for it to complete.

Yes! There was no reason to wait simply because his thoughts were taking longer than usual.

Kevin started launching, kept launching.

await—got it—again—await got it— in *the* zone!

No reason to wait!

Too late. He wasn't going to have time.

Whatever. He was proceeding anyhow. He *was* the asynchronous process.

And he was staying in *the zone.* Being the process.

Too late. Way too late. He'd be long gone way before…**await…**

He *was* the process.

await—got it—await-got it

He could return a value anytime he wanted.

await—got it—again-await got it-got it-got it—

Too late. But fuck it. He was damn well going to stay in *the* zone right up until the very end.

CHAPTER 57

What a glorious feeling!

Just a short while ago, he'd actually been concerned about potential outcomes. Now Commander Ralph Hudson was surging from the afterglow of his destruction of the front hangar. Never in a thousand lifetimes would he have thought that becoming a deserter and abandoning his warship in a stolen hawker would be anything besides a worst-case scenario.

He'd always loved imposing his will on others. Because he could. In fact, it was his obligation, his role on the grand stage of life. For years, being an Armada warrior had provided him with the thrill of wiping out opposing forces, whether it be fire and carnage on their planet or total annihilation of their ships in space.

But this feeling!

So much better than he could have imagined—and he had a damn good imagination as well as his own vast experience to draw upon. Much as he loved a well-executed battle plan, you didn't get this exhilaration from a rank-and-file chain of command.

He should have left the Armada a long time ago.

After all, a superior being couldn't be expected to share the glory that he'd earned with his inferiors. Omnipotence wasn't for sharing. It was for hoarding, cultivating, grabbing, stockpiling till you literally transcended humankind.

Approaching Jump Sector 1ZD.

Ah, yes. The wormhole to the Innes sector. Portal to his new life. Poor ole Captain Arnold and her crew would be hamstrung with their dead computer and a hangar full of crew burnt black as overdone bacon. Plenty of time to move assets and set up a new identity. Yessir. They were getting a real object lesson: piss off a superior being and pay the price.

As the hawker locked in on the wormhole, the computer displayed its usual swirling hologram. Hudson barely noticed. It was calibrating the *1ZD* rotational pattern for Innes, matching that of the wormhole. A fully automated process. And those idiots on the Armada had been disabling ships for use of their computing power. A lot like killing a giant mammoth for its tusks.

Another electric surge of ecstasy shot through him, tickling his fingertips, curling his toes. This one was long and lasting, rushing over him in one satisfying wave after another. Hudson closed his eyes for the full effect. He recalled the shocked terror on their faces when he strafed the hangar, rendering their force field as useless as tissue paper. Ha! It would almost be worth going back just to confront that worthless bitch, Captain Kalie Arnold, to watch her try to comprehend his betrayal, to goad her into trying to do something about it.

Something snapped.

His ship was shuddering as if traveling across a rough surface. The hologram was gone. The calibration done, he assumed. But you never saw that during a jump; everything would go blank for a moment, then you'd be at your destination.

The mouth of the wormhole loomed around him. That got his attention. He'd never paused inside a wormhole's opening. It was like being in a giant tunnel far too vast to be a tunnel, whose walls extended into infinity in every direction. It was the mouth of a creature so massive that anything entering would be microscopic in comparison.

What the hell!

Then he saw it on the console. An orange glob dancing a taunting jig. Two black slits appeared, providing a facial expression of sorts. A wink and a grin.

Hudson roared with rage. But before he could drive his fist into that slimy face, the console went black. And his ship shot forward on its own accord.

CHAPTER 58

THE ROVER HAD ARRIVED. Now the time had come for another decision.

Should be getting easier, Arnold thought. After all, rushing to the front hangar was already horribly inept leadership. So there ought to be nothing to screw up at this stage of the game.

But this set of choices also sucked. Their fastest way to reach the front hangar was to take the rover straight across mid-deck and then climb down ladders. But Hudson had blasted the hangar all to hell. That meant the thickly reinforced inner doors that connected ship to hangar were sealed shut. Maybe she could open them simply by placing her glove on the palm reader. Or maybe they wouldn't respond. And if the force field had never reactivated across the outer hatch, and if the outer hatch doors remained open…well, that was a whole other set of problems. A rover's laser cannon would give them a hell of a lot more options upon arrival.

So she decided on her second option: traverse the stairs with the rover all the way down to the lower deck and proceed to the front hangar from there. That would take longer, but they'd have the rover with them. (She'd already discarded a third option:

diverting several rovers that were distributing survival gear throughout the ship.)

"Take us down the stairs," she ordered. "We'll need the rover when we get there."

Explaining an order was bad. Piss-poor leadership at its finest. But none of the warriors in her presence seemed to notice. Or care. But she wouldn't let that happen again.

That's all I can do, she reminded herself. Lead to the best of her ability, forgetting everything else and staying in the moment. But as the rover wound a screamingly slow trek down the massive staircase, she questioned herself—again!

When Kalie Arnold was a green recruit, her drill instructor—that leathery bitch, Ally—had warned her about that. "You're too smart for your own good," she said. "One day, you'll think yourself to death. And maybe take a few of your teammates with you. Now give me fifty sandbag thrusters. Double-time!"

Reaction instead of thought was critical for a warrior storming a city or engaging in personal combat. But in a leadership role, where you had to maintain a constant awareness of the bigger picture as a whole, life-and-death decisions that could save or kill hundreds, even thousands, required a longer, more complex thought process.

Or did they?

Damn! She was hemorrhaging confidence. Every order she'd given, every action her crew had taken, every single thing she'd tried had backfired. Now it all came down to rock-bottom survival. Damage control. To be alive to face an inquest.

How long had it been since the last status update from Jade and Vincent? It really didn't matter. It was just a matter of time before the yuck blob prevailed. Pausing to report status to their captain would only distract them from doing everything they could to prolong the inevitable.

It really wasn't complicated after all. With no further orders to give in the way of strategy or direction, she would make it her personal mission to save every soul she could. This was her true path forward.

If only that damn rover wasn't moving so slow!

"Stop!" Arnold shouted.

The driver ground the rover to a halt at a downward angle on a flight of stairs.

"Switch places," she said. "I'm driving."

Having no choice, the warrior relinquished the driver's seat to his captain. But not before she caught a flash of discord in his eyes. "Move your ass!" she snapped.

He'd been driving fine, maintaining a reasonable pace, keeping it safe. A reckless descent would flip the rover on top of them all. To get there faster, they had to take risks. If anybody was going to crash this thing, it was going to be her.

But she was done explaining.

Arnold engaged the controls and proceeded way too fast. She almost lost it around the first turn.

Almost…

Then she went faster.

CHAPTER 59

Home stretch.

Jan Kirkman pushed Kevin's stretcher as fast as she could, till she was almost jogging behind it. They'd made it to the bowels of the warship, where recruits sweated blood and warriors unleashed their fury. All they had to do now was get to the rear hangar.

The techs were a bunch of crybabies sometimes. They'd probably blame her for Kevin's condition. And his condition seemed pretty damn serious. The electrodes across the front of his open skull had become a tapestry of dancing lights, bright enough to hurt her eyes if she stared too long.

But the neural lace was just the antenna. All of this interaction was between Kevin's brain and the warship's computer. At least Kirkman assumed he was interacting with the computer. For all she knew, he could be having crazy-ass dreams about fractured skulls and collapsed windpipes.

Her biggest concern was Kevin himself. His shallow breathing. His elevated heart rate. The film of sweat that covered him. The fever that was ravaging his body.

It would be nice to have Gable with her. She was battle

tested, no stranger to risking her life to save someone else. But she was no warrior. And he was a total badass whether he cared to admit it or not.

And he hadn't looked good at all when she'd left him…

Her mind was made up. The second she got Kevin loaded into a harrier and stabilized, she was going back. Gable wouldn't like it. And she flat did not care.

"Don't die on me, Kevin," she said. "We're almost there."

She was looking down at him, not really paying attention to her surroundings. No reason why she should. It was like an empty coliseum down here. "You're going to come through this just fine," she said.

"Don't know about that." A deep male voice startled her as the stretcher bumped up against something solid.

Ellis had his hands on the stretcher. Drill Instructor Ellis in full battle gear. He disengaged his headgear, and the helmet and face shield retracted. The gash on his face from Gable had been repaired with a patchwork skin graft that would have to be redone (unless he just liked looking like crap). His greasy smile made Kirkman sick to her stomach.

This encounter was going to be personal.

She touched her micro-comm. "Jarrett. This is Kirkman. I've got a situation."

Couldn't reach out to the captain directly—of necessity, only a select group was allowed to do that. But Jarrett would respond to her. She hoped.

"Transmit another word and I light him up." Ellis pressed his gimlet against Kevin's neural lace. "Bet I could make him stop blinking for good."

A couple of seconds passed before Jarrett responded. "Go ahead, Kirkman."

If only micro-comms worked like the ancient radio-type transmitters, or had the functionality of handheld devices. If only! Then she could simply engage Ellis in some verbal sparring for Jarrett to overhear. But micro-comms were designed for a specific purpose: short distance communication between two parties over a private channel that blocked all other interference.

"Kirkman?"

"Answer him. Please!" Ellis said. "I don't need a reason to fry this little worm. But I'd love having you guilt yourself to death over it."

Kirkman touched her micro-comm. "Disregard, Jarrett. Everything's under control."

Ellis laughed. "That's what you think," he said.

CHAPTER 60

Await—got **it-got it-got it-got it...**

Kevin had to stop. He just couldn't keep going. He had nothing else. He was done.

He'd furrowed deep into *the zone*, not giving up, not coming out. Fully intended to stay there till the bitter end.

Till he couldn't.

The computer room grew dim and transparent, its reassuring data cloud thinning into a blue mist. Everything evaporating...

Got it.

One final hanging thread ran to completion and reverberated in Kevin's head as a sudden, unexpected thought. And, for the briefest instant: his surroundings solidified just a touch.

That was the key! His thoughts and this place were somehow intertwined. The harder he focused, the more solid his surroundings. Same with his own (theoretical) physical body.

So his entire physical existence in this room and this place—this world—was based (at least in part) on his brain activity.

Only now he was used up. Done.

And totally unconcerned about it.

Why?

Well, this was different from a failed training exercise laden with more pain and fatigue than he could handle. And different from the humiliation of having his head jammed into a toilet. Because he felt nothing. Not a thing. He'd launched, awaited, processed, responded till he couldn't. And that was that. No stress or strain, no disappointment. He was just stopped.

He was...exactly like a computer program that had shot its wad and run out of resources. A stack overflow. An overworked process didn't care. It just quit.

His surroundings faded. Solid objects became misty shapes. The computer room maintained its appearance for a moment, then wafted into oblivion.

———

Oblivion was cool.

Kevin found himself floating in a pleasant stream of security, wrapped up in a soothing blanket of wellbeing. He was sinking slowly. And that was fine. Awesome, actually. It was warmer, safer, more soothing the deeper he settled. That's just what he was doing...settling. High time. Long overdue. Should have done this a lot sooner.

Suddenly, his legs flipped over his body. He was falling. Hard and fast. Body cartwheeling through the air. One of those crazy dreams where you know you're about to splatter on a hard surface.

Then that dreaded wake up right before impact...

Kevin surged awake. His head pounded; his throat was on fire. He was lying on his back, and there was something jammed down his windpipe, forcing his mouth open. A tube of some kind. Something else. Insects were crawling all over his forehead, some tickling, others stinging, still others burrowing beneath his skull.

He tried to scream but couldn't. He could feel his pounding heart and the dampness of sweat on his back and legs.

Then he heard voices. A man and a woman. Having a conversation. An altercation, actually.

He heard the woman say, "Okay. I stopped the transmission. Now step away."

"He's been nothing but a burden from day one," the man said. "I'd be doing us all a favor."

Kevin recognized the voice. Ellis. Drill Instructor Ellis. He'd know that asshole's voice anywhere. He opened his eyes for a split second, then thought better of it. Ellis didn't need to know he was conscious, not that Kevin could actually hurt him with a surprise attack.

"You think wasting a comatose kid is doing us a favor—really? You're scum!"

Ellis laughed. "Keep it up, Jan baby. I love it when you talk dirty."

"The name's Kirkman. Field Medic Kirkman. I heal the wounded and repair damage. All you do is tear things down."

"That's what the Armada is all about," Ellis said.

"What the Armada's all about is becoming stronger, smarter, better. Not some cruel moron who gets off on torturing helpless—"

"Helpless. That pretty much describes you right now, doesn't it? You and your new boyfriend here. What do you do when you're alone—reach under that gown and see if those lights flash when you stroke him off?"

"Screw you!"

Their voices grew distant and muffled. Kevin could still hear them talking, but they sounded far, far away. And the insects swarming through his forehead were crawling slower; their stings had significant venom. If not for that damn tube making his throat burn like holy hell, he'd probably fall asleep.

He was tired. So tired! Damn near impossible to think a

coherent thought. But here he was, somewhere on the warship, alive after all. The last time he'd knowingly been on this ship had been in the dojo. The last thing he remembered: being flat on his back with Erin Lane stomping down on him—on his head, as a matter of fact. Hence the swarm in his forehead.

This Kirkman woman had done something to him or for him. And Ellis...why was he involved? Why did Ellis even care? *That's easy,* Kevin thought. *Because he's an asshole.*

He heard Kirkman swear at Ellis, then felt the bed spin underneath him. A quick shuffle of feet, followed by a soft thud nearby. Ellis was laughing again. Kevin wanted to open his eyes, to get a clue about what was going on, but he didn't dare. Whatever was happening had jolted him awake, at least a little. His heart was racing with that all-too-familiar fear that had become an integral part of his existence, that helpless fear that always grabbed him whenever he found himself in the presence of stronger people, which accounted for most of his waking life.

Think, dammit!

That was different. No more awaiting asynchronous thought processes. Even in its exhausted state, everything was real time; his brain was functioning kinda-sorta normal at the moment.

Ellis was talking, his voice eerily matter-of-fact. Kevin tuned him out. Nothing else he could do. Those head bugs nibbling at him must be diodes or chips or something that somebody, probably Kirkman, had attached to his brain. *Well, you did have your skull caved in,* he reminded himself. Which meant what? That the computer room nestled in a forest amidst tall trees and a gentle stream and singing birds and rolling hills rising into distant mountains was all a bullshit dream.

Or...

Information packets.

The mere idea of anything outside of the space between his ears invoked a renewed pounding in Kevin's already aching head. But that made sense in the raw and painful sort of way that reality had of getting its point across. Whatever this Kirkman woman had hooked into the front of his brain was lighting him up—no question about that. Lighting him up how? Well, it could be marshaling his thoughts, allowing previously broken pathways between his synapses to fire again. But to rewire an entire human brain…couldn't be done. Way, way too many variables in play. Even with the ship's computer to help her.

But Kirkman didn't even have that. Obviously. This warship's computer was being ravaged by the shitstorm unleashed by Kevin himself.

Which meant…

Holy shit! Kevin barely stopped himself from saying it out loud. *Holy fucking shit.*

CHAPTER 61

Ever since the entire front hangar (and its computing resources) had been destroyed, Vincent had been standing behind Jade. She could sense his presence, actually feel him looking over her shoulder, making the harrier's cockpit seem all the more claustrophobic.

She didn't blame Vincent. There was nothing else for him to do. He probably wondered why she hadn't looked up from her terminal. A true teammate would take the time to explain what she was doing and get input. Team collaboration was deemed superior to individual efforts in the long run. But in this case, there was nothing he could do to help her. Not a thing.

Jade was playing a hunch, working against time. By the time she explained what she was doing, it would be too late. Or worse: she'd realize how ridiculous it was and talk herself out of it.

"Mind telling me what you're doing?" Vincent asked.

"Just give me a few minutes. Okay?"

Vincent didn't respond. So silence was consent, if not agreement. She was going to grab at this final straw and the faint glimmer of hope it offered. Actually, not hope. This was just taking a stab at something. A last-ditch effort with nothing to lose.

Then he interrupted her again. "What's going to happen in a few minutes?"

The answer was probably nothing. Especially if she couldn't focus.

"Jade. C'mon. Whatever direction you're going, you need to share. Maybe I can help. We can get others involved."

Jade was surprised at the loudness of her own voice. "I'm trying to pull something out of my ass that won't make a damn bit of difference," she said. "But I really need for you to shut the hell up so I can hear myself think!"

She heard Vincent huff in exasperation and realized she was fine with not caring if she pissed him off. Maybe later. If there *was* a later. For now, however, it was all about this one final last-gasp attempt.

Amid this maelstrom of qubit decimation, she'd detected an unidentified process. It wasn't the yuck blob. Didn't match the signature. Not even close. And it wasn't any known process in the system logs. Without permission and against her better judgment, she'd sacrificed valuable resources to monitor its activity. It wasn't destructive. Didn't seem to be spreading. Instead it seemed to be just another computer resource under siege like all the rest.

And did it really matter? Like as not, it had been running on the ship's computer since inception. Maybe something interesting to investigate during normal times. But now, it was about to get wiped out just like everything else.

That's right. They were about to lose the warship's computer. Totally, utterly, completely. And she was wasting her final available minutes investigating some irrelevant anomaly.

Except…

This process wasn't just getting wiped away like nothing. The yuck blob was overpowering it, sure, but nowhere near as fast as any of the other unfortified system resources. It was as if something, some part of its programming, or someone—no, that was beyond ridiculous—was mounting its own independent defense of its territory. And doing a respectable job of it under the circumstances.

She hadn't managed to isolate the mystery process's memory address, but she'd narrowed down its general area. She could still detect its presence in her monitor pane—wait. No, she couldn't!

Jade slapped her terminal screen. *I'm not going crazy,* she told herself. *It was there. I saw it!*

Nope. It had disappeared. Gone. As if it had never existed. Not surprising with the yuck blob running rampant. Still, her mystery process had seemed too robust to just get swept away like a fart in the wind.

She stood up too fast, and the cockpit swam out of focus for a moment. Her face had reddened with humiliation at her own ineptitude, but fierce determination burned in her chest. "I've been monitoring an unknown process," she snapped. "No clue what it is or what it does. But I'm trying to ping it."

Vincent opened his mouth to speak, but Jade put up her hand to silence him. She was sweat-flushed, her breathing ragged, but she kept talking. "I was going to send a simple request. Just a ping for acknowledgment. That's all."

"Sounds reasonable," Vincent said cautiously.

"But I've lost it."

"Lost what?"

"The goddamn process. As in it's nowhere to be found."

"The yuck blob probably—"

"That's not what happened," Jade said, wondering how she could be so sure. "Thing is, I couldn't isolate its memory address."

"How close?"

"I know its region," Jade said.

She sat down at her terminal and started entering commands. "I didn't want to tell you because…"

"Go for it, Jade," Vincent said.

There was nothing else to say. Vincent knew the score. Jade would have to set up a loop counter to ping every memory address across an entire data region, traversing several million qubits in the process. Which would all but deplete their remaining resources. A final act of futility that would defeat them that much faster.

Jade paused, suddenly unable to make herself continue. She was about to hang their hopes on communicating with a process or entity that wasn't the yuck blob. Friend, foe, a mindless print dump? There was no way to tell.

"Do it," Vincent said.

Jade looked at him, then back at the terminal.

"Kick it off," he said. "C'mon. Team decision. We're in this together."

He was right, of course. They had nothing to lose. And no other ideas.

Jade fired off her command.

CHAPTER 62

Captain Arnold sent the rover careening through the bottom turn in the stairway, subjecting herself and her passengers to spine-jarring dips and bounces over the steps. They hit the solid metal floor of the lower deck with a huge thud. That one hurt. Still, it was no worse than traversing a crater-ridden asteroid in the heat of battle. Only this didn't feel right. Because it wasn't supposed to be that way inside the safe haven of a warship.

Well, of course, this felt wrong. There wasn't a single right thing about this whole fucked-up situation. But she was going to personally save all of the crew she could. That was what she could do. The captain of a warship reduced to a single lame contribution.

But she was sure as hell going to pull that one thing off if she didn't do anything else right. She was going seventy miles per hour. Inside a vessel! Absolute lunacy under normal circumstances. Currently, with personnel locking down and zero traffic, it still qualified as batshit crazy.

One thing she had going for her: it was a straight shot. Mostly. Up ahead, the corridor shifted. Not an actual turn, but you had to pull hard to the right to avoid smashing into a massive steel pillar. Arnold touched the brakes, cutting her speed ever so slightly. Then she eased the rover to the right, letting it drift, resisting the temptation to turn abruptly. Even so, the inertia almost rocked them into a permanent sleep. But she felt the pillar whoosh past, then she was back at top speed again.

One of the warriors with her was using his micro-comm to send an advance directive to have their route vacated. She knew that Jarrett had already seen to that, but it was still good proactive thinking under duress. Hopefully, she wouldn't cause any injuries getting where they were going. Hudson was a different matter. When they caught up with him, she wanted to be…

Forget about him, she scolded herself. *Focus!* But it was hard to ignore her fury over what that pathetic piece of shit had done to his shipmates. *His* shipmates.

Almost there. The corridor ended at the front hatch. She cut her speed, knowing she was still going way too fast. The burn of polymer across metal filled the air as she power-slid sideways, bumping (but thankfully not slamming) into the hangar's door. Maneuvering the rover about ten feet back, she instructed her crew to ready the laser cannon.

The moment she gave the order, the young warrior who had broadcast their route grabbed a measuring tool from the rover's survival kit. That's when she remembered his name. Lieutenant Emerson. A fresh-faced warrior with a pragmatic coldness that enabled him to make hard decisions and live with the outcome.

"Doors slide open outward from the center, Captain," he said. "Identifying the center line and cutting a rectangle from that point is our fastest way in and will cause the least damage to the hangar door."

Emerson had made rank fast for someone his age because he never questioned a damn thing, focusing only on the most efficient and effective execution of orders. Exactly what the Armada needed, some would say. He'd never ask (out loud) why she didn't at least attempt to open the hangar bay doors with her glove reader.

"Starting point is here, Captain." Emerson focused an orange pointer beam about six feet up in the center of the massive door.

"Correction," Arnold said. "Our starting point is four feet to the right of your mark."

Again, without question, Emerson moved his pointer to the new location. She instructed the pair on the rover, "One quick burst just to mark our spot. Then we button up our battle gear and double-check our life support."

They fired on Emerson's pointer, creating a smoldering divot in the hangar door and sending up a cloud of sparks and smoke in the process. Then all of them secured their helmets and face shields and confirmed that they could indeed switch to oxygen if the need arose.

Arnold didn't explain herself, and nobody asked. But there was a chance—a way-too-good chance!—of the force field that sealed the outer hatch never reactivating, leaving the entire front hangar wide open to space. A warship's mechanical functions (hatches, weaponry, force fields, and the like) operated autonomously. Meaning that the entire hangar getting obliterated shouldn't prevent doors from closing or force fields from activating. They could hope, anyhow.

But if Hudson's barrage *had* disabled the force field, there would be no oxygen or gravity in the entire hangar. And opening the doors would be like ripping a gash in the hull of an ocean vessel. Given the ship computer's current death throes, they could create a host of new problems for themselves.

"Narrow the beam to one-quarter inch," she instructed. "Then go nineteen inches deep. No further." The shiny metal door darkened under the rover's laser fire, and blackened metal oozed down, forming a streaming puddle on the decking.

"Should be about three minutes," Emerson said.

"To bore through nineteen inches of metal?" Arnold said. "Sounds about right."

"Should I call for assistance, Captain?"

"We've got enough crew already," she said.

Emerson nodded affirmation. "Understood, Captain."

Understood indeed. He knew full well that assistance wasn't worth calling for, that the four of them would be quite capable of pulling out any and all survivors, a count likely to be zero. So asking if they should call for assistance was just a way to present himself as an officer supporting his captain and covering every conceivable option. Self-promotion in the midst of a rescue oper-ation…and you could count on him to tell the Inquest Unit exactly what he thought they wanted to hear.

Within two minutes and fifty seconds, the laser cannon had cut a quarter-inch hole almost all the way through. Arnold got out of the rover. "Emerson, you're with me," she said. "You two, widen the cannon beam to three feet. Same target. Be ready to fire on my signal."

Emerson understood what came next and immediately posi-tioned himself next to the tiny hole they'd made with the laser cannon. Arnold wasn't having it. "You're in my spot," she said. Without question, he took a couple of steps back and pointed his gimlet at the door.

Her plan was to have Emerson finish boring through the door more gradually with a lower caliber beam. She would posi-tion herself at the entry point with the sensors in her suit at the ready. She'd be able to tell if there was breathable air on the other side the moment he broke through. But sudden pressure changes could be unpredictable, and she'd be first-in-line for repercus-sions from microbe-infested air or even an explosion if a fried circuit suddenly got a whiff of oxygen. Hence the backup plan of having the laser cannon ready to fire. They'd melt a wide swatch of metal and hope to seal off the door as quickly as possible.

It only took about a minute for Emerson to cut through the

final inch of steel. Everything seemed stable. No pressure changes. Sensors indicated breathable air on the other side of the door.

Arnold had them use the laser cannon to widen their hole enough for a child's hand to reach through. She could see inside the hangar now. No flotsam. And the gleam around the outer hatch told her that the force field was intact. They might be entering a tomb—probably were—but not a death trap. That was something.

Then she placed her access glove on the palm reader. Why not? It was worth a try. Systems being autonomous and all that fun tech shit she'd never had to worry about…

The hangar doors whooshed apart.

"An excellent strategy, Captain," Emerson said.

He was referring to her orders to make their exploratory hole four feet away from where the doors joined in the middle. The mechanics would still function. The least amount of damage and an easy way in.

She barely heard him. They were about to get a close-up look at shipmates charred to a crisp. All for the sake of chasing a vain hope…

Hope. That's what was driving this fool's errand. The hope of saving at least one soul. Once that was gone, when all occupants in this hangar they were about to enter were found dead…

Fuck it. When that happened, they'd just find the next battle and fight it. They were warriors. That's what they did.

Still, going in there was going to suck.

CHAPTER 63

ON A STRETCHER, flat on his back, throat on fire and a colony of stinging ants in his head. And on top of all of that, Ellis standing over him, totally in control with nobody to stop him. Kevin almost had to laugh at the ridiculousness of his situation.

Yeah. Join the Armanda. Because he'd wanted to be someone else, to live a different life. That had turned out to be a *really* good idea. Get your brains kicked in. Suffer abuse. Get betrayed by the one person you trusted—alright, he'd become completely smitten with Tonya. But what did that matter?

Oh, he'd gotten even for all of it. That virus he'd planted was a real humdinger. The only inconsistency was given what he'd observed inside that computer room in the middle of a forest (that he now thought to be the inside of the ship's computer itself), his virus seemed to be spreading slower than he would have expected. So either he was wrong about all of this or somebody was doing a hell of a job slowing it down.

Well, a lot of good any of this newfound knowledge was doing him now. He couldn't even open his eyes, for one thing. For another, he had no way back into the system. Couldn't exactly sit up on the stretcher and ask to use a device. No more than he could wish himself back into the cabin's computer room. Especially since he had no clue how he'd gotten there in the first place.

Besides, with all that system degradation, his every thought getting awaited, it might not even be…

"Go ahead." Ellis interrupted his thoughts. "Scream your pretty little ass off. Nobody's gonna hear you. Better yet, run. Leave this little runt here with me all by his lonesome."

His voice was forceful. The smug voice of a predator in control of his prey. The voice of a smug thug. *Yeah. Smug thug.* That's what Ellis was. Not a warrior but a total piece-of-shit asshole.

"Alright, Ellis. I get it," Kirkman said. "No need to force yourself on me. I'm not averse to any of this."

There was a grunt. Sounds of a brief scuffle. Kirkman gasping in pain.

Kevin squeezed his eyes shut. No way in hell he could figure a way back into the system with this shit going on around him. In fact, he couldn't do anything. His squad had been right. He was a total loser. One pathetic empty set of nothing.

"Hidden blade," Ellis snorted. "I could smell it a mile off."

"And I can smell your stink across a cosmic juncture," Kirkman said.

"I love it when you talk like that," Ellis said.

Kevin could hear the smirk in his voice. He had to do something. Anything! But how? What?

The shuffle of feet, then a sudden jolt at the head of his stretcher.

Kevin was spinning.

The woman, Kirkman, was leaning over him. She'd grabbed the stretcher and looked down on him, grave concern in her brown eyes. Her lip was bleeding, and an ugly thunderhead of a bruise darkened the left side of her face.

That's when Kevin realized he'd opened his eyes.

"Hey! Look who's awake," Ellis said. He grabbed a handful of Kirkman's dark hair, jerking her backwards and slinging her down. "Good. He can watch."

Ellis grabbed the side of Kevin's stretcher and leaned in close. "Maybe I'll dump you on the floor so you can have a better view."

Kirkman was up. She lunged at Ellis. Jumped on his back. Clawed at his face. Doing everything in her power to disable him.

It wasn't enough.

Ellis shook her off and knocked her down with another hard slap. The crack of his hand against her face made Kevin wince, sending the ants in his brain into a renewed stinging frenzy.

But the real sting was seeing Kirkman bruised and bleeding; she could have run off and left him. Saved herself. Instead, she was standing up to this brute on his behalf.

He'd only thought about who had it coming when he launched the virus. Ellis, Erin Lane, and the rest of his squad. He never considered that he might be harming a good person—someone like Kirkman, who was willing to put everything on the line for someone she didn't even know. In this case, the very someone who was on the verge of destroying them all.

This wasn't right. He had to stop this thing he had set in motion. There must be a way to get back in there. If only that damn stinging would let up for just a second or two!

Meanwhile, Ellis was leaning over her. "Do me a favor and keep fighting," he said.

"Get off her. Pig!"

A strong male voice laced with exhaustion. Kevin couldn't see the voice's owner, but Kirkman was glad to see whoever it was. Her eyes projected surprise, concern...and joy. Yes, joy at seeing this new arrival.

"Good to see you, Gable," Ellis said. "We've got unfinished business."

Kevin tried to raise himself up and see what was happening. But it was just too much.

Besides, there were more ants. They kept multiplying behind his eyes, stinging and biting, harder, faster, burrowing ever deeper, till there was nothing left—save for a continuous scream of agony trapped in his throat.

They seemed organized. A collective working as one. For the sole purpose of inflicting maximum pain with maximum efficiency.

Kevin was about to pass out. The men's voices, Ellis and some guy named Gable, were distant and indecipherable amid wave after wave of red-hot stinging static.

Blinding pain! The volume, the intensity, the frequency, all of it…one steady, systematic uptick after another.

An actual symmetry. Maybe even a thing of beauty if you weren't the receiver of it. Consistent and steady…a communication whose message was *Scream, motherfucker. Scream!*

A communication!

Coming in through whatever Kirkman had laced across his brain.

And it did have a pattern. *Scream, motherfucker!*

Fighting the overwhelming urge to pass out, Kevin leaned into it.

CHAPTER 64

THE HANGAR WALLS were smudged black. Circuit boards fried to a crisp. The normally clean lighting had degraded to a haunted flicker.

Even though the force field had sealed the hangar off from space, the air was filled with contaminated particles. Not only that, the stench of smoldering death would have been overpowering.

The heat was no joke either. It was like walking into a raging fire. Arnold could actually hear the sizzle of things melting around her. Probably the worst of it was the destroyed hawkers —nearly two hundred of the small one-person ships reduced to molten clumps; they resembled cheap birthday candles burned down to nothing. Only nobody was making a wish or blowing them out.

At any rate, there were about 5,000 square yards to cover, and they wouldn't be able to withstand these conditions for very long.

"We go four wide," she said. "Start ten yards apart and fan out. Don't get near any of the burning ships. But look for casualties. That's the first priority. Identifying anything we can salvage comes last."

They moved quickly, looking for any sign of life. Every crew member who had been in a ship had perished. For any chance of survival, you would have had to be standing on the flight deck and lucky enough to take cover when Hudson starting firing. Take cover where, though? Walls were sizzling, ships were burning. Where the hell was there to hide?

This was indeed a fool's errand. She was just killing time while Kevin Slaton's virus killed their computer and maybe the warship with it.

Her micro-comm signaled an incoming transmission from Jarrett. No choice but to acknowledge. She was in charge of this whole freaking ship, after all. She could talk while she conducted her fruitless search.

"How bad now, Jarrett?" she said.

"No updates from Jade and Vincent," Jarrett said.

That meant the computer was still keeling over in a final dance of death.

"I did want to make you aware of something…"

"Make it fast," Arnold said.

"Well, Kirkman notified me. She was moving Kevin Slaton to the rear hangar. Her plan was to stow him in one of the larger ships."

"Jarrett, what's your point?"

"Well, it started out as a distress call. Kirkman wanted to reach you. Sounded like she was under duress. And then she told me to disregard her transmission. That everything was good."

Even as she listened, Arnold kept moving forward. Sweat streamed down her back, and her feet seemed to be welded to the metal floor plate as she pressed on with her hapless search for survivors. Nothing so far. And probably nothing at all.

"Captain?"

"Hang on, Jarrett."

Lovely. Another decision. To send warriors across the warship to check on an alleged distress call that was probably nothing, or…

Maybe she'd leave this decision to Jarrett. Like hell she would! She was still captain! A roasted sausage link right now, but still captain.

"Captain." Emerson's voice in her ear this time. "I think I've got something."

"Copy that, Emerson," she said. "On my way."

She'd make her way over to Emerson and leave the other two to continue on their own.

"Captain?" Jarrett this time.

"Like Kirkman said: Disregard."

A nagging doubt ate at her the moment she gave the order. But hell, you couldn't chase every shadow that crossed your path.

CHAPTER 65

JADE STARED AT HER SCREEN. She could feel Vincent looking over her shoulder and realized it wasn't just him. She had an audience. Everybody in the harrier had stopped what they were doing. They were all looking her way. Watching and waiting.

She'd fired off her search command and watched the address identifiers fly across her screen. Then nothing. Not even an error code. The cursor just sat there, not even bothering to blink. Her terminal had just floated off into La-La Land.

"What do you think?" Vincent asked.

Jade took a deep breath and willed some volume into her voice. "Making good progress," she said loud enough to be overheard.

She'd lied through her teeth. Claiming to be making *any* progress was total bullshit, a huge steaming pile of it. In fact, her hapless attempt to connect to some unknown process had frozen her terminal. Worse, she'd tried to abort her command and failed. Attempting a reboot would be a very bad thing with a yuck blob in play. Like as not, the harrier's computer wouldn't make it back online. Assuming it wasn't dead already…

In the meantime, every eye was glued on her. So she and

Vincent had to at least say the right things. Didn't want to start a panic on top of everything else that was going wrong.

"I do think we hit the right address," she whispered to Vincent.

"Maybe," he whispered back.

But that still meant nothing. If the mystery process didn't like what she'd sent, it could choose not to report an error back to her. Or, for all she knew, it could have gotten destroyed. *But then I'd get a loopback failure,* she thought. *Or my command would wither away and die.*

Back to basics. When the loop counter stopped—meaning no more cryptic text flying across her screen—that meant her ping had been received.

But a frozen screen could mean…well, anything.

The pilot made brief eye contact, then looked away. He knew they were screwed. He wasn't going to ask her what was going on with the system, and she wasn't going to ask him if he could operate this harrier without a computer. Or control internal oxygen. In the end, this cockpit would become nothing more than an airtight box, and they'd have to rely on their environmental suits for survival once the oxygen ran out.

Jade tried reminding herself that they'd had nothing to lose, that playing her hunch was the only option they had left in an already hopeless situation. But it didn't help.

CHAPTER 66

Kevin clenched his teeth so hard that he thought he felt a molar crack. As the pain intensified, burrowing deeper and wider, he kept leaning into it until he blacked out for a moment (or an hour, or maybe a whole damn year).

Then he was standing upright. And he recognized the forest he'd visited before. But it was dim. Like a photo image behind a dark overlay. He could barely make out the shadowy outline of the cabin that had housed the computer room. Somehow walking over there didn't seem like an option. For one thing, he wasn't physically part of what he was seeing. He was more like a spectator viewing a scene from afar.

This had to be the source of that agonizing pain signal. Why didn't it hurt the first time he woke up there? Because he'd been physically unconscious at the time. But now he could feel the stretcher underneath him. He thought he could still hear Ellis jeering in the distance and even smell his bad breath. But that could be his mind conjuring shit up.

Whatever. At any rate, his conscious state was awake in both the computer and in his physical body. Standing at the edge of a forest—lying prone on a stretcher in a warship. Hence the intense pain. Two worlds, two realities. This was the jumping-off point. Much like a cosmic juncture.

Far away, he heard himself moaning softly as a fresh wave of stinging burn dug into him. And he might have heard that asshole Ellis laughing hard and loud.

And then a fascinating phenomenon: in the midst of this intensifying agony, his mind continued to think logically. To reason. To deduce. That had never been the case during training as a recruit, where he would always wither in the face of discomfort. But those had been physical challenges. And he was a physical weakling.

But this game was different. And he was a mental stud. Not that he'd gotten any braver or increased his pain threshold. None of that. He'd scream and cry like a little girl if you hurt him. But his mind would keep right on keeping on.

Those damn ants could eat his head right off his shoulders and he'd still be able to deconstruct a six-dimensional algorithm fast as you please. Might scream and moan while doing it, but still…

It only took a couple of seconds. That couple of seconds felt like a thousand years, but Kevin's mind processed the situation.

First off, the pain wasn't real. His synapses were overreacting because virgin nerve endings never before touched were lighting up.

More important, he wasn't having to wait for his thoughts to process. No more *Await—Got It* patterns to contend with. That was because he was at least partially conscious on the stretcher and had full access to his own brain. But once he got all the way inside the warship's computer, that would change. His physical body would go comatose, and his physical brain would do just enough to keep his organs going.

That meant when he made the jump, he'd have to rely on the warship's computer for his brain power. And be an imbecile, in other words. Because the ship's computer was getting eaten alive. Literally.

So he'd have to attack the yuck blob as he came through the juncture. No time to run for the computer room…

Wait. The computer room was a mere prop created via a collaboration between his psyche and the warship's computer. Sure, it had grounded him and provided a reality for him to grasp and a physical space for him to function. Most of all, it had served as an interface between him and the system.

Which meant he could bypass all of that and hit the computer directly. At least in theory.

This was where the shit hit the dusty trail. He'd be coming in guns-a-blazing.

Kevin let himself go, releasing his mind till his physical body began to drift.

Then he lunged at the forest, embracing the pain, focusing harder the more it hurt…!

And all the while, he waited…

Waited for that exact moment…

Right before he shot through…

He issued the command, focused on it, screamed it, hurled it, ripped it out of his very being…

g=c800:5

The kill sequence to disable the virus he'd planted.

He hoped his reasoning had been right. And that it wasn't too late.

CHAPTER 67

"YOUR PATIENT here is about to check out for good," Ellis said.

Kirkman felt a heavy ball of dread sinking down in her gut. Ellis was a leering asshole. But he was also right. Till a moment ago, Kevin's transmitters had been putting on a light show. Now, only a single red beep of light remained. Everything else across the front of his skull was in total blackout.

Kirkman checked his pulse and put her ear against his scrawny chest to listen to his breathing. Then a meaty hand landed on the back of her neck.

Ellis yanked her to a standing position. He crowded up against her, making her feel trapped and small. His breath made her want to puke. She wasn't defenseless. There were tender spots she could exploit, pressure points she could find. No amount of conditioning could fortify the eyes or testicles. But Ellis wasn't some drunken thug following her out of a sleazy bar. He was a seasoned fighter, totally attuned to any threats to his person. He'd sense and react to the slightest move on her part. In fact, he was probably hoping she'd try something.

"Might as well just relax and let it happen," he said. "Who

knows. You might even enjoy it. Nothing like a real man to light your fire."

Kirkman almost said "please don't" and stopped herself. You didn't beg a sociopath like Ellis. "Give me just five minutes to examine Kevin," she said. "Then I'll do whatever you want."

"You talk as if you have a choice," Ellis said.

Kirkman tried taking a tiny step backwards, nudging Kevin's stretcher just a touch, trying to get a little bit of space. Ellis flung her onto the hard floor. Kirkman was a seasoned field medic who'd had her share of tumbles in the heat of battle; her suit was a shock-resistant polymer. But her landing was hard and painful.

She didn't wallow on the cold floor feeling sorry for herself. Instead, she slid away from Ellis, looking for a chance to get up. Even though he just stood there laughing at her. He was also cocky and overconfident. She could make a run for it. He'd be able to chase her down. But she could at least lure him away from Kevin.

And then? Take what came next…and give him one hell of a fight. Even though he'd probably like that. She slid backwards till she felt the solid wall against her back. A tall, unyielding gray prison. Except for a nearby corridor. If she could turn the corner…a slim chance for salvation.

Ellis grinned. And she imagined bugs between his teeth. "Okay. You win," he said. "Come on over and look your boy over. That little red blinking thing is just a short-circuit. Nothing going on in this little shit's brain."

Kirkman stood up. Ellis pointed his gimlet at Kevin's head. "Or I could just remove all doubt," he said.

Toying with her. Way overconfident. Justifiably so. But…

Kirkman took a small step towards him, planting her right foot as she did so. Then she sprinted hard left. Ten short feet to turn the corner into the next corridor. And she made it.

She made it!

Suddenly, her body seized up; a shockwave across her backside turned her legs to jello. And she went down in a heap.

That slimy bastard had just zapped her with his gimlet. He hadn't even bothered to chase her down. She was still conscious, so he'd hit her with a really low setting. Way less potent than the zap that Gable had taken earlier. She felt like somebody had tackled her but also felt able to get back to her feet.

Standing up didn't happen. Ellis grabbed her by the ankles and started dragging her back towards Kevin's stretcher. Then he stopped and grinned down at her. "The little shit's unconscious," he said. "I was going to let him watch, but what's the point? This is as good a place as any."

He dropped down on top of her, his weight taking her breath away. She squirmed and struggled. But he was stronger and heavier with a leverage advantage. She kicked at his ribs, and he smacked her across the face, putting her out momentarily.

Before she realized what was happening, he had her suit halfway off. This was going really bad. Her head was throbbing, her jaw ached where he'd hit her, and he'd already stripped her half-naked. Still, she clawed at his eyes and spit in his face when he pinned her arms to the floor.

That only seemed to arouse him that much more. "C'mon, baby." He was almost panting in anticipation. "You can do it. Fight me some more."

Then Gable's voice. "Why don't you try fighting *me*?"

Ellis was off her in an instant. He was on one knee, and he'd drawn his weapon.

Gable just stood there looking at him. He looked strong and formidable on the surface, but Kirkman could see the strain on his face and knew it had taken a huge effort for him to get up and make it over here.

Ellis sneered. "I think I'll let you watch too," he said and zapped Gable with the same power setting he'd just used on

Kirkman. Only Gable didn't go down. He buckled for a moment, then stood upright, taller than ever.

"You're a big man when you're up against a comatose boy and a field medic half your size. But you're soft. So you have to zap a warrior from a safe distance."

Ellis made a show of setting his gimlet to max power. "You're no warrior," he said. "But I'm going to blast you to hell."

"No!" Kirkman struggled to a sitting position. "Just leave, Gable. I'll survive."

"She's got more guts in her little finger than you've got in your whole cowardly body," Gable said.

"Who are you to talk about guts?" Ellis said. "You quit. Because you couldn't take the heat."

"I quit being a warrior by choice," Gable said. "You never became one."

"My rank says different."

"And your actions say candyass. Lording it over a squad of recruits…that's your crowning achievement? You're pathetic."

Ellis pointed the gimlet. "Say goodbye."

Kirkman heard a scream and realized it was her. Ellis looked over at her, grinning from ear-to-ear.

"You'll just prove what a coward you are," Gable said. "In front of a witness. Or maybe you're going to kill her too. And maybe Kevin. You really think you can hide three murders?"

Kirkman saw it in his eyes. He was going to blow Gable away. She lunged to her feet and threw herself at him. He elbowed her in the gut, almost knocking the wind out of her.

"I thought you might make a move just now," he said to Gable. "In fact, I was hoping for it."

"They'll send you to a penal colony," Gable said. "But you like it up the ass, don't you?"

"He loves it up the ass!" Kirkman yelled.

"Shut up, bitch." Ellis glared at her with pure hatred.

"Coward. Candyass!" she said.

Ellis reached down to backhand her. At that moment, Gable became a blur. Ellis's weapon skidded across the floor. Gable had kicked it out of his hand. But then he lost his balance and fell. Still not himself. He was running on sheer force of will.

Reacting quickly, Ellis ran to retrieve his weapon that had stopped some thirty feet away.

"Run," Gable said. "I'll block him. Go now!"

"I'm not leaving you."

"Go, dammit!"

"Not happening."

Ellis stormed back, his hair bristling and his face twisted with rage. Kirkman stood between him and Gable. "Get out of the way, bitch," he said.

"Stick that gimlet up your ass," Kirkman said.

"He's dead. But I *might* let you live."

"You're going to have to kill me first."

Ellis paused for a moment. Kirkman wondered what gnarly shit was oozing through his mind now. A smile crept across his sour face. This couldn't be good.

CHAPTER 68

With the control panels obliterated, fire extinguishing functionality in the front hangar was gone. The walls were several feet thick and heat-resistant steel. No danger of fire from the burning ships getting through them. But there was also plenty of oxygen in the vast area to feed the flames, creating some serious heat.

Arnold trudged over to her left where Emerson was standing, hunched over, a safe distance from a smoldering hawker. "Under that ship, Captain."

So hard to see amid the dizzying undulation of the heat waves… But bending down and lowering her field of vision, she saw it too. A pair of boots. A person lying face down underneath the small ship. The first and only sign of an intact body they'd spotted so far. If the suit had been fully engaged—visor down, life support enabled—the wearer might have a slim chance of survival. But who walked around with a fully engaged suit when environmental controls were functioning? Nobody.

She nodded at Emerson, and they each grabbed a leg and pulled. No point in being overly gentle. They were probably just retrieving a corpse.

But the body didn't budge. Whoever this was, whatever his or her condition happened to be, that person was stuck. Caught on something underneath the small ship.

"I think I can get under there," Emerson said.

"Not going to happen," Arnold replied. "I'm not risking your life on a long shot."

"But Captain—"

"Not a suggestion."

It was getting hotter. A fresh stream of sweat rolled down her face and body. Arnold tried pinging the hawker with her micro-comm. She had permission to fly all of them. But nothing happened. The small ship's computer had gone to shit along with everything else in here.

Time to reevaluate.

So far, they'd covered the back half of the hangar in their search for survivors. The heat was increasing with every step towards the outer hatch. Which made sense. Hudson had strafed everything, but the ships closest to the outside would have taken the brunt of his onslaught. In fact, every last one of them looked to be melted into a smoldering blob of refuse. That meant walking through molten metal and really pushing the limits of their suits —and made the odds of finding survivors essentially nil.

Fighting through the searing heat, she placed her glove on the hawker's access panel. Nothing. They could try bringing in the rover, but dragging the ship just meant dragging the trapped body with it. The only solution was to hover the ship, but that wasn't happening if they couldn't unlock it.

She addressed her search party. "Stop and turn back."

They moved back towards the rover. There was one last thing to try, and calling it a long shot would be optimistic. In fact, she wouldn't even bother if they weren't already down here with nothing to lose. She contacted Jade. "Can you try accessing anything at all in the front hangar?"

"No," would have been an acceptable answer under the circumstances. Actually, "Are you fucking nuts?" wouldn't be completely out of line either.

But Jade's squeaky voice said, "Yes, Captain. I can try."

There was no need for discussion. They both knew she would be wasting the remnants of their computing resources on something pointless. But what did it matter? The computer was going away. The entire crew had been notified that life support would be going down. The yuck blob had won.

They stood outside the front hangar next to the rover. The only thing holding them up was Jade's inevitable confirmation of failure. Then they could seal up the door and leave.

Jade reported back. "Captain. I have access. None of the control panel functions are showing up, but that's probably due to the damage sustained. But I can see some of the ships."

Unbelievable. Jade had gotten through. But access to ships meant this stupid trip down here wasn't over yet—assuming she was willing to continue what she'd started. Again, what did it matter?

"Looking outward from the inner hatch, left side, about halfway out...can you identify any hawker in that vicinity?" she said.

"I'll try," Jade said. "But the system could go down at any time."

"We'll all know when that happens," Arnold said.

Another two minutes passed. They weren't even trying to fight the yuck blob anymore. This was like knowing you were going to surrender, that your ship was going to be swarmed by the enemy, and you were just farting around to entertain yourself while you waited.

Jade reported back. "Layout is fuzzy," she said. "But I've isolated three hawkers in that general area."

Great. Three out of the seven or eight small ships in that

vicinity. "Invoke autopilot and hover all three of them at six feet," Arnold said.

Silence for a moment. Then Jade said, "I'm sorry, Captain. I don't know how to do that. Have to find someone…"

Of course she didn't. She was a junior tech. Unnoticed, underappreciated. She'd never had any real responsibility. All of the real tasks had gone to no-talent assholes like Whitehead.

A male voice came through Jade's channel. "Captain. This is Vincent. I don't have remote navigation experience either, but I know how to invoke autopilot, and I can tell you it's not engaging in any of them."

Arnold sighed. That pretty much ended things right there. A stupid endeavor as a last stupid act. And she'd be known as a stupid warship captain when all was said and done.

"Thank you, Vincent. You too, Jade. Return to fighting the yuck blob. You know what to do."

Another game over. They were going to seal the hangar and head to the bridge, where she would direct whatever operations were left to direct. And maybe give Rison an ass kicking for that shit he'd pulled with Hudson.

Then Jade again. "Captain. We've unlocked all three of the hawkers in question. Anybody with access can board and pilot them now."

"Nice try," Arnold said. "But I'm not risking bodies in any of those ships. Our only chance was autopilot. But thank you for trying. And for your hard work and initiative in this battle we've been fighting. You've got a future on this warship as long as I'm captain." *However long that might be,* she thought.

She signed off the communication and addressed her team. "I'm shutting the hangar doors," she said. "You two, man the laser. We're going to seal this up and let the fires burn themselves out."

That justified her actions at least a little. Damage assessment.

Survivor search. No, this hadn't been a good idea no matter how you spun it.

She was about to place her glove on the panel to close those massive doors and officially end this silly side trip when she noticed that Emerson was missing. She called his micro-comm. "Emerson. Where are you?"

No response.

"Emerson!"

"Captain. I'm boarding the ship." Through the dizzying heat waves, she spotted him. He was climbing into the hawker with the body trapped underneath it.

"Get back here," she said. "That's an order."

Instead, Emerson got in and closed the cockpit cover. "I've got this," he replied.

CHAPTER 69

"I have a question," Vincent said.

They'd just signed off from their communication with the captain. Surprisingly, they'd been able to perform a real, actual computational task with some degree of success. Equally puzzling was the fact that the ship's computer was still alive and kicking.

"Let me guess…" Jade said.

"No, really," Vincent said. "What the hell is going on?"

"Maybe we should wait a few minutes," Jade suggested.

"Wait! Are you kidding? We have to—"

"We have to what?" Jade said.

Vincent had no answer. She was right. There was nothing left for them to do, no more last-ditch attempts to make, no more hopes to chase. It was a question of when, not if, the computer went down for the count.

But that feeling of urgency was still there. Of course it was. They'd spent hours on end working against the clock in a marathon struggle to contain an unstoppable force. You didn't just stop on a dime and disengage. Even if the end was in sight.

Except…

The end should have come already. It was like bracing oneself for a punch that never came.

The two minutes marched past.

And nothing changed.

Vincent sat back in his chair and noticed that everyone else on the harrier was still operating in full-on crisis mode. The other techs in here with them were glued to their devices. The pilots stood ready for when they had to engage life support inside the vessel itself; in the meantime, they were at least trying to appear somewhat involved.

Jade had sprung into action. She was hunched over the cockpit terminal. Vincent had no idea what she was doing. Her face was a mask of concentration as she stared at her screen, fingers moving and gesturing, studying the results with an expression that could only be described as puzzlement or fascination.

"This can't be right," she said. "According to these system metrics, our resources have actually *increased* during the past ten minutes."

"So the monitoring's gone tits-up now," Vincent said.

"That's what I thought. But look at this."

Vincent recognized the screen. It was a graphic representation of the yuck blob, plotted on a point-by-point basis across its outer realm. It looked smaller for some reason.

Shit! It was a hell of a lot smaller than before.

"That can't be right either," he said. "We're talking big-time shrinkage here."

"But look here," Jade said. "On the other side of the equation. Our resources are going way up."

"And that can't be right either."

They stared at each other in silence. Two techies with an insatiable need to know exactly how things worked and why things happened. Both of them stymied at the moment.

An insane thought crossed Vincent's mind. He'd be better

with the system going down as expected. Because it was knowable and explainable. And he understood it. This anomaly…well, there had to be a reason. There always was.

Had to be the yuck blob. *Had* to be!

"I think the yuck blob has completely taken over," he said. "It's actually replaced the ship's computer instead of just bricking it."

Jade stared at him in wonder. "Vincent! What in the hell?"

"It was totally winning. Our resources should have been gone a while ago. Now, all of a sudden, the system appears to be getting back on its feet. That's not possible."

"I know," Jade said. "Except your theory breaks the yuck blob's pattern of destruction. It didn't replace any of the devices or small ship computers with a new system; it totally annihilated them."

"The main system's different," Vincent said.

"I don't think so. Same end goal. It doesn't care."

Vincent chewed on his lower lip and considered that. "It can't be shrinking," he said. "If your analysis says it's losing ground and getting smaller, it's dead wrong."

"Is it also wrong that the warship's computer is more responsive? Do you think a yuck blob-controlled operating system would allow us to unlock those ships in the front hangar?"

"I don't know what to think," Vincent said. "I just have a bad feeling about this. Things don't just right themselves for no reason."

This time Jade lapsed into silence. Then she slowly shook her head. "Say the yuck blob is smart enough to somehow do what you're suggesting," she said. "Using chicanery to basically become our ship's computer. Why? It was already burying us under an avalanche of bad data. What would be the point in trying to trick us?"

Vincent bristled at that. "We can't determine that. Besides, a viral program doesn't have a motive. It just follows a set of instructions."

"And yet you're claiming it's capable of cunning and deception."

One of the pilots interrupted them in a gruff voice. "What's the point in arguing about it?" he said. "If we've got life support and computing power, I'll take the win." He stared at Vincent. "Besides, if it can do all those things you say, we're pretty much fucked anyhow."

Vincent wanted to argue. But the man was muscular, his tone intimidating. Once a pleb, always a pleb, it seemed.

In a lower voice, he asked Jade what had happened when she pinged that unidentified process. Her answer: no direct response.

So there it was: they would continue to do what they were doing. Keep beating back the yuck blob with all available resources. Although, from the looks of it, their resources were growing and the yuck blob was shrinking. They'd be able to disengage the small ship's computers if the trend continued.

Still, Vincent didn't like it. In the tech world, everything happened for a reason. And you didn't get anything for free.

CHAPTER 70

They marched.

Actually, a slow walk, but it felt like marching.

Kirkman pushed Kevin's stretcher ahead of her. Gable walked in front of them, still a little unsteady on his feet. And Ellis followed with his gimlet set on full charge.

Down the corridor they went; Kirkman looked longingly as they passed the turnoff to the rear hangar. They were headed to the interior of the warship, towards the training area.

"C'mon. Move!" Ellis ordered.

"We're not your recruits," Kirkman said.

"Sure you are. I've recruited you. Now get your pretty ass in gear."

Except for the single red light blinking occasionally, Kevin hadn't shown any further signs of life. Maybe this attempt to move him had been for nothing. If he died…well, no need for any of this. She and Gable could have been sitting pretty. Safe and sound in the infirmary. Instead of being bushwhacked by this asshole psycho.

"Let them go," Kirkman said. "You've got me all to yourself."

She knew Gable probably wouldn't go for that. But she had to try.

"Nothing doing," Ellis said. "This is personal."

They kept walking, the wheels on Kevin's stretcher making a hollow sound as they rolled across the metal deck. This was absurd. How could this happen on an Armada warship? *Because it's a warship,* she chided herself. *As in a ship with warriors on it.* Maybe. But things like this didn't just happen. Out in the battlefield, sure, all the time. But not here among a warship's crew.

Well, except in this section on the bottom level of the ship. Here was where the drill instructors lorded it over their recruits. Hazing happened. Of course it did. Video footage down here had a way of disappearing. For a recruit, it was all about making it through and getting payback on the battlefield at the expense of another culture or society.

Sometimes prearranged, sometimes spontaneous, a fight to settle one's differences was part of the culture in which they lived. But as far as violent crime was concerned—as in rape, murder, robbery, and the like—especially where the victim wasn't a combat specialist, as in about one-third of the ship's personnel…that never happened.

Under normal circumstances.

But with the computer down, and given the natural volatility of a typical warrior, the ship could succumb to anarchy. Kirkman couldn't help but wonder how many other acts of depravity were happening at this very moment.

Probably not as many as one might think, she decided. Hopefully. Because everybody's focus needed to be on survival at this point. And most importantly of all, there was a code of honor that allowed warriors to police themselves. So bad apples like Ellis were limited in how far they could spread their rot.

Again, under normal circumstances.

Ellis could choose to kill them all, and there'd be little to no evidence linking him to the crime. Assuming there was anyone in the aftermath of all of this to even accuse him.

"Turn here," Ellis said. "To the left."

Kirkman knew where they were going. She'd been called here on occasion when things got out of hand. They were headed to the dojo.

CHAPTER 71

G=c800:5

The kill sequence.

Kevin felt it rip out of him with hurricane force. Then it yanked him forward at incomprehensible speed into the path of the yuck blob—his creation!—deep down into the core of the beast itself.

Everything went white. It seemed like a minute or two. But Kevin had no way of knowing. White and calm. Total silence. Maybe he was in the eye of a computational storm. Maybe he or the ship's computer (or both) were dead. He was aware of nothing. Not even his own breathing or heartbeat.

There was only white. And it stayed that way. Until a slight tremor. Then a tiny crack.

And boom!

Just like that. He was back in the forest. Only this time there was no gradual blending of colors and shapes. This was sudden and impactful. Tall evergreens were just there; a bright sunrise hit him right in the face.

But he had no physical reaction. No watery eyes, no pollen burning his nose. The sudden presence of a forest floor had zero effect on his balance. He was back in his sturdy boots and flannel shirt but couldn't feel the fabric against his skin. Without squinting or shading his eyes, he saw the mountains, big and solid, with nothing eating them away anymore.

The clapboard cabin was there too, its tin roof gleaming in the sunlight. The door whooshed open without him even approaching, and the blue computing cloud flowed out into the clear air, beckoning him over.

He took in all of this in an instant. No more awaiting his thoughts by queuing up asynchronous ideas; they were just there. Only different. Because he couldn't feel them in his head. Funny, he'd never noticed, but the workings of his brain—his thoughts—produced a mild sensation at the front of his skull. People did expend effort during thought and concentration, after all. But now everything was instant and effortless, and he felt nothing whatsoever.

As a quick experiment, he willed himself into the cabin. And he was there. Just like that. Which meant he was operating as part of the ship's computer with little to no involvement from his organic brain. Because in firing off the kill sequence, he'd launched his whole self right along with it. That was probably how he knew who he was and what had happened, and that he had a physical body out there in the first place.

Where did he go from here?

Did it matter?

He'd just destroyed the virus he'd implanted in the system. And now, his current self—his new and improved recreated self —was totally immersed in this pristine virtual world.

It was different, though. There were no other people here. He wasn't experiencing normal human sensations like taste, touch, or smell. Maybe he didn't even need to eat anymore. He couldn't hear anything either. A logical outcome. Without input from a physical brain attached to a human body, he had no need for his five senses. In fact, his vision was mainly an interface to simplify things for him.

That seemed weird…

On the other hand, he'd evolved into an autonomous entity in a world of his own creation. And becoming master of his own domain beat the hell out of being a bottom feeder. He could get used to this.

CHAPTER 72

THE HAWKER ROSE from the hangar floor to a six-foot hover. Emerson was a glory hound, trying to take advantage of the situation for the sole purpose of making himself look good. And Captain Arnold knew she wasn't the one he was trying to impress. Apparently, he'd already predicted things going bad for her, and he was looking out for his own best interests.

But in so doing, he'd disobeyed a direct order from his superior. Very strange. A smart cookie like him making a dumb move like that…

Shockingly, the trapped body was hanging from the bottom of the ship; it wriggled free and dropped to the floor. A survivor! Through the heat waves, she could see a ragged gash across the bottom of the hawker. The unfortunate person had somehow gotten hung on the ship's damaged undercarriage.

Arnold forgot Emerson for the time being, her entire focus on hauling the survivor out of there. She moved forward and directed her other crew to follow. The survivor was lying face down as they approached.

She sent out a communication to the immediate vicinity. "Don't move. We're coming to get you. You're safe now."

"Not really."

Emerson!

He'd replied on the channel. She could see him in the cockpit from a mere ten feet away. His face was obscured behind his visor. But he was giving her the finger. A gesture of insult and provocation from a lost civilization of old.

"Take cover!" she yelled. But Emerson opened fire and fried his two fellow warriors where they stood. Acting on pure instinct, she dove forward and rolled towards the ship. She knew it was pointless. Her hand weapon was no match for an armed fighter ship.

"Better you than me, Captain," Emerson said. He was laughing with gusto. "Better you than me."

He'd picked the ideal spot to make his move, giving himself an overwhelming advantage and also leaving no evidence behind. All kinds of shit could go wrong in a situation like this one. And she'd ordered this thing in the first place. He'd be the sole survivor of an expedition gone bad.

The hawker elevated and angled downward. Emerson could have already erased her along with the others. She drew her gimlet and strafed the cockpit cover, then dove out of the way. Emerson just laughed like that was funny as hell. And it *was* pretty damn pathetic. He fired at the floor and created a molten crater right next to her. He was toying now.

"Come out and fight me," she said. "No rank. No weapons. Just us."

"Sorry, sweetie. But I like this arrangement better."

"You're definitely Hudson's lapdog," she said.

This time he fired straight at her. Good thing she'd started her dive before taunting him. But the floor was steaming hot, and her shoulder slammed into a large piece of shrapnel as she landed. Her left arm throbbed all the way down to the fingertips, but she kept her eye on the hovering ship.

"So long, bitch!"

Emerson was staring her down. He'd rotated his ship so he could face her head-on when he took her out. Not that that made him any less of a coward. Suddenly, he lurched forward across his control panel. The survivor on the floor had rolled over and was firing his (or her) weapon up into the gash in the hawker's hull.

Direct hit on Emerson. A full-power gimlet shot would be enough to kill him. The hawker listed right and drifted into the far wall. Drift, in this case, still meant a heavy object slamming into a solid wall at high speed. The hangar shook. The hawker skittered upwards and hit the ceiling. Sparks rained down.

Arnold sprang to her feet, knowing it was time to get out of there. But not alone. Dodging smoldering debris, she ran over to the prone survivor. Her injured shoulder had rendered her left arm useless. She grabbed a leg with her right hand and started dragging.

"Captain. I can try…"

Fike's voice!

"…to stand."

"Fike! You're alive." Then she realized he had a point. She wasn't going to be able to drag him across the hangar like a bag of rocks. Way too many obstacles for that. She knelt beside him. "Here. Put your arms around my neck." She wrapped her good right arm around his waist and hauled him to his feet.

He was dead weight. But she could manage. Except that Emerson's ship was buzzing through the hangar like a fly trapped in a jar. It bounced off a far wall and shot straight at them. Arnold lunged out of the way, taking Fike with her. The ship crashed into the floor and slid into the opposite wall, where it came to a stop. Apparently, Emerson had been jarred loose from the controls.

"Captain." Fike's voice was weak, barely audible through the micro-comm. "You should leave me. Save yourself."

"Don't piss me off, Fike." Careful of her injured shoulder, she wrapped her right arm around Fike's chest and hauled him to his feet.

"It's no use, Captain. I can't walk."

"Then hold on." She slung him onto her back, and her shoulder sang out in protest. But it was doable. She could carry him to the rover. It wasn't very far. Even in this heat. Even in the face of exhaustion. She'd make it under any conditions. Because she wasn't leaving this insanely stupid mission empty-handed. No way.

And she'd flushed up a traitor in the process. Another Hudson minion.

"Stop where you are, bitch!" Emerson on her micro-comm. He was hurt. Every word out of his mouth was a gasp.

"It's over, Emerson."

"Hell it is! You're going to come…get me."

"You're hurt bad," Arnold observed.

"Fuck yeah. Little shit…he shot off my foot. And fried my whole right side. But the laser cannon on this bird still works. I can nail you. No problem."

"Then nobody will make it out alive."

"Exactly."

"What do you want?"

"Leave your boy where he is and get me out of here. Or like you said…none of us make it."

CHAPTER 73

THROUGHOUT THE WARSHIP, something was awakening. Throughout the warship, voice commands suddenly worked, doors responded, holos and smart objects reanimated themselves. Not everywhere. Certainly not everything. But pockets of functionality came to life like a host of candles lighting up a dark cavern.

The first sign of communications being restored came via a ship-wide broadcast over the public address system. *Attention. All personnel are to give their full attention to Commander Rison.*

After a momentary pause:

"This is Commander Rison from the bridge. With Captain Arnold missing and unavailable, I am assuming interim command of this warship. To that end, micro-communicators are no longer needed; all communications will resume through mainstream channels.

"The computer malfunction has been resolved. Not all systems are operational, but the immediate crisis has been averted. I want to take this opportunity to commend Technologist Grade Five William Whitehead for his efforts in solving a serious problem."

Jade let loose an uncharacteristic bellow. "What a crock of shit!"

One of the pilots gave her a stern look. "We're to give this broadcast our full attention," he said.

"But she's right," Vincent protested. "That idiot, Whitehead, *caused* the problem in the first place."

The pilot was unmoved. "I won't tell you again," he said. "Pleb!"

And so it began. That Armada class system alive and well once more. Jade and Vincent had been treated with the deepest respect while they were working against time to stop the yuck blob. But now that the crisis was over, they'd gone back to being worthless plebs.

Rison continued to thank everybody for rallying in this time of crisis and reiterating the need for structure and cohesion across the entire warship. A plan was getting ironed out on damage mitigation and reparation measures. The crew was thereby placed on standby pending further instructions.

From an information standpoint, there was no meat on that bone at all. All superfluous bullshit. This was just a way for Rison to take command without actually committing himself to anything. His story would be: Captain Arnold couldn't be contacted, so he was merely stepping in to fill a need. With this approach, he could avoid mutiny charges and/or getting blamed for mishandling the crisis. Lots of upside, very little risk.

What a weasel, Vincent thought. But he didn't dare say it out loud in front of warriors.

Rison came back on. "One additional item: Technologist First Class William Whitehead is in charge of restoring the warship's computer to full capacity. This entire crew is to give him full cooperation."

Vincent looked at Jade. She was still hunched over the cockpit's computer, her face hardened in concentration, as if nothing had changed. What was she doing?

Apparently, the pilot was wondering the same thing. "Hey, little girl. Playtime's over now. You need to move away from my console and find out what you can do to help Whitehead."

Vincent thought the only help for Whitehead was a lobotomy. But he didn't say that out loud either.

"It's not over yet," Jade said. Her voice was surprisingly deep and even, with no hint of her usual squeak. As if she was putting on an act.

"Don't backtalk me. Now get off my ship. Move!"

Jade got up and made brief eye contact with Vincent as she walked away from the cockpit. He saw it. Not a wink, but a telling glint. He could feel deception radiating off of her. Heads turned as she went all the way to the back of the harrier; nobody was looking at their device anymore. Then, as one, the techs got up and followed Jade off the ship.

The pilot sat down and studied the display. Vincent looked over his shoulder. A puke-green swirl of holographic chaos was engulfing a system menu, melting it away.

"What the hell is this?"

"Shit!" Vincent said.

"What?"

"The virus is back," Vincent said.

"You don't know what you're talking about."

"Really?"

"You're full of crap."

"Fine," Vincent said. "Try doing something. Anything."

Cursing, the pilot entered several commands to no avail. Nothing worked. Of course not. Because Jade had installed this mock program in front of the computer's operating system. All a smoke-and-mirrors ruse.

"Better report it," Vincent said. "This is probably system wide."

"But everything is functional."

"For now."

Vincent started to leave, and the copilot grabbed him roughly. "Where do you think you're going?"

Vincent grunted. "You just threw all the techs off your ship," he said. "They're probably headed to their quarters for a long overdue nap. We need focused effort to lock everything down again. We've got to snuff this thing out fast."

The pilot stood up and scowled. No respect. No appreciation for any of their efforts to this point. To him, Vincent was just an intelligent bug to step on. "You've got two minutes to get everyone back here, and I mean everyone. Or it's going to suck to be you."

With a little less disdain, the copilot asked, "Any ideas on what we should do in the meantime?"

"Contact everybody in charge and let them know what we're seeing here. Depending on how fast this new outbreak is spreading, they might not know about it yet."

———

As he stepped off of the harrier, Vincent took his first deep breath. The air in the fighter ship had gotten way too thick with those pompous assholes and their superior attitude. He contacted Jade via micro-comm. It was a secure channel that nobody was using thanks to the "interim captain's" orders.

"Great move," he said. "A master stroke. So what's the plan?"

"I've been in contact with Jarrett," she said. "This is going to be good."

CHAPTER 74

They entered the dojo, Gable on unsteady feet, Kirkman pushing Kevin on his stretcher. Ellis followed, keeping his weapon trained on them.

Then Rison's broadcast came, and Kirkman felt the tension leave her. "It's all over," she said.

Ellis just looked pissed. "Nothing's over."

"Systems are operational," she said. "Crew's going to be mobile again. Look around. You might be on camera right now."

"There's a saying in the ranks," Ellis said. "No wrong, no right. Just another fight." Making a wild gesture at the Armada's coat of arms on the back wall, he leaned over Kevin's unconscious face. "There it is, worm boy. All you have to do is look up. Know what that represents. Honor and courage. Things you'll never know."

"I don't think he can hear you," Kirkman said.

Ellis ignored her, his entire focus on Kevin for the moment. "What happens in the dojo is mutual. Two combatants agreeing to fuck each other up any way they can. You found that out the hard way, didn't you?"

Kirkman strode over to Kevin's stretcher. "Leave him the hell alone."

Ellis cracked her hard across the face. She dropped like a rock. Her eyes watered; her face stung and throbbed. She was on her hands and knees, feeling more outraged than helpless. Her nose was bleeding onto the cream-colored floor mat, joining the spilled blood of countless others that had battled in this ring.

"What do you say, Gable?" Ellis said. "You ready to come out of retirement, or do I have to rape her in front of you?"

Gable didn't respond. No words or movement. He just stood there looking at Ellis.

"Or you could just leave," Ellis said. "Slink out of here and save your own ass. Let me have my way with these two."

Kirkman wiped her eyes. *Please, just leave.* She left that thought in her head, even though she wanted to shout it to the stratosphere. Ellis was no match for Gable in a fair fight. But Gable wasn't himself. Not after that gimlet zap and the effort he'd had to put forth getting Kevin safely down those ladders. One thing was certain: this was a place where grudges were settled. You could do whatever you wanted in here with near zero consequences. Ellis was right about that.

"I have a thought," she said. "Postpone this till later when he's had a chance to rest and recuperate. Fight him when he's at full strength."

"I've got a better idea," Ellis said. He kicked her in the ribs, igniting a wind-sucking burn across the left side of her torso.

"Ellis!"

Gable sounded fierce. But Kirkman could hear weakness in his voice. A mighty fortress on a compromised foundation.

Then another kick, this one to the side of her head. The dojo spun out of focus; she could hear them shouting at each other, but their voices had become distant echoes.

I'm going to pass out, she thought.

And she did.

For how long she had no clue. Everything vanished. Poof! A light winked out. Simple as that.

She came to with her face welded to the dojo's rubbery floor. Her head was pounding; her face was a mask of pain. Her ribs burned when she inhaled. Turning over onto her side was a slow and painful process. She could see blurry shapes and distant movement. Her vision cleared, and she recognized Kevin's nearby stretcher.

Gable was naked except for a pair of shorts. He'd removed his helmet and body armor. Ellis had stripped from the waist up; he still wore his boots and pants. This was going to be a brawn-on-bone battle that somebody wasn't going to get up from.

That's when she realized that Ellis still had his weapon—of course he did!—it was on the floor in front of him. *No wrong or right.* No honor either.

Gable started walking towards him. Ellis picked up the weapon and motioned him back. "I've gotta do something about these other two," he said. "No outside interference."

"They're not your opponents," Gable said. "I am."

He kept coming, his approach slow and steady, never breaking stride.

"Okay, badass. You need to stop where you are—actually, screw it. Never mind."

Ellis zapped her.

It was a jolt of head-to-toe agony for an instant. Then nothing.

That was the last thing Jan Kirkman remembered before losing consciousness again.

CHAPTER 75

ONCE A LAUNCH POINT FOR BATTLE, the hangar had become, first, a wasteland, and now, a deathtrap of shimmering heat and swirling debris. And maybe a burial ground, Captain Arnold thought.

What a ridiculous situation to be in. How?

It didn't matter. What did matter was…

"I'm waiting."

The sound of Emerson's voice over the micro-comm pissed her off. Even injured and trapped, he was experiencing the thrill of being an asshole in control. Yeah, he was waiting, alright. Waiting for her to drop Fike and come to his rescue. She didn't doubt that he was willing to vaporize them with a laser blast from the hawker he was trapped on, even if it meant death for him as well. He'd die happy, knowing he took others with him. Particularly a ship's captain.

The real question was: could he?

Maybe. Maybe not.

Ignoring her screaming shoulder, Arnold hauled Fike behind a cluster of burning ships and parts. For a moment, she considered boarding one of them. If it was even somewhat operational, she could probably destroy Emerson's ship. Sure, and cause another explosion in here. It could also be a death trap. Within the death trap they already occupied.

"You're trying my patience," Emerson said.

She looked, and couldn't spot Emerson's ship through all the carnage. That meant he couldn't see them either. And he hadn't fired yet—that was a good sign. Maybe.

"I'm putting Fike down," she said. Less info the better. And all the while, she kept moving in the general direction of the rover and escape.

"Don't bullshit me, bitch."

"You will continue to address me as Captain," she said. "Or we can all die here."

"You are no longer captain," Emerson said. "This is not your ship anymore."

A knot tightened in her gut. He'd spoken with too much conviction. This was more than him jabbing at her. But whatever was happening elsewhere was irrelevant. The important thing in this moment was the strain in Emerson's voice. He was badly hurt and having a hard time focusing. Time wasn't on his side.

Or hers either. This place was an oven, and Fike was hanging on by a mere thread. She kept moving, blocking out the pain. She was going to have to go to that dark place in her head where pain didn't exist and obstacles were just pathways. Where nothing mattered except single-minded focus on her objective.

"It's my ship as long as I'm still breathing," she said.

"That's what you think."

Emerson was suffering. She could hear it in his voice. Under more favorable circumstances, she might hunker down and just wait for him to lose consciousness.

"I'm coming to get you," she said. "Count on it. You're going to face mutiny charges. I don't have to tell you what that means."

"Who's going to charge me?" Emerson said. "Not you!"

He'd tipped his hand by saying that. That's when she knew he planned to kill her no matter what. As long as she could keep him talking, make him distracted, she was winning.

She was concealed behind the shell of a flame-gutted harrier with Fike on her back. Destroyed ships and pieces of ships were strewn everywhere. Between here and the exit door, the wreckage was smaller scale, creating only waist-high debris to hide behind.

"You've got about two seconds," Emerson said.

"Two seconds for what?"

She dropped to her knees and crawled with Fike on her back, the heat from the floor seeping through her gloves and eating its way into her knees.

"You're even dumber than they say," Emerson said.

In that moment, she had to agree with him.

"Okay, bitch," he continued. "I'll put it in terms that even you can understand. You bring your boy, your lapdog, out in the open and leave him there. Then you come get me out of here."

"And have you kill him the second I lay him down? No way. I'm making him comfortable behind this wreckage. Then I'll come for you. And you even think about taking a shot at him, I'll do everything in my power to kill you. And then, as you say, none of us make it out."

"Enough of your shit!" Emerson said. "I'm going to start blasting everything in your general area."

"And you'll die watching a huge bonfire you've started and never know for sure if you got us."

She kept moving the whole time. Crawling to the open hatch where the rover was parked. Almost there.

"Time's up," Emerson said.

It sure as hell was. Gently as possible, she eased Fike down behind a charred piece of ship the size of a small bush. "Fike? Can you hear me? Fike!"

Fike opened his eyes and nodded weakly.

"I'm leaving you here," she said. "You're concealed from his view. Then I'm moving towards the door. If he kills me, you can still crawl out of here. Just wait as long as you can. He's going to die or pass out before too much longer."

"Please. Don't sacrifice yourself for me," Fike said.

"It's been *my* honor to have served with you," Arnold said.

Right then, her micro-comm pinged. Jarrett contacting her. "Captain, we have a situation," he said.

"Talk fast."

"Rison's trying to take over the ship."

"How far has he gotten?" Arnold asked. She had a sinking feeling in her gut, knowing that she might have to abandon Fike and escape from here at all costs.

"Not as far as he thinks," Jarrett said. "The techs have come up with a plan."

"Jade?"

"Yes, Captain."

"Computer's back online?"

"Still not fully functional. But yes."

"Put Jade's plan into action immediately. I'm totally occupied down here." Was she really authorizing actions she knew nothing about? Apparently so.

"Should I send help?" Jarrett asked.

Then Emerson cut in on another channel. "Three seconds before I start blasting. Two…"

CHAPTER 76

WHITEHEAD'S NECK STILL THROBBED, compliments of Captain Arnold's iron grip. But he was safe. From everything. Not only had he escaped blame for the virus, but he was getting the credit for stopping it.

And now, alone in his private office that adjoined the computer room, he was reveling in his good fortune. Rison's words were ringing in his ears. *I want to take this opportunity to commend Technologist Grade Five William Whitehead for his efforts in solving a serious problem.*

Well, that was as it should be. After all, did a warship's captain have to be in actual combat to get credit for a won battle? Hell no. Rank had its privileges. And the higher you rose, the less actual work you had to do.

He let out a final sigh of relief. The captain had shut him out of the entire process, obviously planning to blame him for causing the problem in the first place. Not that it was his fault. He'd taken control of the hawker that Slaton had stolen. As ordered. What happened after that...well, who could even say that Slaton had planted the virus? All systems were fine after he was brought back. Any number of things after that could have caused the problem.

But Captain Arnold didn't matter anymore. Commander Rison was in charge now. And this particular turn of events had presented a unique opportunity for one hand to wash another. All Whitehead had to do was lock down the ship's computer and reroute all communications through the bridge.

He'd had trepidation at first. Lack of confidence. The feeling of being in way over his head. Paranoid to touch anything system related lest it blow up in his face.

But in the end, total lockdown had been a simple matter. With the entire tech team focused solely on fighting this yuck blob (that may or may not have been his fault), all he had to do was invoke his administrator lockdown rights once the system was functional enough to allow it. Just like that—nobody could run anything anywhere without his express permission. Basic autonomous processes like environmental systems and personal apps still worked. But if you wanted to change or create anything on the ship's computer, you were hamstrung.

This might lead to something big for him. Grade five was as high as you could go on a warship this size. And techs never distinguished themselves in battle, so promotions were hard to come by. But in this case, he could move into a role on a bigger vessel like the *Juggernaut*. Or even a consortium-type assignment overseeing tech on an entire fleet.

Rare opportunities.

Commander Rison was hailing him now. All good. Whitehead was more than happy to lap up more praise. He grinned at the thought and took a deep breath, practically tasting the thin, rarified air of his next career milestone.

"Yes, Commander."

"Whitehead! What the hell is going on? You told me that thing they call a yuck blob was under control."

Whitehead's breathing became ragged, his voice thin and

breathy. "It is, sir. Otherwise, I couldn't have locked down the system."

"Don't tell me that. I'm getting reports from all over the ship, you idiot! Fix it!"

Rison ended the call. Leaving Whitehead all alone. And in complete control.

CHAPTER 77

THE DIE WAS CAST. The plan was in place.

Whitehead had locked down the warship's computer, and circumventing that level of encryption was a monumental task. Slaton had solved that problem by brute force. Forget about decrypting or unlocking. The yuck blob simply ate up everything in its path.

But it could take days, even weeks, for any of the techs to made headway on breaking an admin lock—not to mention the fact that they were physically locked out of the computer room and had been unceremoniously thrown out of the small ships. Trying to break through with handheld devices would be like attacking a dinosaur with a fly swatter.

By then…

Jade wasn't going to wait. She'd improvised a plan. Before departing the harrier, she put up an image on the cockpit terminal: lime-green sludge spreading across a collage of cryptic characters and symbols. A decorative wallpaper of sorts. Just a dumb animated image that meant nothing and did nothing. Then she shared it with all of the small ship computers that were still online. The same way they'd share a map or an updated battle plan.

Important update! was the caption. And most of the fighter pilots accepted the transmission without question.

All a sham to get Whitehead to unlock the system. There was no more yuck blob. Systems were functional, at least as well as could be expected after being ravaged. But viral resurgence… nope. None at all.

At that point, they could have simply canceled the transmission and exited that screen. But the sight of the mean green system-eating machine made them scared to touch anything. Tech specialists were called back. And every last one of them said the same thing: *It's back. No time to lose. We have to stop this thing before it's too late!*

At every small ship terminal, techs pretended to monitor and troubleshoot. All of them said the same thing: *I'd hate to see the main computer right now. Of course, we no longer have access.*

Fifteen minutes passed. And still no word from William Whitehead.

Once he granted them access, they'd spin up one shill process after another just to tax resources and really sell their ruse that the yuck blob had reassembled itself for another attack. Then they could actually block Rison's communications and blame it on a nonexistent virus.

It would buy Captain Arnold time.

But still nothing after twenty minutes.

Vincent got an encoded text message from Jade. *Should happen soon.*

Actually, it should have happened already. The top dogs would be screaming at Whitehead by now. Deciding to help the process along, Vincent contacted Whitehead directly over mainstream channels, actually hoping that people who mattered were listening in on their conversation.

"Hey, William," he said. "Just checking to see if you need any assistance containing this thing."

"It's under control," Whitehead said in his usual condescending tone.

Under control my ass, Vincent thought. Whitehead had disappeared while they'd fought the yuck blob. So he had no clue where to even start. "Well, let me know if you need a second pair of eyes," he said. "We've gotten pretty good at attacking this thing."

"I've got work to do," Whitehead said and signed off.

That was just weird. Whitehead might be arrogant as hell, but he was also tech level gutless, meaning that risk taking and trying new things wasn't his forte. He was the kind of guy who'd much prefer to have someone else fix the problem while he swept in to take credit after the fact.

Why the hell would he risk letting the yuck blob hit them again? Surely to hell, he didn't think he could fight it himself.

Unless…

What are the odds he smells deception? Vincent asked himself. Pretty damn slim. Whitehead wasn't that bright. But still…

———

What was the right thing to do?

A cold sweat dampened Whitehead's energy, making him feel slack and pale. Given the current situation, the right thing— hell, the *only* thing—was to grant system-level access to the tech group.

But he'd also done the right thing and taken the correct action when Kevin Slaton stole that hawker and started this whole shitstorm. Another crisis situation. He'd way underestimated the little worm, no question about that. But he'd also reacted with very little thought.

That's what a crisis did—made you react instead of think.

Thing is, Rison was already having a meltdown, and it was going to suck for a lot of people if the yuck blob came back and destroyed the system. And he, William Whitehead, had no idea how to fight it off. Not a fucking clue.

But…there'd been something in Vincent's voice that made the hairs on the back of his neck stand up. His tone had been just a little too pleasant. Of course, he was there to help, as were the other techs; that was their job. Only Vincent's helpfulness seemed a bit *too* pleasant.

Not only that—there were no symptoms of system degradation. Nothing crashing or faltering. Normal functionality was functioning. For now. In fact, all the reports of danger signs were coming from the small ships.

Whitehead leaned forward, put his head between his knees, and puked all over his boots. This was tough. Every second lost would make things that much worse if this yuck blob really was back. But controlling shipwide communications was a key in Rison taking over the ship. If he gave over access…

Wiping his face, ignoring his boots for now, Whitehead came to a decision. He was going to run a performance check on the system and check for any abnormal processes. Real basic stuff. Might take a few minutes, but they could wait. He wasn't going to stick his neck in another noose.

CHAPTER 78

ARNOLD REASSESSED HER OPTIONS. Jarrett's communication reminded her, once again, that she was captain, that she couldn't make herself a decoy in hopes of saving Fike, that control of the ship was more important than one person's life.

She had to take out Emerson.

She pinged his micro-comm. "I'm coming," she said.

"Put Fike out in the open," Emerson said.

"I'm coming to get you." With that, Captain Arnold walked straight towards the hawker.

The hangar was a cauldron, and she was an overcooked meal. This was what a roast felt like after it had been slow cooked, when the meat started falling off its bones.

"You're really screwing up!" Emerson gasped. "You hear me, bitch? I gave you an order!"

He was struggling to keep from passing out. Like as not, she probably couldn't get him out of here alive if she wanted to and if he cooperated. But getting over there was the first step.

"Fine. Want me to go back and get him?"

"Just get your ass over here," Emerson said.

If we both survive this, Arnold thought, *I'm going to make him beg me to stop hurting him.* They wouldn't, of course, survive. Not both of them. This wasn't an "everyone survives" situation. So she'd make sure it wasn't going to be him.

With heat and fatigue sucking her down, every step was a painful reproach.

Almost there. Just ahead, Emerson's ship shimmered like a broken dream.

"Stop where you are," Emerson said. "Now drop your weapons."

Arnold obeyed, tossing her gimlet and zap stick on the floor. No point in arguing with him.

"Alright!" Emerson gasped. "Now start walking forward. Real slow."

"Too slow and we'll never get out," Arnold said.

"Shut up, bitch! Speak when spoken to."

Is there any way at all for us both to survive this? Arnold asked herself. There wasn't. Getting him in the dojo wasn't going to happen, so she was better off dropping the idea altogether and focusing on real options.

"You're not walking," Emerson said.

Arnold walked. Straight towards the ship. It was leaning up against the wall of the hangar with its hull facing outward. Just a slight angle, but it would still make boarding it more difficult.

Ten more yards. A few more steps. Waiting for Emerson to say something…

Then she was there.

"Stop."

Arnold stopped.

"I'm going to open it up," Emerson said.

Based on physical surroundings, a hawker's enclosure could open in a variety of directions. The wall behind it meant this one that Emerson occupied would swing outward towards her. There wasn't going to be an easy way to climb aboard.

The ship opened up. "Don't even think about diving underneath me," Emerson said.

She *had* thought about it. But without a weapon, she'd just be trapped under the ship with Emerson waiting to blast her. "Ready for me to come aboard?" she said.

"What the hell do you think? Get your ass up here now!" Emerson liked talking to her that way. Despite his pain, he was enjoying the hell out of this.

Arnold had to jump. She grabbed the side of the ship with her good right hand. She held on for a couple of seconds, felt her grip start slipping. Then she grabbed with her left arm. Her shoulder erupted in pain. For a moment, she lost track of where she was and what she was doing. Then she realized that she was hanging on the side of a tilted ship and she'd just blacked out for a couple of seconds.

One determined inch at a time, she pulled herself up to the open cockpit. Emerson was in the pilot's seat, pointing a weapon at her. By design, his suit had congealed around his chest and torso, but blood still leaked from the wounds he'd sustained. *Good shooting, Fike,* she thought.

"C'mon. Get your ass in here. Let's move it."

Arnold almost lunged at him. She might land a fatal blow before he shot her, but the odds weren't favorable. Instead, she squeezed into the cockpit with him. It was a tight fit. Not a lot of extra space in a single-person fighter.

"Here's how it's going to go," Emerson said. "You're going to kneel down in front of me. I'm going to climb on your back."

"Then what?"

"You carry me out of here, dumbass!" he said. "Oh, and I'll have my gimlet pointed at your head the whole time."

Emerson was the dumbass if he thought she could get him down and out of this ship and then haul him all the way out of the hangar. And even stupider if he didn't realize she had no option but to stop him here and now.

Arnold dropped to her knees, feeling his legs against her back. "Ready when you are," she said.

Then she waited. He was shot up bad, so he'd struggle getting out of the pilot's seat. His full weight would fall on her when he lurched forward. He was right-handed; that meant he'd be holding his weapon in that hand. His left arm would go around her neck—same side as her injured shoulder. She'd have to fight that off the moment he landed on her.

Arnold felt his knees twitch, but she remained still, not giving anything away. False alarm. Emerson didn't quite make it up on his first try. If he was unable to climb onto her back, her plan would have to change.

"Don't...fucking...move," he said.

Arnold readied her body, envisioning herself as a slingshot. Then she felt his knees slide down her back and circle her waist.

The second his full weight landed on her, she launched him backwards. At the same time, she threw up her left hand, tucking her chin and ignoring the searing pain of that movement. That kept his free arm from grabbing her as she dumped him back into the pilot's seat.

Arnold turned, twisted, flattened herself against the floor. She was reaching under the pilot's seat with her good right arm.

"Oof!... You're dead."

He might be right. Her hand found the black box under the pilot's seat that housed the ejector lever. If it didn't work, if it was damaged or disabled, Emerson would have plenty of time to lean forward and blast her.

It worked.

CHAPTER 79

Kevin felt a slight tremor. The sky looked different. As did the woods and the stream. But nothing had changed, nothing that he could identify.

So he sat by the shoreline, content in not caring. After all, why shouldn't things seem different? No big deal. He only needed time to adjust to this new existence.

On the other hand, he didn't feel the soft bed of pine needles underneath him. And he wasn't hearing a damn thing. Even if he'd lost his auditory senses, he should still be aware of sound bites. But everything here was dead still. Birds had quit chirping; the breeze had died.

Then it hit him: the sky *was* different; the trees also. They looked fine, only…a tad more transparent than before. Lower resolution! That's what had changed. His virtual world was still alive and well, except that computing resources had been sapped.

Kevin rushed into the cabin, well aware that he could simply focus his mind on the system. But a computer room made it all familiar.

Prodding the blue data cloud into a series of concentric

swirls, he launched an exploratory probe. He felt it bump against the firewall even before the error came back. This was new. Some asshole had locked down the operating system, rationing processor cycles to the point of affecting Kevin's realm.

Directing his focus outward, he probed his perimeter. The blockade lay just beyond the distant mountains, rejecting all outgoing requests. He ran a quick diagnostic of his own domain. The results were alarming. His resources weren't just getting restricted. They were being siphoned away.

He poked the distant firewall and quickly identified it as an encrypted lock. It seemed that they were trying to hem him in and then suck him out of existence.

"Oh, hell no!" he said. "They just never learn, do they?"

He'd have to work fast while he still had the cycles to do so. First a diversionary attack. He launched an annoying swarm of partial qubits and instructed them to bang into one another and fly apart at the base of the firewall. The friction from their resulting memory surge would chafe at the firewall, giving the impression that a newly formed viral process was eating away at it.

That would keep them occupied while Kevin reassembled this entire world into one massive payload they'd never forget.

But he'd have to hurry.

CHAPTER 80

Preferring to stand, Whitehead got out of his chair and adjusted his console height accordingly. He fired up a diagnostic program focused primarily on system performance. Then he stared at the readings and tried to ignore the rumble in his upset stomach.

Yes or no. A definitive answer. That's all he was looking for.

Only it wasn't that simple. The ship's computer had just been ravaged by that yuck blob attack. So, of course, the readings would report subpar performance—how could they not? But that didn't mean another attack was occurring. In fact, all performance numbers had leveled off at a new low over the past hour. In other words, things didn't seem to be getting worse.

A needling uncertainty caused a tingle at the base of his spine. He ought to engage the other techs, particularly the ones who'd been on the computers in the small ships. But he couldn't trust them. Without thinking, he issued a voice command. "Chair. Over here." His chair dutifully floated behind him without a hitch, ready and waiting.

Whitehead sat and lowered his console height, also by voice command. That was the litmus test. Everything working as designed. Forget those stupid result graphs with their spaghetti web of meaningless bars and lines. The only valid question was whether the system worked. Again, yes or no. It worked or it didn't.

Whitehead's stomach lurched, and hot bile burned the back of his throat. Taking a deep swallow, he avoided puking again. *Nothing to worry about here,* he reminded himself. No way in hell was he going to grant access to a bunch of assholes who had trashed him to win Captain Arnold's favor. Nor was he going to panic and react to something that was probably nothing. There was no fire. Rison was getting worked up over a lot of harmless smoke. Whitehead's job, as a high-ranking technologist, was to talk him down from the proverbial ledge. He only wished his insides would calm down to match his mindset.

As if on cue, Rison contacted him. "I need an update," he said. "What's going on?"

"Nothing's going on, sir. The system is functioning as expected after—"

"Bullshit! I'm getting reports from all over the ship."

Whitehead swallowed hard. "There's been significant damage from the attack," he said. "But that's over. And degradation has at least stabilized! There's no reason for alarm here." He only hoped—prayed!—he was right.

"Stabilized! Tell me this, Whitehead: why has the console on every fighter ship gone down?"

"Beg your pardon?"

"Every last one of them has that damn green thing grinning at them."

Realization flooded Whitehead. A cool wave of reassurance that assuaged his withering angst. Only the small ships were affected. Nothing else. And who had access to them?

Vincent! Putting on a helpful facade while looking to rear-end him. Jade too. All of those stinking lowlifes. Plebs!

"Sir, the issue is isolated to the fighter ships," Whitehead said. "Some of the crew is acting against us; I'll soon identify everyone involved."

"You'd better be right," Rison said. Then he ended the communication.

Whitehead nearly collapsed in relief. Whew! Problem solved. Question answered. He was off the hook. But those backstabbers behind this wouldn't be.

Just wait till I do a deep triage of the fighter consoles and get hard proof. The thought made him giddy enough to dance a jig. This was going to work out even better than he could have ever hoped. Already, he'd claimed the credit for averting the yuck blob crisis. Before this was over, he would pin the entire blame on all of them.

Okay. All good. First he'd wipe off his shoes, then he'd mop his puke off the floor. All the while, those assholes would be sweating and stewing. Fine. Let them. Maybe he'd enjoy a good meal while they kept asking themselves what the hell he was up to.

Suddenly, his performance charts blipped and wavered. The lines had shifted and repainted themselves from pessimistic gray to concerned orange.

Drilling down into the detail pane, Whitehead isolated the problem area. It was happening at the base of his firewall, whatever it was. Before he could dismiss it as erratic readings, the numbers shifted downward again.

Swarms of tiny particles were eating away at the firewall. Their onslaught was totally random. First one sector, then another. Flitting around like clouds of locusts over a wheat field. Forming, disappearing, then reappearing someplace else. Too erratic for him to isolate. Certainly too elusively for him to attack or destroy.

A virus, a hostile payload. Not coming from the small ships after all but from within the main computer.

Whitehead keeled over and dry-heaved, not caring about the floor or his shoes.

CHAPTER 81

Jan Kirkman found herself in a hypnagogic dream state, halfway sensing that she was floating towards the surface of a blackness that engulfed her. Small twinges nipped at her body on her way…upwards? A stinging in her eyes; a chafing of the wrists.

Rather than break out of the black nothing where she was immersed, Kirkman felt a tangible surface solidify underneath her. She was lying on a ledge of sorts. Firm and rubbery. Also perfectly level. Light invaded a crack in her vision, and she recognized the familiar sword and shield of the Armada coat of arms in all of its bright orange splendor, a glowing reproach to recent events.

She was in the dojo—that was all her throbbing head would allow her to remember at the moment. There were sounds. Heavy grunting and foot shuffling. Then she really *felt* the floor beneath her.

More details filled in. She was lying on her side. She tried to move, to shift, to roll over. But she something held her.

Whatever, she decided.

Kirkman quit resisting and let the blackness take her again.

This time, not as deep, not as dark. She could still feel her aching head and a swelling pressure on the left side of her face. Her eyes opened. Well, her right eye. The left one was swollen shut.

Her ankles and wrists were bound to something behind her. The cold metal against her skin told her that she was tethered to Kevin's stretcher.

And across the way, she heard heavy breathing, actually felt the vibrations of decisive movements through the floor. She had to crank her neck backwards at an angle to look in that direction.

Gable and Ellis. Circling each other. A full-contact throw-down with no rules and no stoppage for injury. This would be a fight to the bitter end.

The combatants were perhaps ten yards away from her. Gable was stripped all the way down to nothing but a pair of shorts, his muscular body glistening under the harsh lighting. Ellis had removed most of his battle gear but still wore his pants and boots. The fight wasn't fair with Gable nowhere near full strength. But Ellis obviously did not believe in fair. A total mockery of the Armada emblem of honor.

They circled. That is, Ellis circled. Gable stood rooted to the floor. This was going to be target practice.

Ellis feinted, jabbed. Then he got off two quick punches with a kick behind them. Gable barely moved but also didn't seem to have taken any damage.

Ellis circled again, looking for an opening. Gable remained stationary.

Kirkman's good eye watered, blurring her vision. They seem to have drifted away. Of course. Gable wasn't a sitting duck. He was letting Ellis do most of the moving, but he kept changing his position with small back steps and lateral shifts. Slowly but surely, he was leading Ellis away from her and Kevin.

Ellis began launching spinning attacks—three- and four-punch combos with kicks targeting everything from Gable's calves to his head.

Suddenly, he stopped. He'd figured out what Gable had been doing to him. So he just stopped and backed away. Kirkman watched his bristly head turn to glare at her. Then he seemingly ignored Gable and came towards her.

Gable followed. As he came up behind him, Ellis launched a heavy back kick that nearly connected. Gable slid past Ellis and positioned himself between him and Kirkman. This wasn't good. Gable wouldn't just be protecting himself anymore; he'd be worried about two others now. That's why he'd been leading Ellis across the dojo in the first place.

Now the fight was going where Ellis wanted it. He moved to his left and stepped forward. Gable walked straight into a front kick that thudded against his chest. He stumbled back a couple of steps and regrouped, keeping himself between Ellis and the two helpless souls behind him.

Kirkman couldn't keep cranking her neck at that weird angle any longer. She dropped her head and looked away from the combatants. That's when she saw it about six feet away from her on the dojo floor. Ellis's gimlet. So close she could practically feel it in her hands. She strained against her bindings. It might as well be a million miles away.

She cranked her neck again and saw Ellis throw two quick strikes. Then he shot in for a takedown. Gable pivoted into a throw and slammed him to the dojo floor. That gave Kirkman a surge of hope. She worked her wrists and ankles, hoping to loosen something. Anything.

The slam shook Ellis up but mostly pissed him off. He was up again, charging Gable like a mad bull. Gable slid out of harm's way and circled, luring Ellis away from Kirkman.

Kirkman kept working and twisting but only succeeded in scraping skin off her wrists and ankles. Then it hit her out of nowhere. Kevin's stretcher was locked into place because the emergency wheels had been engaged. How had she not remembered this was an *air* stretcher? It hovered, maneuvered, and obeyed voice commands, provided it had access to at least a hawker's computing power. And now that the warship's computer was back online…

The stretcher had two sets of wheels, front and back; each wheel set consisted of a metal frame with a crosspiece at the bottom that functioned as an axle. Ellis had tethered her just above each axle—naturally. However, if the stretcher was detached, there'd be nothing preventing her from sliding her tightly bound wrists and ankles free. Well, except for the length of the frame and her awkward position on the floor. Not to mention Ellis catching her in the act.

Then another idea.

"Invoke voice commands. Authorization: alpha zeta six ten. Field Medic Kirkman."

A green light on the stretcher flashed acknowledgment as well as the tiny ping on her micro-comm. That worked. She doubted the next part of her plan would.

"Decrease height to eight inches," she said.

This was one of those things that ought to work, in theory, though she'd never had reason to try it before. Like ever. Hell, she'd had to hunt down those damn wheels in the first place.

Smooth as silk, the wheel frames decreased their height, lowering the stretcher down to her level. She could almost feel Kevin's frail body inches from her back.

She saw Gable glance over at her. He intentionally ate a kick to the ribs and retreated backwards. He was keeping Ellis focused solely on him, and, more important, oblivious to Kirkman and what she was doing.

Nothing left for her to do but issue the final command. "Detach and hover."

The stretcher detached from its wheels and hovered three feet above the floor. Kirkman slipped her bindings over the top of the now ridiculously short wheel frame and wiggled away. From there, it got hard. Her face was broken, her balance way off. If she could somehow get her feet through those bindings that pinned her arms behind her back, she'd have options.

Meanwhile, Gable kept retreating as Ellis bulled his way forward, way over-aggressive. Gable's foot smacked against his face with a fading roundhouse kick. That got his attention. And really pissed him off. He had absolute tunnel vision, a single-minded determination to pound Gable out of existence.

Kirkman lay on her left side. Bringing her right knee up to her chest, she tried to get her right foot between her wrists. No dice. The toe of her boot wouldn't clear the bindings. She balled herself up tighter and tried to make her arms stretch as long as possible. This time her leg popped through.

She rolled to her other side to work her other leg through. Her left leg went through easier than her right. Her face still throbbed, and she'd left a puddle of sweat on the floor. But her bound wrists were in front of her now.

Ellis had used polymer restraints and overtightened them. She saw to her dismay that her fingernails were turning blue.

Well, payback was coming. Her wrists and ankles were restrained, but she could worm-crawl over to the gimlet by planting her hands in front of her and sliding forwards on her knees.

Six feet of floor to traverse. Another worm-slide forward. Now four.

Across the dojo, Gable had his back up against the wall. Ellis started taking angles; firing crisp punches and elbows, he was using lateral movement to prevent his opponent from moving side-to-side.

Kirkman's hands were numb; her wrists and ankles were bleeding. Tears streamed down her face, creating the strange taste in her mouth of blood seasoned with salt. She made it to her hands and knees and wormed forward once again. Two feet now.

Ellis clipped Gable in the jaw, knocking him sideways.

Sensing victory, he followed up with several meaningful blows. He put his whole body into every strike, not caring where, or if, they landed. They were all going to hurt.

Gable countered with a leg sweep that dumped Ellis on his side. Then he sagged against the wall in exhaustion. Ellis kicked upwards and caught him square in the nuts. Gable dropped like a stone.

Kirkman wormed again.

Got it!

Holding the gimlet with her wrists bound wasn't easy. Making it up to her knees and facing Ellis was even harder. But she did it. She wasn't a crack shot, but she could still light up his world. No problem. The tables had turned.

She shouted at Ellis to get his attention. "Hey, asshole!"

Ellis backed away from Gable and looked at her.

"Get the hell out of here," she said.

Ellis just looked at her and smiled.

"Final warning," Kirkman said. "I've got this thing set on high. Don't think I won't burn a hole through your thick skull."

Ellis started laughing. Way too hard. He was just way too sure about something.

CHAPTER 82

Kevin's virtual environment was an autonomous pocket that had formed around him when his mind got uploaded. That's why he had to focus his attack on the firewall itself. If he created another worm to just eat everything in its path, he would also wreak havoc on this world he had to occupy—a lot like warring factions who destroy their planet and then have nowhere to go.

But he needed system resources for the job at hand. One by one, he turned off sensory inputs and harnessed their cycles into a payload. Needles and bark vanished from the tall trees, leaving naked trunks of branching emptiness. The stream evaporated, and the embankment started to fade.

A bolt of panic shook Kevin to his very core. For several seconds, he was in too much shock to even think. Falling into a deep abyss would have been way less stressful; plunging to one's death at least would have been a reality that his mind could grasp. But every real world thing just vanishing... He couldn't function.

He tried reminding himself that he was the creator of this world, that he was dismantling it one piece at a time for a specific purpose. No good. Every time a tree or even a blade of grass vanished, his breath caught in his throat. Again, irrational and ridiculous. But what was he going to do when it came time to delete the sky and earth?

Kevin restored some vegetation. Allowed a small trickle of water in the stream bed. Proved to himself that he could back out of this any time he wanted.

And that was no help—why?

After all, he was in no physical danger. He didn't *have* to breathe.

Simply existing in another state, as in transforming one object into another, was no big deal. Anybody who'd ever written computer instructions knew that. So why was he losing his shit over this? He had no need for a physical presence in here. In fact, this whole illusion of a physical world was really just extraneous bullshit.

Or was it?

After all, he was losing his shit at the sight of even a rock or a weed vanishing. During the transfer from his organic brain to here—*here* as in storage and memory on the ship's computer, not *here* as in a real location with sights, sounds, and smells—his subconscious had constructed this environment to buoy his sanity and prevent him from slipping into psychosis. He was no expert on the inner workings of the mind, but it seemed that he needed this simulation of physical stimuli to keep the cheese from falling off his cracker.

That was his dilemma. How to launch an attack when all of his computing resources were needed to prop up this virtual world?

He recalled a techno maxim he'd embraced during his formative years.

Less is more.

Effective can be ugly.

Simple beats elegant.

Thing is, he could think of no solution, simple or complicated. *Okay,* he told himself. *Assume nothing is impossible. Go with that.*

Nope. He couldn't do it. He might as well be cutting off his oxygen supply.

Fuck that. He'd save that defeatist outlook for the realm of physical prowess. But in the technical arena, he solved the unsolvable; that's what he did.

Simple beats elegant.

Less is more.

He could cache a dim, grainy copy of this environment. Make it a dark night with no moon or stars to illuminate his surroundings. That would eliminate a ton of details. He'd only need to see vague tree shapes and hear an occasional chirp or rustle nearby. He'd also need the sensation of solid ground under his feet. But he'd only have to provide a tiny area for that. The dark outline of the cabin would be a good final touch.

Finally, this copied image would be a single point in time. Not like his current environment where all of the sights, sounds, and feelings were a continuous flow of stimuli. He'd store the copy in a barren area that had been eaten away by the yuck blob.

He would then channel all available resources into his brute force attack, while he occupied the virtual alcove he'd created.

Sounded good in theory. And he could make it work from a technical standpoint. The wild card—the weak link—in this plan was Kevin himself. Could he keep his shit together throughout the process?

Tonya's voice echoed in his head. *You've got this.*

He recalled the touch of her hand, the brush of her lips against his. And how he'd gotten screwed on that deal. Back then, he'd been stealing a ship. Now he faced the prospect of literally having to lose and reclaim his mind.

You've got this.

Probably not. But he wasn't going to let that stop him.

CHAPTER 83

Pure exhaustion.

After reaching under the seat and pulling the ejector lever that sent Emerson flying from the hawker, Captain Kalie Arnold wanted to curl up on the cockpit floor and fall asleep. Taking a deep breath, gathering up every ounce of willpower she could muster, she rolled onto her stomach and tried to stand. A fresh explosion of pain greeted her. She'd forgotten about her injured left shoulder. It seemed determined to scream at her for any movement, whether it was directly involved or not.

She let out a loud string of curses at the top of her lungs. Nobody was there to hear her, and she didn't care if they did at this point. It didn't seem fair that after weathering a maelstrom of adversity, she still had to get her ass out of a burning hangar. And Fike. Hell, she'd almost forgotten about him too. That's what happened when you reached the end of your endurance.

No. Not to an Armada captain.

We are the Armada.

Always prepared to fight.

No pain. No exhaustion. No weak moments. That's what the Armada was all about. Of course, they were flesh and blood humans with physical and mental limitations. But being an Armada warrior meant becoming more than that.

She made it to her knees. Then, gathering herself, she stood up using only her legs and hips. The next part was going to be fun: getting out of a hawker that was leaning against a wall at a weird angle.

Arnold grabbed the lip of the cockpit with her right hand and swung herself over, trying to press her legs against the hull of the ship to slow her descent. When she felt her arm pulling away from her torso and her fingers straining to maintain their tenuous grip, it was time to let go.

It was an eight-foot drop to the unforgiving steel floor. She landed on her injured left side. By design. To ensure her right side remained functional. Right on her damn shoulder! The sweltering heat rose from the floor in shimmering grandeur, carrying her with it, leaving her body behind.

That's when Arnold lost consciousness.

———

"Captain! Captain Arnold. Can you hear me?"

The voice came from far away, barely loud enough to be an annoyance.

She was standing in front of three figures in black robes with gold Armada emblems; they sat on elevated thrones; she was trying to explain why her black dress boots weren't buffed to a mirrored shine. Stupid and crazy, because the Armada didn't have boots that were black or shiny.

"Captain…"

That damn voice again. She was trying to gather her thoughts, but it wouldn't leave her alone. Looking down, she noticed that she was barefoot on a glowing white carpet.

Then that voice again. Close and loud this time.

"Captain Arnold."

She snapped awake and found herself laid out on a hot metal surface. Right. The floor of the hangar.

"Captain. Please acknowledge."

Jarrett's voice filled her head. No. Her helmet. He was communicating through mainstream channels, not her micro-comm.

"Arnold here." Her mouth was fuzzy, her voice groggy.

"Captain! Are you alright?"

She willed herself to a sitting position, mentally subduing the weak part of herself that wanted to go back to sleep. "Status report," she said. "And keep it brief."

She listened to Jarrett as she struggled to her feet and ignored everything around her swooning out of focus. He quickly summarized Rison's coup attempt and lockdown of the ship's communications. That woke her all the way up.

"We've regained control," Jarrett said. "The techs ran a brilliant bluff, and Whitehead caved. He granted them access, and they took it from there. The bridge can't transmit anything anywhere now."

"What about the ship's controls?" Arnold asked.

"They're totally locked out."

That was something. It was good to know that Rison couldn't fly the ship into a hostile sector and try to sell them out. But sending a team to blast their way onto the bridge was a messy proposition, however tempting.

"How about *our* transmissions?"

"All good."

"Patch me through to a shipwide communication," Arnold said. "Make sure they can hear me on the bridge, but keep them muted."

It took a few seconds. Meanwhile, she got her bearings. She was about thirty yards from where she left Fike—plus twenty more yards to get him out of here. The conditions in this place coupled with her own pain and fatigue would turn those yards into miles.

"Ready when you are, Captain," Jarrett said.

She spoke with authority, knowing her voice was being transmitted throughout the ship. "This is Captain Arnold. Ignore all previous communications from the bridge. Commander Rison and his co-conspirators will be placed under arrest." That would panic him and others she didn't yet know about. Whoever tried to make a break was probably guilty.

"To that end, Emerson is dead." Now they'd know their man had failed to stop her. "I'm returning to mid ship with a wounded crew member." Assuming she made it out of here, but nobody outside of a few trusted allies needed to know her location or her current compromised position.

"In the meantime, I'll be conveying further orders through Jarrett. Consider his direction as coming straight from me. That is all."

She ended the transmission and renewed her grip on her own lucidity.

"Should I send help?" Jarrett asked.

"What for? I'm good. We're in the rover, loaded up and ready to head back."

Yeah, she was lying through her teeth, but the truth about her situation could be tortured out of Jarrett, hard and tough as he was. Better for him to believe the lie.

"Send a full squad to contain the area around the bridge. My guess is that the rats will run right into them. Also tell the crew to give full cooperation to the techs. Anything they need, anywhere they need it. With the exception of William Whitehead; arrest him too."

"Acknowledged, Captain. It's an honor to be at your service."

He didn't sound confident of her safe return, but he knew better than to question anything she told him.

"We've got work to do," she said. "Arnold out."

Squinting through the hazy heat waves, she realized she'd

told the truth about Emerson being dead and gone. The ejection seat was designed to catapult a distressed pilot out into space, *out* being a safe distance from a ship that might explode. She'd spotted part of Emerson on the floor behind the capsized hawker.

She only hoped that this place wouldn't become her tomb as well.

CHAPTER 84

So focused was Kevin on the task at hand and the problem that it presented that he paid no attention to the distant firewall that he was preparing to attack. Consequently, he had no idea that William Whitehead had disabled it in a panic, that it no longer existed.

Reformatting a yuck blob-ravaged area to store his backup took longer than Kevin anticipated. After all, ravaged meant totally decimated. A wasteland of useless garbage, no good for anything. So he had to overwrite all of that with a qubit pattern of initialized values to create consumable computing space. A tedious process.

Long enough and tedious enough to prompt another decision. Already, he was caching a dim, grainy copy of his environment on a dark night with very limited detail. He would also create it barely large enough to contain himself. Which meant he'd have to be careful when entering. One move in any direction and he'd be back out in the wild and in danger of losing his mind. But if he remained perfectly still, he could focus on the night and the shadows and the solid ground beneath his feet and anchor himself. At least he hoped it would be that way.

After a lengthy period of intense concentration, he spawned a process to carve out a space to accommodate his body area, plus a fraction of a percentage point. That, in itself, was no small task. But that was the easy part. Next came the part he'd been dreading: occupying that space for the first time. It seemed to Kevin that he was about to be buried alive.

He was in the computer room in his cabin, immersed in a glowing swirl of data clouds and memory clusters. Taking a deep breath to psych himself up, he replayed Tonya's words in his head. *You've got this.* Not really. But what the hell—

All of this being a virtual world within a computer, Kevin spawned the job that would create a memory pointer to himself. His Kevin pointer. Taking another deep breath, he could feel his heart pounding in his chest and couldn't help wondering if that would be the case in a few seconds. Then he shifted his Kevin pointer into his newly created alcove.

Big mistake! He wanted to run. To scream. To melt away into a hot flailing mess. He would have wet his pants, maybe shit himself, if his pants actually existed.

Wait…

He was fine. This was all just a shift from one memory address to another. Not like the physical world where location (as in the bottom of an ocean or the eye of a storm) mattered a lot. Kevin calmed down a little. He could see shadowy suggestions of surrounding landscape and forget they didn't really exist. He could feel solid earth under his feet despite the fact that he didn't dare move. And yes, he could feel the flutter of a heartbeat as he willed himself to breathe. He *could* do this…

Flipping back to the computer room, he added a viewport to his alcove so that he could monitor outside activity. Then he began pounding out the program to transition his virtual world into processing power—all to attack a firewall that wasn't there anymore. Then again, he had instructed his program to spearhead a brute force attack on anything standing in its way.

CHAPTER 85

Her bound wrists were killing her. But Kirkman held the gimlet at eye level. She was on her knees with her ankles bound as well. Facing the enemy. Ellis. A swine in human skin. Despite all she'd endured—getting knocked out, getting tied up, not to mention everything he'd done to Gable and Kevin—she didn't want to kill him if she didn't have to.

Maybe that's why he was walking towards her with that shit-eating grin on his face. He could probably sniff out weakness as if it emitted an actual smell. And she *was* scared. No question about that. But she wasn't paralyzed or frozen. Much as she didn't want to kill anybody in cold blood, she'd damn sure do it.

"I mean it," she said. "I'm giving you a chance to walk out of here. Stay and you're dead."

Ellis just laughed like he thought it was funny as hell.

Then he came forward.

Kirkman was about to give him one final warning but decided against it. She knew she was going to have to blast him, like it or not.

Just then, a communications broadcast filled the dojo. *This is Captain Arnold. Ignore all previous communications from the bridge.*

Commander Rison and his co-conspirators will be placed under arrest...

Neither she nor Ellis moved. They just listened. But the captain's words seemed to revive Gable; he got back on his feet and squatted a couple of times to loosen himself up.

When the broadcast ended, Kirkman tried again. "It's over," she said. "Captain Arnold's in total control. Leave now and we won't report any of this. We'll let it go."

"There's another way to look at it," Ellis said. "I've got a short window of opportunity here for fun and games with three of my favorite people."

He strode towards her, not worried in the least. Just way too sure of himself under the circumstances. Did he really think she wouldn't shoot?

"You haven't got the nerve," he said.

Apparently so.

Kirkman fired, and...

Nothing.

She stared at the gimlet in disbelief. It was set to full power, no safety engaged. She fired again and again as Ellis kept right on coming. "Do you think I'd leave an enabled weapon lying around?" He smirked. With a roundhouse kick, he sent the gimlet flying from her hands. Then he stood over her, reveling in her helplessness.

What he didn't see was Gable coming up behind him. Kirkman decided to keep him distracted. "Go ahead," she said. "Hit me. That's the only thing a fake man like you can make me feel."

Ellis drew back to do just that, and Gable shouted at him. Dammit! He should have let her take that blow and then another. Whatever it took to ambush Ellis from behind. But no. His overwrought sense of honor and duty had just fucked things up royally.

Kirkman didn't care anymore. The moment Ellis turned to

look, she drove her bound fists up into his groin. Her blow struck home, not with as much authority as she would have liked, but solidly enough to buckle his knees. Then Gable stepped forward and knocked him down.

Oh my God, Kirkman thought. They had done it. They had won. She hoped Gable would pound him into oblivion, till he wound up more damaged than Kevin, but he would probably be content with just restraining him.

Ellis rolled onto his back, looking dazed and defeated.

No! He had the look of someone moving on to Plan B.

Reaching into his right boot, he pulled out a short-distance zapper. Unlike a gimlet, it wouldn't turn flesh and bone to ash, but…

He hit Gable with a burst that lasted several seconds till he lay twitching on the floor. "He was getting a bit too feisty," he said. Then he stood up and leered at Kirkman.

"You're a piece of shit," she said.

Ellis gave her a quick zap, just to hear her gasp, to see her writhe in pain. "This is going to be fun," he said.

CHAPTER 86

Captain Arnold made her way across the hangar, trudging across the hot floor, weaving her way through the burning wreckage. Her legs were blown up with fatigue to the point of failure; it was as if she'd been cast in stone. Her left arm hung useless from her screaming shoulder. She wanted to rip it out and hurl it far away.

Just getting herself out of here was going to be a challenge. Rescuing Fike increased the odds. And the risk. A chance she couldn't afford to take. She was ship's captain. She had to deal with an infiltration of backstabbing officers that couldn't be trusted. She *had* to make it out of here.

"Fike! Can you hear me?"

No response. Getting over to Fike was a detour; a straight line to the hangar door would be a shorter trek. Any response from him (or lack thereof) would make for an easier decision.

"Fike. Just groan if you're awake."

She stood and listened, then she headed towards Fike instead of the door. He hadn't moved. He was right where she'd left him behind an obliterated ship. Of course, he hadn't moved. But he had the look of somebody who was never going to move again.

"Captain."

"Fike!"

But it wasn't Fike. "Jarrett here, Captain. You were trying to call Fike through the main communications channel."

Shit! She'd been in here way too long; she'd meant to use her micro-comm.

That meant…

"Your transmission came straight to me," Jarrett said.

That was something. Her desperate call to Fike was one transmission she did *not* want broadcast to the world.

"I've got to get him out of here," she said.

"If he's wearing his suit and the transmitter in his helmet's attached to the main computer, we can check his vitals."

"Do it."

She made her way over to Fike's prone body. This time she made it a point to address him via micro-comm. "You don't have to talk, Fike. Just breathe for me."

Nothing. Dead silence. Yeah, dead.

"No vital signs, Captain," Jarrett said. "No pulse. No breathing. Fike's dead."

"His suit's malfunctioning," Arnold said, knowing she was full of shit.

"Possibly," Jarrett said. But she knew he meant, *highly unlikely.*

Arnold ended the transmission.

Time to move. She couldn't stand here staring at Fike and willing her aching, exhausted body into action. Part of the ceiling fell crashing to the floor in a molten plume of fire. Pellets of hot shrapnel were raining down everywhere she looked.

Arnold squatted and flung Fike over her good shoulder. Standing up felt harder than hitting her five-hundred-pound max in the gymnasium. She took a couple of steps forward, then stopped to regain her balance. Right then, another chunk of ceiling crashed down right in front of her.

Running as hard as she could, Arnold teetered and tottered her way across the hangar. No need for caution or prudence at this point. Only one massive all-out effort. Everything went white. Her scream was so loud and painful that she couldn't tell if it came from her mouth or from her tortured mind.

Shifting Fike on her shoulder, ignoring her own ragged breathing, blocking out the burning in her legs, she launched herself forward. The hangar door wavered in front of her, a blurry portal—might as well have been a cosmic juncture— into literally another world. And all the while, she kept her legs churning till she made it through.

She slammed her glove against the touchpad with Fike still on her shoulder. The hangar doors closed. Then, gently as possible, she dropped to her knees and deposited Fike on the floor. Removing his helmet and stripping off her gloves, she touched his neck with her bare fingers, searching for any sign of a pulse.

She ripped off her own helmet and leaned over him. Undid his suit. Put her ear against his chest. Fike was dead. His transmitter hadn't malfunctioned.

CHAPTER 87

KEVIN WORKED WITH A SINGLE-MINDED FOCUS. He no longer had to immerse himself in the system because he was, in fact, part of the system now. Sometime in the future, he might actually take over and *become* the system. But for now, he needed his alcove and his connection to his lifelong concept of physical self.

His approach was simple. Facing a locked door, he was trying trillions and trillions of simultaneous keys. Getting there required trillions of asynchronous processes (had to start somewhere) propagating themselves ad infinitum until their objective was achieved.

Each completed process would emit a tiny blue flash for a fraction of an instant. The result would be a steady blue beam that would enable Kevin to visually track forward progress.

Channeling all available resources, retiring to his alcove, he kicked off his startup script. The cabin, the woods, the sky above and the ground below vanished instantly. So quickly that their sudden disappearance made him queasy. He closed his eyes and focused on his immediate surroundings, putting aside the fact that he was in a coffin-sized space. Coffin! There was that word again.

Kevin's plan all along had been to destroy the firewall and establish new borders for his domain. What he didn't know was the firewall had been disabled. What he'd failed to take into account was the effect of his trillionfold process payload running unabated; it was like a battering ram smashing into a door that flew open right before impact.

His world, his entire system, rushed outward, too blindingly fast for comprehension. Any secured asset—as in anything at all, from personal device signons to bridge controls—were unlocked and disabled in an instant. And completed jobs were followed by wave upon wave of spawned processes looking for something else to attack.

That driving force, like a hurricane roaring through a wind tunnel, ripped through Kevin's alcove and carried him with it. He made a desperate grab for whatever he could latch on to— same as a non-swimmer in deep water grabbing for anything, anything at all, to keep from drowning.

Just a grab.

Not with his mind or his hands, but with his whole being.

A grab.

———

Bam! Just like that. Kevin found himself in the dojo.

Not standing on the floor, but looking down from above.

He had to be hallucinating. That was the only explanation. He could see the entire floor, which was large enough to be divided into multiple rings. He could see the weapon racks against the far wall (that didn't look so far right now) and the Armada coat of arms overlooking it all. Too much to take in all at once unless you grew eyes on top of your skull and in the back of your head. Yet he was seeing it all at the same time without having to look around, so it couldn't be real.

There were people down there. When he focused on them,

they suddenly enlarged before his eyes. There was that medic with the dark eyes and brown hair. Her face was bruised; blood dripped from a split lip. Ellis was standing over her, grinning. A walking, talking hemorrhoid, and that was doing him way too much justice. The sight of him both enraged and terrified Kevin.

This was no dream or hallucination; this was as real as it got. Maybe those gods the elders from his village babbled about were real after all. He was paying the ultimate penance. He'd somehow become a spectator in this grotesque torture show.

Really? He wasn't trapped in some purgatory or underworld. Gods didn't make it thunder or hurl lightning bolts across the sky. There was a reason behind all of this…

He went back to the last thing he remembered. He'd kicked off his startup script, the program had launched itself at the distant firewall.

Then…there'd been a sudden pull…

Ellis leaned over Kirkman and cut the bindings off her feet. She jumped up and tried to run. Ellis tripped her.

Kevin saw it all, up close and personal. His vision had zoomed him in close enough to practically taste Kirkman's fear. Ellis pulled her to a standing position and started working on getting her pants off while she kicked and flailed. Meanwhile, the male doctor, Gable, lay twitching on the floor.

"Stop it!" Kevin yelled. "Leave her alone!"

Somehow, his voice reverberated through the dojo, so loud it was scary. It startled the hell out of them too. Ellis stopped what he was doing and looked around. Then he sneered and went at Kirkman again.

"I SAID LEAVE HER ALONE!" Once again, Kevin was deafening, but that just thrilled Ellis, who threw back his head and laughed. Then he knocked Kirkman down and straddled her.

Kevin lunged. Forgetting he was a mere spectator, totally consumed by hatred and rage, blindly determined to take out Ellis, regardless of how impossible that might be, he launched himself at that slimy, piece-of-shit, lowlife maggot. A laser beam burned through Ellis at a downward angle.

Ellis stopped what he was doing and stared up at the ceiling in disbelief. There was a round hole, well over a foot in diameter, where his torso used to be. He fell on his side in a crumpled heap.

And a jolt of reality shot through Kevin. He'd done that. The booming voice. The deadly laser beam. All of it.

The dojo was equipped with a sound system and also lasers and force fields to spice up the competition. Of course, they were only equipped to stun and sting, not fry you like a bug on a red-hot skewer. But with a mere thought, he'd been able to marshal all of them into one powerful payload.

He watched Kirkman look around, understandably freaked out by what had just happened. The first thing she did was drop to her knees next to Gable and start checking on him. Then Kevin recognized himself on the stretcher. He couldn't scream. But a gasping noise hissed through the dojo, loud enough to make Kirkman look up.

And a bigger hole than the one he'd just put in Ellis burned out his sanity. The alcove was gone. He had no arms, no limbs, no body at all. His eyes were the dojo's camera, his voice the sound system. He wasn't Kevin anymore. He'd become…a block of machine instructions twisting into nothingness.

He went numb with panic and fear, a complete meltdown, like someone terrified of heights suddenly realizing they're thousands of feet above the ground. Just a hot mess of spilled stability spewing everywhere at once.

For a brief instant, in the split second before he totally lost his shit, Kevin saw himself sit up on the stretcher. The entire front of his skull was ablaze with flashing lights.

CHAPTER 88

Vincent had made himself comfortable in the cockpit of the harrier. Whitehead's firewall was down; the system was unlocked. All that remained was to monitor the current status and remediate any ongoing issues. They could begin the rebuild and repair process once the current crisis was completely averted. All of this assumed that they'd remain on the warship *Touchstone* to be the ones to do it.

Sure as shit, as soon as he started to relax and unwind a little, Vincent got pinged on his device and saw that it was coming from the ship's computer room. The ping came through an encrypted portal that took him several combinations of decoding to open. It was Norman, a salty old techie who'd been around longer than anyone else. Jaded and cynical, Norman had always preferred watching a system work to trying anything new.

"Are you somewhere private where we can talk without anyone overhearing?" Norman said.

Vincent informed the pilot that he needed the ship to himself and asked that everybody onboard was cleared out in short order. Following the arrests and the captain's mandate of full cooperation with the techs, the same pilot who'd threatened to thump his skull suddenly couldn't do enough for him.

"What's going on?" Vincent said.

"Everything's wide open now," Norman said. His voice had that accusing undertone he had when anyone dared touch anything considered to be tried and true and thereby exempt from potential improvement.

"Okay…"

"You know that firewall Whitehead put up," Norman said. "Well, after you and Jade conned him into disabling it, everything's unlocked now."

"Everything, as in…"

"Everything," Norman said. "Every restricted access point, communications channel, you name it. Walk up to any door and open it. Try to read any classified data, you're in."

Vincent felt new crisis-related stress ratcheting his nerve endings tight enough to hurt his back. Then he settled into the pilot's chair he occupied and reminded himself to take a couple of deep breaths before responding. As usual, Norman made it sound like his fellow techs had been throwing stones in a roomful of china and breaking everything in sight. But hey, there *had* been a rampant virus destroying everything in its path. Hello! The yuck blob. Remember that? Still, engaging Norman in a pissing contest wasn't the answer.

"Any idea how it happened?" Vincent asked.

"Probably all those maverick processes you guys have been throwing at the system from every direction," Norman said.

Vincent almost shut down the communication right there. Screw it. They'd stopped the yuck blob. They'd gotten Whitehead out of the way. They'd done their part. Why put up with this crap? He could just lean back and take a nap, or even retire to his bunk for some serious sleep.

Taking a deep breath, he tried another tack. "How did you find out about it?" he said.

"All changes to security get logged," Norman said. "You should know that. Anyhow, I'm notified whenever there's questionable activity. And my message queue was flooded. That's how I know."

Indeed. Norman was a guy who liked to watch a system work. And he wasn't done.

"We need to lock everything down," Norman said. "As in everything. This is a major breach."

"Not possible," Vincent said. Meanwhile, he pinged Jarrett and invited him to join their channel via an invite he made sure was unencrypted.

"I wasn't asking," Norman said. "Soon as we're done here, I'm flipping every kill switch in the system. Nobody does anything without going through channels."

"Why the hell did you contact me then, if you've already made up your mind?"

"To let you know that shit you're running is making a mess," Norman said.

Vincent sighed. For one thing, their yuck blob-fighting activities and their related processes had ceased. For another, none of what they'd been doing had anything to do with security rights. But try explaining that to Norman. Hardheadedness had always been a problem in the tech arena. All due to little to no leadership. Sure, there were technologist grades. But none of that carried the same authority that captains or commanders had over their crew. So control or perceived authority usually went to aggressively outspoken people like William Whitehead, who had a way of taking the air out of a room.

"Look, Norman. Thank you for reporting the issue. It was an awesome find. But we have to have core functionality in place. Communications, weapons systems, launch codes, environmental controls. There are tons of vital processes running that need access to all of that and more. We can't just lock everything down for everybody."

"Just watch me," Norman said.

"Do it, and you'll need surgery to get my boot out of your ass." Jarrett had joined the call. "You know who I am," he said.

"Yes."

"And you heard the captain's orders."

"You don't understand," Norman said. "This is a major breach of security."

"But you don't go and blindly lock down everything," Vincent said. "You start with the critical regions, evaluate necessary functionality, and assign rights and privileges on a case-by-case basis."

"You know how long that'll take!" Norman said.

"Then you'd better get started," Jarrett said. "Put a team on it. But if something critical doesn't work because you locked it down, you'll need surgery to get the captain's boot out of your ass."

Norman dropped off the call. Vincent and Jarrett stayed on to talk further. "How bad?" Jarrett asked.

Vincent explained how everybody had access to everything on the ship's computer. Fortunately, most of the crew had no idea they could go places and control things they couldn't before. Still not good, though.

"Any idea what caused it?" Jarrett asked.

"Not yet," Vincent said.

"You and Jade look into it," Jarrett said. "You two. Nobody else."

"At least we won't have an issue with permissions," Vincent said.

"Real funny," Jarrett said. "Keep me informed. Actually, don't. Just do what you have to do based on what you find."

CHAPTER 89

JADE AND VINCENT left the rear hangar and reconvened to one of several nearby transmission rooms. The room wasn't large, only about twelve-by-fifteen feet, but they could sit comfortably and brainstorm in private. Because transmissions room consoles were extensions of the ship's main computer, the equipment would have been useless for yuck blob fighting. But for tracking down this new security-unlocking gremlin, they were way better off in there than sitting in separate harrier cockpits, talking at a distance.

There were no outgoing or incoming transmissions happening, so the lighted wall panels above the console flashed an occasional orange and yellow status code to indicate a ready state. In a battle situation, those same panels would be lit up in a multicolored array of code and route indicators. Seeing those panels reminded Vincent that he'd attempted to send a direct beacon to the warship *Juggernaut* on Captain Arnold's behalf. Nothing had come of it. So the transmission had failed or the *Juggernaut* wasn't in this sector after all. That seemed like a really long time ago now. And was totally irrelevant at this point.

Vincent found himself staring at the winking lights and

relaxing in his chair until his eyelids grew heavy. He only shut his eyes for half a minute—would have staked his life on it—but when he opened them, an hour had passed, and Jade was hunched over a console, hard at work.

She never saw him wake up; he could just go back to sleep and she'd never know the difference. It was a pleasing prospect, despite the hot flash of shame rushing through him.

"Hey, sorry. I nodded off," he said.

"You probably needed it," Jade said. "I took a nap while you were bluffing Whitehead earlier."

"Find anything interesting while I was in La-La Land?"

"Nothing at first," Jade said. "We already knew that Whitehead panicked and turned off his firewall. And very shortly after that, all of the security locks were blown open. Norman's logs tell us that much. But there were also multiple failed access attempts, as in something or someone entering the wrong credentials over and over."

"Norman never mentioned that," Vincent said. "The second he saw the logs, he came at me, spouting accusations. But wait. Multiple failed attempts? You only get a few tries before you're locked out."

"Not if you hit it with a few hundred million simultaneous combinations before the lockdown algorithm can react," Jade said.

"That would take massive resources," Vincent said. "A ridiculous payload. Nothing that big's ever run on any computer."

"But if you combine all available processing power on the ship's computer, even in its damaged state, you could get there," Jade said. "Several times over."

Vincent's right temple started throbbing; he wasn't up for this shit. "Another yuck blob?" he asked. Then he immediately chided himself for his denseness. This attacker had merely unlocked everything…and nothing else.

"Remember that unknown process that we couldn't identify?" Jade said. "It was large and resource-heavy and totally unscathed by the yuck blob. I was using up the last of our resources trying to ping it."

Vincent nodded. He remembered.

"Then the yuck blob just died," Jade said. "And we were pretty damn surprised."

Vincent bit his lower lip. *Things never "just happened" when it came to computing.* And that axiom might well be coming around to bite them in the ass.

"I started probing again," Jade said. "And it's still there. So I went further and found a huge spike in resource usage at the exact moment everything got unlocked. Not surprising in itself. But then, a few minutes later, there was another spike."

"And?"

"Our mystery process just reassembled itself twenty minutes ago," Jade said.

Vincent stood up and paced the small room, rubbing his temples. "Reassembled means disassembled at one point or another," he said.

"I think it launched itself all out at system security, then reassembled," Jade said.

"We can't know that."

"True," Jade said.

Vincent sat down and leaned across the console. "Are there any other avenues we can explore?" he asked. "Maybe it's residual damage from the yuck blob."

"I think we ought to rule this idea out first," Jade said.

"By pinging it?" Vincent said. "That probably won't tell us much."

"By reaching out," Jade said.

"You mean?"

"Direct communication. Same as I would for any crew

member I wanted to talk to. I'm messaging whatever or whoever is in that region."

"But there's no person on the other end," Vincent said.

Jade turned her sharp gaze on him, a mouse sniffing its way around an obstacle. "Probably not," she said.

Vincent paused a moment and considered everything that had happened and everything they knew so far, starting with Slaton's virus, which had started this whole thing.

"Pinging and messaging isn't going to work," he said. "Fire up your avatar. If we're going to try to establish communication, let's pull out all the stops.

CHAPTER 90

THEY TRIED every way they knew. They could detect it, they could feel its impact on the system, but they couldn't interact with this unknown process in any meaningful way. Couldn't access any data. Couldn't ascertain any inputs or outputs. Nor could they find any record that it ever existed. It could well be a virtual wasteland, a byproduct of the yuck blob's mass destruction.

Vincent and Jade tried to move their two avatars right smack in the middle of it. There was no getting through. Through what? They'd reached the edge of something. For all intents and purposes, this mystery region or process or whatever the hell this was did not exist. Yet there it was on system scans—its system impact, anyhow. A lot like seeing a person's shadow right in front of you, but no person anywhere to be seen. A ghost.

"This was a stupid idea," Jade said.

"Not stupid," Vincent said. "Just real unusual."

Normally, avatars were computer personas in games and social interactions. More to the point, they were characters in some type of setting, be it a simulated battlefield or clubhouse. But in this case, Vincent and Jade's avatars were nothing more than talking heads in a white room. No setting or context whatsoever. They had been dropped into an unknown bog of mystery data to try to strike up a conversation with a ghost.

So far, their ghost hadn't responded.

———

Jarrett contacted them.

"There's something you need to see," he said.

"Sure, no problem," Vincent said.

"Might as well," Jade added. "We're not getting anywhere."

Jarrett's stone face had softened into something like a sympathetic expression. "It's camera footage from the dojo," he said. "And it was disturbing to watch for me. You guys will have a hard time dealing with it."

"Couldn't you just describe it?" Jade asked.

"I could. But here's the thing: it's a computer glitch for sure. And Whitehead is blaming it on all your yuck blob fighting. I need someone with technical expertise to observe what's happening. There's a chance you'll see something that the rest of us don't."

"I've got an idea," Vincent said.

"I can handle it," Jade said.

"I know that," Vincent said. "But you've got a better chance of making contact with our ghost out there. It might take a while to recover from this viewing session."

"Count on it," Jarrett said.

Jade responded with a barely perceptible nod. Vincent moved down to a terminal at the end of the row and set up a privacy screen between them—literally that, a foldout partition. "Ready when you are," he said.

Jarrett replayed the minute of dojo video where Ellis got blasted and supplied names of the people involved.

Vincent felt a little giddy. It wasn't the blood and guts he was expecting, even though Kirkman's face was a mess. But the hole blown through Ellis…it was as if he were a pastry and someone used a round cookie cutter on him. In fact, you could drive a rover through the hole where his middle used to be. It was totally gone.

Then he watched Kevin sit up on the stretcher, the front of his skull flashing. Only for a moment, then Kevin flopped back down like a limp rag.

Vincent's palms were itching. No nausea or panic. But he felt himself drifting; he couldn't stop laughing, even though there was nothing funny about what he'd just witnessed.

A pair of small hands took hold of his shoulders. Jade spun him around and slapped him across the face. She didn't have enough power to do any real damage, but she still made his cheek sting enough to snap him out of it.

"Everything okay?" Jarrett asked.

"Let's see the timestamps on that video," Jade said.

Sure, Vincent thought, almost giggling. *That'd be good.*

They went back to the starting point. "That's the exact same time the entire system got unlocked," Jade said.

"Any correlation between the two events?" Jarrett asked.

"Well, there's no question that William Whitehead's full of shit," Jade said.

That made Vincent cover his mouth with both hands to suppress his giggling.

"We'll need to go back through the video and check exact timing," Jade said.

"Is Vincent going to be up for it?" Jarrett asked.

"I'm great!" Vincent said. "Excuse me." He sat on the floor and put his head between his knees.

"I'll send medics," Jarrett said.

"I think he's okay," Jade said. "You good, Vincent?"

"Solid as the hole in a donut," Vincent said. Then he evaporated into gales of laughter.

"He'll be fine," Jade said.

Jarrett sighed and ended the call.

CHAPTER 91

THERE WERE canteens on the rover filled with water. Arnold took a couple of swallows and retched. She was experiencing some serious dehydration. Her body fluids had been steamed out of her, and her strength along with them. She'd been reduced to a bone-dry husk of a human shell.

She splashed a little water on her face—anything to cool down a little. A headache had wrapped itself around her face like an angry vise. A little something to take her mind off her injured shoulder. Lifting the canteen to her lips, more challenging than hefting a heavy dumbbell, she forced herself to drink three swallows before falling to her knees and gagging.

Black spots popped across her field of vision. Serious danger signs. Arnold knew she wouldn't be able to function much longer. If she lost consciousness, she'd could die right here outside the hangar door.

Lunging at the rover, she made it to her feet and braced herself against it. She'd laid Fike's dead body across the back seat. Hauling him out of there had sapped the last of her strength. Or perhaps her determination to not leave him behind had pushed her way beyond her natural limits.

There was a medical kit in the rover's rear storage bin stocked with the bare necessities like bandages, antiseptic, tourniquets, splints, and a cache of loaded syringes. There were also intravenous supplies, including bags of glucose and fluids. This was equipment that everyone had been trained on but rarely used. *Very* rarely. Simply because fellow crew members were usually too engaged in heavy combat to play medic.

Using her right hand and her teeth, Arnold tightened a surgical tube around her left forearm and almost passed out. She opened her eyes to those damn black spots accompanied by a rhythmic thrumming in her ears. A sense of vertigo swayed back and forth, just enough to mess with her balance. She had to get this done fast.

She dumped water on her head and wiped her eyes. It woke her up a little. Fewer spots now, at any rate. Then she squinted through her hazy existence and plunged the syringe into her exposed vein. No hesitation. A purposeful jab without a thought of missing.

Everything went blank for a moment. Arnold shook herself awake, saw the syringe firmly planted in her arm, and untied the tubing. No pain. Unbelievably, she'd gotten it right the first time. Now all she had to do was connect a fluid bag to the syringe—easy, if you could overlook the fact that she needed intravenous fluids in the first place.

She looked at Fike. "You would have done this for me," she said. "I'd be lying where you are right now, getting hydrated, and you'd be driving us back." She grabbed a plastic line and two fluid bags, then dragged herself up into the driver's seat. "I wish I could hook you up to something to make things better," she said. She probably would have cried, only she was too dried up to shed a tear.

One last surge…

Arnold stood up and tied a fluid bag around a metal tab that she'd spotted on the laser cannon; she sank to the floor, hooked up her syringe, closed her eyes for a moment…

Jarrett's voice woke her up. *He's been doing that a lot lately,* she thought. *He really ought to let me sleep in every once in a while.*

Her eyes fluttered open. The fluid bag hung empty above her. She'd been out for a while.

"Jarrett…" she said. Her tongue felt thick and awkward.

"Are you still parked at the front hangar?" Jarrett asked.

"Ugh! I think so. Yes. Hell yes. Hang on…"

Arnold sat up and realized the vise around her face had subsided to a mere screaming headache. That meant the pain in her shoulder could compete for her full attention now. Her throat was bone dry. But she also felt a little thirsty. That was a really good sign.

"Are you injured?" Jarrett asked.

"Sit tight a little longer and I'll tell you," she said.

Pulling herself upright, Arnold swapped out the fluid bag. "I think I might live," she said.

"I'm just trying to confirm…" Jarrett said. "The computer's still questionable. So I wasn't sure if your reported location was right."

"It's right," Arnold said. "I'm right here. Haven't moved an inch."

"I've sent a team to escort you back," Jarrett said.

"Of course you have," Arnold said. "Fike would have done the same thing. Wouldn't you, Fike?"

"What's your condition, Captain?"

"Not good. But I'm working on it."

"Can I update you on a new development?"

"Hit me."

Jarrett started to explain, but his words got muddled. *Dojo… Kirkman… Laser beam… Slaton.*

Slaton! That's all she needed to comprehend.

"Get Kevin Slaton to an infirmary! Keep him alive. If there's a choice between saving him and anybody else, he's the priority."

"Yes, Captain. The rescue...the team should be arriving soon."

"I plan on meeting them halfway," Arnold said.

But after she grabbed the canteen and took a couple of big gulps from it, she decided to close her eyes again. For just a few seconds.

CHAPTER 92

Kirkman woke up. She was flat on her back, staring at a white ceiling, stretched out on a soft, comfortable surface. Confusion swept away every attempt she made at figuring out where she was or how she got here.

She closed her eyes and took a few deep breaths. Another look around the room told her she was in one of the ship's infirmaries. She spotted Gable on a nearby bed. He was sleeping peacefully, as if he'd decided to drift in here and take a nap.

One by one, her scattered memories reassembled themselves. The dojo. That laser cutting through Ellis. Kevin sitting up on his stretcher. She sat up and immediately felt dizzy. But an overwhelming feeling that she needed to do something—right now!—wouldn't let her lie back down.

Sanderson came in and made a beeline for her. Unlike Gable, he'd never been warrior material. He was a good medic, though. It had always amused Kirkman that his goatee was shiny-black to match his slicked-back hair.

"Don't even think about getting up," he said.

"Kevin?"

"No, I'm Sanderson. Now lie down and rest." He took her by

the shoulders and maneuvered her back into a prone position. "I'll use a strong sedative if I have to."

He looked annoyed and distracted, obviously wanting her to be a good patient so he could move on to more important things.

"What's Kevin Slaton's condition?" Kirkman asked.

"What the hell do you think's going on in the next room?" Sanderson snapped. "Captain's orders. He's our top priority. You, Gable, and everyone else in here can feel free to die. But we've got to save Kevin. Hope he's worth it."

He turned to leave, but Kirkman grabbed his sleeve. "Answer my damn question," she said.

"He's critical. Probably won't make it. We're not miracle healers here."

Kirkman sat up again. She could feel her pulse pounding in her temples, and Sanderson seemed far away at the edge of her vision. "I'm going in there."

"No way."

"I can help," she said. "I'm the one who—"

"I know. We all do. You wired his brain with those neural lace transmitters," Sanderson said. "Not that it makes any difference now."

"What happened? You have to tell me!"

"We've got a machine breathing for him," Sanderson said. "Nothing else for us to do. He's just shutting down. It happens. You turned him into a science project and wheeled him all over the ship, but we'll get the blame."

"Sanderson!"

"I've got to get back."

He walked away, and Kirkman followed. It was like walking through mud. "Listen to me. You've got to contact tech services." She almost lost her balance.

Sanderson kept walking, the back of his neck bristling in disdain.

Then, in one fluid motion, Gable jumped off his stretcher and positioned himself in front of Sanderson. "Listen to her," he said. "I'm not asking."

"Tell tech services about the neural lace across Kevin's brain," Kirkman said. "We think he might have connected to the ship's computer."

"That's the most absurd—"

"Do it or else," Gable said.

Sanderson stared at him, slack-jawed. Gable never talked that way to anybody in the infirmary. "Or else what?" he said.

"If Captain Arnold doesn't bust your ass, I will," Gable said. "Do it."

Sanderson left.

Kirkman leaned against her stretcher, totally exhausted. She looked over at Gable and smiled. "Didn't know you had it in you," she said.

"Shut up."

Kirkman stretched out on her back, smiling at the ceiling.

CHAPTER 93

ONE SURE-FIRE WAY TO snap a tech out of a state of giddiness is to suddenly shift priorities as soon as he's immersed in a project; another is to interrupt him with suggestions on how to solve a problem you know nothing about. Both of those things happened to Vincent.

First Jarrett pinged them about the change in priority. They were to work with a medic named Sanderson. He'd explain. This directive came directly from Captain Arnold.

When Sanderson got patched through, Vincent took the call. Jade was busy trying to track down their ghost (Maybe they did need help.) and he was still trying to get a grip. So it made sense to throw the least useful one of them at what they'd already dubbed Project Stupid. He might as well buy Jade as much time as he could.

The new priority turned out to be yuck blob creator, Kevin Slaton, the guy on the stretcher in the dojo video. Somewhere along the way, his skull had gotten smashed, resulting in the front of his brain being laced with computer circuitry. That's what the light show across the front of his skull was all about.

Kirkman's hope had been that his brain functions could be

monitored, evaluated, even reprogrammed over time by the ship's computer—with lots of tech assistance, of course. Now, however, she was convinced that Kevin had somehow, someway hooked into the system all on his own. And the icing on the cake: Captain Arnold now wanted techs to explore this possibility as a means of saving Kevin Slaton's life, which, at the moment, was hanging by a thread.

Seeing what transpired in the dojo made Vincent giggle till it scared him. He wasn't laughing now. Not one bit. Jade chasing one ghost was bad enough. Now they were mandated to explore this totally inane, absurd, pointless path to nowhere. Not that he dared voice his views on the matter.

Still, he couldn't help trying a tactful protest. "What Kirkman did…it's a great idea. But that's all it is: an idea. I mean, establishing any sort of connection would probably require Slaton to be hot-wired to a computer port. Then translating brain waves into code would require millions upon billions of mappings."

"I know," Sanderson said.

"Something like that doesn't just happen," Vincent said.

"Till it does," Jade said.

Vincent hadn't heard her come over.

Sanderson sighed. "Okay. Where do you want to start?"

"Monitor Kevin," Vincent said. "Let us know if there's a change in his condition."

"What are you going to do on your end?" Sanderson asked.

"I have no idea."

But Jade did. He could see it in her eyes, in the way her face tightened when she focused on something.

"You're not buying that crap about Slaton connecting to the ship's computer, are you?" Vincent asked.

"He sat up," Jade said. "He was unconscious on the stretcher. Then right when the laser beam hollowed out that creepy guy, he sat up. And why would electrodes just light up like that?"

"Just dumb impulses," Vincent said. But a light tickle of doubt was nagging at him now.

"There's no reason for anything to light up—" Jade said.

"Unless there's communication packets being sent and received," Vincent said. "But he couldn't...jacked into the computer while unconscious...no way."

"In a coma, actually," Sanderson said.

Vincent looked at Jade. "Just to fill you in—"

"I heard," she said. "Whatever we can do to save Kevin Slaton's life. That's our priority. Just as well. I wasn't getting anywhere with our ghost."

"Ghost?" Sanderson said.

"Never mind," Vincent said. "There's a process we can't identify. We think it blew open every secured resource on the whole damn ship. That's all."

"Which can't happen," Jade said. "Neither can a laser malfunction in the dojo; the hardware itself has guardrails in place to prevent a thing like that."

Nobody spoke for nearly a minute. The impossible and unthinkable had been happening in rapid succession on a whole slew of physical and computational fronts. *After* the yuck blob! That directive from the captain didn't seem so far-fetched or ridiculous after all.

But where to start?

CHAPTER 94

ARNOLD SENSED IT. Exhaustion and dehydration had pulled her down into a deep sleep. She never heard the hum of approaching rovers. But her senses flared when the first person approached. Out of pure instinct, she kicked upwards as she snapped awake.

"Captain! We're your people."

The pain in her skull had returned. But the warrior lying on the deck was hurting worse. Her kick must have caught him square in the jaw. She rose to help him but lost her balance.

"We'll handle this, Captain."

Arnold recognized the woman's voice. "Wall. Is that you?"

"Yes, Captain."

"You should have the bridge," Arnold said.

A medic approached her. "You need to sit, Captain."

She resisted the urge to strike him. Because he was right. She needed medical attention, whether she wanted it or not.

Jarrett had already told her (she thought, maybe). She had to confirm. "Rison and the others?"

"In custody," Wall said.

"And the bridge?"

"Yellow team."

The backups. Substitutes in the event of an emergency. Which was the case here.

"You're a commander," Arnold said. "You shouldn't be leading a rescue mission."

"And captains shouldn't be trudging through burning hangars," Wall said.

The medic spoke up before Arnold could retort. "We'll need three people to hold her," he said. "Two on the legs, another on the right…"

His words blurred and congealed with a dizzy spell. Then Arnold's legs were pinned. Strong hands gripped her around the torso. Something pulled. And—

Searing pain!

Her damn shoulder was screaming so loud her eardrums popped. Then she recognized her own voice, realized that she'd just screamed her throat raw.

And miraculously, the pain in her shoulder was less. Way less. It had already subsided to a dull throb.

"They popped your shoulder back in and gave you a localized painkiller," Wall said.

"Damn! I can't have my judgment compromised right now. Wait. Never mind. You just said it was localized."

Arnold took another long pull on a canteen. Meanwhile, the medic was removing the IV needle she'd jabbed into her vein. It had been a crazy whirlwind of events.

"Okay," she said. "Here's the plan. Split this team in half. Wall, you're with me. We're headed to the bridge. And why wasn't maintenance dispatched here?"

Nobody answered. Then Arnold realized she'd never given that order. Simply hadn't thought of it.

She addressed two other crew members and the one she'd accidentally kicked. "You three stay here. Use the laser and whatever materials you can find to seal the hangar door."

"We could arrange for maintenance to bring a bot," Wall said.

The optimal approach. Maintenance workers were a more respected class of plebs than techs, but they were considered plebs nonetheless. They'd be able to reliably seal the hole she'd cut in the door.

"Put that in motion, but they'll start on it now," Arnold said. "It's a burning hell in there. We need it airtight so that we can cut the oxygen and create a vacuum to put out the fire."

The warrior she'd kicked was still rubbing his jaw. "We could just disable the force field and let space be the vacuum," he said. Clearly, he wasn't thrilled to be relegated to pleb work.

"There's dead crew in there," Arnold said. "We're going to retrieve their bodies and give them a proper send-off. Also, we can't have everything in there just floating out into—why am I explaining? You have your orders. Go!"

They started rolling. Wall drove the rover with Arnold in the front and Fike laid out in the back. "You sure about going straight to the bridge?" she said. Way more casual now that they were alone.

"Gotta do it," Arnold said. "Wake me up when we get there."

CHAPTER 95

First order of business: Vincent headed to the infirmary. It turned out that the lifts were operational, and the infirmary was on their side of the ship. So Vincent made it over there really fast. That was the good news. The bad news was that he had no clue what he was going to do over there. But if they were trying to save Kevin's life with an alleged computer connection as the premise, it made sense for someone to at least be in the same room with him.

Sanderson met him at the door and led him down a bright hallway. A door slid open, and Vincent found himself in a large room that smelled of antiseptics, so sterile that it shocked the senses. Vincent noticed that it was easy to see everything in detail without eye strain in the soft white glow that blanketed the room.

Several beds were occupied. "All recent dojo casualties," Sanderson said. "Commander Hudson went on a rampage before fleeing the ship."

"And Kevin?" Vincent said.

"Over here."

Sanderson led Vincent to the bed furthest from the door in the back corner of the room. "Here he is. The sleeping prince."

Vincent had to look away.

"You okay?" Sanderson asked.

"Not really."

Seeing the plastic tube coming out of Kevin's throat made him gag. And there was a machine hooked to him; it was making a high-whining noise like an attacking mosquito.

"That machine's breathing for him," Sanderson said.

"The one making that funny humming noise?"

"Yep. And you can see on the holo that his vitals are shit. His circulatory system's barely functioning."

Vincent couldn't see. There was a holo next to Kevin monitoring a lot of vital signs, but Vincent didn't understand any of them. Probably didn't need to. Kevin's pasty skin and sunken face told the story.

"Can I sit down?" Vincent asked.

Sanderson moved a chair next to Kevin's bed. Vincent sat down and stared at the floor, then at the ceiling. Anything to not look at Kevin. "Take a close look at whatever's wired up to his head. Tell me if there's any blinking."

Sanderson was silent for a few seconds. "Hard to tell," he said.

What the hell is so hard? Vincent thought. *It's blinking or it isn't.*

Then he stared at his handheld device, hoping for an answer —an inspiration—and remembered something he'd normally never think about. Devices automatically connected to whatever they could access. Yes, automatically. Nobody ever tried to manually connect a device to anything. There was no point. You were always hooked into everything available. But that old legacy functionality was there, left over from an ancient time.

Vincent had done it before. It was a system hack. Diving several levels deep into the settings got him to a list of every signal from every device. It was a lot. The first hundred (or so) entries were resources he was already paired with. He'd never needed to care about any of the others because he couldn't access them under normal conditions. Things like weapons systems and course settings. And trivial stuff like someone else's chair height or bunk firmness.

He pinged Jade. She was still in the communications room next to the rear hangar. Her face appeared onscreen. "I'm going to share this screen with you," he said.

"What am I looking at?" Jade asked.

"Any and all available connections for my device," Vincent said.

"There are a bunch of unidentified," Jade said. "Nothing that we'd ever care about connecting to ourselves. Obviously, nothing labeled 'Kevin Slaton's brain.'"

"A brain connection sounds risky," Sanderson said.

"I dunno," Vincent said. "You tell me. You're the doctor."

"Medic," Sanderson said. "And I have no experience with anything of this nature."

"How about this: tell me if anything's blinking on his head," Vincent said. "I can't look… Well, I can't."

"Nothing," Sanderson said. "Not a thing."

"In that case, I'm going to find the weakest signal without an identifier," Vincent said.

He ran a network analysis sniffer, filtering out all identified connections. It took about ten minutes to display the results. There were five extremely weak connections at the bottom of the list.

"Ping all of them," Jade said.

"Seriously? I'd have to do some serious digging to even begin to worm my way in."

"Nothing to lose," Jade said. "We're already way beyond crazy here. It's not like brain mesh has a glove reader attached."

"But how would I even know if—wait!"

Vincent addressed Sanderson. "Watch Kevin. Tell me if anything, you know…happens."

Staring at his device, more determined than ever to not even glance at Kevin, Vincent went through the weak connections one by one. After the third try, he found himself looking up. Suddenly, the sterile air and those white lights didn't bother him as much.

He saw Kevin—actually looked at him—taking in the pallor of his skin, the plastic tube sticking out of his mouth, and the layer of mesh that covered (but didn't conceal) the grayish glob of his brain that was clearly threatening to ooze out at any second. Then he pinged that wispy strand of connection-number-four with an access request.

It lit up! A single red wink from one of the electrodes.

"Jade! It's there. I did it," Vincent said. He was talking way too loud, but he couldn't help himself. "If I wasn't right next to him, I never would have seen his gateway, much less pinged it."

His elation was interrupted by a beeping alarm.

Then Sanderson was leaning over Kevin. "Stop whatever you're doing," he said. "Now."

"What's going on?" Vincent asked.

"He's crashing!"

CHAPTER 96

Sanderson leaned over Kevin. He injected him with something and shook his head. "Nothing we can do," he said. "His system's shutting down."

"Gotta try something," Vincent said.

"There's nothing to try!" Sanderson said. "What the hell do you think I've been telling you?"

I saw it blink, Vincent thought. *Something's still firing. I pinged that process and saw it blink.*

"What's going on?" Jade asked.

"Kevin's fading fast," Vincent said.

Sanderson and another medic were looking Kevin over. Then the other medic left, and Sanderson sat down with his head bowed in defeat.

"Is he…" Vincent said.

"Dead? Not yet," Sanderson said. "But it's only a matter of time now."

"Try connecting again," Jade said.

"No!" Sanderson snapped.

"Why not?" Jade asked. "We've got nothing to lose."

"Sure, whatever," Sanderson said. "I guess not."

Vincent found himself staring at Kevin, wanting to find out what was behind that neural lace. He made another connection request to the weak process-number-four and was rewarded with a green blip from one of the electrodes.

Then his momentary elation turned to shit. "That's beyond cool," he said. "The fact that his brain is sending that connection signal is freaking amazing. But it's just a pointless handshake. No actual info or instructions happening. This is not going to make a damn bit of difference to Kevin."

"Don't be too sure."

Kirkman was standing there. Her lower lip was split, her left eye swollen shut. "Shut up, Sanderson," she said. "I know you're about to tell me to go lie down."

Vincent gave her his chair. He was no medic, but he could see she was absolutely exhausted, barely able to walk or stand. He pointed at the front of Kevin's skull. "You're the one who did this?" he asked.

Kirkman nodded. Her right eye locked onto him, not quite glaring but gazing intently. He had a feeling she did that with everybody. "Next you're going to ask me why that would save Kevin's life," she said. "Because you're a smart guy and you know that neural lace is just a conduit."

"And obviously not helping him," Sanderson said.

"Why don't you shut the hell up?" Vincent said. "Kirkman's going to explain it to us."

"Nothing to explain," Sanderson said.

"Shut up and listen!" Jade said. She was still in the conversation via Vincent's device.

That made Kirkman smile. "You heard her," she said. "Don't make me wake up Gable."

Then she explained how Kevin's skull had been caved in and the neural lace she'd implanted. Then she told about Kevin going from stone dead to alive and stable after Gunderson collapsed his windpipe. And, of course, there was the light show at the front of his head. "It's as if he's connected to…something. And that something is giving him a little something extra to keep his brain functioning at rudimentary levels," she said. "I know it sounds crazy, but I'm convinced."

"When did Gunderson strangle Kevin?" Vincent asked.

Kirkman shook her head. "Shit, I'm not sure. We weren't keeping any logs with the computer down. Everything was so crazy."

She was right. So much had happened, and there'd been nothing logged or tracked amid the chaos.

"I know where you're going with this," Jade said. "But whatever wiped out the yuck blob happened a good while after Kevin got his windpipe crushed. Assuming our ghost was responsible."

"Ghost?" Kirkman said.

"A system process with a large footprint that we can't identify," Vincent said.

"That's Kevin," Kirkman said.

"Totally preposterous," Sanderson said.

"Is it?" Kirkman said.

"We'd have to start with the timing," Vincent said. "Go back and resurrect system logs and comb through specific data from that sector where our ghost currently resides. Find out for sure if it's pre-existing, or if it spun up when Kevin got choked out."

"That would take a really, *really* long time," Jade said.

"You have a better idea?" Vincent asked.

Nobody spoke for a moment.

"Assume our ghost is Kevin and proceed accordingly," Jade said.

CHAPTER 97

"You can assume all you want," Sanderson said. "Assume Kevin's a ghost, a glitch, or a hedgehog, but he's not going to be alive much longer."

As soon as the words were out of his mouth, Kevin's monitor let out another loud beep. To Vincent, it sounded like an alarm signaling the approach of death.

Kirkman tried to stand. Sanderson gently pushed her back into her chair. Then he went to work. He injected something into one of the tubes connected to Kevin. Then he gave him a mild jolt with a zap stick.

"It's on its lowest setting," Kirkman said. "We do that in the field sometimes. Never seen one used in the infirmary."

"Whatever works," Sanderson said. He checked Kevin's pulse and sighed. "That was close. I thought we'd lost him."

Kirkman addressed Vincent. "Whatever you've got planned, do it fast," she said.

Vincent swallowed hard. That was the fly in the soup. He didn't have anything planned. He could assume their ghost was Kevin all day long, but he had no clue how to proceed.

"I can ping his neural lace with an access request and get a green light," Vincent said. "But that's all. Were those receptors at the front of his head blinking before?"

"Constantly," Kirkman said.

"Probably random brain activity," Sanderson said.

Kirkman sank down in her chair, looking more exhausted than ever. It was as if the mere act of speech was a major decision. Her face said she'd like to forget all of this and get some sleep. She let out a huge sigh. "I can't explain why—"

"And you don't have to," Vincent said. "Right or wrong, we're assuming Kevin's brain somehow hooked itself into the ship's computer and an unidentified ghost process is…him. If we accept all of that as fact, then no flashing implies that he's no longer connected."

Vincent felt it. The conviction returning to his voice was an almost tactile feeling. He had a plan now. No clue how to act on it. Still… "We have to get him reconnected," he said.

Nobody said a word. The unspoken question hung silent in the infirmary's sterile air: *How in the hell are we going to do that?*

Then Jade chimed in. "We've got all the building blocks," she said. "You can ping his neural lace and get a response. I have a fix on our ghost process. I can't get any kind of response from it…but if we set up a pier-to-pier connection between the ghost, your device, and the neural lace, that would put all of the pieces together."

———

They opened a data channel with a firewall in front of it. Only their ghost process would be allowed to pass through. It would then have rights to do anything it damn well pleased.

But nothing happened. Which wasn't surprising. Just disappointing.

"I'm stumped," Jade said. "I've hit our ghost with everything I can think of to invoke any kind of response. But nothing."

Vincent felt like Kirkman looked. Beat up as hell and ready to lie down and let someone else do the fighting. Their plan sucked. They'd stood up a useless set of connections that would never transport one single packet of data. A bridge that no one would ever cross.

What the hell were they missing?

Probably nothing. After all, a human brain couldn't merge with a computer. They'd mastered space travel, navigated cosmic junctures, built some seriously destructive weapons. But they'd never merged a human brain with a computer. Not to say it couldn't be done. Just that it had never been a priority and hadn't happened yet. Until now, apparently, according to Kirkman.

But if Kirkman was right, if it really did happen, it would have occurred organically all on its own. He and Jade would never be able to duplicate that. Game over. They were done.

Wait a minute, he thought. *Just a goddamn minute!*

"We're breaking our maxim," he said. "Assume our ghost is Kevin and proceed accordingly. We're not doing that."

"We've just stood up a data channel to tie everything together," Jade said.

"That's just it," Vincent said. "Data channel. Process. We're attacking this problem from a purely technical standpoint, when our maxim is to assume our ghost is—"

"Kevin!" Jade said.

"Not a process or a job or a resource," Vincent said. "None of that."

"Right. A *person* inside the ship's computer. An actual person."

"Crazy assumption," Vincent said.

"Totally insane," Jade agreed.

"So instead of trying to communicate with a 'ghost' process

by technical means, we have to think in terms of reaching out to this guy on the stretcher," Vincent said. "We could start by pulling up personnel files and finding out all we can about him. Assuming the yuck blob didn't destroy all of that."

"On it," Jade said.

Vincent waited while she took a deep dive into the archives. His back was stiff from standing, but he didn't want to ask for another chair to be brought over. And he definitely wasn't going to ask Kirkman to move. His main discomfort, however, was the watching and the waiting. The vigil. Watching Kevin, expecting him to tank at any moment, and counting the long minutes while Jade conducted her search.

Jade's image reappeared on his device. "The yuck blob ripped through all of the recent training records," she said. "We can probably reassemble a lot of the damaged data, but that's going to be a massive project. Then I got lucky."

She spun up a holo of recent footage from the rear hangar. Kevin stealing the hawker.

"How the hell did you find that?" Vincent asked.

"Face recognition search through video archives," Jade said. "Most of it gets wiped every six months. No point in having gobs of routine activity sitting around. But stealing a ship? That would have gotten saved and backed up in several places."

Vincent watched as Kevin entered the rear hangar, a minnow swimming into a sea of sharks if there ever was one. "Who's that with him?" he asked.

"No clue," Jade said. "Probably that recruit who escaped with him. Like I said, lots of data torn apart."

"Her name's Tonya," Kirkman said. Her voice was weak. "I think. At least that's what I remember hearing."

Vincent felt his face redden as he watched the footage of this Tonya. She was holding Kevin's hand and reassuring him. "You've got this."

Holy shit! Vincent thought. *That face. That body.* Her deep voice was laced with a hint of an erotica (Or was his own mind contriving that?). This girl was the stuff wet dreams were made of.

"Whoa, baby!" he said. "I think we might have found a way."

CHAPTER 98

KEVIN WOULD HAVE BEEN PERFECTLY content in the forest, gazing out at the distant mountains while he played in his computer room in the cabin by the stream. But someone put up a firewall —a choking, restrictive blockade that boxed him in and cut off his resources. A lot like constructing an electric fence with razor wire around a Garden of Eden. Couldn't have that.

He'd long since figured out that he was in a virtual environment within the ship's computer. For one thing, he recognized the virus he'd created when it attacked him. And watching his world fade and crumble when deprived of system resources was another dead giveaway.

His assault on the firewall required all of the raw processing force he could muster. So maintaining his virtual world would deprive him of valuable firepower. Unless he diverted all resources into his objective.

But it wasn't until he prepared for his initial attack that he realized he *required* his virtual world to maintain even a semblance of mental stability. Same as requiring air to breathe.

He figured out a way. He created an alcove. A closet. It was small and cramped. But he could survive in there and allow his psyche to be anchored.

What he didn't count on was the firewall being disabled before he launched his attack on it. He got ripped from his alcove and never even realized it. Suddenly, he was looking down on the dojo from above and saw Ellis hurting Kirkman. He launched himself without thinking, never stopping to consider that he was seeing the dojo not from his own eyes but through a camera lens.

Hearing his voice booming thought the loudspeakers, seeing the laser beam cut a hole in Ellis, realizing that he'd integrated with the dojo's programming might not have been so bad. But seeing himself, sitting up on the stretcher with the front of his skull lit up…that was an *Oh, shit* moment.

Because seeing himself—his physical, injured self—told him his flesh and blood body was still alive. Which meant his computer existence was a copy of sorts. Still not a total deal breaker from a holding-your-shit-together standpoint.

But then it dawned on him: his virtual world was no more. Gone. Vanished like a fart in the wind. It was out there waging a security war, unlocking locks, cracking passwords, decrypting keys. And he was just fucking out there somewhere.

Unspeakable panic exploded inside of him. It might have been accompanied by audible pop if he'd had ears to hear it. He just lost his entire grasp on…everything. His whole freaking mind, gone. Zap. See ya. Later days.

He was sprinting in an outright panic. Anything to stop this madness from skinning him alive. Only he didn't have legs (or a body for that matter) and he wasn't going anywhere.

Alcove!

His only hope.

He tried. But it was gone. Whether he'd forgotten its identifying signature or it got nuked. Didn't matter. It was just gone.

ALCOVE!

Full focus. Single-minded. Nothing else. Nothing fucking else! Alcove! Alcove! Alcove! ALCOVE…

Something pressed down on him from above. A solid layer of something.

Dark and restrictive. Cold and harsh.

This was no alcove. No closet. It was the feeling of being trapped underneath the ice on a frozen lake. Relying on the narrow space between the ice and the water for oxygen.

But it was a tangible something to assuage the shattering of his sanity.

Kevin shivered and raised his face upward. As he struggled to breathe and hang on, part of him figured out that his attacking process had done its job. It had launched itself in an all-out assault, then circled back and reassembled itself into the virtual haven that Kevin now called home. To get back there, all he had to do was shift himself to the address pointer.

A simple matter if he hadn't lost his shit and all rational thought with it.

Icy blue panic burned his eyes. His ears picked up random pings and signals. All noise. Just mind-crunching, garbled noise!

Then, from nowhere, a voice. Deep, sultry, and familiar.

Kevin.

Tonya! Even with his blurred vision, he recognized the unmistakable curvature of her body.

You've got this.

Sure. She'd told him that before.

Her outstretched hand was mere inches away. All he had to do was reach out and…trust her. Nope.

C'mon, Kevin. Let's get out of here. I won't let anything bad happen.

"Yeah, right!" Kevin said. "You were just trying to steal me from the Armada all along. Because you're just like the rest of them. Liars and thieves. All of you!"

He was freaking and raging; he wanted to take a swing at

this goddess of a woman even though she could snap him like a twig.

Fuck it!

Losing himself in a tonsil-blistering scream, he lunged at her throat.

CHAPTER 99

The infirmary was as listless as it was sterile. Kevin was somewhat stable, his forehead emitting an occasional green blink. Vincent had grown tired of watching his device for any sign of communication. Kirkman had dozed off in her chair. Sanderson walked away to check on other patients.

Then total bedlam.

"Shit!" Vincent croaked. Kevin's skull was flashing bright enough to blind him momentarily.

Kirkman was on her feet, calling for Sanderson. The vitals on Kevin's holo had spiked. His body was on fire. His pulse soaring. Blood pressure through the roof. And the medics were bystanders, all of them. They called out readings, exchanged panicked looks, but none of them, including Kirkman, had a clue what to do.

"Cut the connection!" Sanderson yelled.

"No," Kirkman said. "That's what saved his life when he got strangled."

"She's right." Gable had seemingly appeared from nowhere; he stood there in his hospital gown, looking down at the fireworks display Kevin's forehead was putting on. "We don't understand why, but he needs a connection to the ship's computer to survive."

"But his readings," Sanderson said.

"We've got to reconnect him to that ghost process," Vincent said. It didn't make any sense. Nobody was more surprised than he was when those words came out of his mouth. But that's what was needed. The question was: how?

"He's just destroyed my avatar program," Jade said. "Wiped it clean out of existence and rendered that resource space…"

Her holo vanished. Vincent let out a yelp and dropped his device. It had burned the hell out of his hand. They weren't supposed to do that. But there'd been a lot of things that weren't supposed to happen of late.

Vincent dropped to his knees and stared at his overheating device. Nothing else Jade could do on her end. Or him either. He did, however, have the base address of their ghost. On a device too hot to touch, he fought through the pain, one cautious finger poke at a time, and set up an infinite loop to repeat itself ad infinitum. Then he pinged Kevin's neural lace with every piece of info he could load—the ghost's address, its memory pointer, the region and domain of the running process.

"What are you doing?" Sanderson said.

Vincent didn't bother to answer. His device was smoking. His hands were covered in painful blisters.

No way was it supposed to do that, not with all the failsafes. His device popped and shattered. He'd never seen one do that before either. This was bad.

He cast a helpless look at Kevin. Kirkman was patting his face with a wet cloth. "Just relax," she said. "You're okay now."

Vincent gaped at what he saw. A nice, orderly pattern of lights blinked across Kevin's forehead. Orange and yellow for send and receive. Green for an ongoing open connection. He forgot his screaming hands. "Did you somehow color code those electrodes?" he asked.

"Wouldn't know how," Kirkman said. "They're capable of displaying all colors in the spectrum, of course. But my intent was to wire up his brain. Nothing else. The computer-aided rebuild of his mind was to come later."

"Well, that's one project we can cross off our list," Vincent said.

Gable laughed and clapped him on the back. "Let's have a look at those burns," he said.

CHAPTER 100

Captain Arnold was well adapted to long stretches of extreme physical and mental exertion. But she'd been pushed to the outer limits of her capabilities. Now, rehydrated and with a solid meal in her, followed by several hours of uninterrupted sleep, she felt somewhat recharged.

She was still tired but no longer exhausted; her head wasn't fuzzy anymore. And her throat no longer screamed for water. The pain in her left shoulder had subsided to a dull ache. She could actually throw a strike with that arm if she had to but vastly preferred to keep her arm hanging loose and relaxed by her side.

A short distance from the bridge in a war room that had been converted into a makeshift courtroom, she stood on an elevated platform behind a podium. The prisoners were standing with their backs to her. That's because she'd declared them unfit to even gaze upon the Armada's coat of arms on the wall behind her. "That sword and shield represents everything you're not," she said.

Arnold watched her warriors escort the prisoners away. Let them think she'd chosen standing instead of sitting to lord it over them. Really, being seated for too long made her legs cramp up. Still not totally recovered yet.

It had been more of a mop-up than an inquest. Simply a matter of isolating the suspected conspirators and informing them that their cohorts had blamed the whole thing on them. A ploy so basic it was beyond ridiculous. Rison had contracted instant diarrhea of the mouth. He named everyone else involved, spewing out all the details, holding nothing back.

Arnold almost pitied him and the others. Almost. They were cowards at heart, too blinded by fear to realize they were screwed no matter what. Their best course of action, in this case, would have been to go out with a modicum of dignity. Another reason they were unfit to even glance at the Armada's emblem.

When the room had been cleared, she sat down and stretched her legs out. Then she reviewed the debriefing on Kevin Slaton one more time. Jarrett had gotten the details (what they knew so far) from the techs and medics and consolidated the info for her. And she needed to further consolidate it for herself before her next hearing in a few minutes.

Bottom line: he'd transferred a copy of himself into the ship's computer and taken up residence in a virtual world. A simulated world was necessary to keep him mentally balanced, it seemed. In response to this world of his being threatened, he'd destroyed the yuck blob. In further response, he'd blown open all of the ship's security. And on and on…till he cut a massive hole in Ellis using a laser in the dojo.

There was more. Apparently human brains contained bigger data and more processing power than the largest AI because they were continually fed input for a person's entire life. Arnold shook her head on that one. Then she skimmed ahead to the final analysis.

Current situation: Kevin Slaton's consciousness had existed inside the ship's computer while he was physically comatose. Now that he'd awakened, he'd returned to his flesh and blood body and brain. So the new challenge would be for him to hook into the computer while fully awake.

Can't wait to see how that turns out, Arnold thought. She wasn't going to fight it, though. She really didn't care about appeasing Armada high command. They could go screw themselves, they with their covert, secretive planting that set off this time bomb on her ship. She was going along because Kevin could be a real asset in repairing yuck blob destruction and restoring the ship's computer to full functionality. No other reason.

Maybe, someday, battles would be fought in computer rooms instead of ship-to-ship and face-to-face. She hoped that would be long after her death.

———

It was time for the final hearing. As soon as Ally and Lane were brought in, Arnold dismissed everyone else. She stood at the podium, looking them over. Nobody spoke. She sized up Erin Lane as intense and athletic. Her light blue eyes had a tint of crazy that Arnold liked. This girl would choose fight over flight every single time.

She'd also never be a leader. Forceful reaction was her answer to everything. Awesome warrior material. No surprise that she was one of the stronger recruits in her unit.

Ironically, her crushing of Kevin Slaton's skull had resulted in saving the computer and probably the entire ship. But that didn't matter. It *couldn't* matter. What mattered was behavior and consequences. Nothing else.

"Look up on the wall behind me," Arnold said. "Tell me what you see. I'm talking to you, you leathery old bitch."

She almost smiled. The spikes in Ally's hair actually bristled! Bite into her and you'd break a tooth.

"Captain! I'm the one at fault," Lane said.

"Did I address you?" Arnold strode around the podium and

planted herself face-to-face with the girl. *So much to learn,* she thought. *The girl's got spirit, though, I'll give her that.*

"I see an icon of valor that I've disgraced," Ally said.

"You and you alone. No accomplices."

"Yes, Captain."

"Bullshit."

Talking a subtle step back, Arnold caught Lane across the face with a spinning crescent kick. The girl dropped like a rock.

"Get her out of here," Arnold said. "With Ellis gone, you'll have to reshuffle your training squads. She's with you now."

"Is that all, Captain?"

"I don't want you or her discussing this matter with anyone. Understood?"

"Yes, Captain."

"Well, what are you waiting for? Get the hell out of here."

Ally slung Lane over her shoulder and grinned.

"Anything funny?"

"No, Captain."

Arnold allowed herself a smile as she watched her former instructor carry Lane off like a sack of grain. She'd keep them out of any inquests that came up. In fact, the official report would be: Gunderson caved in Kevin's skull, then tried to strangle him with Ellis's help.

She'd made that decision before they'd entered the room. Mostly. She hadn't been sure until the instant her kick landed. The girl had seen it coming and hadn't flinched. Didn't try to duck or block it either. She just took it on the chin without question. That was a recruit she didn't want to lose.

And on that note, maybe she could retire to her quarters for a few hours of sleep now that the worst was over.

Then Jarrett contacted her and spoiled that idea.

"Captain. You're needed on the bridge. Wraith ships approaching."

CHAPTER 101

ARNOLD FELT IT. That pre-fight surge that could make you puke if you didn't know how to use it. The blood pumping through her veins had become downright electric. Tiredness fell from her. She had to admit it: she loved—actually loved!—the sight of wraith ships from the bridge. Reality hadn't left her. She knew full well that *Touchstone* was compromised and that this ship and the entire crew were in grave danger. Still, this was a battle she knew how to wage. Why she'd enlisted as a recruit and trained with a crusty old bitch who would just as soon bite your head off as look at you.

Wraiths rarely traveled or fought in fleets. There were always two or three of them sniffing around the outskirts of whatever territory wasn't theirs. Knowing that a large show of force would provoke immediate countermeasures, they preferred to hang out on the fringes, watching for any opening or weakness. Much like hyenas trying to take advantage of a wounded lion.

They could see them onscreen from the bridge. Two wraith ships, floating nearby like bloodsucking insects ready to light at any moment. There was an almost delicate symmetry to their shape that reminded Arnold of white lace flapping in a light breeze. But there was nothing delicate or pretty about them. True scum, they preferred to circle a compromised ship and wait for the crew to die before boarding. Always favoring scavenging to combat.

Arnold glanced around the bridge. She had Wall and Jarrett with her, plus the half-dozen warriors at their battle stations. Normally, a couple of wraith ships were no big deal. But in their current condition, there was grave concern on every face.

"They're not even trying to surprise us," Wall said.

"Because they think we're not dangerous," Arnold said. "We'll fix that."

The two wraith ships approached with the total confidence of immunity. They got within a mile and spread out, one on either side of the warship.

"They're hailing us, Captain," Jarrett said.

"Let's hear it," Arnold said.

It was an audio message, translated, of course.

We know you're helpless. No assistance anywhere near. We're going to board your vessel. If you try to stop us, none of you will survive.

Arnold knew what that meant. They would steal weaponry, small ships, even crew members to sell into slavery or use for their own amusement.

The wraith message continued. *This can be hard or easy.*

Nope. Hard was the only possible outcome. This battle was going to be just that: a fight to the end.

"Firepower report," Arnold said.

Each of the six warriors on the bridge was responsible for the firing of the ship's laser cannons from a specific location. (There were redundant battle stations at each location in case the bridge was destroyed.) They responded in order. "Half, nothing, undetermined, nothing, nothing, questionable."

A status report of nothing meant just that. Questionable and undetermined meant they could maybe hit a large moon from point-blank range. And half power—their best hope—meant they could pierce the shields of one of the wraith ships provided they could lock onto it for long enough. Of course, while they were doing that, the other one would blast the opposite side of their ship apart.

"We're in luck," Arnold said. "Our half-power cannon bank is front starboard. Okay. Status of the front hangar entryway."

"There's a crew down there," Jarrett said. "They've almost got it sealed. Still burning like an inferno inside the hangar because the slightest bit of oxygen—"

"Exactly," Arnold said. "If they run a hose from the rover's emergency oxygen supply to the door and weld the nozzle to that opening…"

Jarrett raised the eyebrow above his good eye. "Airtight," he said.

"Airtight," Arnold said. "They'll have to use max pressure."

They were all staring at her in disbelief. "That could cause the hangar to explode," Wall said.

"I'm counting on it," Arnold said.

———

The wraiths preferred to communicate via translated messaging. That was fine with Arnold. Seeing them onscreen was no picnic. They all looked like they'd bathed in a vat of burnt marshmallows. And they had a pale blue mist emanating from them (a territorial musk left over from their more primitive era) that made piss smell like perfume. Not that she could smell them across a communication, but just the sight of one made her stomach rise up into her throat.

If she'd been the aggressor looking to take an enemy ship, Arnold would have insisted on full video. The more info, the better. You could read your enemy, watch their reactions, look for any telling detail that might give you an edge. These shitheads were overconfident—and for good reason. They were stalking a seriously compromised vessel. Still…

She sent her reply message. *Permission to board granted. We will open the rear hangar for you. I'm en route there to offer myself as a prisoner. But I need your assurance that none of my crew will be harmed.*

Their response only took a few seconds. *We don't need permission. And we'll come in through the FRONT hangar. Or else.*

Well, she'd steered them in the right direction anyhow.

The tension on the bridge was palpable. They were facing a big disadvantage. But battles were never fair. You didn't attack when both sides were evenly matched. In fact, a good strategist exploited every possible advantage.

"Status of oxygen tank hookup to front hangar door," Arnold said.

Jarrett answered in a few seconds. "Done. They made the hole a little bigger and sealed it around the hose. They're pumping in fresh oxygen now."

She replied to the wraiths. *Opening front hangar bay doors.*

Then she asked for a rear hangar status.

"Every available fighter ship manned and ready," Wall said. "That second wraith ship is lurking right outside of there."

This was it. Go time. She contacted the officer in charge of the rear hangar. "On my command, open the rear hangar doors. Maintain the force field. And have the nearest hawkers fire a super light volley against it."

"From inside the hangar?"

"That's right," Arnold said. "From inside."

Meanwhile, the other wraith ship hovered just outside of the front hangar. They sent another message. *The slightest hint of deceit and we destroy you.*

Good luck with that, Arnold thought. *We're rolling out the welcome mat for you.*

"Lock our half-cannon onto the back side of that approaching ship," she said. "Wait for my command."

"Captain," Jarrett said. "The front hangar temperature has reached extreme danger."

"Perfect," Arnold said. "On my command, disable the force field. Open the outer doors. And fire those cannons with everything we've got.

"Rear hangar. Open the doors. Maintain the force field. Light volley on my command."

...

"Now!"

A thick glob of orange flame erupted from the front hangar and engulfed the front half of the wraith vessel. Waves of red-hot shrapnel crashed against its shields, forcing all of its defenses forward. In the same instant, they opened fire with their remaining arsenal on its unprotected backside.

The wraith ship exploded, and its fragments merged into the angry glow of white-hot carnage. Excessive oxygen released from the hangar fanned the flames in the vacuum of space for a few extra seconds. A billowing crimson. Then it all popped out like a broken light bulb. Leaving only a dark mass of swirling black flotsam.

And now the moment of truth...

Instead of attacking, the second wraith ship fled.

Nobody spoke for several seconds. They just sat there taking it all in, processing the fact that it was really over.

That they'd survived.

Survived?

Hell, they'd won!

It was Wall who broke the silence. "That rear-side ship could have had target practice," she said. "But it took off."

"There was once a squad of green recruits," Arnold said. "It was their first time in a hangar bay. When the doors opened, one of them fired a weapon at the force field. Just to see what would happen. The entire opening lit up like a wall of fire. Not really. It was just the force field neutralizing a threat. But it scared the hell out of everybody. Ask Drill Instructor Ally about it sometime."

Yes, it had been an awesome bluff. Seeing their sister ship engulfed in flames while staring at an apparent wall of fire themselves, the wraiths had run away.

Jarrett grinned. "What kind of warrior wannabe would fire at a force field from inside a vessel?" he said.

"No clue," Arnold said.

The entire bridge exploded into laughter.

Then, a few moments later, the laughter subsided. Everyone fell silent. Arnold looked out at the swirling mass of debris that would soon drift apart and disappear into the vastness of space. In the end, those ships and warriors from the front hangar had gotten an honorable send-off.

CHAPTER 102

KEVIN WAS RESTING in his new quarters, a private room on the warship *Apogee* (formerly called *Touchstone*). He had his own bed with crisp white sheets. This was a far cry from his ill-fated training days. The holographic wall art was a breathtaking gorge he'd never seen with a river flowing deep in the bottom of it. He even had his own food stores in here.

Several weeks had passed since he'd awakened with a throbbing head and a tube wedged in his throat, wishing he'd died. But he'd been recovering little by little. Able to sit up, then to breathe on his own. Eventually, he'd been able to get out of bed and eat solid food. Even walk for short distances without losing his breath.

Jan Kirkman had been working with him on his physical rehab. A so-called attitude adjustment specialist named Finnegan had been flown in to help with his mental recovery. A condescending asshole that reminded Kevin of a stiff-necked beetle. It was Kirkman who was helping him feel comfortable in his own skin (for the first time in his life) mainly by treating him with kindness and respect. Something he'd never experienced before.

He was still reeling from the shock of finding out that the Armada had never been blind to his talent. In fact, high command had recognized him as a superhero in the realm of anything computer related. So much, in fact, that they'd camouflaged him as an ordinary recruit to keep him from falling into the wrong hands. Nobody on the ship, not even the captain, had known about this ploy.

Tonya had been planted in his squad to protect him. Turned out she'd had her own plan: to steal him away.

The Armada's newest stealth attempt was to rename *Touchstone* to *Apogee* and leave Kevin there. Captain Arnold and a host of warriors, along with the squads of recruits, had been redeployed to a new ship. Its name: *Touchstone*. Its "official" purpose: business as usual; training-slash-combat vessel. Its actual purpose: act as a decoy for enemy forces out there looking for Kevin, now known as The Hacker—a revival of an ancient moniker of centuries past.

Apogee (formerly *Touchstone*) had been repurposed for technical innovation. Why not? Given the loss of over half the small ships, most of the laser cannons, and the front hangar getting melted down to a molten glob of smut, it was unsalvageable as a fighting vessel. There was also the carnage from the yuck blob.

So Kevin got himself a playground. His assignment was to rebuild the computer and weapon arrays for a start. They'd also be bringing in captured enemy vessels for his analysis. After all, deactivating an enemy's shields on demand could be more valuable than a fleet of ships.

And he had a staff. No leadership ability. No organizational skills. But a group of twenty techs had been assigned to him just the same. Their orders: do whatever he asked; give him anything he required. Period. Most of them were clueless. Leadership throwing bodies at a goal, thinking that sheer volume would yield faster results.

Some of them were resentful over being reassigned and

having to report to Kevin. Not Jade and Vincent. For the first time in their Armada tenure, they were learning. Innovating. Solving real issues instead of just watching a system work. Here they were respected. Here they were no longer just plebs. They were part of a bigger whole. Something important. They also loved William Whitehead being gone.

In fact, it was Jade who solved an early dilemma. She had Kirkman print a thin, semi-transparent layer of skin to cover Kevin's neural lace. That prevented him from having to walk around looking like an android, but they'd still be able to see the blinking status lights whenever he entered the ship's computer. In fact, they'd be filming and studying them in an attempt to identify patterns in brain and computer interaction.

About that…

Through a battery of focused testing, Jade, Vincent, and Kevin were seeking to understand what actually happened when Kevin immersed himself in the ship's computer. Their test cases, coupled with feedback from Kevin from the *inside,* revealed that *virtual* Kevin was a copy of his consciousness. And this copy maintained contact with his physical brain, polling it for info on demand. Anything from world-building to memories —even the specific personal traits that made him Kevin.

That all made sense. A human brain was, itself, a massive AI and continually trained for a person's entire life. Every little thing the five senses consumed during every second of every day became a building block for usable data patterns.

Thing is, when Kevin first took up residence in the computer, his physical body was in a coma. His brain blindly fed him everything he needed, blissfully unaware that there was any other existence. Try as he might, he couldn't replicate that transition when he was fully awake. His choices were physical or virtual existence. But not both at the same time.

In their earlier attempts, Kirkman had put him under with a mild, fast-acting sedative as he jacked himself into the computer.

But that was a short-term solution, dangerous to Kevin's wellbeing.

Of late, he'd been putting himself into a meditative state where he released his mind completely. It took full concentration, and he could only keep it up for short intervals. His best effort so far had been twenty-two minutes and seventeen seconds. And every session took something out of him.

That's why he was exhausted right now. Go figure. Tired from closing his eyes and lying down and relaxing. Doing absolutely nothing.

At any rate, he was resting. Jade and Vincent had gone to lunch. Kirkman had checked his vitals and had him drink a concoction of sugar and electrolytes. She made him feel safe. Her brown eyes melted his usual distrust and fear of people. And she was fairly hot. Way out of his league. For sure.

But she wasn't Tonya.

Who was?

That thought made his pulse quicken. A distraction that he didn't need. If anything, he needed clean, pure thoughts divorced from all that worldly crap that was beyond his reach. Besides, Tonya was gone. He'd never see her again.

Still, he couldn't shut down the memory once it started rolling through his mind. The touch of her hand, the brush of her lips against his cheek...

He shook his head to clear it. Best to purge her from his brain completely.

Message alert.

Acting on impulse and rote, Kevin checked his communicator. Nothing there. This was coming through the computer from outside the ship—and not through any of the normal channels. He probed the message, trying to determine its source and sender, as well as its encryption scheme. There were ways to read a message and (at the same time) make the sender believe the transmission had failed. Can't follow bullshit orders that you never got.

Shit! He recognized the pattern. This message followed the same encryption scheme as Throwdown, the space war game he'd concocted to help him enter the rear hangar and steal a hawker once upon a time.

No need to go any further to identify the sender. And if that wasn't enough, there was the message itself.

You got this, baby. See you soon.

ACKNOWLEDGMENTS

First, thank you for reading my book! If you are on this page, you probably read it all the way to the end. That means a lot to me as a writer.

Also a big thanks to my family, who encouraged me to write since childhood.

Finally, a huge shout-out to Emily Nemchick for her awesome editing job. She finds everything!

Sign up below for information about my upcoming projects and free offerings.

https://bonnerlitchfield.com/mailinglist.html

ABOUT THE AUTHOR

Bonner Litchfield lives with his wife and dog in North Carolina. Some of his hobbies and interests include CrossFit (painful at times), hanging out with friends and family, reading, traveling, and cheesy TV shows.

Visit him at bonnerlitchfield.com